MURDER SO FOUL

A ROB SOLIZ AND FRANK PIERCE MYSTERY

LARRY ENMON

Print ISBN 978-1-957529-13-4

Ebook ISBN 978-1-957529-14-1

LCCN 2023940832

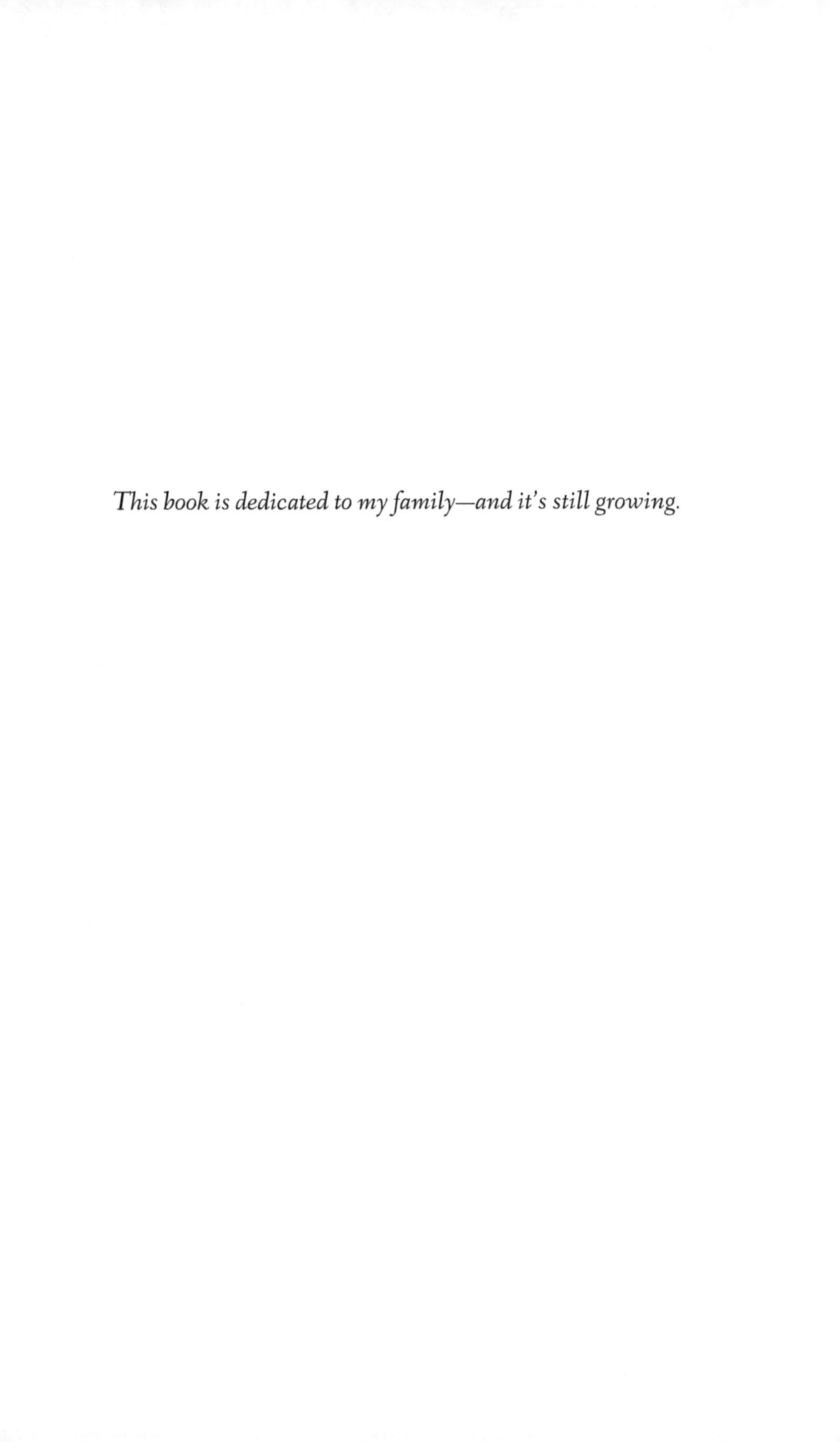

This book is dedicated to my family—and it's still growing.

I was getting the feeling again, and it was bad this time.

DENNIS RADER, BTK SERIAL KILLER

ONE

At 3:45 Monday afternoon, Detective Rob Soliz had a bad feeling when he parked behind the last police cruiser on the lonely street in South Dallas. Hated these *meet the detective* calls. Never knew what you'd end up with. There were at least half a dozen vehicles already there. Marked patrol units, detectives' unmarked cars, and two CSU vans with the back doors open. A uniform officer in short sleeves, holding his cap in one hand and a bottle of water in the other, wiped sweat from his brow. He had a bored expression and nudged closer to the shade of a small live oak. To his right, a narrow trail led into the creepy dense woods. Yellow crime scene tape stretched from the street to the dirt path and forest beyond. The officer eyed them as Rob turned off the engine.

"So, this is the Great Trinity Forest, huh?" Rob said as he got out of the car and swatted a mosquito. He stared at the horizon of trees. "What's so great about it?"

Frank Pierce rose from his slouched riding position, raked both hands through his long brown surfer hair, and took a swallow of water before getting out. He stood beside the passenger door and slipped on a pair of sunglasses. "Largest urban hardwood forest in the country—six thousand acres." He tore a stick of chewing gum in half, handing a piece to Rob as he walked around to the passenger side. Rob popped the gum in his mouth, carefully folded the silver wrapper a few times, and pocketed it. Frank wadded up his wrapper and tossed it on the floorboard before slamming the door.

Rob loosened his tie and unbuttoned his top button. Frank never wore a tie. A Polo shirt and khaki Dockers served as his business casual. Neither took their jackets. The badges and guns on their belts were all the identification necessary. The August afternoon, with humidity tracking just over eighty percent, left the air rich with earthy loam smells after the passing shower. The high-low chirp of katydids deep in the forest made Rob think of camping as a kid. He didn't mind the heat as much then, but now...

"Criminal Intelligence," he said as they ducked under the yellow tape.

The uniform officer changed hands with his cap, wiped his brow, and shot a passing glance as he motioned with his head toward the dirt lane to his right.

Rob led the way into the gloom, following the narrow, winding trail. He ducked under a honeysuckle and caught a whiff of the sweet fragrance. The impenetrable green canopy stretched for miles. Only slim streaks of sunlight found their way to the ground. Felt like they were entering a dark tunnel. A tunnel where tragedy hung in the air. The hum of crickets echoed high in the trees and blended with the katydids, and Rob swatted another mosquito buzzing his ear. Thick air surrounded them like a choking veil.

"Place reminds me of training in Panama during my Marine days."

Frank said nothing. Not much of a talker—more of a thinker. Bushes and woods weren't his happy place. Guy didn't even like stepping off the sidewalk. He walked carefully up the woodland trail, making sure he knew where each footfall landed—had a snake phobia. But the strangest thing about Frank wasn't his looks, phobias, or miscellaneous idiosyncrasies. The strangest thing was his sex appeal. Women found the guy irresistible. Rob never understood it. Frank was a chick-magnet and didn't even appear to recognize it —crazy.

The leaves of a Dwarf Palmetto raked the cuffs of Rob's pants as he maneuvered around a puddle of water in the middle of the trail. Several sets of muddy mountain bike tracks marked the path as they moved through the forest. The lane took a turn and the sound of retching—someone vomiting their guts out—drifted through the trees. When they made the second turn, a uniform officer leaned against a sturdy oak, wiping his lips with the back of his hand. He spotted them and straightened up. A flush crept across his cheeks.

"You okay?" Rob asked.

The officer looked like a rookie—face a little too soft, uniform a little too new. He nodded and cleared his throat. In a weak voice he said, "Yeah, I'm fine." His sallow complexion gave him a sickened appearance.

"Here," Frank said, and handed him his half-empty bottle of water before marching further into the abyss.

"Just relax. Get out into the fresh air," Rob said and followed Frank.

"Hey, mister," the uniform called.

Rob turned back and faced him.

The rookie's mouth twisted into a frown. "If you don't have to see *that*, don't."

Rob felt that tug in his gut he got when he suspected it was going to be a bad scene. He nodded and pulled in a breath. "We were called."

Rob caught up with Frank and a whiff of cigarette smoke mixed with the woodsy scent. Kelly sat on a fallen log, finishing his smoke.

"Hey, guys," Kelly said.

He wore his white CSU Tyvek crime-scene coveralls halfway unzipped. A particulate face mask hung around his neck, and perspiration dripped off his nose and chin. Kelly was a big man with a buzz cut. Every time Rob saw him in the white crime-scene coveralls, it reminded him of the Stay-Puft Marshmallow Man from *Ghostbusters*.

"Bad?" Frank asked.

Kelly stood, took one last puff, field-stripped the cigarette, and dropped the filter into his pocket. "Worst I've ever seen. Come on, I'll take you in. Here." He handed Frank a small jar of Vicks VapoRub. "Do yourself a favor."

Kelly's voice had a tired, worn-out quality, and his huge body moved with sloth-like speed. If Rob had seen as many grisly crime scenes as Kelly, he couldn't sleep nights. Frank dabbed a generous portion of Vicks around his nostrils and between his nose and upper lip. Rob did the same. The assault on Rob's mucus membranes by the Vicks took him back to childhood, sick, staying home from school. They followed Kelly as he moved up the trail, pushing aside overhanging foliage. Rob braced himself for what might be there. *Worst I've ever seen.* Kelly had seen some pretty bad stuff.

Frank said, "Thought you gave up smoking."

Kelly grunted. "Did until about an hour ago."

Muffled voices of several people drifted through the trees up ahead. When the stench hit Rob, it was like walking into a wall of death. That sweet, putrefied odor of decay mixed with the Vicks, and Rob almost gagged. Frank stopped, his sensitive nose twitched, and he swallowed hard.

The crime scene was on the left side of the path. Not exactly a clearing, but an area with less brush. Rob halted and stared. A large Muscatine plant with plump, dark grapes served as a backdrop for the horror. "Madre de Dios," Rob mumbled.

She was a white female, naked. A rope tossed over a tree limb held her upside-down by her ankles. Her long, black hair shielded most of her face, but the cut along her throat stood out. The arms were free and dangled just above the surface of the hole. Her cheeks had been cut, and that caused the mouth to hang open, allowing the lower jaw to form a macabre, bloody frown. She'd been gutted with a Y-shaped incision like a medical examiner uses. The pile of intestines and blood pooled in the pit below her. Hundreds of big, black flies buzzed the corpse and blood-soaked ground.

Rob crossed himself as he choked down the bile.

Frank stared at the woman with an open mouth, eerie expression. Sort of like that of the victim. When Rob worked homicide, he'd seen lots of ugly crime scenes. But nothing could prepare you for this. Frank's time in Missing Persons and Vice hadn't hardened him. The color drained from his face as he fought the wave of sickness that threatened to overtake him.

Alton's familiar voice echoed across the crime scene. No mistaking it. Had that gritty, grinding sound. Alton was a homicide detective in DPD. Being black and heavy set, he and his voice remined Rob of Louis Armstrong.

"Yes, sir," Alton said into the cell phone. He glanced in Rob's direction and nodded. "They're here now. I'll let you know."

"How much longer?" Kelly asked the CSU team.

The tall, skinny photographer squatted and adjusted the lens on the camera before snapping another picture. "Just a few more minutes, boss."

There were four other CSU types in Tyvek coveralls, hoods, and masks searching the area, bagging evidence. A line of squatting, white ghosts covered by the same shroud. Couldn't tell if they were male or female from their head-to-toe baggy white suits.

Alton dropped the phone in his pocket and strolled to Rob and Frank.

"Why did you call us to something like *this*?" Frank asked. His voice had an angry or disgusted tone, Rob couldn't tell which. But he was just about to ask the same question. Criminal Intelligence officers didn't do homicides unless there was a serious extenuating circumstance.

Alton's lips stretched into tight lines. He raked his hand across his short hair before saying, "I didn't. My lieutenant called CIU and requested assistance on this one—blame Edna."

Alton motioned for Rob and Frank to follow him closer to the victim. She was young, and her slim body had begun taking on a dark, bruised-like color. The oppressive heat had transformed the once pale skin into a palette of large irregular blotches. Her hair shined black and sticky from matted blood. The scene was bad enough, but the thing that caused Rob's greatest disgust were the flies around the corpse. Just like the thousands of flies that swarmed the dead Iraqi soldiers his unit encountered during their race across the desert in '91. After initially seeing the corpse, Frank made an effort to ignore it—that was Frank's way. To the side of the pit, a blue tarp draped over something about two feet tall. Alton pushed back a vine and carefully lifted the tarp, revealing a makeshift spit made of two Y shaped tree branches with a quarter-inch rebar lying across the top. An unusual piece of half-cooked meat with parts sliced off was impaled on the rebar resting above the cold ashes.

Having field dressed his share of deer, Rob identified it first. "Good god," he said and took a step back.

Frank's crinkled brow soon gave way to a wide-eyed look. "Is that—?"

"A human heart," Alton finished the sentence.

In his seventeen years of law enforcement Rob had never seen such a thing. This was a murder so foul it could cause a new officer to resign. Maybe even a veteran officer. Frank closed his eyes, probably wishing he could un-see it.

Alton laid the tarp back over the spit and brushed off his gloved hands. "The reason you were called wasn't because of the murder, but because of what else we found." He pointed to the right side of the blue tarp. "We found it in the bushes, over there." He reached into his jacket and produced a clear plastic evidence envelope sealed with a strip of red tape at the top. Inside was a bloody, crumpled newspaper clipping and photo. Rob had seen the same one in last Sunday's edition of the *Dallas Morning News*. The photo was part of a feature article about the city. Four people sat smiling for the camera.

The Mayor of Dallas, his wife, and two children.

TWO

"Thanks for not bringing any crime scene photos," Lieutenant Edna Crawford said, after hearing Rob's account of the murder. She reared back in her executive leather chair in the Criminal Intelligence Unit of the Dallas Police Department and squeezed her stress ball a couple of times before looking across the desk at Sergeant Terry Andrews. He sat in the chair by the door—his usual spot. Terry didn't speak; he only stared back. His eyebrows were low and pinched tight. He released a slow, even breath when Rob finished the story.

Rob had worked for him so long he understood that was his disgusted expression. Terry and Edna had been Rob's and Frank's supervisors for the last five years. Terry was senior in time to everyone, and Edna still had her eye on being the first black female major to lead the Criminal Intelligence Unit.

Frank had hardly spoken on the ride back to CIU or during the briefing with Edna and Terry. A few grunts were about all he contributed. The scene back at the woods had taken the starch out of him. He lounged his six-foot-three frame in his trademark slouch position on the couch while Rob described what they'd witnessed.

Edna's new scented plug-in this month was vanilla. Rob

thought it smelled like Bluebell Homemade Vanilla ice cream. Even giving a description of the horrific murder scene, he couldn't stop his mouth from watering. Funny how just a smell could tease people with a happy memory while listening to something so awful.

"I'm waiting on Higgins to decide how he wants to handle this," Edna said. "He's on the sixth floor now."

Rob nodded. Since the mayor's security fell to CIU's Dignitary Protection Section, Major Higgins was probably angling for an ass-kissing position with the chief right about now. Higgins was a dick. The kind of person that if you strolled into his office and found him choking to death on something, you'd just leave and softly close the door behind you without saying a word.

Edna pursed her lips and dropped the ball on the desk. "The question is, does this constitute a direct threat to the mayor? It's obvious the newspaper article is some kind of indirect communication, but is it an actual threat?"

Terry pulled himself up in the chair and crossed his legs. "I don't see how it could be interpreted any other way. Has to be a threat."

Edna picked the ball back up and gave it another couple of squeezes. She leaned closer to Rob and Frank before saying, "Sorry you guys had to go out there, but I wanted our people to have eyes on the scene in case we end up getting involved through the back door. Did Alton offer anything of value?"

Rob started to answer, but Frank spoke up for the first time.

"No one offered anything of value." His voice had a beat-down, angry tone. He stared at Terry and Edna through hollow eyes. "She'd been butchered, and he'd begun eating her heart. That was it."

Edna eased back and lowered her gaze as a blush rushed up her neck.

There were a few awkward seconds of silence before Terry asked, "Do we have an ID on her yet? Does she have any connection to the mayor?"

"Lori Mathews," Rob said. "That's what's on her driver's license in the jeans found at the scene. Alton said he'd check into any connections to the mayor's office and get back with us."

Edna leaned forward again and rested her forearms on her desk. From her expression, it was clear she wanted to end the discussion. She puffed her cheeks and blew out a breath. "We'll see what the sixth floor plans for tomorrow. Anyway, it impacts the dignitary protection guys more than us." She looked Terry's way. "We'll talk later."

Terry rose. "Thanks, lieutenant."

Rob and Frank followed Terry back to his office. While Edna's space had a cold, impersonal look, with everything in straight lines from the awards and certificates on the wall to the uncluttered desk with only the bare essentials, Terry's was the opposite. Rob always felt at home here. The smell of fresh brewed Costa Rican Blend pulled you into a cozy place with oil paintings on every wall. Edna's office tempted you with ice cream, but there was none. Terry's office promised hot, black coffee and there was plenty. The piles of reports and stacks of papers looked like the average detective's desk. That's why everyone respected Terry. He was one of them.

"Grab a cup, boys," Terry said before plopping in the chair behind his desk.

Rob filled Terry's cup first and passed it to him. After filling his and Frank's, they took a seat.

Terry rubbed the back of his neck and grimaced. "This couldn't have come at a worse time. The mayor has enough on his plate now, with his father on his death bed."

Rob blew on the coffee before taking a sip. "It's a miracle the guy's alive at his age. How old is he, anyway?"

"Hmmm, let's see now." Terry stared up at the ceiling a few seconds.

"Ninety-seven," Frank answered. "Turns ninety-eight in November."

Rob stared at Frank, took another sip, and grinned. "How *do* you keep all that useless shit in your head?"

Frank shrugged and also sipped his coffee. "It's a gift."

"Thing is," Terry said, "when this hits the media, no telling what will happen. I expect that's one of the things Higgins and the chief are discussing right about now. "

"Think the details will show up in the news?" Rob asked.

Frank chuckled and went into his slouch position. "Always does. We have more leaks than the Titanic."

Terry nodded. "But no use speculating this early." He checked his watch. "Let's go home, Miller time."

Rob and Frank meandered back to their cubicles. Rob didn't want to go home. He didn't want to lie or try to explain what he'd seen an hour ago when his wife, Carmen, asked, "What did you do today?"

The office hum had changed. Instead of coffee perking, computers being powered up, and lively chatter from other detectives, it had the more subdued sound of closing down, throwing on sports jackets, and quietly moving stacks of case paperwork for another day. Through the glass window of Edna's office, Rob saw her gathering her files and ramming them into her black, shiny briefcase. Frank swallowed the last of the coffee, slipped on his jacket, and straightened the collar. "Ready?"

Rob cleared his throat and didn't meet eyes with him. "No... I have a few things."

Frank sauntered out the door, and Rob dialed his home phone number.

When Carmen answered, he said, "Yeah, running a little late. Please keep supper warm."

Rob would hang around until well past rush hour. After this afternoon, didn't have an appetite anyway. Either catch up on work or have a few pops at a downtown bar. His chest tightened as memories flooded back. Disturbing memories. Memories forty-seven years old—before Rob was even born. Stories the family still told, faded photos, and frightening recollections from aunts and uncles. Rob ran a hand across his Marine high and tight haircut and opened his email, but he couldn't concentrate. Of all the homicides he'd investigated, this was the only one that triggered the recollections. Why this one? Why today?

FRANK PARKED in his building's underground garage and took the elevator up. Even being below ground level, the garage was a furnace during the summer. Living in a high-rise in uptown had its advantages as well as a few disadvantages. Frank had hipster and yuppie ways, but never thought of himself as one. Wrong job, wrong education, wrong political views. But his building was full of them. Most made more annually than Frank made in five years with the city. They were friendly until they learned he was a cop. Frank couldn't care less—they always threw boring parties. He took the elevator to the top floor and ambled into his loft. He released a breath —his sanctuary. He changed into a T-shirt and gym shorts then poured a glass of red. Frank stood for several minutes staring out onto his plant-filled balcony. The green palms, elephant ears, and climbing vines gave it an inviting quality. His hanging baskets of blooming plants and ivies shielded the grill and hammock from the baking sun. Only half the balcony was in the sunlight this time of day. The plants had that saggy look they took on just before wilting and dying. Needed to water again this evening. He was half tempted to turn on the ceiling fan and wade onto the superheated patio. But with the temperature still over a hundred, it felt more like an oven than the green oasis he loved in the spring and fall, even most of the winter. He cracked the sliding glass door open and poked his head out. Even twenty floors above the street, the air had a hot, dead odor—no breeze.

Frank flopped on the sofa and sipped the glass of red. He'd tried pushing the vision of the woman from his mind on the drive home, but it still flashed in his memory. Why would someone do that to another human? One thing his years in law enforcement had taught him, there was nothing he could imagine that a person wasn't capable of. Frank was happy the investigation would land in someone else's lap. *Not the kind of thing I'm cut out for.* That's why he avoided going to the Homicide Unit as a detective. Working things like that depressed him. Criminal Intelligence suited him—more cerebral. Monitoring criminal patterns, figuring things out, and predicting future trends kept his active mind engaged. Frank sometimes speculated whether he was really suited for police work. He'd had no interest in it until he left the restaurant in New York. If his wife hadn't died, he'd probably still be a chef. Her death had changed everything.

Someone knocked quietly on his door twice, waited a couple of seconds and knocked another three times. This brought a smile to Frank's lips. He wasn't expecting her but was happy she'd chosen that particular evening to stop by—good distraction. Didn't feel like being alone tonight. But she was more than just a distraction, and she knew it. More importantly, so did he.

He opened the door, and Katrina Wallace waited with a bottle of red. She grinned, and her dark blue eyes had a mischievous twinkle. She wore a bright yellow tank top and cutoff designer shorts shredded to look a decade older. Her blond hair hung in a loose ponytail. She stood on tiptoes and wrapped her arms around his neck, giving him a long, wet, deep kiss. Her hair had a citrus shampoo fragrance. He reached behind her, grabbed her butt, and lifted her off the floor as a giggle escaped her lips. He was twice her age, and someday, someone at the PD would probably discover their relationship and he'd get yelled at by supervisors, but he didn't care. Dating the mayor's twenty-two-year-old daughter came with risk he was willing to accept.

Katrina was the one thing in his life he didn't have to explain to anyone. Social status, age, and perceptions aside, she had a calming effect he'd only experienced from one other woman. But that woman was gone. Katrina hadn't erased her memory, just made it easier to live with.

THREE

The next morning at nine o'clock, Frank and Rob were back in Edna's office, waiting on Terry. Frank studied her and pulled in her scent. Her olive complexion, the tilt of her head, the knock-out figure. Edna always stimulated something in his psyche he couldn't explain. If she wasn't married and his lieutenant... She wore another short skirt this morning. She turned as she chatted on the phone and crossed her legs —Frank accidently got an eyeful.

She was talking to another lieutenant from Homicide about his ideas on the case. Frank and Rob politely acted like they weren't listening. Rob had bags under his eyes this morning, and his ramrod straight back had a noticeable bend. Didn't see him like that very often. Rob usually exemplified all the things Frank aspired to but was too lazy to do.

Terry rushed in and took a seat in the chair by the door. "Sorry."

"I have to go," Edna said into the phone and hung up. She took a moment, scanning a stack of papers before speaking. Using her *command voice,* she read from the notes.

"Higgins and I met earlier. The chief briefed the mayor personally on the dead woman. Showed him a DL photo of the victim.

Mayor doesn't know her or why she would have an article regarding him and his family." Edna's brow folded. "So, we have to assume the worst—it was left by the suspect. As a precaution, two additional detectives are being laid on each shift of the mayor's protective detail for a while." She looked up from the papers at Rob and Frank. "You two will liaise with Alton in Homicide on his investigation. Can't afford to have anything fall through the cracks. He's been instructed to share all investigative material with you. Higgins, the chief, and the mayor want regular updates."

Rob groaned and lowered his head.

Edna cut her stare to him. "Problem?"

Rob straightened a little and took a breath. "No, ma'am."

Terry broke in. "It's either that or rotate you guys to supplement the mayor's protective detail." Terry made a face. "Not a lot of excitement there—mostly hurry up and wait stuff."

Frank came awake—didn't need that action. "I love liaising. We both do."

A grin eased across Edna's lips. "I bet you do," she mumbled.

Terry followed Rob and Frank back to their cubes. He motioned at Frank. "Better shoot Alton a call. Get the latest update." Terry glanced at Rob. "This shouldn't be too bad. Just monitor what's going on in Homicide so Higgins doesn't get blind-sided in a staff meeting. You know the CYA drill."

Frank hated busy work. *So, Higgins doesn't get blind-sided.* Yeah, right.

Frank's phone rang. The caller ID showed Alton Brady.

"Hey, Frank," Alton said. "Looks like we're joined at the hip on this dead woman. I'm swinging by Sarge's for lunch. Wanna meet me?"

Frank placed his hand over the receiver and stared at Rob. "Sarge's?"

Rob showed the double thumbs up sign.

"Just about to call you for any new information."

"Yeah, got a couple of things. Tell you over lunch."

FRANK AND ROB sauntered into Sarge's a few minutes past eleven o'clock. Frank gazed at the green, leather barstools and red booths all squeezed into the narrow space, looking for Alton. The small bar and sandwich joint was filling fast. A full-length mirror behind the bar gave it the illusion of a larger space. The sweet smell of honey-baked ham and Dijon mustard wafted past Frank's nose. Alton's reflection in the mirror, waving from the last booth in the rear, caught Frank's eye.

Sergeant Jimmy Bielstein retired from the PD five years ago. His dream had always been to open a bar. He wanted a quiet place cops, prosecutors, and jailers could drink or grab a quick bite without being around the assholes who occupied the other downtown places. His dream came to fruition with the opening of Sarge's. Sarge envisioned a big, stylish place in a trendy area of downtown, but his budget didn't allow it. Ended up with a tight, understated space a lot closer to the Greyhound bus station than he'd desired.

As Frank led the way to the back of the place, Sarge, stationed behind the bar with a bar rag hung over his left shoulder, looked in his direction.

Frank held up two fingers. "The usual."

Sarge nodded and started working on their orders.

Rob and Frank slid into the booth opposite Alton. He already had his notebook out and a cola in a glass. Alton's hair grayed a little more each year on the sides. Kind of gave him a professor-like distinguished look. He had almost twenty years with the PD.

Rob nodded at the Coke Alton held. "Cherry or vanilla?"

Frank sniffed the air as he slid beside Rob. "I'm guessing vanilla."

Alton glanced at the drink and grinned. "Always vanilla."

The running joke in Dallas PD was Sarge's colas. He'd retired out of Vice. Everyone drank in Vice, on and off-duty. Hell, the city gave them a weekly allowance for drinks and money to slip into the G-strings of dancers and ladies in massage parlors who they were trying to make a prostitution case on. Sarge wasn't a health nut, but believed alcohol helped with digestion and kind of took the edge off a stressful job like law enforcement. His rule was simple. One alcoholic beverage if you were on duty and working plain-clothes. None if you were in uniform. Everyone chose something mixed with Coke. Since every drink looked exactly alike from a distance, it was a good plausible deniability tactic if the wrong supervisor walked in—like Higgins.

The way the game was played made sense in a perverse sort of way. Coke equals regular Coke. Cherry Coke equals Coke plus a shot of bourbon, and vanilla Coke equals Coke and vodka—simple. Sarge arrived with their cherry Cokes and said, "Sandwiches won't be long." His shock of thick blond hair streaked with gray was a mess, as usual. The aroma of beer and bread wafted off him. He wiped a crumb off the table with a bar towel, and the big German spun around and headed back to the counter.

"The woman from yesterday, Mathews, was a local lounge lizard from East Dallas," Alton said. "Thirty-three years of age. Worked in a number of ice houses, beer joints, and honky-tonks all her adult life." He licked his finger and turned a page in his notebook. "Arrested twice for solicitation, once for PI, and once for shoplifting." Alton closed his notebook, slipped it back into his jacket pocket, and took a drink. He smacked his lips. "Nice."

"So, she's a nobody?" Frank asked.

"Pretty much," Alton added. "No known connection to the mayor or his family."

Rob dropped his chin and mumbled. "Bad way for a somebody or a nobody to die."

Everyone nodded. They sipped their Cokes without talking for a while.

After a few seconds, Alton sat back in the booth as Sarge delivered their sandwiches.

"Here you go, guys," Sarge said. "Can't visit. Jan had a doctor's appointment—running late. Just trying to keep caught up."

He rushed toward the bar without another word as a group of four uniformed sheriff's deputies strolled in.

Rob crossed himself and attacked the ham sandwich. Frank rested his elbows on the table and kept sampling his Coke. He eyed Alton. "Got the ME's report yet?"

"Yeah, preliminary, at least. Still waiting on a few tests." Alton stroked his throat and grimaced. "Poor thing got the whole treatment. Tortured and murdered. Someone must have really hated her. Crime of passion, most likely. Probably an ex-lover or husband. We're checking that angle."

At Alton's description of the death, Rob stopped eating. He looked up, laid his sandwich on his plate, and frowned at Alton before drinking all his Coke in one long gulp.

After lunch, Rob and Frank spent the rest of the afternoon on administrative paperwork. Frank didn't mind paperwork. He enjoyed the office noise—the hum relaxed him. Voices blending with the sounds of typing and coffee cups dragged across desks. The only time it bothered him was when he wanted to do a deep think.

Just before five, Terry meandered up to Frank's cube and sat on the edge of his desk. He looked around and lowered his voice. "Edna called a minute ago. FBI has invited us to their office tomorrow morning for a special briefing on the murdered woman." Terry stretched his neck and looked like he might say something else but didn't.

Rob popped his head and neck above the low cubicle wall. "What?"

"Not you," Terry said. "This is Higgins' party. Him, Edna, me, and Frank."

A slow smile moved across Rob's mouth. "Breaks my heart I can't come—especially since Higgins will be there."

"Any idea what it's about?" Frank asked.

Terry shrugged. "Edna just said us four were invited for a ten o'clock meeting—no details." He eyed Frank up and down and pursed his lips. "Probably should wear a suit tomorrow."

Frank had been to the FBI office only once, for a Missing Person's seminar when he'd worked that unit. Never thought he'd go back. Never wanted to go back. Something must be seriously messed up with this case. Something so big the FBI was asking for local assistance. They didn't do that very often. In fact, they'd acquired a reputation over the years of not including the locals in anything they could do by themselves. No use sharing credit when you didn't have to. No, this was something they couldn't do alone.

FOUR

Frank came in early Wednesday morning to finish catching up before the meeting. Terry was already in his office and had put on the squad coffee pot. The aroma of fresh brew drew Frank to the coffee bar before going to his desk. Rob wasn't there yet. Probably still in the gym. Besides lifting weights, Rob boxed every other day. Frank never could keep straight which were boxing days. Rob did weights and boxed; Frank did yoga and drank wine. How did they ever end up partners?

A few minutes before nine, Rob walked in. He was in full cowboy attire. Western cut brown suit, starched white shirt with white, pearl snap buttons, and ostrich cowboy boots. The way he dressed would look better on someone who was taller than five feet seven. But Rob's stout physique still looked better than Frank's—tall and skinny.

Frank grinned and did an impersonation of riding a horse. In his best John Wayne voice he said, "Giddy up, cowboy."

Rob ignored him, grabbed his cup, and headed to the coffee pot. When he returned, he said, "You're one to talk," motioning at Frank's business suit.

Frank had chosen a navy-blue suit, light blue shirt, and a black and burgundy regimental tie. Frank hated suits, wore them as seldom as possible, but always got compliments when he wore one.

"You look like you're either running for office or about to preach a sermon," Rob said before taking his seat.

Frank didn't answer.

After waking up his computer, Rob draped his jacket over the back of his chair and gazed over the top of the cubicle wall. "Wonder why Higgins only wanted you at the meeting and not me?"

Frank had also considered this. Higgins hated them both equally, but he never did anything without a reason. If not for the fact they were the best case solvers in CIU, he would have transferred them years ago. Frank let another grin ease across his lips. "Only thing I can figure is he suspected you'd wear that outfit and didn't want the embarrassment at the bureau."

Rob made a face before going back to his computer. "Smart ass cracker."

A half hour later, Frank drove to the FBI building on One Justice Way. The five-story white building was a fortress in the middle of a large open field and surrounded by a vehicle-proof rock and metal fence. Since 9/11, new FBI offices were about as close to reinforced camps as they could get. Closest neighbor was the DEA building, which was equally fortified. Frank never liked visiting federal law enforcement offices. The feds never asked you over unless they'd get something in return. He badged his way through the gate and walked into the front doors. After he displayed his credentials and receiving a visitor's tag, his female escort agent scanned her ID badge on the keypad and buzzed them into the secure rear lobby. They entered just as Frank's FBI pal David Ford walked past.

Ford did a double take. "Frank, what are you doing here?"

"Invitation to a meeting."

Ford turned to the female agent. "I'll take him."

"Great," she said.

Frank had worked with Ford on more than one case in the past.

He always played fair and never tried to BS Frank. Ford held the distinction of being the office heartthrob. Six foot, muscular, with black hair, he was the most eligible bachelor in the Dallas FBI, and that's the way he liked it.

Ford motioned with his head for Frank to step into the elevator. As the door closed, Ford asked, "You here because of that murder yesterday in the forest?"

"Think so. Any idea why they called a meeting?"

Ford nodded and lowered his voice even though they were alone in the elevator. "BAU's here."

"Huh?"

"Behavior Analysis Unit at Quantico—Layla and a team arrived last night."

When the door opened to the fifth floor, Ford led Frank down the hall toward the SAC's Conference Room. Several other FBI types meandered down the hall, and Edna and Terry stood outside the conference room door, talking to an agent with a short, blond beard.

As he and Ford walked, Frank whispered, "Who's Layla?"

Ford slowed his pace and hesitated a moment. He turned his back to the group in the hall. In a quiet voice he said, "The newest wunderkind from BAU. Someone to steer clear of."

The way he said it made Frank believe Ford and Layla may have had a past run-in. "Really. Did they send her down because of the murder?"

"Yup. She's the new go-to gal."

"Interesting."

Ford grinned as they approached Edna and Terry. He lowered his voice again. "Just don't let her get you alone."

"What...why?"

Ford stopped and drew closer. He winked before saying, "Likes playing mind games."

"Mind games?"

"Coming, Frank?" Edna called and motioned as she walked into the conference room.

Ford nodded and slapped Frank on the shoulder. "Good luck."

Frank followed Terry and Edna into the conference room and took a seat at a big mahogany table with black leather chairs. There was a large video conference screen and several FBI agents, all wearing dark suites and serious faces. The scent of lemon furniture wax wafted up from the shining conference table. Sitting there were Alton, his lieutenant, and a sergeant from DPD Homicide. None looked all that excited to be in attendance. Alton held a keyring and kept spinning it on his little finger to see how many rotations he could make it turn.

Frank leaned closer to Edna and whispered, "Thought Higgins was coming."

Edna shrugged. "Last minute meeting on the sixth floor." She smiled. "Unhappy?"

Frank grinned and slid into the chair beside her. "I'm devastated."

At that moment, the FBI agent with the blond beard that had been talking with Edna and Terry in the hall broke away from the other agents and addressed the police visitors. The agent introduced himself as Supervisory Special Agent Ben Stroud. Besides the blond beard, he had short blond hair and angry eyes. He sat several navy-blue binders on the table, thanked everyone for attending and introduced the other FBI agents in the room. There were two from Atlanta, a couple from the Dallas office, and two from BAU in Quantico. When he introduced Layla, the corners of her mouth turned up into a quick, mischievous grin before settling back into the serious expression they were probably told to exhibit at the first meeting with the local cops. Agent Stroud took ten minutes rehashing the crime scene from yesterday.

Something felt wrong with this whole setup. Frank hadn't been aware the Bureau even knew about the murder until yesterday. No FBI agents on the ground in the hot, sticky woods. That, combined with what Ford said about this Layla person, caused Frank's suspicion meter to ping a little higher. Whatever the FBI had in mind, it probably wasn't good for the local cops.

Layla stood behind and to the side of Agent Stroud. She was young, around thirty, and attractive, with shoulder-length black hair and dark intelligent eyes. She wore a black jacket and skirt with a white silk blouse, the top button undone. Reminded Frank of the actress Krysten Ritter. Seemed a little antsy. Almost bouncing, as if she wanted to say something. But she didn't, just studied each member of the DPD contingent as Agent Stroud spoke. When her stare fell on Frank, he stared back and didn't blink. She didn't either. She held his gaze for a few seconds before giving someone else the once-over.

"...and at this time, I'd like to introduce Supervisory Special Agent Layla Barbee with the Behavioral Analysis Unit," Stroud said.

Layla stepped forward. "Thank you, Ben. And thank you all for coming on such short notice." She pointed a remote at the video-conference screen and the image of the dead woman hanging from the tree flashed on with all its horror. Seeing it today was as impactful as yesterday for Frank. Like something from a scary movie in real life. He lowered his eyes and opened his notebook.

Edna winced at the young, murdered woman strung up like a side of beef.

Layla gave everyone a chance to absorb the picture before saying, "I'm afraid I have some bad news." She walked to the end of the screen with her head down. Looked like she might be thinking about what she wanted to say next, but Frank knew better. The confident way she stood, her expressions, and her overall demeanor screamed strong power-woman. She knew exactly what she was going to say, probably been rehearsing it for hours in front of a mirror. Frank gave her credit—she'd played it perfectly. Building up suspense and tension with the small pause until she had everyone leaning forward in their seats. She looked up with a pensive expression and a gleam in her eye. "We believe this—" She motioned to the screen. "Is the work of a serial killer."

Edna's brow creased and she leaned over, whispering something to Terry. He whispered something back and clasped his hands, digging the tips of his fingers into his knuckles.

The lieutenant from homicide cleared his throat before speaking up. "Excuse me, ma'am, but we have no indications that's the case here. True enough it was a heinous crime, but there's no reason to believe it was committed by a serial killer." The sergeant seated next to Alton gazed at him. Alton had stopped playing with the keyring and stared blank-faced at Layla like she just said fairies were real.

Layla allowed another quick, confident smile before continuing. She eyed the lieutenant, and in a patient and confident voice, she said, "But it was." She touched the remote again and a second image popped on the screen. This one was a colored map of the Southern United States, from Georgia to Texas. Eight numbered red flags dotted the map, with the last in Dallas. Layla gave everyone a moment to digest the implication.

Frank got that sick stomach churning feeling he got sometimes when surprised and knew he wasn't going to like whatever he heard next.

Layla spread her feet shoulder-width apart and held her hands behind her back. She raised her chin and stared at the group. "We believe the killing spree began approximately twenty-seven months ago outside Atlanta." Photos of eight women appeared below the map. Frank leaned forward, studying them. All were young and attractive, with dark eyes and black hair, like Layla.

"The victims ranged in age from nineteen to twenty-eight," Layla said. "We believe the killer is a young, white male and has some sort of skill or job that allows him to easily find work in or near large metropolitan areas." She flipped the picture back to the map and pointed. "Atlanta, Montgomery, Jackson, Shreveport, and now Dallas. He kills one or two every few months and then moves on. A drifter, but not necessarily a transient. Someone without anything holding him in one particular area—no family, no obligations, and free to travel when he wants."

Edna sat a little straighter before speaking up. Her voice had that quiet, unsure quality she showed when she wasn't certain of her facts. "Why do you believe he's the same person responsible for all those murders?"

Yeah. Frank had been about to ask that same question. Something wasn't adding up. From her cool expression, Layla was ready with an answer. "He takes trophies," she said. She turned back to the photos of the young women. "Besides their overall similar appearance, these victims have one other thing in common." She again paused for dramatic effect. "They all have four or more missing teeth. Always rear molars."

"Good god!" the sergeant from homicide murmured, and his mouth dropped open.

The clanging sound of Alton dropping the keyring on the table caused a few to jump. Alton quickly scooped it up and put it in his pocket.

Layla appeared unfazed. Her too-cool demeanor and blank expression caused Frank concern. She paced in front of the screen to the opposite side. When she got to the end she turned and said, "We also believe the suspect has some basic knowledge of dentistry. No evidence to suggest he's a dentist, but he knows how to extract teeth that are some of the hardest to pull in the human mouth without appearing to break them—which isn't easy."

The question that Frank wanted answered was *how does she know?* He was about to ask it, but Layla didn't give him the chance.

"We've consulted with experts in the field. They believe he's either seen teeth extracted or someone explained or showed him how. Most probably has extraction forceps in his possession."

Terry had the look of a man who'd just been told there was a bloated, dead possum in the pool. His mouth twisted into a disgusted grimace.

"Have all the murders been like yesterday?" Frank asked.

Layla showed the flicker of a smile. "Best question of the day. The short answer is no. We've seen an escalation of the guy's psychosis and violence toward his victims as time progresses." She flipped off the presentation and stood with her hands behind her back again. "The murder near Atlanta was a straight strangulation and removal of teeth. Over the last two years, things have only gotten worse. He's added torture. And now finally, dismemberment and cannibalism. But all the victims have missing teeth. That's the common denominator. It's never been reported by the press. We've kept that as our secret verification fact. That's why we believe it's the same guy."

Everyone was quiet until Alton put both hands on the table. "So what kind of insane schizoid should we be looking for?"

Layla showed another pensive expression. "Not necessarily insane or schizoid. Most serial killers, while suffering from a psychosis, aren't the schizophrenic or bipolar types you'd expect. We refer to them as having an antisocial personality disorder."

Alton grunted, smirked, and settled back into his chair. "Antisocial—you can say that again." He stared at her with a Cheshire Cat grin.

Layla didn't return the grin. Her forehead creased and the dark eyes bore in on him, giving Alton the most *go to hell look* Frank had seen in the last few years. She quickly regained her composure and threw her shoulders back, again lifting her chin.

"We believe he's most likely a white male, probably between twenty and thirty, very powerful, and we think he lives in an apartment."

"Why?" Frank asked.

"Why, what?"

"Why do you believe he lives in an apartment?"

"Because of the nature of his crimes," Layla said. "Doesn't live anywhere long enough to put down roots, establish credit or maintain a steady career, or purchase a residence. Probably lives paycheck to paycheck. And all the victims appear to have been tortured and killed at the scene, indicating he didn't have his way with them at a private residence before dumping the bodies."

Alton mumbled. "Paycheck to paycheck. Sounds like most cops I know."

Layla ignored him. "We'd like to work with the PD on this. If he follows his usual MO, he'll be here awhile—probably kill again in a jurisdiction this big."

That remark left the room with an eerie silence before she said, "We believe we know the kind of places this guy likes to look for victims. Dark, out of the way bars and ice houses, in the low-rent part of town. The places that don't always know their clientele and he could blend in. Most of his victims have histories of working in or frequenting those places. Probably targets them while drinking there."

Frank turned toward Alton to gauge his reaction. He wasn't the most sophisticated homicide guy on the force, but he knew his business. The muscles in his neck had tightened, and Alton opened and closed both hands into fists.

"So, we're just waiting for another victim then?" Alton asked.

From her look, it was clear Layla had had just about all of Alton she could stand for one day. She took a deep cleansing breath before saying, "We'd very much appreciate the department's assistance locating this guy. Talk to your sources; send plain clothes Vice, Narcotics and CIU officers to drinking establishments this guy probably visits. FBI can post a reward. There's a lot of work we can do on this one. We're putting together a task force." Her gaze fell back on Frank. When he returned the stare, she blushed slightly and turned away.

No one spoke. This was one of those pincer movements the Bureau was so good at. Bring everyone together, drop a bag of crap in their laps, and ask for help. Of course, in reality, it was also probably the best way to get the guy off the streets before he killed again. But it sounded like a long shot to Frank. At least the Bureau had a plan— not a good plan, but a plan.

After a few seconds Edna asked, "What do you need us to do?"

Layla perked up. She laid her hand on the binders on the desk.

"Take one of these briefing notebooks back to your units and share it with your people. Our SAC has a meeting scheduled with your chief tomorrow to formalize the task force. We'd like this kicked off ASAP." Layla showed a courteous smile and ended with, "And thank you in advance for your assistance."

Edna's lips drew into tight lines, and she looked at the others at the table. One by one they stood and headed for the hall, picking up a notebook on their way out. Frank received a text as he strolled to the door. He stopped to read it—Rob.

How's it going?

Frank texted back, *Great. Heading to the PD now.*

When he looked up, only he and Layla remained in the room.

"Detective Pierce," she said, stepping toward him. "I need to talk to you, please."

She knew his name. From a distance she was more attractive. Up close, the eyes were a little too big and the mouth a little too small. Reminded Frank of a doll his sister used to play with. He slid his phone back into his pocket. "About what?"

Layla glanced at her watch and frowned. "Not enough time now. Could I meet you somewhere in a few hours?"

She'd had her eye on him since he walked in. The top of her blouse cracked opened just enough that the outline of a white frilly bra appeared. Frank had no idea what this after-hours meeting might be about, but it went against his nature to avoid attractive women. He must have considered it too long because she lightly touched his arm. "It's very important—won't take all evening."

"I suppose we could have a drink later."

"Great," she said. She handed him a card. "Call or text me where we'll meet. I should be available after five."

Her relaxed stance spoke volumes. *A woman used to getting what she wants when she wants it.* Frank nodded, took the card, and wandered into the hall. When he got to the spot he'd left Agent Ford, the guy's last words echoed in Frank's ears—*Likes playing mind games.*

FIVE

Late Wednesday afternoon, Perry walked into the kitchen and filled a big glass with ice before topping it off with water from the faucet. He downed it with one long gulp. Crew had run out of water today and the foreman refused to go get any more. Perry filled another glass and drank half while he lifted his face inches from the air conditioner vent, letting the cold air bathe his skin. One of the advantages of being tall—breathe better air.

"Hey, Perry," Raul said as he passed.

Perry eyed him as he took a plastic container from the refrigerator and set it on the counter. He dug out a sauce pan and dumped the contents of the container into the pan.

"Want some chili?"

Perry answered in his quiet voice, speaking just above a whisper. "No, thanks."

"What?"

Perry spoke up. "I said no."

Mrs. Cleveland walked through the kitchen with a basket of clean clothes and stared at Raul. "Why you about to eat before we have supper?"

"I'm already hungry," Raul said, setting the pan on the stove and lighting a burner.

"Mind you don't scorch that pan—it's one of my good ones," she said, heading to the living room with the basket.

She always carried the clothes into the living room and dumped them on the sofa. She liked watching game shows as she folded.

Perry weaved his face back and forth, letting more cold air blow his long, silky blond hair and dry the sweat. Raul hummed some silly tune while mixing the chili. Perry hated Raul. If it wasn't for him, Perry would have the nice bedroom with the full bath and view of the back yard. As it was, he had to walk down the hall just to take a leak. Actually, it wasn't too bad though. Finding a boarding house this nice after arriving in Dallas was lucky. The two-story was clean and comfortable. For something built in the '40s it was in excellent shape. Be even nicer if he had Raul's room. Raul wasn't all bad. Let Perry use his computer when he wanted, but he could be a pain. He needed to move.

Raul stopped humming and started whistling the same stupid tune as he kept mixing. Guy was always happy. He finished warming the food and turned off the burner. He emptied most of it into a bowl and set the pan back on the stove, then headed for the living room. Over his shoulder he said, "Left about a cup if you change your mind."

The smell of chili made Perry's stomach ache for food, but he didn't want anything from Raul except for him to leave. Guy was self-ish, didn't respect Mrs. Cleveland. She was such a nice old landlady. How could someone treat her the way Raul did? He was lazy, never offered to wash the dishes or clothes, never helped with yard work or offered to wash her car. Mrs. Cleveland gave Perry a break on his rent for helping out. He didn't mind doing a few things around the place.

Perry finished his water and set the glass in the sink. The music from the game show *Jeopardy* floated into the kitchen. Mrs. Cleveland and Raul always watched it every afternoon after doing laundry. They had this thing going. Seeing who could out-guess the other and beat the contestants. Perry only watched it a couple of times. For someone who never graduated, the answers were too hard. Perry preferred reading the paper for entertainment.

"What is Mount McKinley," Mrs. Cleveland shouted before the voice of the host repeated, "What is Mount McKinley."

Laughter sounded from Mrs. Cleveland and Raul.

Raul would never move out. And she'd never kick him out. Just before leaving the kitchen to grab a shower, Perry turned the burner back on under the pan of chili. Made sure it was nice and low. After it started bubbling, he removed the lid and smirked.

Perry headed for the stairs. Needed to get cleaned up. Didn't mind operating the saw at work even though it was the dirtiest crew job. Made him feel special—knowing everyone had to wait on him to finish his work before they could do theirs. But the caked drywall dust made his back itch as he marched up the stairs. With each step, the swaying necklace under his shirt tickled his chest hairs, the teeth making a quiet clicking noise as they knocked together.

SIX

After work, Frank waited at the Uptown Pub off McKinney Avenue. It wasn't far from his loft and he liked it because of its rustic character. A younger crowd usually hung out there, lots of yuppies, and it was a lively place to relax after a long day before attempting the commute home. Frank never had that problem. Just another advantage of living in uptown. In a past life, the restaurant and bar had been a 1920s home. Frank never came during karaoke night, but he'd made friends with the cook and passed on a couple of his favorite recipes from his professional days in New York. Chef always sent out a complimentary appetizer for him when he came for dinner. Frank grabbed a quiet table and gazed at the deserted outdoor patio. Sunshine streamed across it like a spotlight, giving it a glaring, almost luminous appearance. Nice place to relax during most of the year, but not today. There were tables and large umbrellas shading them, but no one ventured outside in this oppressive heat. The crowd had started building around the bar, and the noise level rose with each new arrival.

Frank had filled Rob in on the briefing after returning to CIU. Rob showed a strange expression after hearing about the serial killer theory. Seemed quieter than usual and declined to meet Frank and Layla for drinks—weird. Rob never passed up after-work drinks.

Frank had debated canceling the meeting. He didn't have a clue what she wanted to discuss, but Ford's warning still lingered in the back of his mind. *Likes playing mind games.* What did that even mean? Frank was king of the mind games. Other DPD units would call him once a month or so if they had a suspect who wasn't cooperating. Frank would talk with the guy for several hours about a dozen things that had seemingly nothing to do with the crime. Make them relax while discussing their childhood, school, family, jobs, relationships, likes, fears, doubts. But all the while he was probing, cataloging, looking for that one chink in their emotional armor that was the eventual key to a confession. Was that the reason he wanted to meet Layla for a one-on-one? To check her mind games?

He'd waited less than ten minutes before she arrived. Layla marched inside and jerked her sunglasses off while slowly scanning the place as her eyes adjusted. Like someone memorizing every detail. When her gaze caught his, for reasons Frank couldn't explain, he felt elated. Frank seldom felt elated. That faint smile crept across her lips as she wove between tables toward him. Place was almost full of uptown workers grabbing a drink or two to fortify them for the evening drive. Conversations quieted as heads turned her way.

Layla took a seat at the table and looked around the crowded room. "I'd forgotten how bad traffic can be in big cities. Work at Quantico, so my commute's easier."

Frank didn't answer. He studied her a moment. She'd flown down super early this morning, conducted god knows how many briefings, and been in meetings all afternoon. Her light shade of red lipstick had faded during the day. Probably didn't have time to touch it up. Just a trace remained on the sides of her lower lip. Her black hair had a little wave he'd not noticed earlier. Gave her more of the child's doll look. And her pale skin was stretched tight on her cheeks and below her chin—the wonder of youth. There was just a whiff of sweet floral perfume. It hadn't been there this morning.

Frank already had a glass of red. The waiter rushed up and asked for her order.

Layla motioned at Frank's glass. "I'll have what he's having and a shot of Casamigos mezcal."

The waiter's head snapped back and he said, "Yes, ma'am," before heading to the bar.

Frank grinned. Was this just a show for him, or did she really drink mezcal with a red wine chaser?

She sighed. "Thanks for meeting me." She sat back and laced her fingers across her mid-section. First time Frank saw her not standing ramrod straight.

Frank still hadn't figured out her game, so he also sat back, mirroring her pose. "Couldn't imagine what you wanted to talk about. Seems you made things clear enough at the briefing."

Layla nodded and a blush filled her cheeks. She spoke just above a whisper. "My reasons for wanting to meet you were not just professional, but also personal."

"Personal?"

"Yes, you have a bit of a reputation in this town."

Frank had no idea what she was talking about, and that made him pause before answering. He waited a moment too long to answer before they were interrupted.

"Here you are, ma'am." The waiter sat the wine and shot glass of mezcal on the table. "Just holler if you need something else," he said as he retreated.

Layla snatched the up the mezcal and, without a word, downed the whole thing in one gulp. Frank kept a steady gaze on her. She didn't flinch, didn't make a face, and didn't make that *grrr* sound in the back of her throat that he did after drinking the stuff.

Layla dabbed her lips with the paper napkin. "As I was saying, I wanted to talk to you because your name was at the top of the list." She reached for her wine.

Frank tilted his head. "And what list is that?"

She was taking her first sip as he asked the question. When she stared back at him, he got the feeling he should have known the answer. Her eyes squinted. "You don't know about the list?"

"No. What kind of list?"

"Hmm..." She held up the glass of wine. "This *is* delicious. Good choice."

Frank didn't answer. He took a swallow of wine instead.

After a few awkward seconds, she said, "Some departments know about the list and some don't." She gave a good-natured shrug. "My bad for not checking first."

Frank still didn't answer.

She smiled and leaned closer. "The Bureau rates police agencies across the country. We determine the level of professionalism and competence of each so we can better know how to work with them. Within each department we pick a half dozen or so detectives that are the best at what they do—the list." Layla took another quick sip, leaned her forearms on the table, and lowered her voice again. "When we have a high-profile case, like a serial killer, we attempt to get the department's best people involved."

Frank just stared at her. He'd never heard anything about a list. Of course, there probably was a lot of stuff above his pay grade he'd not heard about. Kind of made sense when you thought about it. He'd elected to meet with her one-on-one not only because she was attractive, but also to see if her mind game was up to his. Now he'd been snared in her mind trap before he realized the game had even started.

Frank didn't show any surprise or satisfaction at being named the best as he slowly said, "I'm probably on a lot of lists. This is a new one for me." A clever thought suddenly occurred to him. "And can I also assume Alton's somewhere on the list since he's the homicide case detective?"

"Ha!" Layla eased back and took another sip. "Not on your life. That mope was assigned to the case by DPD before we were even aware of it." She shrugged again. "Sometimes we get lucky, sometimes we have to make our own luck." She pointed at Frank.

Whole thing sounded far-fetched to Frank, but he decided to play along. "What exactly do you want me to do?"

Layla showed her trademark grin. "You've worked undercover, been highly decorated for valor, and have a sharp, analytical mind. We need someone like that to help investigate this case. Killer's going to strike again—we know that. We have to intercept him before he slaughters someone else. It's only a matter of time. If we can catch him here in Dallas, who knows how many lives we can save. Guy's only half way across the country and already killed eight."

After saying that, she took a breath and blinked a couple of times.

Frank shifted. Something about the way he was sitting suddenly became very uncomfortable. How did she know so much about him and his career?

"What about my partner, Rob Soliz. He on your list?"

Layla swirled the last of the wine in her glass and looked over the rim. "Nope, didn't make the cut."

"We're partners, work as a team."

She downed the remainder of the wine and slid the glass to the side. "Sure, bring him along if you like. Everyone needs an assistant."

Frank bristled. "He's not an assistant—he's my partner."

Layla nodded and smirked. "Okay, I get it. I apologize. Your partner is more than welcome, as long as you're there."

Frank settled down. She was in his head. Finally, another question popped into his mind. "During the briefing, you mentioned the killer wasn't necessarily insane. Didn't understand where you were going with that. Who else but someone insane would do that to another human?"

"Alton used the term schizoid," she said. "Clinically, that's incorrect. The person we're looking for most likely doesn't suffer from schizophrenia or some bipolar disorder."

Frank knew about the criminal mind and criminal ways. Mental disease played a large part in some of the most horrific crimes. "Why do you believe that?"

"You see, when someone is schizophrenic or bipolar, their mental abilities are seriously impaired in most cases." She glanced around and spoke in low tones. "This killer has showed the ability to calculate, plan, and execute complicated murders. That's difficult or impossible for someone suffering from a serious condition such as schizophrenia or bipolar. They have difficulty focusing for long periods of time unless they're on their meds. And if they are, chances are they're not thinking about such things." Layla straightened in the chair. "Not saying the guy isn't a crazy, but he's most likely a different kind of crazy. That's why I referred to him as antisocial. That's the clinical term associated with that particular type of disorder."

Frank's mind searched its reference file for all he knew about abnormal psychology. Hadn't worked a lot of crazies, mostly gang and organized crime stuff in CIU. Layla had him at a big disadvantage on this—figures.

"Who are we looking for—exactly?"

Layle grinned. "Same profile I outlined in the briefing, but with some interesting anomalies."

Frank finished his wine and moved the glass to the side. "Such as?"

Layla leaned her forearms on the table again and let out a breath. She had her mouth open to speak when the waiter rolled up.

"Another round?" he asked.

Frank glanced her way. She hesitated a second before the nod.

"Yeah," Frank said. "Two more reds."

As the waiter retreated, Layla eyed Frank. In her lowest voice of the night she said, "What I'm about to tell you should not be repeated, not by us at least. The job of disseminating it will be up to the big dogs." Layla's shoulders tightened as she pushed her head closer to Frank's. "The guy's invisible."

"Huh?"

She drew back a bit. "He leaves a forensic evidence trail everywhere. Never makes any attempt to hide anything. Fingerprints, DNA, footprints, you name it. It's all there. We have everything we need to make a solid case except a suspect. We've run the forensics through all the indices. Attempted to match them in a dozen different ways, but no luck. The guy's invisible, like he doesn't exist. Never been in the military, never filed for any license requiring prints to be submitted, never work for a federal, state, or local entity where prints are required. Not in the Combined DNA Index System. Never arrested or served time. Nothing!"

"Have you checked for a relative match on 23andMe and Ancestry?" Frank asked.

Layla nodded as the waiter delivered their new wine. The place was rocking now. Every seat was taken, and a big crowd stood around the bar. The bar noise and laughter drowned out their conversation. Still, she lowered her voice. "Yeah, we checked those and a half dozen similar sites. Have several leads out, but nothing's come back yet." She picked up her wine and took a hefty swig. "We're flying blind here, Frank. Any ideas?"

"How many states require prints for a driver's license?"

"Four," she said, "including Texas. Well, a thumb print at least."

Frank considered this. "He probably hasn't bothered getting a new license, if he ever had one."

Layla nodded. "That's how we see it."

"Any witnesses or videos that might help us?"

"This guy works in the shadows, places people don't pay much attention and don't bother installing cameras. But we do have something we can use." Layla exhaled. "Waiting for the SAC to discuss it with your chief before we reveal it. Cutting-edge DNA stuff."

"Tell me," Frank said.

Layla stared at him a moment. "Okay, but not a word until it's officially released by the brass. Don't need my butt in a sling with the Dallas SAC or headquarters." She leaned closer and her eyes narrowed. "We don't have a photo but have something almost as good."

Frank didn't say a word, just waited for the big reveal.

"A relatively new forensic DNA analysis method that can give us a better than average description of the suspect."

"What?"

"It's called *Snapshot*. It can help with genetic genealogy, DNA phenotyping, and kinship inference."

Frank didn't deal in DNA too much, but he'd heard about the new technique a couple of years ago. "What is DNA phenotyping?"

"That's what we'll use to identify the suspect. It's the predictor of someone's appearance from just their DNA signature."

"They can do that?"

Layla sipped her wine. "Yeah. Like I said, it's not exactly new, but they've shaken the kinks out enough that it's extremely reliable now."

Frank leaned closer and whispered, "What's the description of the guy you're after?"

"We believe he has an oval-shaped face with Northern European ancestry, fair skin, either blue or green eyes, and light-colored hair. Could even be a nice-looking guy who'd find it easy to pick up women."

"What if he dyes his hair?"

"There are some environmental things we can't control. Dying hair, using colored contacts, *et cetera*. But here's the thing." Layla winked. "I don't believe this guy realizes we're on to him. He's probably just going around living his life the way he wants without regard to anything, including when he kills, or cleaning up the crime scene. Either he doesn't know or doesn't care, I can't decide."

Frank was intrigued, but also disgusted by the whole serial killer aspect of the thing. Didn't know how many more crime scenes he could handle like the one yesterday. Something about the way this whole case was unfolding didn't quite feel right. The idea he might be on a special list and Ford's warning about Layla playing mind games gave him pause.

She pursed her lips and met eyes with him. "So, what do you think? Are you in? Can we include you and your partner in the task force?"

Frank started to say no, but hesitated. This was something he really didn't want to get involved with. He knew if he said no, that would mean he and Rob would wind up sitting in a hot unmarked police car in front of the mayor's house as personal security while other investigators worked the case with the Bureau. He hated sitting in hot cars.

"I can't obligate to anything with discussing it with my partner."

"Fine, discuss it, but push him to do it. I want you on the team."

The mezcal and two wines changed Layla's appearance. Her forehead had relaxed; the small tension wrinkles in her face disappeared, giving her more of a delicate child look. The eyes had a glassy, sensuous sparkle he'd not noticed before, and the ripe lips took on a delicious looking pout Frank found exciting.

"Okay, I'll broach the subject, but no promises."

Layla showed an expression Frank didn't understand—sort of a smirk. Was she pleased? Or was she just satisfied she'd scored another victory. He had the feeling if he sat with her all evening he'll still not figure it out. He drank the last of his wine and pushed back from the table, leaving thirty dollars on the edge. "I have to be going."

Layla's shoulders slumped and she flashed the pout again. "So soon?"

"Yeah," he said. "Have to meet someone for dinner." As he told the lie, there was no one he'd rather have dinner with than her. But it was too late to go back. *Jerk. Next time, think before you speak.*

"You'll let me hear from you tomorrow?"

"Sure."

The waiter walked up.

Layla kept her eyes on Frank and lifted her shot glass. "I'll have one more."

Walking out the door, a profound sense of loss descended on Frank. His FBI pal had been right. Allowing himself to be alone with her had been a mistake. Whatever happened with this case, Frank vowed not to make that mistake again. There was just one problem— he wanted to.

SEVEN

The next morning, Frank got to the office extra early—even beat Terry by ten minutes. He powered up his computer and started the unit's coffee pot, making the first perk extra strong. He loved being the first one in the office, making the first pot of coffee. The rich Arabica bean smell signaled the start of a new day. Mornings, when no one was there and quiet, were the best times to think. Frank had a lot to think about before the mob arrived. When Terry walked in, Frank nodded as he passed.

"Morning, Frank," Terry said.

Frank waited until Terry got settled in his office before making his move. He'd pondered this all last night and made sure he got in early enough to talk to Terry before Rob arrived. Frank sauntered to Terry's door and took a last look over his shoulder before going inside. Terry had his personal pot of Costa Rican blend brewing and was behind his desk, reviewing a folder.

"Got a minute?"

Terry looked up and slipped off his reading glasses. "Yeah, what ya' got?"

Frank swiveled his head again, checking the squad area. "Does the FBI keep any kind of list on local PDs?"

Terry's eyebrows squished together. "What kind of list? List of what?"

Now Frank felt stupid. He'd figured he would, but thinking about it was one kind of stupid and actually feeling it was another. He didn't understand why being on someone's list bothered him so much, but it did. He cleared his throat and said, "List of top investigators."

"You mean detectives?"

"Yeah."

"Never heard that one before. Who told you that?"

"Agent Barbee, yesterday."

Terry chuckled. "Sounds like a bunch of FBI BS—know what I mean?

"Kind of what I thought."

Terry held up a finger and stared at a point on the floor. He gnawed his lower lip before saying, "Hold on. I just remembered something." He looked up at Frank. "It could be true."

"Huh?"

Terry nodded. "I don't know about the Bureau, but from working with Secret Service, I know they rate police departments."

"What?"

"Yeah, when the president plans to visit a place, the Secret Service checks their list to determine the professionalism and overall effectiveness of the cop shop of the city he's going to. If it's up to par, they send the typical number of agents to cover the event. If it deficient, they send extra guys... you know, to fill in any weak spots."

"So, if the Secret Service does that with PDs, what's the chance the Bureau does it with individual officers within a PD?"

Terry shrugged. "Got me. All the feds are crazy. Do their own thing."

Frank's gut twisted. He'd hoped for a confirmation the whole thing was made-up. Now all he had was a deeper suspicion Layla might be telling the truth. "Thanks, Terry."

Frank finished off the last of his paperwork as Rob strolled in a little before nine.

"Morning," Rob said and hung his jacket on the back of his chair. He tapped the power button on his computer before heading to the coffee bar in the corner. When he returned, he sat in his chair and turned to Frank. Because Rob was short, Frank only saw what appeared as a disembodied head looking over the top of the cubicle's half-wall.

"What?"

"We need to talk," Rob said.

Oh, crap! Did someone mention the list to him?

Rob continued. "You know that task force thing you told me about yesterday?"

"Uh-huh."

"I think we should try and get on board with them."

"Really?"

"Yeah."

"Why?"

Rob rose and leaned his arms on top of the cubicle. He turned his head toward the far wall, breaking eye contact before saying, "We just need to. This guy needs to be taken off the streets."

Frank was intrigued. Rob hated working anything with the feds, except with their mutual friend, David Ford at the FBI. Suddenly he wanted to work on a task force and take orders from them? No, something was definitely afoot. Might be fun figuring it out.

Frank nodded. "Okay, if that's what you want, but one condition."

"What?"

"First, I want you—"

Edna marched into the unit and past Frank's desk on the way to her office. She pointed at him. "I need to see you, now."

As she took a seat at her desk, Rob eyed her through the glass wall separating her office and the cubicle jungle where they lived. "What the hell did you do, Frank? Is she pissed? I couldn't tell."

"Who knows," Frank said. "We'll finish this later."

Frank stuck his head around the corner of Edna's office. She looked especially nice today. He loved the light shade of lip liner she favored. Even with her hair in its signature bun, she exuded a sensuousness. *Why did she have to be married and his lieutenant?*

"Wanted to see me?"

Edna slid her briefcase into the corner. "Yes, come in and take a seat."

Frank dropped into the chair across from her.

She opened a folder. "Just left a meeting on the sixth floor. Looks like the chief's going for this task force business the Bureau discussed the other day."

Frank remained silent. When he didn't respond Edna continued.

"Anyway, it appears they've requested you, Rob, and half a dozen other detectives as task force members." She grinned, reviewing the names on the paper. "Wonder if the chief has any objections to the feds cherry picking his best guys and gals?" She tilted her head to the right, and her nose did that cute crinkle Frank found endearing.

He checked the skirt she wore today and pulled in a deep breath.

"Know anything about that? Why they're asking for specific detectives?"

Frank honestly didn't know if this was some test where he was expected to give a correct answer, or if it was only idle curiosity on her part. For Frank's part, he didn't care. May as well come clean. Besides, he had nothing to be ashamed of. "I think there's a list."

Edna laid the folder on her desk as her forehead crinkled. "List?"

"Yeah." Frank went on to tell her about meeting Layla for a drink after work.

Edna's lips parted slightly and then turned up into a devious smile. "Chumming and gumming with the FBI, Frank?"

Frank shifted in the chair and coughed. "Naw, more like drinking and thinking."

Edna wiggled her finger at him. "That girl had her eye on you the minute you set foot in the meeting yesterday. Undressed you right in front of the whole group." Edna's eyes widened. "Better watch out, Frank."

Frank didn't think Layla had been that obvious. "Seems to know a lot about me."

"There's a lot to know. You've been shot, stabbed, rescued damsels in distress, and been awarded the medal of valor. Doesn't take much to discover your history." Edna leaned her elbows on the desk and clasped her hands. "I bet you've never bothered googling yourself, have you?"

Frank didn't answer. He'd googled other people, but never himself.

"I can't tell you how many people have asked me about how you went from being a professional chef in a high-end New York restaurant to a detective in Dallas. You're a bit of a curiosity," she said. "A conversation piece."

Frank didn't like being a conversation piece, but everyone gossiped in the department. He should have figured he'd wind up in the mix sooner or later.

Edna held up the folder. "As far as any list, I've got one right here. The one the Bureau presented to the chief. Looks like we have our marching orders. You want to tell Rob, or do you want me to officially inform him he's on the task force?"

Frank stood up. "I'd better be the one to break it to him. You know how much he hates working with the feds."

Frank had lucked out. He wasn't looking forward to having the conversation about the list with Rob in the first place. Rob's feelings were easily hurt, and Frank never wanted to be a source of distress to him. Since they'd both been included on the list, that was all the cover he needed. But he still wanted an explanation from Rob as to why he was so hungry for the case. That wasn't Rob's way. Frank slipped into his inquisitor mode. This could be fun.

PERRY STOOD on the stepladder and, using the measuring tape, got the measurement for the next sheet of drywall. The sound of hammering in the next room vibrated through the wall at a steady beat. It was another hot day. Working inside the enclosed room with no air-conditioning, even with the big industrial fan blowing and windows open, was bad. Perry wiped a line of sweat from his forehead as he examined the next cut. This would be trickier. The way the wall curved and the weird angle of the corner meant the cut had to be precise. Wasting a four by eight sheet by making a wrong cut always meant an ass chewing by the boss. That's why Perry did all the measuring and cutting himself. He climbed down and raked his long blonde hair behind his ears. He took a quick swallow of water from the bottle as more sweat tickled his neck and back. *Had to be a hundred.* His necklace swung under his shirt, pushing beads of sweat back and forth across his chest. Perry grabbed another fifty-pound sheet of drywall and laid it across the saw horses. As he used his tape to mark out the cuts, the sound of a Mexican radio station echoed through the house being renovated.

Perry liked Norteño music. Something about the rhythm and beat gave it a happy uplifting quality. He grabbed the track saw and positioned his feet shoulder width apart. He started the first cut as Diego and Alejandro walked in. Diego munched his last breakfast burrito, and Alejandro finished a cigarette. They were good with hammers and nails but couldn't measure or cut a straight line for shit. Drywall dust billowed from the sheet as Perry followed the pencil line he'd drawn with the track saw blade, dust so thick he tasted it even with his mouth closed. The dust collection holder on the saw had a hole on the top and the boss refused to buy a replacement as long as the saw still worked.

After finishing, Perry leaned the cut piece against a wall as the boss outside hollered.

"Need everyone out here to unload the truck."

Diego and Alejandro grinned and mumbled a few words in Spanish. Perry's Spanish wasn't very good, but he could pick up a word or two. Thought they said something bad about the boss.

Diego pointed at the tooth necklace which had flopped out from under Perry's shirt and said, "Man, that's badass. Where'd you get that thing—are those human?"

Perry tucked the necklace back inside his shirt and, using his quiet voice, said, "My dad was a dentist, he made it from patient's teeth he pulled. Kinda reminds me of him when I wear it."

Perry walked through the kitchen with Diego and Alejandro to the open garage, and everyone gathered around the unloading area. The boss stood near the back of the garage and directed the truck driver as he backed inside with the load of new drywall sheets. The smell and growl of the diesel engine died away, and the workers began loosening the straps holding the sheets. The load had shifted in transit and looked unstable on the flat bed.

The boss stepped around the side of the truck, eyed the load, and pointed. "You guys watch out when you loosen that back strap—might shift on ya'."

Pedro dropped his cigarette on the concrete floor and gave it a twist with the toe of his boot before popping the back strap. The load began sliding his way. That's when he did something stupid. Instead of running, he braced himself and pushed back against the hundreds of pounds of sheetrock slipping off the side of the truck. It rolled over him like a tsunami. Pedro screamed and fell back as the full weight settled on his lower legs and chest.

"Get him! Get that weight off him!" the boss screamed.

Everyone scrambled to help, but with the fallen sheetrock, there wasn't enough room between the truck and garage wall for them all to lift at the same time.

The boss called 911 while the rest of the crew tried unsuccessfully to lift the stacked sheets of drywall. Perry grabbed Diego and pulled him back to get in closer. He squeezed between the wall and truck. Alejandro strained but couldn't budge the load.

Perry pushed him aside and said, "When I lift, pull him out."

Perry situated himself in the middle of the fallen load. He bent his knees and squatted, just like he'd been shown by the high school weight coach. His gaze drifted to Pedro, pinned by the load. The small man screamed and panted like a dog as Perry calmly said, "Gonna get you out of there, amigo." Perry slid his hands under the bottom sheet, pulled in a breath, and let out a scream as he stood—lifting the entire load three feet off the garage floor.

Perry's arms felt like they were being torn from the sockets. He gritted his teeth, and the pulse beat so hard in his temple it made his head hurt. His back was about to snap under the strain. A half dozen hands reached under the drywall and dragged Pedro to safety. Once his legs cleared, Perry dropped the sheets and fell back against the garage wall—totally spent. He took in long breaths and leaned forward with his hands on his knees. *Out of shape for this kind of lifting.*

A siren down the street screamed in their direction. The boss gave Pedro a swallow of water and made him as comfortable as he dared. A bloody bone poked through the top of his jeans on his right leg and his left arm was twisted to an unusual angle. Diego laid a hand on Perry's back and handed him a cold bottle of water.

"Man, you saved his life."

Perry took a long swallow and nodded, still catching his breath.

Alejandro shook his head. He eyed the fallen sheets then stared back at Perry. "Dude, there has to be eight hundred pounds there. I've never seen anyone lift that much."

Perry poured the last of the water over his face. He rested his head back against the garage wall and in his quiet voice mumbled, "I've always been strong."

Perry's strength and size had always been women magnets. They sensed his raw male power. Craved for him to share it with them. Allowed him to do anything. He'd always been a generous lover, giving them over an hour of wild pleasure before allowing his explosive release. But every now and then, when that uncontrollable urge for more took over, all during sex he kept only one desire in mind. All he really wanted from this one was to choke her until the last beam of life faded from her eyes.

———

WHEN FRANK WALKED out of Edna's office, Rob expected him to ask about the serial killer task force and why Rob wanted to join. Instead, Frank ignored him and dropped into his chair. Looked like he was going into another deep think. Probably wouldn't speak or breathe for the next couple of hours. *Wonder what Edna told him?* Whatever he had on his mind, Edna probably put it there.

A few minutes before eleven, Frank's phone rang. He came out of his self-induced trance long enough to answer it. "Pierce."

Frank looked over the cubicle wall at Rob and mouthed the word, "Sarge's?"

Rob nodded.

"Okay," Frank said. "See you there."

"Who was that?"

"Alton. Asked us to meet him at Sarge's for lunch again. Says he has the full ME's report."

On the drive over, Frank was silent, still pondering something. Rob would give him time. He'd spill it sooner or later. Frank always thought things through before speaking. They found a booth in the rear and slid in. Place wasn't very crowded, but by the time they left, it would be shoulder to shoulder at the bar, with everyone trying to get a Coke and sandwich. Rob always liked how the malted smell of beer welcomed him back into the place. Gave the joint a homey, comfortable feel.

Sarge's wife, Jan, took their drink orders and marched back to the bar.

Frank settled into the booth and stared at Rob. "Tell me why the sudden interest in this serial killer task force?"

Rob fiddled with a coaster on the table and didn't look at him. "Just seems like the right thing to do."

Frank nodded. "You were quiet after I told you about it yesterday. Why the change of heart?"

Rob hadn't planned on sharing this, but he trusted Frank's discretion. Rob rested his arms on the table and leaned forward. "Because a serial killer murdered my uncle."

Frank's confident expression faded. "What?"

"You ever heard of the candy man killings in Houston in the early seventies?"

"I read about it a few years ago in a crime journal but don't know many details."

Sarge delivered their drinks. "There you go, boys."

"Alton's walking through the door in a few minutes, Sarge. Might want to work on his usual," Frank said.

Sarge frowned and slapped the bar towel against his leg. "You could have told Jan when she took your order."

"I know," Frank said, "but Alton hates if his ice melts and dilutes the Coke."

Sarge grunted, spun around, and made his way back to the bar, grumbling under his breath. "Uh-huh. Wouldn't want to disappoint Alton."

"Finish your story," Frank said.

"It's not much of a story." Rob rubbed the back of his neck and picked up his Coke. "Happened before I was born, but the family still talks about it sometimes."

"What happened?"

Rob downed a long swallow of bourbon and Coke. "My uncle, Francisco, was my mom's older brother. In 1973 when he graduated high school, he hitchhiked to Houston, looking for work. The story goes, he was staying with a friend in the Heights neighborhood while he searched for a job. Called his mom after he arrived and told her he was safe and doing fine. That was the last anyone ever heard of him."

Rob felt funny telling the story because he never knew the man.

Never experienced any life with him. Didn't know if he'd even like the guy. He was a stranger to Rob, like someone you'd read about in a book—not a real person.

Frank leaned in closer, ignoring his drink. "What then?"

Rob shook his head. "No one knows for sure. What they do know is that between 1970 and 1973, Elmer Wayne Henley, David Brooks, and Dean Corll tortured, raped, and murdered twenty-eight young guys in Houston." Rob tilted his head to the side. "My uncle was one of them. Found him buried in a boathouse with his hands tied behind his back and a bag of lime dumped on him. He'd been strangled to death according to the ME."

Frank's eyebrows narrowed. "Why did they call it the candy man killings?"

"Because Corll used to hand out candy to the children in the neighborhood. His mom owned a candy store."

Frank eased back in the booth. "So, what? You're on a mission all of a sudden to rid the world of serial killers?"

This was probably Frank's way of drawing Rob out—making him further explain why he wanted to do this. Rob knew all Frank's interview and interrogation tricks. Fortunately, Rob was saved by Alton's arrival.

"Hey, guys," Alton said, sliding beside Frank. "You ordered yet?"

Sarge sauntered up with Alton's drink. "Here you go."

"Thanks, Sarge."

"Three ham sandwiches?" Sarge asked.

Everyone nodded.

As Sarge retreated, Frank asked, "What ya' got from the ME?"

All humor left Alton's countenance. "It's all bad. Turns out the cut throat and disembowelment wasn't the cause of death. That was all postmortem. The official cause of death was strangulation."

Frank shot a look at Rob. Probably remembering what he'd just told him about the way his uncle was murdered in the '70s.

Alton sipped his drink and flicked the straw a few inches farther away from his glass. "Looks like she had several rear teeth pulled out by the suspect. Didn't find those. But the most disgusting thing was what they found in her mouth and throat." Alton made a face.

Neither Rob nor Frank asked. Rob wasn't even sure he wanted to know.

"Traces of semen," Alton said. "Also postmortem."

Frank twisted his lips. "You mean the guy...?"

Alton shrugged. "Looks that way. No other sexual penetration—sick bastard. By the way, just heard on the radio on the way over. The cat's out of the bag."

"What?" Rob asked.

"News just reported about that picture of the mayor and his family being found at the murder scene."

"Edna's going to be pissed," Rob said.

Frank's face took on a sad, weary look as he shook his head. "This place has more leaks than the White House."

"Looks like I'm on that FBI task force forming up to catch this guy," Alton said and took another sip.

"I expect Rob and I are also going to be on it, according to Edna," Frank said.

Rob gawked at him. Frank was sneaky. Guy could have told him after the meeting with Edna. "You knew it all along?" Rob said.

Frank rendered a half-ass salute. "Guilty as charged."

Sarge delivered their ham sandwiches, and they talked of other things while eating. Serial murder and ham didn't go well together.

A half hour later, as Rob and Frank stepped into the hall outside of CIU, Terry sat in his office enjoying his sandwich, chips, and ginger ale. Through the glass door, the vision of Edna running into Terry's office caught Rob's attention as they walked in.

EIGHT

Frank hated seeing Edna rush anywhere. Nothing good ever resulted. In her haste, she'd not noticed that Rob and Frank had returned from lunch and walked through the door. She and Terry conferred for a moment, and Terry looked over her shoulder and pointed in Rob and Frank's direction. Edna snapped her head around and dashed from Terry's office. She did this complexion thing when she got excited. Frank referred to it as her chameleon face. Her dark olive skin lightened, except for her cheeks. They took on a bright red tone like she'd overdone the blush. Frank loved that look.

"Thank god you're back," she said in a high-pitched voice. "We have a witness."

"Witness to what?" Rob asked.

"Someone who may have seen and spoken to the suspected serial killer."

Terry stuck his head from his office. He had the office phone pressed to his ear. "He's in Homicide now."

"Get to Homicide and sit in on the interview. Find out as much as you can," Edna said. "I'm calling Higgins." She turned for her office. As an afterthought, she looked back, "Good luck. Bring back something good."

Rob and Frank each picked up notepads as Terry approached. His forehead wrinkled and he spoke slowly. "Hey, guys. Be skeptical, be really skeptical. Know what I mean? Chances are, this is some moron who read about this in the morning paper and decided it would be a good day to jerk our chains. Make sure you pin him down on specifics—details. Because we'll put him on the box if his story sounds about halfway credible."

"Okay, Terry," Rob said as he followed Frank out.

Rob and Frank walked through the door of Homicide as detective Chelsea Bradshire walked out of interview room number one. Frank knew her story. She was one of a handful of female detectives working Homicide. Tall, thin, and imposing, she was still on light duty after being shot in the leg by a suspect a month ago. The limp was almost gone, but she still favored the leg. She softly closed the interview room door behind her, showing a grim expression. She walked toward Alton and his supervisor, Sergeant Allen.

"I got all his identifiers." She held up a notebook. "I'll run him while you guys conduct the interview. If what he says is true..." She shivered and shook her head.

Standing off to the side, Layla was on her cell. She wore another dark outfit today, her raven hair and skin so pale it almost shone, giving her the porcelain doll look Frank liked. She glanced in his direction but didn't acknowledge him as she spoke quietly into the phone. She turned her back and took several steps away from the group.

Frank slowed his pace. Who called her?

A dozen detectives sat in their cubicles watching the show. The smell of popcorn filled the large room as the mini popcorn machine by the coffee pot finished up another batch. Rob licked his lips as he stared at it.

Layla disconnected from her call and joined Alton and his sergeant as Frank and Rob walked up.

Frank caught Layla's stare. He nodded and she nodded back.

Sergeant Allen said, "Alton, you're the lead on this one. Choose one person as your support. Don't want a room full of detectives. Take it slow and easy."

"Great," Alton said. "Frank, I'd like you with me."

"Sure," Frank said.

Allen cleared his throat before addressing the group. "We probably shouldn't get our hopes up too much. Chances are this will be a bust. It doesn't go down this easy too often." He looked at everyone like he expected an answer, but no one spoke.

Alton cleared his throat again. "Anyone who wants to watch, we have a two-way mirror and audio in the adjacent interview room." He glanced at Layla. "You're welcome to observe from there."

Layla had a pinched expression, and she quickly crossed her arms after Alton's comment.

"You ready?" Alton asked Frank.

Frank nodded.

"I'll take the lead and you jump in whenever you want," Alton said before opening the interview room door.

Frank was a little surprised by the man waiting across the table from the two chairs where he and Alton would sit. He wasn't sure what he expected, but the short, slim man with close-cropped gray hair and looking like an unemployed jockey wasn't it.

Alton greeted the man and stuck out his hand.

"Good afternoon, Mr. Price. I'm Alton Brady."

The man shook Alton's hand. He nodded and in a shy voice said, "You can call me Tom if you want to."

Frank introduced himself and took a seat. Tom Price was dressed in jeans and a white T-shirt with The United Way logo printed on the left breast. He had a deep Southern twang, a two-day growth of beard, and a lot of acne scars. Body odor drifted across the table and slammed into Frank's sensitive nose.

"Okay, Tom," Alton smiled. "Want to tell us a little about why you're here?"

Tom was nervous—real nervous. Frank caught him taking furtive glances toward the two-way mirror and brushing the side of his face. Of course, most folks are nervous being interviewed by the cops.

In a quiet, almost apologetic voice he said, "I think I might know the man you're after."

Alton leaned both forearms on the desk and interlaced his hands. "Which man is that?"

Alton wasn't going to make it easy. Knowing the interview was being recorded, he intended to make Price spell out everything.

Price broke eye contact—not good. Sweat formed on his upper lip even in the cool room. "You know," he mumbled. "The man who killed that woman in the woods the other day."

"Yeah, sure," Alton said. "I know the one you're talking about. You say you know the dude who did it?" Alton slowly leaned back into the chair and posted his hands on his hips.

Price kept his head down and nodded. "I may."

"You're going to have to get a little more specific here. Knowing and may know ain't the same," Alton said.

Alton appeared to also believe what Frank did about this milk toast idiot. Just decided to stroll over to the police station and tell a BS story that could never be confirmed. Started chickening out after the initial interview with the first detective and would soon ask to leave and request them to just forget the whole thing. These types dwell on the fringe of society with no lives of their own and try to pick up a little notoriety by involving themselves in big news events—figures. But that's not what happened.

Price swallowed hard and looked Alton in the eyes. In a soft, even voice, he told his story.

"It was about two years ago that I may have met him. I was hitch-hiking from Atlanta one cold night in the rain." Price shook his head and grinned. "Haven't seen rain like that before or since. Anyway, I decided to hole up under an overpass 'til it slacked." Price's eyes stared at some point on the table and his lips curled as he recalled the details. "It was real dark—nasty. In the distance, I could just make out the shadow of someone walking on the side of the freeway, coming toward me, from the lights of the passing cars. Had to chuckle to myself. Appeared I wasn't the only fool walking in the rain at night."

Alton picked up his pen. "Which freeway?"

"Eighty-five west, coming out of Atlanta."

Frank thought back to Layla's briefing. Killings started twenty-seven months ago, murders in Atlanta and Montgomery.

Alton rolled his shoulders and from the look on his face, he also made the same connection.

"Go on with your story," Alton said.

"Well," Price said, "I watched the man in the headlights of the cars getting closer and closer to the overpass. Didn't seem to be in no hurry. Wasn't even holding out his thumb. Wearing an overcoat and hoody. Kept his hands in his pockets and his head down. So, when he got to the overpass, he never slowed up. Appeared like he was going to walk right through and keep going. I was wedged up high in the shadows of the girders, but I guess some reflection must have given me away because he stopped and stared in my direction for a second. Just stood there staring at me in the darkness." Price hugged himself as if a chill passed through him.

"I had an old jacket pulled tight against the cold, eating a can of sardines with some crackers as he walked up the concrete ramp and stood in front of me. Have to admit I was a little scared at first."

"Scared? Why were you scared?" Frank asked.

Price shrugged. "You know. Dark night in the middle of nowhere —stranger. But it was his size that scared me. Big man. Tall and wide shoulders."

"What else did you notice? Hair, eyes?" Alton asked.

"No, couldn't see much. Just what the passing car lights showed. He may have had a full beard. Couldn't tell because of the hoodie, but he had a light-colored mustache and goatee for sure."

Alton motioned with his pen. "Go on with the story."

"It was pretty dark under that overpass. Guess he must have seen me eating or smelled the sardines because he asked if I could spare a can. I hesitated for a few seconds until he pulled a pint from his coat pocket and said, 'Trade you a couple of swallows for a can.'" Price's neck turned red, and he looked at Frank and Alton with a sheepish expression. "That was during my drinking days. Before Jesus saved me." He lowered his head and talked to the table. "I gave him an extra can, and he passed his bottle." Price smacked his lips. "Sure tasted good on that cold night."

Frank had grown impatient with the story. It had a ring of truth, and that was why he wanted to get to the point. Just before he was about to say something, Price surprised them all.

"And you'll never guess what he did with that can of sardines." Price grinned as if someone just told a joke and he already knew the punch line. "Fed 'em to a dog."

"Whoa," Alton said. "He had a dog?"

"Yeah, but I never saw it 'til he pulled it from inside the folds of his overcoat. Little bitty puppy. Couldn't have been more than a week or two old."

Alton shifted in the chair. Crossed his legs and sat on just his left hip. "What?"

"Yeah," Price said. "Thing didn't make a sound the whole time he was talking to me."

"I'm still a little unclear about how you inferred anything about murder or the mayor so far from this drifter's actions," Alton said.

Frank released a sigh. Thank god! Get him back on point, Alton.

Price smiled a sad smile. "Oh, sorry, that's what I was coming to. It's just that... well, I haven't told this to anyone since that night." Price rubbed his arms like he was cold and gnawed his lip. "Tell you the truth, still freaks me out a little. So, me and this man talked for a little while. I told him I was heading to Dallas or Houston, looking for work." Price's forehead wrinkled. "Then he said the strangest thing. Said his dad was the mayor of Dallas and he was going there to tell him because he didn't know."

"Didn't know what?" Alton asked.

"Huh? Oh, yeah. The mayor didn't know the man was his son. Or that's the way I took it."

Alton situated himself squarely on the chair and locked eyes with Price. "He said he was his son?"

Price nodded. "Uh-huh. Said he was."

Alton turned to Frank and showed a wide-eyed expression.

Frank jumped in. "Okay, now I get the connection to the mayor, but you still haven't explained why you think he could have murdered that woman."

Price wiped a hand across his mouth before jamming both hands into his armpits. He licked his lips and sucked in a deep breath. He didn't say anything for a few seconds, just stared at the edge of the table. Another shiver passed through him just before he spoke. "It's what he did next that scared the bejeebers out of me and started me thinking about him when I heard that report on the radio today. The whole time we talked, he fed sardines to that little puppy and stroked its head. Kept saying it just wasn't right how someone should put a dog out on a busy freeway at night in weather like this. That it would have been more merciful to just put the poor animal down. I gave him back his bottle and rolled over to get some sleep. Next morning when I woke up, he's gone. The puppy's still there, asleep, so I'm thinking, oh, great, now I have to do something with that thing. But it never woke up. When I got ready to leave, I lifted it, and its head just lolled from side to side." Tom looked into Frank's eyes and shook his head. "Man had snapped its neck before he left."

Price shifted his stare to Alton and in a hesitant voice asked, "Someone who'd do something like that to an innocent little puppy is capable of anything, don't you think?"

A tingle rushed up Frank's back and he slowly released his breath.

Alton made a strange sound in the back of his throat and said, "Shit. You kidding me?"

"No. That's why I made the connection between the mayor and the murdered woman."

Frank received a text. It was Layla. *Meet me outside.*

Alton would be with Price for a while. Going over the complete story again. Clarifying details. Pinning him down on things for the polygraph test. But Frank had one last question.

"Tom," Frank said. "What physical feature or mannerism stuck out the most about this man? I realize it was dark, but what's the one thing you might be able to identify him by if we were to call you in for a lineup."

Price blinked a couple of times. "Oh, that's easy. It was the voice. Kind of a Clint Eastwood, Dirty Harry quiet voice. You know how he said, 'Go ahead. Make my day.' A low, threatening voice like that. Just a whisper."

Frank excused himself and stepped out of the room.

Rob and Layla waited outside. Rob had a pissed-off expression Frank knew well from their years as partners.

"First impression?" Layla asked.

Frank glanced at Rob before answering. "His story fits the facts we already know."

"My thoughts exactly," she said.

Rob said, "We'll have to wait to see how he does on the box, but I can tell you that story is enough to scare a drunk sober."

Layla checked her watch. "I need to make a couple of calls. Will you let me know how the polygraph comes out?"

Frank nodded. "Yeah."

As Layla marched out the door and into the hall, Rob grunted. "What?"

Rob said, "I stood in that room with her through the whole interview. She never introduced herself and didn't utter a word the entire time. What's her problem?"

Frank didn't say anything, but that wasn't a bad question. Layla was a strange one. It was almost as if they were all actors in a play she was directing. If she didn't want to interact with the hired help, she didn't have to. Five minutes later, Frank briefed Edna and Terry on the interview of Tom Price. When he mentioned that the suspect had said he was the mayor's son, Edna laughed.

"Reminds me of the imbecile my partner and I pulled out of a car dealership early one morning when I worked uniform," she said. "Dude was drugged up and naked, sitting in a Jeep, singing. When my partner asked him what he thought he was doing, he said, 'Just waiting for my mom and dad.'"

Everyone just stared at her. Frank didn't get the connection.

Edna stopped laughing; probably realizing she left out a critical detail. "Oh, then he says his mom and dad were Clark Kent and Lois Lane."

Terry smiled.

"Anyway," Edna continued, "what did you make of the interview?"

Frank shook his head. "It had a ring of truth, but without knowing more about Tom Price, I couldn't say."

Rob chimed in. "It was spooky, lieutenant—real spooky."

"Okay, we'll just cool our heels while Homicide checks out Price," Edna said. "Write it up. The chief said he wanted to see all reports on the case because it involves the mayor. Watch out for your commas, Frank."

"Yes, ma'am," Frank said.

Edna could have been an English teacher. She kept a red pen on her desk, ready to swoop down at any time on those who dared transgress by using too many, or too few, commas. Edna was an Oxford Comma girl. She challenged subject-verb agreement at every corner and stood up for the right of every American to use an em dash at least once in an official report.

By the time Frank completed his paperwork and double-checked the grammar and punctuation, it was going home time. Rob had already begun the daily ritual of preparing to leave. He powered off his computer, straightened the piles of papers on his desk, and slipped on his jacket.

"When is this task force thing supposed to start?"

Frank slid into the full slouch position and propped both feet on his desk. "Beats me."

Rob fished around in his pocket and drew out his Copenhagen can. "We need a name for this suspect until he's identified. You know, something to call him other than, 'the suspect.' Any ideas?"

"I guess the FBI probably already has some case name they've attached to him—usually do."

Rob thumped the lid of the can twice and removed it. He grimaced and said, "I never like FBI names. No imagination."

Frank loved it when Rob went on one of his creative pilgrimages. He always came up with something interesting. Except for the time Frank introduced him to the wonders of the $200-a-bottle Extravecchio Aceto Balsamico Traditional di Modena DOP Gold Seal Balsamic Vinegar on a salad he'd made for them at his loft during lunch one day. Rob had dubbed the stuff with a new descriptive name: *Awsamic,* a word meaning *awesome balsamic.*

Rob's brow creased and his lips twitched as he mentally sorted through the possibilities. After a few seconds, he said, "Got it. If Price's story checks out, I have the perfect name for the suspect." Rob took an extra big pinch of snuff and tucked it between his lip and gum.

Frank didn't respond, just stared at him, grinning.

"We'll call him *Whisper* because he's a low talker."

Frank nodded. Rob had captured the essence of the killer. Someone who moved in the shadows, talking low, never drawing attention. The kind of guy you could pass on the street and never suspect might follow you home, murder you, and jerk out a few teeth. The predator who stalked his prey and gave no warning or mercy.

NINE

Friday morning, Edna informed Rob and Frank the first serial-killer task force meeting would be at the PD at one o'clock that afternoon. The more Frank heard of this, the less he wanted to be a part of it. He liked controlling the cases he investigated. Not being a gofer for some federal agency. He knew if he backed out, Rob would also be asked to leave. Pretty sure Layla wouldn't keep him around if Frank wasn't there. Since this appeared to be a holy crusade for Rob, Frank didn't want to be the one who got him kicked off the task force. Partners looked out for each other—that's the way things worked.

Just before ten o'clock, Alton walked up with a satisfied look and wad of papers.

"He passed," Alton said.

"Who? Price?" Rob asked.

"Yup, with flying colors. The examiner says no deception. Story hangs together. His information about meeting the suspect that night looks righteous."

"Did you check him out?" Frank asked.

Alton nodded as he fumbled with the papers. "Hand me your stapler, Rob. Before the polygraph, we contacted his employer,

United Way. They couldn't say enough good things about him. Got you a transcript of the interview right here."

Alton carefully arranged the two stacks of papers and stapled the first, handing it to Frank.

"His boss at United Way says he's a regional truck driver. Shows up on time, always dresses appropriately, and maintains a good attitude." Alton stapled the second stack and frowned. "You out of staples, Rob?"

Rob stood. "Can't be. Just filled it up a couple of days ago."

Alton clicked the stapler a couple of more times on the papers. In an uncertain tone, he said, "Must be a jam. Here hold these." He handed the papers to Rob.

Frank sat back and gazed in pure fascination as this comedy skit played out. Everyone but Alton knew he was a little psychoneurotic. If something wasn't right, he had to fix it.

"Here," Frank said, holding out his stapler. "Just use mine."

"No. I got this," Alton mumbled, trying to figure out how to open the stapler. "This some new rig here?"

Rob reached over and touched it. "Just push this slide back as you lift the top—"

"I got it... I got it," Alton said, pulling away from Rob's reach.

Rob rested his hands on his hips and leaned closer.

Alton fiddled with the thing a couple of more seconds before a loud snap sounded.

"Son of a bitch!" Alton screamed, dropping the stapler like a red-hot coal and dancing in place.

"What?" Rob asked.

Alton gritted his teeth and held up his left thumb. A staple had impaled itself into the top of the skin.

"Oh, for god's sake," Rob said. He grabbed Alton's hand and snatched out the staple.

"What's going on here?" Edna asked, stepping out of her office.

She could have been excused for asking the question. Alton had teared up and was sucking his thumb, Rob held a bloody staple between his fingers, and Frank was in the full slouch position, laughing.

When no one answered she said, "Okay, boys, play time's over. Get back to work."

ROB WOULD NOT BE PLACATED. He demanded tacos for lunch. Knowing tacos weren't Frank's favorite, Rob only insisted on them once a week. The way he figured it, if Frank needed fried chicken every week, then it was only right they should do tacos on a Friday. Sometimes it's the little things that contribute to the success or failure of a marriage—or a police partnership. Rob understood these things.

After lunch, Rob and Frank arrived in Homicide and were directed to the conference room. Several detectives mingled outside the door. As they approached, Alton's grinding voice echoed from inside.

"What a crock of shit!"

Rob peeked around the corner, and Alton stood toe to toe with Layla. They both looked a little stressed—well... a lot.

"I'll talk to the captain about this," Alton shouted in a voice shrill enough to shatter thin glass.

Layla shot him an intense, fevered stare. "I believe your chief already has."

Alton turned and walked out, mumbling, "I need a cup of coffee." When he passed Rob and Frank, he gritted his teeth and shook his head. "Bitch!"

Frank and Rob walked into the conference room. Place held the odor of old hamburgers and fries. Detectives used it as the lunchroom when no meetings were in session. Frank walked up to Layla.

"Good to see you and Alton are still playing nicely."

She ignored him and thumbed through a stack of papers.

Frank didn't move. He just stood there towering over her with a cherub expression like a big dumb kid. The inquisitor's stare finally took its toll, and she broke.

She looked up and sighed. "Alton appears to have a few concerns about the logistics of the task force. Probably needs to discuss it with his supervisor."

So there. Layla just answered Frank's question with the most bureaucratic response possible. Guess she showed him.

Frank said, "Tom Price passed the polygraph—story hangs together. The United Way says he's their most dependable man."

Layla didn't answer, but offered a quick nod before saying, "Yes, I know."

Frank and Rob took their seats at the conference table. The dozen chairs quickly filled as a gaggle of other detectives from several DPD units drifted in. Vice, Narcotics, Homicide, and Criminal Intelligence were all represented. Layla was the only stranger in sight—the lone FBI agent in the room. From her expression, this pleased her.

"If everyone will take a seat, we'll get started," she said.

The room quieted and everyone found a chair. There were ten guys and four women.

Layla spoke up, "For those of you who don't know me, I'm Supervisory Special Agent Layla Barbee with the FBI Behavioral Science Unit at Quantico. As you are aware, you've been selected to participate in the search for the suspect in a string of serial murders across the south. We have reason to believe the killing of the woman in the Great Trinity Forest is connected to this suspect." Layla did another one of her famous pauses for dramatic effect before finishing with, "Everything heard, everything seen, and everything said in this room, stays in this room."

Several detectives did their version of a full eyeroll. Like this was the first time they ever heard that one.

Layla showed her signature smile. The friendly *I'm from the government and here to help you* smile.

Rob wasn't buying it. She was a fraud.

She held up a stack of papers. "I've put together an information packet for each of you. Please keep it in a safe place and don't share the information with anyone. Several items in here are things that we've held back from the press. Things we can use to verify information received from a tip line. We've released just enough information to the press to ask for public assistance but haven't disclosed the fact it is probably connected to a serial killer." She handed the stack to the nearest detective. "Take one and pass them down."

Alton ambled back into the room with a large cup of coffee. He'd loosened his tie and appeared noticeably less excited as he stood in the back of the room.

"If you'll turn to page three of your packet, we'll do a quick review of what we know and what we believe that might assist us in locating the suspect," Layla said.

The sound of pages turning was the only noise in the room for the next few seconds.

Layla waited with her hands behind her back and a self-confident smirk glued to her lips. She held no notes. Probably knew the material well enough to brief them in her sleep.

Frank had slipped into one of his after-lunch sitting positions. The one that caused Rob, on more than one occasion, to fear him dropping off during an important meeting. Mundane things bored Frank. Meetings, briefings, and anything to do with politics. He was a Sergeant Friday type of guy. *Just the facts, ma'am, only the facts.* He scooted back from the table and stretched his long lanky frame out to its fullest. If this meeting didn't pick up speed soon, Rob feared his partner might miss the whole thing. Finally, Layla spoke.

"First, what we believe. The suspect is a white male in his early 20s to early 30s. He's most likely tall—over six feet. Well-built and powerful. From DNA analysis, we think he's from Scandinavian stock. Light-colored hair and blue or green eyes." She turned to the females in the group, who were sitting in a row. A quick smile raced across Layla's lips. "Sounds hot, right?"

A couple of the female detectives grinned. Rob figured they thought it was a stupid and corny remark, as did he. Layla didn't know how to seriously interact with real street police. She'd been in the federal bubble too long.

Layla continued. "He most probably produces, transports, or works with drywall—sheetrock. Could very well be in construction or just a driver who delivers and handles it."

"How do you figure that?" a guy from Homicide asked.

"Traces of gypsum have been recovered from more than one victim." Layla paused again and then added, "As *we* know, gypsum is the prime ingredient in drywall. We have a team from the Bureau canvassing multi-family construction projects and all commercial sites which use drywall in the metroplex. We're expanding it to include private construction as well."

Layla stopped talking and stared at the group. More for effect than anything. Rob couldn't imagine she'd forgot her lines. Her eyes pinched and she crossed her arms.

"We believe he's a drifter. Seldom stays anywhere too long. Keeps moving from one town to another. Never gives us a pattern to track him or any means to predict where he might strike next. A big city like Dallas is a target-rich environment for his kind. Might keep him around long enough to get him in our sights. That's our hope."

From the corner, Alton let out a grunt.

Layla ignored him.

Alton interrupted. "You've told us a lot about what you believe, but what do you actually *know*?"

Every head in the room turned toward Layla. Girl never missed a beat. Without realizing it, Alton had just given her the perfect lay-up. She leaned against the wall. "We have a real opportunity to take him right here, right now." She punctuated her statement by jabbing her finger at the audience. She then pushed off the wall, removed her jacket, and faced Alton. "So, here's what we *know*." She turned back to the assembly and held her arms out. The tight, dark blue blouse outlined her slim figure.

"Take a look. I fit the description of all his victims to date." She leaned both hands on the table and met eyes with the group. "Probably hangs out in cheap honky-tonks and ice houses in the rough parts of town. He selects his victims from women with my physical description. We know about what he looks like and we know who he's looking for. Our job is to find him."

Layla shifted her stare back to Alton, daring him to try a comeback.

He remained silent.

Rob had to admit, while he didn't especially care for the woman, she did put on one hell of a show. Probably the best dramatic briefing he ever attended. He looked over at Frank. He was wide awake and had his chin propped in his palm with his elbow on the chair's arm. One thing about Frank—always admired good stagecraft.

Layla said, "At the FBI, we've broken this task force up into groups. Some agents will check out in-town leads from the tip line. Others are handling out-of-town leads. Some will be with the sheriff's department. And my assignment is to liaise with DPD. FBI Special Agent Sanders will be with me. He was unable to make this briefing today." She leaned on the table again and cast a solemn stare at the detectives. "You people know this city best. You have an idea of what the killer looks like, who he's probably looking for, and the places he's most likely to be found. Go get him."

Frank sat up and, using his feet, rolled his chair closer to the table. People collected their notebooks and began standing just as Layla said, "We all work with partners on this one. He's a predator hunter. Don't take any chances. He's got nothing to lose by killing a police officer, and he knows it."

Everyone paused a moment before continuing to drift out of the room. As the place cleared, Layla strolled over to Frank.

"Thought I was losing you there for a moment."

"I like to get comfortable during briefings."

Rob laughed to himself. Frank got comfortable everywhere.

"I was wondering," Layla said. "You like Vietnamese noodles?"

"Huh?" Frank said. "Oh, yeah... I do."

Layla again flashed another one of her cute smiles. "Thought so," she said before walking away.

***

ROB AND FRANK spent the rest of the afternoon writing supplements on their current cases, putting them to sleep for a while. *All hands on deck* was the order sent down from the sixth floor. With a serial killer in town, who may or may not have the mayor in his sights, everything else got put on hold. Just before five, Edna called them into her office.

Edna would have been a terrible poker player—didn't have the face for it. She sat hunched over her desk, staring wide-eyed at a piece of paper as Rob and Frank walked in.

"Take a seat, guys." She motioned Rob to close the door.

Now Rob was almost certain he and Frank had done nothing to ignite the lieutenant's wrath, but it still felt uncomfortable to be summoned and then have the chamber sealed behind them. Rob hated being called to her office. He sat beside Frank on the sofa, and his left leg bounced. She didn't say anything at first, but the pain in her eyes told Rob she had a decision to make. She must have noticed his leg. She cracked a smile.

"Relax, guys." Edna exhaled and reared back in the executive chair. She squeezed her stress ball and eyed Frank. "Since Tom Price passed the background and polygraph, it looks like the information he's provided has been corroborated. You guys are assigned to the task force until further notice. I've worked out a new work schedule for you, but I want your opinion."

Rob was taken off guard. This was the first time in history Edna had ever asked their advice. She usually bounced ideas off Terry first. Being a senior sergeant put him in a sweet position. But Terry had taken a half-day off, so she was left to her own devices. She handed them two pieces of paper and interlaced her fingers across her midsection.

Rob saw the problem at once. A straight 6 PM to 2 AM schedule which allowed for no variances. He didn't want to sound too critical, so he waited a beat before answering. "It looks good to me lieutenant, but we might want to make it a little more flexible."

Edna fought it, but just the trace of a frown crossed her lips. "Flexible?"

"Yes, ma'am." Rob leaned forward and pointed at the times on his sheet. "We don't know this guy's schedule, work hours, or living arrangements. May I suggest we be allowed to work our hours as the investigation dictates? If this guy gets off work at five and pops by an ice house for a couple of beers on his way home, we might miss him if we're not signing on until six."

Frank didn't say a word but nodded his approval.

Edna grabbed the schedule away from Rob and wadded it up. She grinned. "Just an idea. No big deal. You guys know what you're doing. Work when you feel you're most effective. Put in as much overtime as it takes."

That was the reason Edna remained one of Rob's favorite supervisors of all time—no big ego. But *as much overtime as it takes* was new, especially in light of the memo from the Chief's office last week instructing all supervisors to cut overtime hours. Edna was under the gun to have her guys catch the guy first, and she wasn't taking any chances.

TEN

Frank made it home a half hour later. The summer depressed him. The heat waves shimmering off the roadway, the stuffy heavy air, and sweating like a field hand brought misery every summer in Dallas. It was especially bad this year. Had to wonder if he was becoming allergic to the heat or if the summers were just hotter. He could live in the cold better than blazing hot temperatures. But with late August in Dallas, this was to be expected. After a refreshing shower, he poured a glass of red. Never had much of an appetite in hot weather, but he'd had a craving all day and intended to satisfy it.

Frank removed the stems from the fresh spinach leaves and washed them. He kept a few hard-boiled eggs in the refrigerator at all times. As he sipped the red, he peeled a couple and sliced them into thin circles. He also kept a supply of fried bacon, doubled bagged, in the freezer. He removed four pieces and crumbled them in a saucepan. Now for the secret ingredient. Frank dug around in the back of the refrigerator until he found the glass jar of rendered bacon grease. He scooped out a teaspoon of the creamy, white fat and added it to the saucepan and then turned the burner to low heat. As the saucepan warmed, Frank sliced mushrooms and red onion. When the crumbled bacon began to sizzle, he whisked in a little red wine vinegar, sugar, and Dijon mustard. He dropped in a pinch of sea salt and coarse black pepper. But the job had to be put on hold at that point.

He stopped and poured another glass of red.

He divided the vegetables into two large bowls, pouring half the contents from the saucepan on top of one, and tossed the salad. *Love that smell.* He'd have enough for dinner tonight and tomorrow night. His instructors at the Culinary Institute of America would have been horrified at not boiling the eggs and frying the bacon fresh that day. And the thought of saving dressing for later would have made them scream, but they didn't count anymore. He was a detective now, not a New York chef.

Frank sprinkled a little Sunlight goat cheese and Kalamata olives on top of the salad. Not exactly your traditional spinach with warm bacon dressing recipe, but he liked it. He'd just sat at the bar to devour his feast when tragedy struck. The only thing he hated worse than the phone ringing when in the shower was the doorbell ringing when he was about to eat. He could have easily avoided what happened next by simply looking through the peephole, but in his haste, he didn't. Building security always stopped solicitors, so it must be someone he knew.

As he swung the door open, Layla waited in the hall. She held a white paper bag in her hand. Before he could speak, she smiled and lifted the bag.

"Vietnamese noodles. Will you join me for dinner?"

PERRY DIDN'T LIKE craft beers. Never developed a taste for them. Besides being too expensive, most of the places that served them wouldn't let the likes of him through the door, all sweaty and covered with construction dust. But he felt right at home here at

Lady's Choice. He loved dive bars—cool, dark, and quiet drinking holes. Those titty clubs had too much noise, too much going on. Perry glanced at the clock on the wall, six fifteen—time to head home. That's when he saw her.

She'd walked in when he wasn't paying attention. Small girl, with shoulder-length black hair and a skimpy blue halter top. She meandered to the bar and took a seat. She and the lady bartender talked and laughed about something. He'd not seen her here before. His breath shuddered as he took in the resemblance to the first woman in his life.

He still remembered his mom when she was a young woman like that. The likeness was amazing. Perry kept his gaze on the new girl in the bar mirror and ordered another beer. He always wished his mom and dad had stayed married. *Yeah, things would be so different.*

Five-year-old Perry peeked around the corner into his dad's home lab. It was late, but Perry loved watching him work. His dad had been a dentist for a long time, at least that's what Perry's mom said. He hunched over his workbench holding a pair of false teeth and, using a silver pick, scraped at the gum line. A cloud of smoke hung like a fog over him as the cigarette burned down in the ashtray, which was already filled with burned-out butts. He picked up a magnification headset and fitted it over his head before lifting the teeth to the light. He pulled his lips tight and leaned closer to the bright bulb as he gave the dentures one last pick. His dad laid them on the workbench, removed the headset, and took a puff off the cigarette. The man always seemed to know when Perry was near. Must have felt him in the room. Without looking in Perry's direction, he spoke.

"Want to come in?"

"Uh-huh," Perry said.

His dad turned in his chair and welcomed Perry into his waiting arms. Perry loved the man. His familiar touch, the smell of smoke on his clothes, and his comforting soft voice all relaxed Perry and made him feel loved and safe.

"I added two more today," his dad said. "Can you find them?"

Perry's gaze shot up to the fishing line strung above the workbench. He searched the teeth the fishing line passed through, looking for the new additions.

"Here, get a better look." His dad lifted him onto a knee as Perry examined the gnarly specimens suspended above him. Had to be fifty or more. After extracting a tooth, his dad would use his Dremel tool and drill a small hole through the side. He'd run the invisible fishing line through the hole and string it back across his workbench.

Perry pointed. "Those two?"

His dad playfully mussed Perry's blond hair. "That's right. You're so smart."

Perry's mom hated the tooth rope, as his dad called it. It *was* pretty gross. Many of the teeth were rotten or discolored. And many of the roots still had traces of red bloodstains. But Perry liked it. He didn't know why, but the fascination of the thing stayed with him. Just thinking about how they were once part of someone's body filled him with excitement and a little fear.

Perry turned to his dad. "Can I practice?"

"It's late. You need to get to bed."

Perry showed his angel expression. "Please."

His dad relented. The angel look always worked on him. "Okay, but just one." He sat Perry on the floor and reached under the workbench. He pulled out the silver metal box, placed it on the bench, and opened the snaps. Lifting the lid revealed what fascinated Perry. A full mock-up of a person's open mouth, with all the teeth numbered. His dad had taught in a couple of dental schools, and the mock-up mouth was a teaching tool leftover from those days.

His dad situated Perry on his knee again. "Which one tonight?"

Perry studied the setup. He knew, if he asked to do an easy one, his dad would say, "Where's the challenge in that?" No, Perry would have to go after one that presented some difficulty.

"I'll try for the lower left wisdom tooth."

"Make it the upper right instead."

Perry understood why. That was the toughest tooth to pull in the human mouth. Never easy to get to and sometimes required cutting the gum.

His dad handed Perry the extractors and Perry's little fingers slipped into the loops as he lowered his head to get a better look. He eased the extractors around the tooth, taking care to stay as close to the gum line as possible.

"Don't forget to wiggle it first," his dad said. "That will tell you which side to pull from. One side will feel looser than the other—you'll know."

Perry nodded and moved the extractors side to side. The tooth seemed to give when he moved it to the left. "Okay, I'm ready."

His dad anchored the box with his hands. "Go ahead."

Perry tilted the extractors to the right and gave a slow even pull. The tooth didn't budge. He tried again. This time exerting more pressure. Still no luck. He looked at his dad.

The old man smiled and winked. "Okay, you know what to do."

Perry latched onto the tooth and, with a sharp tug, the thing popped out. "Got it!"

His dad pulled him into a strong embrace and kissed the top of his head. "You sure did."

Very few things gave Perry as much satisfaction as pleasing his dad. He loved and respected the guy. One day, Perry would go to dental school and make him proud.

"What are you two doing?"

Perry's mom stood in the open doorway wearing a housecoat over her pink nightgown. Her arms were crossed and she wore a good-natured smile.

Perry held up the extractors with the practice tooth. "I did the upper right one tonight."

"It's late." She fixed eyes on his dad. "You didn't show him any more of those god-awful videos, did you?"

"No, he's well past that. Almost a real dentist now." His dad mussed Perry's hair again.

The videos his mom didn't like were the ones from the dental school. The ones of an oral surgeon calmly lecturing while extracting a patient's tooth as a group of dental students gawked at the procedure. His mom always shuddered when she talked about such things.

She took Perry's hand. "Come on, off you go."

Perry broke loose and gave his dad a quick hug and kiss.

"I love you," his dad whispered.

Perry's mom led him back to his bedroom and tucked him in. Her long, black hair tickled his nose as she bent over to give him a good night kiss. Her breath smelled of mint toothpaste. Perry didn't understand his mom. He and she had silky blond hair. The kind that seemed to glow when the light hit it just right. The kind that people tried, without success, to color their hair to match. What confused Perry was his mom's insistence on dying her hair raven black. She hated the blond color everyone else loved.

There was something else going on in the household Perry didn't understand. The raised voices of his mom and dad fighting late at night sometimes woke Perry. His stomach bubbled with anxiety, and he would roll over and pull the pillow tight around his head to block the screaming. His mom had started going out at night several times a week. She told his dad she was visiting girlfriends, but she came home smelling of smoke and beer. His dad didn't like it when she went out. That's what most of the fights were about.

The next summer, Perry went to stay with his mom's sister, Aunt Grace, and Uncle Steve in Biloxi. He and his cousins had fun hanging out together, and they taught him how to fish and catch minnows at the creek. But by the middle of August, he was ready to go home. He would start first grade this year and the thought excited him.

When he arrived home, everything had changed. His dad had moved out. His home lab was nothing but an empty storeroom now. Bits and pieces of trash littered the dirty floor where the workbench once stood. The smell of smoke that clung to the walls was all that was left of the old man. Perry walked through the room and tears formed. In the corner, under a wadded-up piece of paper, he found a single tooth from the tooth rope. His dad had secretly left him a small token. Perry folded the tooth in the paper and slipped it into his pocket. *Someday, I'll make my own tooth rope.*

His mother sat Perry down and tried explaining how sometimes people change. Their likes and dislikes change. How people could fall in and out of love. Perry didn't exactly understand what she was saying but understood she was talking about his dad. They'd gotten a divorce. But Perry could still see him on weekends and holidays. That was also the day she told him his dad wasn't really his dad. His real father was a rich man living in Texas. Perry didn't understand back then how someone could have two dads.

Perry was sick with grief. It was like his dad had died and only his ghost would appear every so often during scheduled visitations. This new information about another father only served to confuse Perry more. Two months after school started, his mom received a phone call just before Perry's bedtime. She answered it and listened for a moment before saying, "I understand." She turned to Perry and embraced him. Her sobs stilled echoed in his ears to this day. His dad had killed himself. And it was all because of her. She didn't say that, but Perry knew.

Perry took another swallow of beer and continued studying the young woman with the raven black hair in the bar mirror. She was drinking something mixed with Coke. That old hunger, the old urge almost overwhelmed him. His skin tingled as if a million needles pricked just below the surface, sending electric waves through his body. Just staring at her wasn't enough. He had to have her. She had to be his tonight—right now. He picked up his half-empty beer and walked in her direction.

The door opened and several guys sauntered in. "Bella," one shouted.

The young woman turned, and a wide smile spread across her full, luscious lips.

"Thought you'd never get here." She lifted the glass. "Started without you."

Perry kept walking past her. He finished the beer in one long gulp and sat the bottle on a table as he headed for the door.

ELEVEN

To say Frank was surprised at Layla's appearance would have been a huge understatement. He was more put out than surprised. Never gave any indication she might drop by—should have called first. How did she even know where he lived? Federal agents have more access to indices to locate people than most city police. Should have expected something like this.

She didn't move but stared at Frank. "Can I come in?"

Frank woke up. "Oh, yes, sorry. Didn't expect you is all."

When Layla stepped into the loft, her attention, like everyone who enters for the first time, was automatically drawn to the wall of windows on the right. Being on the twentieth floor afforded Frank a view few others enjoyed. Layla's mouth hung open.

"Oh, my god," she said, handing Frank the to-go bag without taking her eyes off the view of downtown and beyond. She slowly walked to the window. She whirled around and giggled. Not a grown woman giggle, but a teenage giggle. "How in the world do you afford this?"

Frank took the bag into the kitchen. "*I* don't. Trust from my grandparents paid for it."

She gave a passing glance to the other wall with the floor to ceiling bookcase. She leaned her head toward it and her brow rose. "Now I know how you got on the list—walking encyclopedia."

Frank began unloading the bag. The aromas arising out of it made his mouth water. His suspicion about Layla's sudden appearance hadn't abated, but he wanted to be a gracious host. Inside were a couple of hot soups and two dinners. She'd brought stir-fried chicken with garlic noodles. The second box contained sautéed filet mignon with red, spicy noodles. If Frank had ever entertained the thought of sending her away, that went out the door when the sweet smell hit him.

Layla took a seat at the bar as Frank plated the dinners. She showed a tight, nervous smile and fidgeted in her seat. In an apologetic voice, she asked, "Are you angry with me for arriving unannounced?"

Frank almost spoke his mind. He could play this two ways. Admit he was put out or let it run its course. Layla never did anything she hadn't fully thought through. "That depends on two things," Frank said.

Layla sucked in a low, short breath and leaned closer.

Frank smiled. "Will you help me eat this salad?" he said lifting the spinach salad bowl. "And can I have the chicken with noodles?"

She laughed and the worry lines around her eyes relaxed. Frank liked her laugh.

"Yes, to both," she said.

"In that case, we may begin," he said, placing the plates and bowls side by side on the bar. As he took a seat, he asked, "Red wine?" and handed her a glass.

She studied him a second with a stare that seemed unnatural before saying, "Thought you'd never ask."

Frank wasn't a big eater, but chicken and garlic noodles were one of his favorites. Just like having barbecue and fried chicken every week was a tradition, so were noodles. He'd not had his fix this week.

"So, how did you know this was my favorite?" he asked.

She whirled a few noodles and forked some beef while staring at her plate. "You look like the type."

He laughed. "No seriously, how did you know. Ask Rob?"

When he looked her way, he caught a micro-expression he wasn't expecting. A frown flashed across her lips before she recovered. "No. I just knew."

Frank's alarm bells began a soft jingle like you hear in the distance on a cold Christmas night in New England as a horse-drawn sleigh approaches. The bells that should be warning him something wasn't right. But Frank had a blind spot when it came to beautiful, sexy women. He knew it but couldn't help himself. He and Layla chatted about everything from the weather to favorite vacations. Frank told her about his cruise to Greece. She told him about climbing the Matterhorn. She admitted the guide never took them to the top, but she'd climbed half the fourteen thousand seven-hundred-foot mountain. Not once did she bring up the case. This surprised him. Frank had assumed the case consumed her every waking minute, but here they were having wine with dinner and casually discussing things a normal couple might talk about on a first date. *Was this a first date?*

Frank had to admit, for a small girl, she could put away the food. She matched him bite for bite. He had to admit another thing—he liked her. Without the stiff façade of FBI Supervisory Special Agent, she was gregarious and a great conversationalist. They finished off the food and wine in a chorus of laughter and joking. She cleared the bar while Frank opened another bottle. The wine had relaxed them both. It was the time of the evening when Frank enjoyed the company of a woman most. Cuddling on the sofa, drinking wine, listening to jazz. Always led to the evening's climax, in multiple ways.

Layla motioned to the balcony. "Can we sit on the patio?"

Frank checked the digital thermometer. "Bad idea. Still over ninety-eight out there."

Layla pouted and flopped on the sofa. "I have an idea. Let's play a game."

In all the years Frank had owned the loft, not one girl ever said those words while not referring to something sexual. He was awestruck and couldn't think of a quick comeback. Had to be a set-up. Was she serious? "Game?"

Layla patted the sofa beside her. She had that mellow look that showed after a good meal and a few glasses of wine. She flashed the same disarming smile she'd shown all evening. "Yeah, you'll like it."

Frank topped off their glasses and took a seat to her left. "What kind of game?"

Layla sipped her wine before saying, "I call it the nonpolitical correctness game. The way it works is I tell you a fundamental belief I have which, in this day and time, is not held by the rank and file and put forth a convincing argument to support it. You are free to question me and try and knock down my argument. Try to change my mind if you want."

Frank's antennas rose. What the heck. "So, it's like a debate?"

She shrugged. "Not necessarily. But you can turn it in that direction if you want." She gave him a good natured shove and grinned.

That glint in her eye served as a challenge. *Likes playing mind games.*

"Afraid of debating me, Frank?"

Frank had that same feeling he had as a kid when he and his friends had snuck into the abandoned concrete plant that had been closed for years. His parents warned him not to go there. Too many dangerous things in an old, dilapidated plant like that. But when everyone crawled through that hole in the fence, he did as well. And when, after poking around the place for an hour, everyone decided they'd jump the wide pit filled with dirty water, he went along with the crowd. Couldn't be accused of being a chicken.

"Okay, but you go first," Frank said, reclining back into the cushion.

Layla also reclined and seemed to collect her thoughts. Her shoulders tensed and brow creased before saying, "I'm against abortion."

Frank didn't believe her. A fully independent, successful woman doing what was up to a few years ago only a man's job? *No way.* "Do you expect me to believe that?"

She kept her eyes fixed on him and raised her glass in a salute. "It's true."

This started feeling more like an academic exercise that the kind of things Frank, and women who came to dinner, usually did. By this time of the evening, there were usually articles of clothes on the floor. But he was curious and wanted to see where this was going. He needed to tread carefully, though. Her game was at least as good as his, perhaps better. "Okay. Go ahead," Frank said.

Her voice had a husky tone. "What is murder? Taking of human life, right?"

Frank nodded.

She positioned herself on the cushion so she faced him. "So, then the question becomes *what is human life?*"

Frank didn't answer. Still had the feeling he was being played.

"A fetus has a heartbeat that can be observed by ultrasound at three weeks. Three weeks later, electronic brain activity begins to occur. If an organism, any organism, has a beating heart and brain activity, it's alive in my book and, therefore, if it's human, killing it is homicide, whether it's officially born or not."

Frank had met and dealt with his share of feminists. While respecting their beliefs, he didn't necessarily agree with all of them. What Layla just said was either the biggest surprise or biggest lie he'd heard in a long time. She was putting out the same tired arguments that had been going on since Roe v. Wade. He tried reading her expression, but she gave nothing away. Frank loved a challenge. But he still must proceed with caution. Something still felt very wrong here. Her spine stiffened and a whiff of that floral fragrance he'd noticed the other day drifted under his nose.

Frank wasn't sure where to go on this. He figured a woman had a right to choose what happened to her body. And an unwanted preg-nancy could throw many into poverty, or deeper into poverty, but he had to admit he'd had some of the same doubts Layla expounded. In his opinion, her basic argument was still pretty weak. When he didn't challenge her, she grinned.

"Won you over yet?"

He shrugged. "I'm fairly liberal on most social and religious beliefs, but you've got me thinking."

Layla finished her wine and held out her glass. "Good—thinking's good, Frank."

Frank filled it and topped his off again. He already had a little buzz going, but he took a long swallow. "So, is it my turn?"

Layla again offered a salute with her glass. "That's how it works."

He settled deeper into the sofa. He'd never expressed what he was about to say to a soul. To do so was more than just heresy. It was almost sacrilegious. But he'd agreed to this ridiculous game. If she was playing straight, and he had no reason to believe she wasn't, it wouldn't be fair if he threw a softball when he had a hardball already in his hand. Frank sipped the wine again. "I think the whole global warming debate is a lot of hooey."

Layla's brow released and her mouth fell open into a wide smile. She sprang forward almost spilling her wine and gave him another good-natured shove. "You do not!"

Frank loved her animation. Something she'd never shown or even hinted at since he'd met her.

"Yeah. I do."

Her eyes widened. "Frank, that's science. How could you not believe in global warming?"

"That's not what I said. I *do* believe in global warming. I just think the debate is hooey. Besides, it's more history than science."

She blinked, pulled back a little, and showed a blank look. "Okay, you lost me."

Frank laughed. "Stay with me on this." He held up four fingers. "Four factors affect global temperatures: carbon dioxide levels, volcanic eruptions, Pacific El Niños, and the sun's activity, otherwise known as sunspots." With each point, Frank folded a finger. "Lower solar activity seems to cause temperatures to plunge. Higher activity has corresponded with temperatures rising."

Layla's eyes stayed fixed on him in some mesmerizing stare that made him feel uncomfortable. She didn't say anything, but Frank got the idea she thought he might be crazy.

Frank took a breath and said, "What I'm having problems with is—"

She pointed at him and interrupted. "Whether the warming is the result of man."

She was quick. "Yes, between 1300 and 1870, the sun entered a period of low activity known as the Maunder Minimum, causing earth's temperatures to drop on average twelve degrees. We know this time as the Little Ice Age."

Layla sipped her wine and nodded. "Yeah, I've heard of it."

Frank continued. "Temperatures were warmer before it started and warmer when it concluded. It lasted five hundred and seventy years. There were no combustible engines in operation. Did man do something to cause it, or was it just the natural cycle of the earth's heating and cooling like we may be currently experiencing?"

She just stared at Frank. No expression. No words—nothing. After a moment she leaned forward in a way that told Frank the wine had finally taken hold. Layla rested her hand on his thigh. Her bedroom-eyes expression excited him. She spoke slowly, taking care to make sure each word didn't come out slurred. "You just blew my mind."

Frank was confused. "In a good way or bad?"

Her sexy grin pulled him closer. "Good way." She pointed at him and squinted. "If I've got this straight, your contention is we don't know what the true average earth temperature is based on data collected over the last hundred years or so, then."

Layla surprised him. Most people with as much wine in them as they'd consumed couldn't multiply five times five. She'd kept up with him easily—almost too easily.

"Correct," Frank said. "But we might just get a chance to find out pretty soon if the theory holds up."

Layla slipped her shoe off and ran her toe up Frank's pants leg, massaging his shin. She had the look.

Frank cleared his throat. "The Royal Astronomical Society has put forth an idea that the sun will re-enter another Maunder Minimum in the 2030s. We should see a significant temperature drop by then if they're correct."

Layla's foot moved a little higher up Frank's leg—felt good.

Frank's throat went dry, and he edged a little closer to her.

Layla sat up and put her wine glass on the end table. She turned back to him and eased her head to within a few inches of his. Their lips were almost touching. Her breath was warm and sweet. She dropped her hand to his crotch and began rubbing in tight circles.

Frank hadn't made love on a sofa in a while. He wasn't about to start tonight.

She softly kissed him. "I'm tired of talking."

Frank sat his empty glass on the floor and took Layla in his arms. He kissed her hard. A moan deep in her throat washed through the condo. The heat of their bodies bonding felt as if Frank had a fever. He was lightheaded from too much wine. Needed to get to a better place—fast. Layla had his pants halfway unzipped. He broke their kiss, sliding her hand away before scooping her into his arms. She reached up and softly kissed him again, holding his face in her hands. Her tongue wiggled past his lips and tickled the top of his mouth in a way that sent little shocks of electricity through Frank's head, directly into his brain.

Frank carried her down the dark hall into his bedroom, lit only by a single lamp. They removed their clothes without speaking, never taking their eyes off each other. For reasons he couldn't explain, Frank found this more stimulating than the best strip-club performance he'd ever seen during his undercover Vice days. Frank had cared little about Layla a couple of hours ago, but now a hunger rose in him and he wanted to consume her. From her expression, she felt the same.

By the time she dropped her bra to the floor and slipped out of those panties, Frank was about to explode.

She ran her stare over his lean, naked body, and below his waist. Her lips pursed and she nodded before saying, "My, that's something to be proud of."

They started slow. Frank had a secret he never shared with other men. A secret so simple, and yet so effective it never failed. Women want things slow—very slow. Guys were ready right off the mark. But women's plumbing, emotional conditioning, and hormones were better suited to someone who took their time. Frank not only took his time but teased them with sensations they'd never felt. Sometimes he'd spend over an hour in foreplay just to get a lady to the peak of excitement. His goal was first to hear her ask, then plead, and finally, demand he consummate the act. His "slow hand" method took patience but paid big dividends.

Layla was an aggressive alpha woman at the office, but in bed, she started off as a submissive mistress. Her breath came in sharp pants as she squirmed beneath his tongue. She ran her fingers through his hair and pushed his head down. He added his fingers to the action and kept it going until she pulled his head up. "I want it now, Frank. Now!"

It quickly became obvious that this was an 'anything goes' night. She released sensuous moans and groans during the lovemaking. The sensation of her sweaty body in perfect rhythm to his kept Frank focused. But soon after straddling him, she got her first climax. Frank had never seen such a thing. Her black hair was askew, partially hiding her face when it happened. She let out a wounded animal scream and bared her teeth.

Layla fell off him and lay on her back gasping. A satisfied grin swept across her lips as she held her arms out, welcoming him again. Frank rolled on top, and they made love another half hour. She had several more orgasms, but nothing like the first one. Frank was glad—

it had been unnerving. When she headed for the bathroom, he stretched and rolled over, dreamily imagining doing it all again. He closed his eyes, and when he opened them, ten minutes had passed. Frank turned to the bath and the light was off. He sat up in bed and scanned the room. Her clothes lay in a heap on the floor beside his.

"Layla?" When he received no answer, he slipped on a pair of gym shorts and walked into the hall. "Layla?" Frank strolled toward the living room, checking the extra bedroom and bath on the way. She wasn't there either. *Where did she go without clothes?* His mind drifted back to her earlier question. "Can we sit on the patio?" The lights were down in the condo, and Frank squinted as he walked to the sliding glass door leading to his balcony. A faint glint of light reflected off something from the bright, summer moon. There in the darkness, among the forest of plants, Layla lay naked in the hammock. She sipped from a wine glass as she stared at the lights of downtown. Frank slid the door open, and she turned her head his way. A serene expression encased her face.

"Just enjoying the view."

Frank walked outside, and the heat radiated around him. Almost too hot, even at this time of the night, to walk on the concrete floor. The balcony stored the sun's heat, and the place felt like a health spa's sauna. The earthy smells of plants mixed with her perfume as a light breeze blew from the south. He squatted beside her.

"Aren't you hot?"

She showed a flat-lipped smile. "I love the heat."

Frank ran his fingers along her breast line, over her long nipple, and down the sweaty stomach to her navel. Amazingly, her skin was cool—like a snake. Frank had wanted to ask her a question since this investigation started, but never figured he'd get a straight answer as long as she was in full FBI mode. Now seemed like a good time. "How much chance do you give us of actually catching this guy in Dallas?"

A small frown moved across her mouth before taking a quick sip of wine. "Honestly, not much. We've tried this task force thing twice before—it didn't work."

Frank nodded. "Seems like a long shot. If this guy has any sense, he's lying low right about now after a fresh kill. Maybe even left town."

Layla faced him. From her expression, she looked like a sensual goddess about to offer an official edict. He ran his hand along her narrow hips and massaged her butt. In the distance, the scream of a siren cut through the silence of the still night.

"That's just it, Frank. He doesn't have any sense. He's driven by an inner rage or hunger, or both, I can't tell." She stared at something on the floor and sighed. "Because of the physical likeness of his victims, it's almost as if he's killing the same person over and over again. Like he's forced to do it—against his will."

Frank just stared at her.

She reached out and stroked his cheek. "This guy's dangerous in more ways than one. That's why we went with the list in Dallas. We needed the most stout-hearted investigators we could get."

"I don't understand."

Layla took a moment before answering. "This case will work on your mind, Frank. Don't let it get to you."

Frank shook his head. His confused expression probably caused her to explain further.

She took his hand. "A cop already died because of this guy."

"What?" This was the first Frank had heard of this. Why was he just now finding out over pillow-talk? If the suspect killed a cop, this should have been disseminated during the briefing. He withdrew his hand from hers. "Why did you wait 'til now to say anything? This shouldn't be kept secret."

She looked at him with an empty stare. Speaking just above a whisper, she said, "The suspect didn't physically kill him. The case did. Stress brought on by the investigation caused the officer to take his own life. Family said he became despondent soon after getting into the worst of it. Stopped sleeping or eating, barked at family members, always seemed to be on edge."

Frank sat back on his heels. *What have I gotten myself into?* "Hey, that guy probably had other underling mental things going on. Cops don't kill themselves over things like this."

Layla's sad eyes blinked before she took his hand again. "Some do."

FRANK WOKE at his usual time Saturday morning. Blazing sun filtered around the blinds and sent little lasers of light shooting across the carpet in sharp bright lines. He shook the last of the cobwebs from his mind. The loft was quiet and still. Only the air conditioner blowing broke the stillness of the room. Took him a minute to realize Layla wasn't there. Her clothes weren't piled in a heap on the floor anymore, and no sounds from the hall. He searched each room, calling her name, but there was no sign she'd ever been there. In his half-awake state, Frank could easily have been convinced it had all been a dream except for two things. There were two wine glasses near the couch and a note by the coffee pot.

Frank, last night was a mistake. Forget it happened. We have to work together on this case and being in this kind of relationship isn't healthy. I'll see you later. Layla

Frank's suspicions had just been confirmed. Layla was a strange duck. Something else was confirmed. Her challenge to play the game the night before was a calculated move. He saw it now that his mind wasn't a jumble of wine and sexual energy. His memory drifted back again to that time as a kid when they snuck into the old, abandoned plant through the hole in the fence. That deep ditch filled with green, stagnated water they'd jumped across. Frank was the last to jump. He was the smallest, with the shortest legs. Everyone waited on the other side, taunting him to do it. The twisting sickness in his gut as he sized up his chances of making it. From the other side, someone yelled.

"Chicken."

That was it. Frank got a running start and charged ahead. Just as he planted his left foot at the edge of the ditch to begin his jump, loose gravel caused him to lose his footing. He tumbled into the nasty water, impaling his leg on a sharp piece of submerged rebar and getting a mouthful of disgusting water. All he got for his effort were three stitches, a tetanus shot, and diarrhea for several days.

Sometimes when a person calls you chicken or asks if you're afraid to do something, the best course of action is to just say, "Yup," and walk away.

Frank began his usual half hour of yoga, but his mind stayed on Layla. Had he totally misjudged the relationship? No. She was all in last night, but after she slept on it, she was all out. Why? This just further complicated things. Having this kind of drama in the middle of an investigation wasn't good. But Frank wouldn't take it back. Last night he'd seen something in her. When he cracked her tough outer shell, he'd seen a vulnerability he'd not recognized earlier. Was that what she wanted to keep hidden? She wasn't who she said she was. He still wasn't sure who she was, but last night he liked what he saw.

Frank finished exercising, drank coffee, and ate breakfast. Usually, on Saturday nights he cooked for a lady friend. If he weren't on this task force, he'd invite Katrina over. They'd begun seeing more of each other the closer she came to graduation. He'd given her time to mature and decide what she wanted in a relationship, and she'd given him time to decide if he wanted her exclusively. They both saw other people, and Frank suspected she'd go for a graduate degree, so he didn't have to make up his mind immediately. He was relieved. Being the mayor's daughter, she was in a class that shouldn't fraternize with the likes of him. But that was her choice, not her father's.

Frank never figured he'd take an interest in another woman. Since his wife died in New York, he'd made a special point of not getting too close to members of the opposite sex. Never wanted to feel that kind of loss again. That empty, hollow feeling he'd experienced drove him from New York to Dallas and a change of careers.

Frank relaxed on the sofa and watched a little TV until the restlessness took hold. He showered and went out for a long Mexican food lunch. Working the evening shift wasn't what he liked. Didn't like it when he worked patrol; didn't like it when he worked Vice. Evenings were best spent at home. But this Whisper investigation demanded he get out of his happy place. Time to get his head around the idea again.

TWELVE

Rob checked his watch as Frank strolled into CIU. How can a guy who gets to the office before everyone on weekday mornings be ten minutes late on a Saturday afternoon?

Place was almost deserted. The usual gaggle of detectives and their ambient noise had the weekend off. Carmen, Rob's wife let Rob go to work grudgingly on Saturdays and Sundays. She wanted him to herself on those days. She loved his Saturday grill nights and then snuggling together while watching a favorite old movie on the sofa. She looked forward to going to Mass with him and then relaxing on lazy Sunday afternoons. Carmen hated being alone on weekends. Rob hated it, too. Since she'd defeated a three-year bout of post-menopausal depression, he made it a point to stay as close to home as possible.

Rob looked up as Frank ambled toward their joined cubicles. "Oversleep?"

Frank glanced his way with a neutral expression but didn't bother answering. Only drawback to working with Frank was his moodiness.

Frank flopped down in his chair and released a breath. He looked sleepy today. Of course, Frank looked sleepy most days. Most laid-back guy Rob knew.

But Rob also knew that particular look. "Hot date last night?"

Frank powered up his computer before saying, "Yeah, hot."

It was going to be one of those days where Rob would be forced to carry the conversation again. Frank often went hours without uttering a word. But that didn't mean he wasn't thinking. Could see it in his eyes. Computing, analyzing, studying some problem, trying to make sense of it. That's what Rob saw today.

"Decided where we'll start?" Frank asked.

Rob tossed him the FBI briefing sheet over the short cubicle wall. The idea was that each partner team would take a few gin joints and surveil them during Saturday night in hopes of spotting the suspect. Rob dusted a smear off his shiny ostrich skin boots and said, "They've already assigned us the ones we're supposed to check. Our only choice is in what order."

Frank stopped staring at the computer screen and gave a cursory glance at the list before tossing it back. "Whatever."

"Ready when you are," Rob said. He stood and adjusted his holster under the untucked Western-cut shirt.

Frank wore the same outfit he wore every day, except he'd left the polo hanging out to cover his weapon. Resembled a homeless, unkept yuppie. Together with the khaki Dockers and deck shoes, he gave the appearance of being on vacation in Martha's Vineyard, not gearing up to visit low-class bars and ice houses in Dallas. Not exactly the look most people in the places they were about to visit sported.

Frank switched off the computer and stood. "Hope Layla's satisfied with the results tonight." He yawned and stretched.

"Ask her yourself."

"Huh?"

Rob motioned with his head toward Edna's office. She and Layla sat there chatting like best pals behind the glass wall. Rob had never seen Frank embarrassed, but when Edna and Layla laughed about something and they turned and stared at Frank, blood rushed up his neck and colored his face.

"Let's hit the street," Frank said, before heading for the door.

Rob smirked. Yeah, he was upset about something, already using cop-shop talk. Rob led the way across the enclosed walkway to the employee garage. A trace of a breeze blew through the garage and tried, with little success, to cool the parking area, but the place was still a roaster. As usual, they took Rob's unmarked patrol car. He leaned over and dialed the police radio to the Southeast patrol channel.

Frank took a long swig of bottled water. "Why you doing that?"

Rob shrugged before tapping the top of his Copenhagen box and twisting it open. "Might come in handy if we need quick help." Rob took a pinch of snuff and situated it between his cheek and gum. He had an alternative motive for switching the radio—he loved listening to dispatched calls. He often missed riding patrol. It was a simpler life. A life where, at the end of the shift, you didn't leave things undone. No pending cases, no leads to run out later, less paperwork. He hadn't been caught up on his paperwork since arriving in CIU. But patrol also had its bad side, which he didn't miss. Being first on the scene when five people are killed in a head-on, seeing a mother and her six-year-old daughter hysterical after both have been raped by the same home intruder, and viewing the charred corpses of three young children after an apartment fire. Come to think of it, patrol wasn't all that great after all.

Frank probably never missed patrol. He viewed it as dirty, dangerous, and boring work. He was the quintessential detective. A man who liked puzzles and mysteries. Whose inquisitive brain became restless when there wasn't a case worthy of his abilities. A man who would quickly become inpatient visiting bars, beer dives, and ice houses looking for someone who might never show up. Rob glanced over at Frank as they pulled out of the garage. He had sunk in the full slouched riding position—head on the rest, knees on the dash, and eyes closed. He'd be asleep soon if Rob wasn't careful.

Rob took the RL Thornton Freeway and exited Dolphin Road. He knew a place on their list Frank would like. Frank had a confidential informant who owned the joint. Pretty sure Frank hadn't visited her in several months. As he turned right on Dolphin, the dispatch announced, "Any unit clear and close. Have a street disturbance 3400 Forney."

When no one volunteered, dispatch sent a one-man unit to the call and asked if anyone was clear to check by.

Rob bumped Frank's shoulder. "Hey, want to check by with that one-man?"

Frank turned his head Rob's way, slid the sunglasses down with his index finger, and opened an eyelid. "Sure."

Rob snatched up the mic. "Five-seventeen, we're in the area and can check by."

"Roger that, five-seventeen—have you checking by. Thank you."

Frank sat up in the seat. "How far?"

Rob pointed straight ahead. "Just on the other side of Haskell."

A minute later when Rob pulled into the working-class neighborhood, the action was still going strong. A young, angry white man with a scraggly beard and wearing a wife-beater A-shirt stood in the front yard screaming at the house next door. The grass in his yard was almost a foot high, and a dilapidated Ford truck sat in the driveway on blocks. The guy downed the last of his beer and, cursing, threw the empty can at the house next door. Neighbors watched from yards and porches, sipping beer and smiling at the free drama across the street.

Frank smirked. "Six-thirty on a hot, summer, Saturday evening. What're the chances alcohol is involved?"

One thing about Frank. He had a master's in sarcasm, even though he acknowledged it was the lowest form of wit. The patrol unit hadn't arrived yet, but Rob and Frank strolled toward the guy as he screamed obscenities at his neighbor's home.

"Is there something wrong?" Rob asked.

The slim man swung around, almost losing his balance, and his eyes had a beer glow. Tattoos lined both arms, chest, and back. His hands were balled into fists, and something brown stained the front of his shirt. The odor of beer sweat wafted off him in waves. Before he could speak, Rob held out his ID and badge.

"Dallas Police. What's the problem?"

The man took a step back and his expression softened. "Bout time you got here. Called a half hour ago."

"Do you have a problem, or do you want to discuss our arrival time?" Rob asked.

The guy pointed at the neighbor's house and said, "Have someone harassing my wife—that's all."

"What's your name?" Rob asked.

"Will Pickens."

The one-man patrol unit rolled up, and Frank broke off from the interview to meet the officer.

"Hold that thought a minute," Rob told Pickens.

Frank and the uniform walked to where Rob stood.

"Go ahead with your complaint," Rob said.

"Gerald Sykes—" The guy pointed at the house beside his. "Was in our back yard a minute ago with a sack over his head, naked, and howling like a dog!"

"Who's Gerald Sykes?" the uniform asked.

The guy motioned toward the house he was yelling at. "Well, who do you think? He lives next door."

"Did you see him?" Frank asked.

The guy did a double take. "No, but my wife did."

"Where's she?" Rob asked.

Pickens motioned at his house. "Inside."

Rob stared at the uniform. "We'll talk to her, while you get his story."

"Thanks."

Rob strolled to the house, and Frank followed. The place was a '70s ranch with a huge Live Oak shading the whole front yard. The lawn consisted of every kind of weed known to Texas and Oklahoma.

Behind the screen door, an attractive woman in her mid-twenties watched as the scene out front unfolded. She wore Daisy Dukes and a low-cut top with no bra. Sweat beaded on her upper lip and chest and wormed its way down her abundant cleavage.

"You Mrs. Pickens?" Rob asked.

"Uh-huh." She twisted a strand of blond hair and had a mischievous smirk.

Rob said, "Did you see someone in your back yard naked?"

"Uh-huh."

"Can you identify him as your neighbor, Gerald Sykes?" Frank asked.

The woman grinned and gave Frank a look. "Sure can."

"About how long ago did this happen?" Frank asked.

She shrugged. "Forty-five minutes or so."

Rob pulled out a note pad. "What did he say to you?"

She giggled and sucked on the end of her hair. "Didn't say nothing—just howled."

Frank glanced back at the uniform interviewing her husband. In a low voice, he asked, "Was he wearing any distinctive clothing?"

"Nope, naked as a jaybird wearing a sack over his head with two holes cut out for eyes."

Frank winked at Rob.

Rob said, "So let me get this straight. There was a naked man in your back yard with a sack over his head, howling, wearing no clothing, who didn't speak to you? Is that about right?"

She nodded. "Yes, that's correct."

Frank said, "But you believe it was your next-door neighbor?"

"Uh-huh."

Frank smiled and motioned toward Rob. "Grounder, be my guest?"

Rob looked at her husband and back at the woman. He leaned closer and in a soft voice asked, "How did you identify the suspect as your neighbor?"

She opened her mouth to speak and her eyes widened. Her head snapped toward her husband, still talking to the uniform. She stepped back from the door. "I... I just knew, that's all."

Frank had trouble keeping a straight face when he asked, "How?"

Her eyes quickly shifted back to her husband, and she stiffened. After a moment she glared at them. "Well don't believe me then. See if I care!" She slammed the door so hard it shook the frame, and her husband looked in their direction.

Rob and Frank strolled back and pulled the patrol officer aside, briefing him on what they'd discovered from Mrs. Pickens before clearing the scene. At least the encounter had awoken Frank. Always got a kick out of domestic things like that.

"Where we headed?" Frank asked.

Rob flipped on his blinker. "Ruby Dare's."

Frank nodded. "Good, been meaning to drop in on the old girl."

Ruby Dare ran a washed-up club off Military Parkway and Jim Miller Road. Owned the place since the '80s. In her younger days, back in the '60s, she sang in the club. Bought it twenty years later. She tried to add a little elegance to the working-class neighborhood joint by keeping it clean and clear of riffraff. Which wasn't easy. Ruby was known to be a friend of the police. Patrol cars stopped by often to check in on her. Community had done a one-eighty in the last fifty years, but not in a good way. But Ruby wasn't ready to throw in the towel yet. She would fight for her club to the end.

The blazing afternoon sun shined on the front door, and the handle was hot to the touch. Frank followed Rob inside. The welcoming cool darkness with the whiff of beer and whiskey in the air was a working man's paradise. The kind of place Rob felt comfortable. The small stage to the left only hosted local country and western bands on weekends now. The glory days of scoring big-name stars were long gone. A group of musicians was setting up their equipment for tonight's performance. Looked like a grandpa, son, and grandson trio. Everyone was decked out in western attire. Ruby, like always, was serving behind the bar. Upon seeing Frank, a broad grin swept over her wrinkled lips. In a smoky, raspy voice she said, "Frank, where you been?"

Frank lazily approached the bar. He slid his long frame on a stool and accepted her outstretched hand. After softly kissing it, he answered, "Pining away for you."

Rob waited patiently as the traditional greeting continued. Always amazed him how Frank could make this crusty, old gal melt like a snowball on a hot Dallas sidewalk. Ruby was pushing seventy—probably already there, but she always blushed when Frank came near. *Weird.* Ruby's long hair had been dyed so many times probably not even she knew its true color. She styled it in a sixties bouffant with loose strands cascading around her ears. Always wore the same red lipstick and heavy caked makeup. Especially on her left cheek—where she'd been shot.

According to Sarge, in '76, Ruby lived with a real asshole. Guy had run-ins with the law every week. One of those weeks, he robbed a gas station and didn't bother telling Ruby. She found out later that night when officers stopped them in the same car he'd used to hijack the business. Ruby's old man jumped out of the sedan shooting. The officers returned fire. A stray police bullet took a bad bounce and ricocheted through the back window, grazing Ruby in the cheek about the time she realized there was a serious problem. She knew her old man kept a gun in the glove compartment. Ruby was so pissed he had gotten her shot she grabbed the automatic and pointed it at him as he stood outside the driver's door blasting away at the cops. She was about to give him the warning to surrender when she looked over her shoulder just in time to see him shoot one of the officers. After that, she claimed she really didn't recall what happened next. The last thing she remembered was squeezing the automatic's trigger. What resulted was her plugging her live-in four times in quick succession, which allowed the second officer to render aid to his fallen partner. She calmly dropped the pistol into the driver's seat and raised both hands before someone took the opportunity to shoot her again. The wounded officer recovered, she was recognized for helping to save him, and everyone just sort of forgot about her killing the guy. That's how Dallas did business in the seventies.

Rob swung on to another stool as Ruby said, "Rob, you still drinking the usual?"

"Yup."

Ruby served him a Michelob and Frank the best house red.

"What do I owe the pleasure, gents?"

The place was mostly empty, so Frank didn't bother keeping his voice down. "Looking for a young guy who didn't grow up around here. Big blond dude. Might stop by for a drink now and then."

Ruby shook her head. "Doesn't ring a bell. What's he done?"

Rob finished taking a long pull of beer. "Might be that guy involved in the Trinity Forest murder."

"Figured as much," Ruby mumbled. "Was that as nasty as rumor has it?"

"Nastier," Frank said.

Ruby shook her head. "Hadn't seen him in here, but one of my girls said she saw a creepy guy down at Bigelow's last week."

"Fit the description?" Frank asked before taking a sip.

"Don't think so. Old and fat."

"Lots of creepy old fat guys in Dallas." Rob chuckled.

Frank had a photo of the guy from the Snapshot DNA profile the FBI printed, and he slid it across the bar. "This hasn't been officially released, but we're passing one out to every place that might come into contact with him."

Ruby unfolded the photo and nodded. "Nice looking."

The door to the left of the bar swung open and an attractive twenty-something Hispanic girl walked in, carrying a tray of clean glasses. She set them on a shelf behind the bar and nodded at Rob.

Ruby passed the Snapshot photo to the girl. "Lucia, this guy ever come in here?"

Lucia picked up a glass half full of orange juice and took a sip as she studied the photo. She slowly shook her head. "Haven't seen him around." She swiveled her head from Rob to Frank and her forehead wrinkled. "You cops?"

Frank extended his hand. "Detective Frank Pierce." He nodded toward Rob. "Detective Soliz."

After finishing off the juice, Lucia asked, "What's he done?"

"He kills women," Rob answered.

Lucia showed a tight grimace before returning to the back room.

Frank visited Ruby another half hour. The interior of the car was like a blast furnace when they pulled out of the parking lot. Took twenty minutes to cool it down.

And that's pretty much how the rest of their evening went. Between 7 PM and 2 AM, they hit six more dives on their FBI list in East Dallas. Passing out photo flyers to the bartenders and keeping their eyes open for anyone who came close to the description they had of the Snapshot photo. Frank lost interest in the futile exercise around ten and was rotten company the rest of the night.

THIRTEEN

Perry woke up early Sunday morning and for a second didn't know where he was. He was naked in bed, and the soft, warm arm lying across his midsection finally refreshed his memory. He glanced down at the short, brown-haired woman with her face buried in the pillow as her steady breathing seemed to match his. Picked her up at a beer joint in South Dallas about one this morning and she took him home with her. Girl acted like she hadn't had a man in ages from the way she made love. They didn't get to sleep until almost three.

Perry turned toward the window. The soft light of dawn peeked around the edges of the blinds, and a low rumble of distant thunder echoed through the room. The steady dripping of rain off the roof caused Perry to relax and try going back to sleep. After ten minutes, he gave up the idea. Better to just be gone when she woke up. Didn't need to hang around a place he had no intention of staying. Perry slipped out of bed without waking her and got dressed. Had things to do. Couldn't lie around here all day. As he eased down the hall, the sound of a TV drifted toward him. In the living room, a small boy about five sat cross-legged on the sofa watching cartoons. Perry didn't remember any kid when he brought the woman home last night. The little guy gazed at Perry with a curious grin.

"You mama's new friend?"

Kid had curly brown hair and wore Spiderman pajamas while eating a bowl dry of cereal.

Perry darted his head left and right, making sure they were alone. "Yeah, sure."

Kid touched the top of a gallon milk jug sitting on the coffee table. "Can you open this?"

Perry stuffed his shirttail into his jeans and twisted the jug lid open. "There you go."

"Thanks." The kid steadied the jug and carefully poured the milk over the cereal. He went back to watching the cartoon and didn't say another word.

Perry stepped outside into the rich humid air and the smell and sound of light rain greeted him as it filtered down the gutters and off the leaves. He fired up the truck and tried figuring out exactly where he was. The beer joint had been off Ledbetter and Marsalis. He hadn't been paying much attention when she directed him in the dark to her house. Nothing around here looked familiar—a dead-end street. Perry drove to what looked like an intersection, and that's when he saw the first street sign. He was at Travis Trail and Telephone Road, wherever that was. If he had one of those expensive phones like most people, he could just plug into its GPS app and it would take him right home. But his cheap flip phone didn't do that kind of stuff.

Acting on instinct more than knowledge, he swung left and headed down Telephone Road. The roads were just wet enough that you could spin out if you goosed the gas too much, so Perry drove the speed limit and squinted through the front windshield through the low fog that hung over the road. Just after passing a sign that read Newton Creek, a red blur shot across the road in front of him from the trees to Perry's right. He slammed on the brakes and skidded as the crunch of something under his tires was followed by a scream.

Perry's heart almost stopped as he put the truck in park and slowly opened the door. His was the only vehicle on the two-lane road this foggy Sunday morning. Holding onto the side of the truck, he carefully walked to the rear to a chorus of moans and groans. All scrunched up in the road were a red racing bike and a man dressed in a red sports outfit. A dirt path on each side of the road led off into the woods—hidden bike trail. The guy looked to have compound fractures on both legs and blood seeped from the corner of his mouth. The metal from the bike was wrapped up in his legs and his head bled from under the helmet.

As Perry approached, the guy's eyes flashed open. In a pleading voice filled with pain, he said, "Call 911—please hurry."

Perry knew what he had to do. It was the only merciful thing he could do. He squatted down and carefully removed the helmet from the injured biker. "It's okay," he whispered. "I'm sorry, I just didn't see you."

The man raised his head a little from the pavement and screamed, "For god's sake, call 911. I'm all torn up inside—can hardly breathe!"

Perry stood up and looked in all directions. "I know, I didn't mean to hurt you, mister." Perry twisted his head again, making sure they were alone, just before placing his boot over the biker's neck and shifting all his weight to that foot with one sudden motion.

FRANK SLEPT IN SUNDAY. Wasn't used to staying up into the wee hours of the morning anymore. He did his yoga routine and drank a little coffee with a piece of toast smeared with almond butter and wild honey. He'd spent the majority of Saturday night pondering Layla. What was her real game? Oh, he knew her official game. Catch Whisper and make Dallas safe. But that wasn't her real game. There was something else. He'd have a talk with his FBI pal, David Ford.

Frank turned up the volume on the TV as the weather report started. A new tropical storm had developed in the Windward Islands. Storm warnings were posted for Dominica, Barbados, Martinique, Saint Lucia, Saint Vincent, and the Grenadines. The World Meteorological Organization had already assigned it a name —Kate.

Frank's phone rang.

"Hey, want to chill?" Katrina asked.

Frank usually thought about Katrina every day, but the case and the distraction of Layla had caused him to focus on other things. "Little early to start fooling around. People aren't even home from church yet."

"They're not invited, just you and me. Fixing lunch if you want to stop by."

Frank hesitated a second before answering. Didn't know why... just hesitated.

"Of course, if you have other plans—"

"No, no other plans. You know I'm working evenings, now?"

"When did that start?"

"Long story, tell you over lunch."

An hour later, Frank got out of his car and spent a few seconds studying Katrina's apartment building near SMU. It was built back in the eighties, but someone did a major makeover a decade ago, and it had a stylish retro feel with its sweeping arches and large central patio and pool area. He seldom went to her apartment. But every time he did, he recalled his first visit. She wasn't home that April afternoon two years ago when he first visited. In fact, she was missing, and he and Rob were investigating her disappearance. The memory flashing across his mind caused him to slow his pace as he took the stairs to the second floor. Katrina met him at the door with a long kiss. The kind that makes you wish you could stay in those arms forever. The place still pretty much looked the same. Open and airy, with nice furnishings and several modern oil-on-canvas pieces of art that gave a splash of color to the living room walls.

"Hungry?" she asked.

"Starving."

She'd made tuna sandwiches on toasted whole wheat, cubed an avocado, and thrown a handful of grape tomatoes on the plate. Had an open bag of Lays and a small jar of gherkin pickles on the table. Simple meal, and for a college kid, more than healthy. As she poured the iced tea she asked, "When did you start working evenings?"

Frank shrugged. "It's this Great Trinity Forest murder."

"Oh. Any leads?"

Frank took a swallow of tea and shook his head.

"Daddy doesn't seem too worried about it. Thinks the guy's a nut."

Frank didn't hold the mayor in too high a regard. Something about the man just rubbed Frank the wrong way. "Yeah, probably, but when a murder scene has a photo of the mayor and his family, cops tend to take notice."

Katrina showed a dark expression and got very quiet at the mention she might be in danger.

Frank quickly said. "Don't worry. We're going to scoop this dude up pretty soon. He won't last long with me after him."

Katrina let out a short breath and nodded, letting her hand slide into Frank's. He softly kissed it. He shouldn't have said anything. After what she had been through with the kidnappers, she still felt a sense of insecurity. "Don't worry, I'll always protect you," he whispered.

After lunch, they spent the rest of the afternoon making slow, wonderful love. Katrina wanted to be held and assured all would be well. Frank didn't blame her. Everyone wanted that kind of assurance. When they finished and lay together on the cool, sweaty sheets, he held her tighter and showered her with soft kisses on the cheek and lips.

"I'm worried about Poppy," she said.

"Who?"

"My grandfather, Poppy. My mom called and said he's sinking fast."

With everything else going on, Frank had forgotten about the mayor's dad. Kinda felt sorry for the family, especially Katrina. "I'm sorry. From what I've read, sounds like he's lived an exciting and productive life. A legend in Texas." Frank tossed that legend thing in based on an article he'd seen last week on the old man. Ernest Wallace had indeed lived a full life. Outlived two wives, made almost a billion dollars, and built a gas and oil empire that guaranteed his heirs would remain wealthy for many generations to come. Katrina's voice took on a quiet *little girl* quality.

"The thought of losing him fills me with such dread. He's been the family rock for so long. The anchor we all attach ourselves to."

Frank had no words. Never met the man. Never knew him. But the fact he gave several million dollars annually to children's hospitals and charities was enough to gain Frank's endorsement.

Katrina leaned on an elbow and faced him. Through misted eyes, she said, "I don't think I can stand to lose him without another rock to hold on to." Her forehead tightened. "You have to be that rock for me, Frank. You have to be there for me when the time comes, promise."

Frank's heart swelled with emotion. They had just entered a new level in their relationship. She trusted him completely. He would not let her down. "I promise."

She laid her head on his chest as a chill must have washed over her and she shook. In a monotone voice, she asked, "Do you ever think about the cave?"

At the mention of the cave, a chill also shook Frank. Of course he did. Not a day went by that something didn't remind him of that terrible place. Many nights, he'd wake in the same cold sweat he had kneeling in the damp sand in the dark, waiting for the whackos outside to come in and kill them. The overpowering stench of putrefied human remains still lodged deep in his nostrils.

Frank pulled her a little closer. "Yeah, I think about it now and then."

Katrina wrapped her arms tighter around him and didn't speak for a few seconds. Finally, in a hoarse voice, she said, "When I imagine hell, the cave always pops into my head."

She was right. Nothing in Frank's experience or memory compared to it. He'd probably missed a great opportunity not talking about it at his mandatory meeting with the police shrink. Might have gotten some better peace of mind if he had. Frank had learned to live with his demons, and Katrina must as well.

Frank sucked in a lungful of confident air and in his most convincing voice said, "You can forget it. You'll never be in another dark scary place again with someone out to kill you."

Katrina shifted herself and rolled on Frank, forcing his legs open with her knees. She began a slow back and forth movement. Her familiar grin eased back across her lips. "If I do, I want you with me."

***

SUNDAY EVENING when Rob and Frank left the station to go on their evening patrol, Frank noticed a change in Rob. His enthusiasm wasn't like last night. Didn't have that old spark of energy. "You okay?" Frank asked.

Rob put the car in reverse and backed out of the parking space in the police lot. In a voice devoid of emotion, he said, "This isn't what we should be doing. We need to be running out leads. This isn't our thing. Feeling useless."

"What did you expect?" Frank said. "We're not calling any shots, making any decisions, turning over any rocks. We work for the feds; they're the boss."

Rob glanced at him. "This was a mistake."

Frank started to agree when his phone rang. Terry calling. Frank put the call on speaker.

"Hey, Terry."

"Frank, you guys work 'til about ten tonight and come into the office around ten o'clock tomorrow morning. Been a change in plans."

"What kind of change?"

"I'll know more tomorrow. We'll talk in the office," Terry said before disconnecting.

"What do you figure is going on?" Rob asked.

Frank shrugged, but Terry's voice held that conspiratorial tone it occasionally took on when he was up to something.

The FBI list they had that night called for them to check clubs and gin joints in South Dallas. Just as well they were quitting at ten. Sunday nights, even in the summer months, were for the most part usually dead. Everyone had spent their money and energy Friday and Saturday nights. The ne'er-do-wells had probably bonded out of jail and the victims had probably been released from the hospitals while everyone else was getting ready to go to work Monday morning. There were a couple of exceptions to the rule. You could always count on trouble from the Grovites and Tushhogs. Those two groups never took a rest and always came back twice as strong. They weren't gangs as such. Being a Grovite or Tushhog was more a state of mind. Just a bunch of middle-aged white guys that enjoyed drinking and a good fight. Wasn't much difference in the two except that the Grovites ran in the Pleasant Grove area of Southeast Dallas, and the Tushhogs stayed strictly south of Loop 12. If one crossed the border and got caught drinking in the wrong bar, the police and at least one ambulance always got called.

One of the joints assigned for Rob and Frank to check that night was the Down and Out Bar. With a name like that, it was a wonder it had thrived in South Dallas for over a decade. Had a very loyal clientele of Tushhogs. These older middle-aged bikers, construction workers, and rednecks paid loyal allegiance to the place like a shrine to individual liberty and freedom. Lots of fights, mostly with folks outside of the Tushhog community. But the crazy thing about the Tushhogs? If they couldn't find an outsider to fight, they'd fight among themselves.

The Texas Alcoholic Beverage Commission had tried to close the Down and Out numerous times, but like a Phoenix rising from the ashes, they always reopened. Since it was most likely the place they would encounter trouble, Rob and Frank elected to check it first. No use letting the patrons get any drunker or meaner than necessary. Frank had been to the club only once. During his Vice days, his partner, now retired, decided The Down and Out would be a great place to do a liquor violation. Frank had heard of the club and knew its reputation. His senior partner assured him it was overblown and they could make a quick case there and take the rest of the night off. Things didn't exactly go down as planned. When they attempted to arrest the bartender for serving intoxicated persons, a mini riot erupted. Frank and his partner retreated to the cover of the back storeroom and called for backup. It took a half dozen patrol officers to restore order and rescue Frank and his partner. Frank hadn't been back since.

The Down and Out was in the 7300 block of Bonnie View Road, just before the I-20 service road. The small, white cinder block joint had a flat roof and gravel parking lot. After his encounter a few years earlier, Frank wasn't keen on just strolling into the place without doing a recon first. They drove by slowly, crossed I-20, and came rolling back up at a few minutes after seven o'clock. Everything looked quiet. Hot Sunday evenings in Dallas meant everyone pretty much stayed indoors. A few Harleys, a couple of work trucks, and several pickups occupied the parking lot.

"How you want to play it?" Rob asked.

Frank didn't want to play it at all, but he wasn't going to be intimidated into ignoring an assignment. "We go in, leave a Snapshot photo of the suspect, and leave. No one orders anything. Clean in and out with no problems. Keep your eyes on the door and my back. Don't let 'em get behind us." In the back of his mind, an old worry lingered. Would he encounter the same bartender from five years earlier that chased them into the cover of the storeroom? Would they recognize him? Frank pulled in a breath and said, "Let's go."

Just as they got out of their car, three shots echoed from inside the club. Rob ducked behind the open car door and had his pistol out.

Frank squatted beside the right front wheel well and also drew his weapon. They waited a few seconds, but nothing else happened. Rob glanced Frank's way. He had his mouth open to say something when the door busted open and a fat guy with long thinning gray hair, wearing a bright yellow T-shirt and olive-green cargo shorts staggered out, holding a bloody Buck knife. The guy's eyes were wild with fear and pain as he clutched his blood-soaked chest with the other hand and fell to his knees. He dropped the knife and gasped for breath.

Frank stood. *Oh, shit.*

Just as Rob stood, a mob of Tushhogs stampeded through the front door, heading for their rides. They trampled the shot guy in their enthusiasm to get away, grinding him into the gravel. Rob and Frank took a tactical stance on each side of the door and Rob did a quick peek inside. He looked back at Frank and nodded. They rushed in with pistols drawn to a surreal scene of mayhem. Everyone but three people had gotten out while the getting was good.

The front of the Formica bar faced the door. Every wall sported a mix of faded Playboy and Hustler fold-outs and Confederate and Texas flags. Over twenty different beer advertising signs glowed from the walls, offering the only light source to the gloomy interior. Frank blinked several times to help his vision adjust from bright sunlight to the dark bar. Traces of gun smoke still hung heavy in the beer and blood-soaked air. A small bushy-headed guy was laid out on the floor, unconscious and bleeding from the chest. Air bubbles formed and popped at the site of the stab wound with each breath he took. Another guy, bigger, with a cowboy hat, leaned against the bar holding his left leg. Blood oozed between his fingers. He loosely held a small automatic in his other hand.

Rob aimed his pistol center mass of the guy. "Police. Drop it!"

As Rob tightened his finger on the trigger, a female voice behind the bar screamed, "Better do it, Brian. He'll kill ya' for sure."

The guy let the gun slip from his grip onto the floor and used his gun hand to put more pressure on his bleeding leg. He gritted his teeth but had a weird grin.

Rob kept him covered until he picked up the weapon and moved away.

Frank rushed to the man with the stab wound. Frank pointed at the screaming, hysterical bartender. "Call 911."

She was in shock. Kept babbling, "They done kilt Daryle, they kilted him."

Rob made the 911 call from his cell as he searched under the counter. He identified himself to the 911 operator and asked for backup and three ambulances. When he emerged from behind the bar, he had an empty plastic ice bag. He dropped beside Frank who had both hands pressing down on the sucking chest wound of the bushy headed guy on the floor.

"Here," Rob said, passing Frank the plastic bag.

Rob's time in combat had taught him to bring exactly what Frank needed. Had to seal the hole in the lung to let the guy breathe. Frank snatched the bag with his bloody hands and slapped it over the hole in the chest as another red bubble began forming. "I got this one, check the one in the parking lot."

Rob nodded and bolted for the door. When he opened it, the distant sound of police and ambulances filled the room.

Less than a minute later, Rob returned. He shook his head when Frank looked his way.

The police and ambulance response was great, considering it was a weekend and the department was still short-handed. A sergeant led the troops in, and they quickly took control of the scene. After an hour and several interviews, they were finally able to piece together what happened from the evidence and witnesses. The dead guy in the parking lot was a suspected Grovite poaching on Tushhog turf. He'd had words with the guy that got stabbed, Daryle, over whether the Cowboys would go to the Super Bowl this year, and the Grovite stabbed Daryle in the chest. Defending Tushhog territory and the questionable reputation of the hometown team, the guy with the cowboy hat jerked his Remington .22 automatic from his boot holster with such enthusiasm he managed to shoot himself in the leg. But it spoke well of his marksmanship that, after wounding himself, he still had the presence of mind to drill the attacker with the knife twice from twenty feet away with a short barrel pistol.

Frank and Rob hung around until Homicide detectives arrived. They gave their statements to the lead detective and outlined how they believed it all went down. It was a quarter past nine by the time they cleared the scene. Frank dug his phone from his Dockers and called Terry. He explained the details of the shit show they'd walked into. Terry always wanted to hear the story from his guys first before the information had a chance to get filtered through headquarters.

"You guys okay?" Terry asked.

"Yeah," Frank answered.

Terry's voice took on a concerned tone. "Sure, neither of you discharged your weapons?"

Frank had to grin. "We're sure, Terry."

The sound of Terry releasing a slow breath drifted from the phone. "You guys call it a night and get some rest. We'll talk tomorrow."

The ride back to the police department was quiet until just before they took the Lamar exit. Rob said, "It just doesn't make any sense."

Frank didn't bother answering. Of course, it didn't make any sense. Two hundred and twenty homicides last year, all over senseless, stupid stuff. Life was so cheap on the streets, it was sickening. The term misdemeanor murder had been coined to account for the senseless killings every week. The chief was struggling to keep his job with an increasingly skeptical city council and mayor. When Frank got out of the car at headquarters, it felt like he had a fifty-pound weight across his shoulders.

Rob didn't look any better. "I'll see ya' tomorrow, Frank," were his only words before he backed out of the parking garage and headed home.

FOURTEEN

Rob was just pulling into the police parking lot Monday morning, ready for his hour workout in the gym, when his phone rang. It was Terry.

"How close are you to the station?"

"Just pulling into the garage. Why?"

"Frank will be there in a minute, already spoke to him. You guys beat feet over to the Bureau. They just had a walk-in confess to being the Great Trinity Forest killer."

From the corner of his eye, Rob caught Frank's car sliding into a nearby parking place before the door swung open and Frank bolted for Rob's car.

Rob said, "He's here now. We're in route."

"Hold on. Remember what I said before the Tom Price interview. Be skeptical of everything—real skeptical," Terry said.

"Got it."

Frank flopped into the passenger seat and pointed to the garage exit. "Hit it."

Reminded Rob of Jake Blues from the *Blues Brothers* movie.

Twenty minutes later, they were checked through FBI reception, and an agent led them to a first-floor interview room. Layla and five other FBI agents gazed through the one-way mirror at the agent in the next room interviewing the guy across the table. Rob was a little shocked as he and Frank squeezed into the confines of the small room. Frank spoke Rob's concern as he approached Layla.

"Figured you'd be conducting the interview."

Layla didn't take her eyes off the subject. "Would, but this isn't the guy."

Rob leaned around a taller agent and peeked through the mirror. Man being interviewed was average height and weight with a crew-cut and black stubble outlining his head. Frank must have also noticed. He cleared his throat and whispered, "You certain?"

Layla's jaw was set and she nodded. "Idiot doesn't know the first thing about the details, just repeating what was in the media. He's just a serial confessor, looking for attention. We're about ready to kick his butt out."

Frank glanced Rob's way before saying, "Okay, keep us in the loop."

Layla didn't meet eyes with him or answer, only nodded.

As they exited the building, Frank scratched around in his pocket. He found his phone and dialed a number. Without introductions, he said, "Can you meet me in the front parking lot in five minutes? Yeah, the FBI parking lot. We're here now."

"Thanks." Frank turned to Rob. "Let's wait in the car."

LESS THAN FIVE MINUTES LATER, Rob and Frank waited as their pal, Agent Ford, made his way down the front steps of the FBI. Ford gazed in all directions, craning his neck around just before Frank reached over and tapped the horn twice. Ford's head snapped in their direction. He strolled toward them and slid into the back seat. After greeting him, Frank got down to business.

"Tell me the story on Layla."

Ford chuckled. "Didn't take you long to figure out she had a story."

Frank eyed him. "No, seriously, what's going on with her?"

Ford let out a long breath and stared back at the FBI building a few seconds before answering. "Layla's had a few problems."

Rob spoke up. "Ford, saying that's like saying General Custer had a few problems. What kind of problems?"

Ford lowered his voice. "This stays between us, right?"

Frank understood agents talking about other agents out of school could have serious career consequences. "People talk to us because we talk to no one."

Ford nodded and took a few moments collecting his thoughts. "Layla had an OPR that really raked her over the coals awhile back. But that's only the latest thing."

Frank draped his arm over the front seat and eyed Ford. "The beginning of a story is always a good place to start."

Ford grinned. "When Layla applied to the Bureau, they were elated to get her application. Girl's a genius. Not every day you get a clinical psychologist walking through the door wanting the kind of pay-cut you have to endure to become a new agent."

Frank nodded.

"Anyway," Ford continued. "They were so excited about having someone of her caliber, they waived the requirement for several years of field experience before sending her straight to BAU. Rushed her right into the program. Lots of on-the-job training going on there. She did well the first couple of years until they gave her the White Mountain killer case in New Hampshire."

"Refresh my memory on that one," Rob said.

Ford brushed lint off his dark suit pants and said, "Some nut murdering hikers and campers out in the woods. Killed at least five we know of before we put an end to it... well, Layla put an end to it."

"Huh?" Rob asked.

"She killed the guy. Worked night and day on the case for weeks.

When they executed the warrant, she was the first one through the door of the suspect's house. Clearing a back bedroom when the suspect popped up from behind a bed with a pistol." Ford's brow wrinkled and he bit the inside of his cheek. He shot a furtive glance their way. "Well, that was her story, anyway." Her partner said he never actually saw the suspect holding the weapon. He was behind Layla as they entered the room, and she fired so quickly, he didn't see the gun in the guy's hand before she shot. Might have just been laying on the bed."

Frank slowly looked over at Rob. He was running his tongue back and forth along his inside lower lip. His standard sign of doubt and concentration.

"Was the shooting righteous?" Frank asked.

"Yeah," Ford answered. "Everything checked out clean. Forensics put him at the scene of the crimes, and one surviving witness even identified him."

"So, where's the problem?" Rob asked.

Ford relaxed in the back seat and crossed his legs. "It was the next shooting that was the problem."

"Next?" Rob asked.

Frank had the kind of feeling he got just before someone was about to deliver really bad news. That flutter in the gut and tightness in the throat that signaled *beware*.

"Less than a year later, Layla was working as a co-case agent with another BAU member. Dude they were looking for cruised I-95 truck stops looking for runaways. Found the bodies a few days later, usually in a ditch near water. Without informing anyone and without backup, Layla took it on herself to also cruise I-95 truck stops on her days off. Smoked the guy about a month later. Guy was a trucker that had a weekly run between Virginia and North Carolina. Again, all the forensics checked out, but this time he didn't have a weapon. Unless you consider a pocket knife a weapon. Layla said it was a *him or me* situation, had the bruises to prove it."

Rob was doing the rolling lip thing again.

"Anyway, they treated her pretty rough for failure to follow Bureau policies. Almost got her fired over the OPR. Got transferred out of BAU to the Baltimore office. But she fought back."

"Huh?" Frank said.

"Yeah, called her dad, and the next thing anyone knows, she's back in BAU."

Frank poked his head further over the seat. "I'm not following, who is her dad?"

Ford smirked. "Ever heard of Clarence Barbee, the senior Senator from California?"

"So, she's wired," Rob said.

"About as tight as they come," Ford replied. "I warned you to stay clear of her."

"That's not working too well since she's in charge of the investigation and assigned to coordinate stuff at DPD," Frank said.

Ford uncrossed his arms and straightened his jacket. "Hey, well I gotta get back. Keep all this under wraps and stay clear of Layla. Word in the Bureau is she's as crazy as the people she's hunting. Enjoys killing—blood sport. Even with her father's backing, probably heading for a short career."

As Ford closed the car door, Frank's stomach knotted, and his skin turned cold. He wanted out of this thing before something happened he couldn't foresee. Something that could get him or Rob hurt. This news about Layla explained a lot—too dangerous to be around. Frank had met cops like her. Always managed to get someone else injured or killed while skating by on stupid blind luck themselves. He found it difficult to fathom the sexy, gregarious woman he held in his arms the other night capable of the things Ford described.

Rob probably said it best. "This suddenly feels very wrong. Sorry I encouraged you to jump in. You telling Terry any of this?"

Frank slowly shook his head. "No, but I say we jump out the first chance we get."

PERRY SAT in the shade of the big oak in the front yard of the house being renovated and munched his sandwich. Crew always ate an early lunch. A food truck pulled up at eleven o'clock every morning and the boss called a break. Perry's favorite was the roast beef. One of them, a bag of Doritos, and Coke was all he needed 'til supper.

After hearing the news of the dead woman in the woods, Perry understood he'd screwed up big time. Hadn't realized he'd lost the newspaper clipping about the mayor until the announcer talked about it the other night on TV. Perry wished he had that photo back. Those people were his family, his kin. The ones he'd traveled halfway across the country to see. But now they would be frightened of him. According to the papers, it had disturbed the mayor and his family so much they were avoiding public appearances, and the police had increased security. Not at all what Perry had intended. Now they'd think him a monster. Maybe he was a monster. But then again, maybe he wasn't. Sometimes he did bad things when the uncontrollable urges took over, but the rest of the time he was a nice guy. Helped Mrs. Cleveland around the house, helped Pedro under the drywall. Even opened the milk jug of the little kid in the house the other morning. Yeah, he wasn't all bad. No worse than anybody else. At least he'd admit his faults, if only to himself. More than most people would do. Perry felt nothing for the dead woman he'd left in the woods. A piece of useless street refuse the world was better off without.

Perry sometimes wondered how it would be if he were like everyone else. Not everyone had need-to-hunt urges. But the strange thing was, he never had the desire to *just fit in*, be like regular folks. The world was controlled by rules and laws. The way Perry figured it, he never got a vote on what rules he was supposed to follow, so he just followed none of 'em. Which was fine with him. Only did what he had to do to get by, just like everybody else. The rest of the people went through their miserable lives never feeling the elation one feels being a god. That was the best description he could offer of his behavior. A god who held the power of life and death in his hands.

Yeah, leaving the newspaper clipping was a screw-up. Which still left him with the problem. *How can I get close enough to introduce myself to the mayor?*

Perry checked his watch. Fifteen minutes before going-back-to-work time. A dark blue Chevy Impala pulled up in the driveway, and Diego rushed over and jumped in, chatting with the attractive twenty-something Mexican girl in the driver's seat. As she backed out, she shifted her gaze to Perry sitting under the tree. She tapped the brake and stopped for a second as she eyed him. Perry didn't know her, never seen her around the worksite before. After a few seconds, the girl quickly averted her eyes back to the rearview mirror as she swung the Impala into the street. Just as she shifted the car to drive, she took another long hard look at him.

ROB AND FRANK walked through the door of CIU and straight into Terry's office. Rob would have preferred lunch first, but Terry expected them.

Terry looked up as they crossed his threshold. "What happened with the walk-in at the Bureau?"

Neither took a seat. Frank answered. "It's a bust. Layla says the guy's a fraud. Knows nothing more than he heard on TV."

"Crap," Terry mumbled under his breath. "You guys still okay after that little dust-up yesterday evening?"

"Yeah," Rob said.

Terry laced his fingers and leaned his forearms on the desk. "We might pull you off canvassing the clubs. Mayor's dad is about to die. Everyone's expecting him to go this week. Old man lives in the Hill

Country, out around Leakey somewhere. The department expects they'll bring him back to Dallas to bury him. Probably Highland Park Methodist. We'll need two experienced guys to organize the security arrangements. You know, church, funeral procession, graveside service—the usual VIP funeral package when the mayor's in attendance."

Rob tried not to express any emotion, but he wanted to laugh out loud with relief. They were getting off the investigation without even asking. Frank didn't react, but from his relaxed expression, Rob figured he felt the same.

"So, what do you need us to do now?" Frank asked.

Terry showed his pained expression. "Afraid we still need to cover the clubs until we get the word about the old man. Don't worry, once he croaks, we'll pull you guys off to do the funeral advance. Shouldn't be that much longer."

Terry probably suspected Rob and Frank weren't being used to their greatest potential, having them cruising bars and clubs, but the manpower-slots had to be filled and their names were still on *the list*. He'd pull them out as soon as he could justify it to the brass. But the news from Terry was still disappointing because, just as quickly as he had thrown them a lifeline, he'd jerked it just out of their reach until some indefinite point in the future. Rob was heartbroken.

With them doing a short turn-around and reporting back to work tonight, Frank wasn't in the mood for lunch at Sarge's. He moped out of the office on his way home. Rob wasn't in the mood to drink alone, on or off duty, so he figured he'd head home, eat a sandwich with Carmen, mow the yard, and try and grab a short nap before reporting this evening. He cranked the car and headed down the ramp of the parking garage as he flipped on the radio.

This just in from the National Weather Service: Tropical Storm Kate has just made landfall in Barbados and St. Vincent, with maximum sustained winds of fifty-two miles per hour. Early reports indicate there was no loss of life, but severe flooding and beach erosion.

Now that it's entered the Caribbean Sea, we'll be watching this rain-maker and post regular updates.

Rob flipped off the radio and grinned. Growing up on the Texas Gulf Coast he'd seen his share of hurricanes. He didn't miss all the excitement and drama surrounding an approaching storm. That was another great reason for living in North Texas. Being almost three hundred miles inland gave him peace of mind.

FIFTEEN

Frank drove home and took the garage elevator up to the top floor. His loft was cool and quiet. As he strolled down the hall toward his bedroom, Layla popped back into his mind. He slowed his pace. Was she waiting for him in the bedroom? He eased to the door and peeked inside. No Layla. *Get a grip, Frank—forget her.* He shucked the polo and dockers for just a T-shirt and gym shorts. The news from Terry left him disappointed. He was so ready to see this case in the rearview mirror. When Frank was disappointed or upset, he knew what he needed to do—cook. He dug in the back of the refrigerator until he found the freezer bag of beef bones. He was a bit of a purist when it came to soups and stews. He refused to use that thirty-two-ounce slop in cardboard containers called bone stock. Soup and stew weather was still months away, but just doing something in expectation of the colder fall and winter temperatures made Frank feel cooler.

Before he got down to business, he opened a 2018 Trivento Argentina Reserve Malbec. Nothing complements cooking on a hot summer afternoon like a refreshing red. Frank took the six grass-fed beef bones and dropped them in his slow cooker. He covered them with water and then added four tablespoons of extra virgin olive oil, one rough-cut onion, one sliced carrot, three stalks of celery, two cloves of garlic, one bay leaf, two teaspoons of salt, and a twist or two from his pepper mill. As an afterthought, he also added a splash of red wine. *Bone stock always tasted better if you added a little acid to the mix.* He'd bring it to a boil in his slow cooker then drop the temperature to a simmer until he got home from club-hopping tonight. He typically grilled the bones first to enhance the flavor, but the temperature on the patio still tracked out at 102 degrees. Just this time, he'd skip the grill part of the recipe.

The steamy day had robbed him of an appetite, but he figured he'd better eat something. He threw a handful of mixed greens into a salad bowl, added a half dozen grape tomatoes and half of an avocado, and julienne-sliced some red onion on top. A drizzle of extra virgin olive oil with some of Rob's *Awsamic vinegar,* and Frank had the perfect light lunch.

Frank felt better now. He finished the red, pulled the drapes, and dropped on his bed. Grabbing an hour or two nap before work might put him in an even better mood. He stared at the ceiling fan doing its lazy turns and admitted he did miss cooking professionally, well, maybe a little. The stress of the line cook or even the head chef wasn't a job he relished as he did almost twenty years ago, but there were things he still missed. He'd always loved cooking. His earliest and happiest memories revolved around summers cooking with his grandma on the Florida ranch. From the time he was three until he left for the Culinary Institute of America in New York, his grandma had been his inspiration and teacher.

Strolling with her for an early morning trip to the garden to collect the day's fresh vegetables still brought a smile to his face. The sweet scent of tomatoes ripening on the vine, sweet corn ready for harvesting, and okra plants in bloom still stirred his olfactory memory. He still heard bees buzzing around the squash and the taste of fresh dug onions and carrots. His grandpa tried enticing Frank out of the kitchen to help with ranch chores, but that held no interest for him. Swimming in the pond and riding horses were the only reasons he saw fit to leave his grandma's side. Something about her presence gave him a warm cozy feeling he got from no one else. Her confidence in the kitchen astounded him. She was the one who taught him the difference between a pinch and a dash of spice. Her rule of *you can always add more later, but you can't un-add it* stayed with Frank to this day.

Frank understood he had been a great disappointment to his grandpa and especially his dad. The guy was a brawny construction superintendent who wanted his son to follow in his footsteps. Again, Frank's grandma came to his rescue. She explained to her son that Frank had a special talent, and it would be a shame to waste it on something he wasn't passionate about. The old man finally relented and agreed to help fund Frank's culinary education at the CIA.

Frank ran his hand down his face and checked his watch. *Not sleepy.* He could lie here for hours and not drift off. The aroma of bone stock cooking drifted in through the door. He hated the evening shift. Just as the day was coming to a close for the rest of the world, a new shift of first responders was going to work. Not enjoying a relaxing evening at home with their families, but on the street, handling people and their family problems that defied explanation and control. The sooner he and Rob got relieved of this assignment and away from Layla, the better. She was right—this case was getting to him. But he still didn't fully understand why. It was a gut feeling more than anything. Something he couldn't quite put his finger on, but knew it existed—and it wasn't good.

ROB MET Frank at the police parking lot at four-thirty. Rob had insisted they get an early start because he figured the suspect, Ol' Whisper, probably wasn't going out drinking on a Monday night— few do. That's why the clubs and bars sponsored Monday night specials, Tuesday ladies' nights, and half-price Wednesdays. But if the killer was stopping off for a drink, he'd most likely do it on the way home from work. Most drinking establishments were pretty dead until Thursday. People could sniff out the weekend by then, and a thirst developed. But there were a few guys who liked to swing by the local joints on their way home for a beer or two. Rob and Frank still needed to finish off the clubs on their Sunday night list since they'd been interrupted by the unexpected shooting.

Frank dragged himself into the car. The oppressive heat pulled everyone down. Needed a rain shower to cool things off. Frank stowed his gear and immediately went into his favorite riding position in the seat. "Okay, let's do this," he said in a weary voice.

Rob didn't answer but pulled out on Lamar and got on the freeway. Frank looked like he was drifting off. Better start some interesting conversation. Just as Rob made the hairpin turn off US 175 onto CF Hawn Freeway heading east, he said, "Does it bother you at all this used to be called Dead Man's Curve?"

Frank pulled his sunglasses down with his index finger and stared at the construction cones and barrels. He pushed the glasses back into place and mumbled, "Not in the least."

Rob gave up. Let him sleep until they got to the first club. About five o'clock, they parked at the It's Me, Not You bar in the nineteen hundred block of Belt Line Road South. Several pickups, work trucks, and half a dozen sedans were in the lot and street. Rob poked Frank. "We're here."

Frank grumbled under his breath a few seconds before sitting up and looking around. They didn't spend a lot of time in the dingy dive. Rob passed a copy of the Snapshot photo to the owner and asked him to keep an eye out. Frank leaned against the bar, keeping Rob's back covered. And that's pretty much how the early evening stops went. They hit a few more clubs before Frank demanded fried chicken from Hall's Chicken. Frank loved the place. Got the two-piece dark with fries, bread, pickles, and pickled jalapeño. Rob got a wing basket.

After the meal, Frank's mood greatly improved. Just as they

pulled out onto Lancaster, Frank pointed at the blinking neon sign up ahead past Ledbetter.

"Hey, let's check in with TJ while we're out here."

Rob hadn't noticed TJ's Lounge down the street until Frank reminded him. "They on our list?"

"Naw, but I check in on Ted any time I'm out this way."

Rob shrugged and put on his right blinker. The lot was only about half full. Looked like the usual South Dallas crowd. Several young guys leaned against the building discussing something as Rob and Frank eased through the door. They headed to the bar with the sound of pool sticks snapping cue balls from the corner and a younger Merle Haggard crooning *Today I Started Loving You Again* spewing from the jukebox. Even though there were only a few cars in the lot, the place was still pretty crowded for a Monday evening.

Frank meandered up to the bar and asked, "TJ around?"

The bartender shook his head. "Always takes Sundays and Mondays off—wife makes him."

Frank turned back to Rob. "Want to have a beer here?"

Rob had been checking out a group of Hispanic guys whispering and passing something in a plastic bag back and forth at the other end of the bar. When he turned back to answer Frank, he caught sight of Layla laughing and leaning with her back against the bar, talking to a big blond dude. Layla's black hair was loose and hung naturally almost to her shoulders. She wore a white lacy low-cut top with no bra, jeans, and light blue cowboy boots. She chatted with the big, strapping blond guy as if they were old friends.

Rob's jaw dropped and he bugged his eyes her way.

Frank's lips pursed at Rob's expression before turning to look behind him at what fascinated Rob so much. Frank took one look and jerked his head back to Rob. "What the hell's she doing?"

Rob moved to a spot so Layla wouldn't catch sight of him. In a quiet voice, he said, "What does it look like she's doing?"

Frank shook his head. "Naw, she wouldn't."

Rob said, "Don't be so sure. Let's get out of here."

They wove their way through the crowd and to the parking lot. Then, they waited in their car for over a half hour, keeping an eyeball on the front door. It had just started getting dark. That time of day in the summers when twilight engulfed the landscape and gave everything a soft, hazy-yellow glow. About five minutes later, the big blond guy Layla was talking to left in a beat-up Ford truck, but Layla was nowhere in sight. A few moments later, the club door swung open and she strolled out, swinging a clutch on a chain.

Frank bolted from the car in her direction, catching her on the blindside about halfway across the parking lot. He was almost on her before she spun around with a Glock in her hand. Her face held no expression, the eyes were sharp and clear, and the jaw set. Frank had stared killers in the face many times. He did so again now.

She lowered the pistol and her head flinched back. "Frank, why are you here?"

Rob came trotting up in time to spot the tall, bald man get out of a car and head their way.

"Why are *you* here?" Frank asked and grabbed for her arm.

"Hold it right there," the bald guy yelled. He also had a Glock and it was pointed at Frank.

Layla waved the newcomer down. "Relax, Sanders, they're cops."

The guy had a confused look, but lowered the pistol, still keeping his finger on the trigger.

"I got this," Layla said to him. "Wait for me in the car."

The guy gave Rob and Frank another hard stare before heading back to his sedan.

Layla turned back to Frank. "This club isn't on your list. Why are you here?"

"Our badge says the city of Dallas," Rob said. "We can go into any place, any time."

Layla blew Rob off and stared at Frank, who'd yet to answer her question. Frank finally found his voice.

"You're playing a dangerous game. One mistake and you're

dead," Frank whispered. "He kills little girls like you, cuts them into pieces, and eats them."

Layla advanced on him. "Who the hell you think you're talking to? Some rookie? Dallas is this guy's last stop. We're ending it here! Understand?"

Frank regained his composure. "Stop this now. You'll get yourself or someone else hurt. It won't be like before." *Oh crap.*

Layla's look changed from anger to curiosity. "Like before, Frank? Who you been talking to, huh? Some loudmouth asshole in the FBI who's still pissed about not making the promotion cut. Jealous of someone else's success? Is that who you're talking to?" She stepped back and smiled. "Well, never forget one thing. I'm the one BAU sent to finish this guy. We've missed him twice and headquarters has decided on a more direct approach."

Rob had no idea what she was talking about. Sounded like she was sanctioned to snuff the guy. Only a conspiracy theorist would believe something that crazy. No, this was all in her head. The feds were indeed crazy, but not that crazy.

Frank edged closer and said, "This guy is invisible. You said so yourself. And while he's deranged, he's also smart. He'll see you coming a mile away."

Layla got in his face again. "He won't see me until it's too late. I always have a backup like Sanders."

Frank had his mouth open to remind her she didn't have a backup on the I-95 incident but stopped himself. He'd said too much already.

Layla stepped back, and the sarcastic smirk bloomed. "You worry about your list, Frank, and I'll worry about mine." She glanced at Rob and then back at Frank before turning to leave. Over her shoulder, she said, "Besides, I don't need advice from a climate change denier."

Frank's whole expression collapsed. Never seen a blanker look from anyone.

Rob touched Frank's elbow. "Time to call it a night, partner."

PERRY WATCHED FROM THE SHADOWS. Something had felt wrong from the start with that girl. Good thing he made his excuse and left when he did. He'd driven down the street a few blocks before turning around and pulling back into the club's lot from the rear. This time he didn't park in the main lot, but on the side of the building—the street lights didn't reach into the shadows. He wanted to see if his suspicions were correct. She had the look he liked. Perry felt it in his groin and a tingling sensation sent electric pinpricks across his skin. The urge grabbed him by surprise and the predator response took over. But he'd pulled back at the last minute. *Something about her.* About the way she stood and talked. She was trying hard to fit into this cowboy bar scene—too hard. Wasn't who she said she was. This one was educated, and smart. When faced with something he couldn't figure out, Perry fought the predator, hunting urges backing down. There was danger here, a danger he didn't know and couldn't see.

Once she walked outside, he almost jumped her. Took all his strength to hold back. Good thing. When those two guys approached and then another guy from the car, all with guns, Perry knew he'd been right—cops—a trap. So, they were seriously looking for him. He'd have to be extra careful in the future. But still had to figure a way to get close to the mayor. The thought of the girl cop in the club popped back into his mind. He still liked her looks. Let's see, she had three guys backing her up, but two of them didn't appear to know the other one. And she carried a pistol. Wondered if she'd turn up somewhere else later. He'd keep an eye out for her. Maybe he'd have another chat, but this time not excuse himself to go home and check on his sick mother. No, not next time.

SIXTEEN

Tuesday morning, as Frank did his yoga, he got a text from Alton. *Meet me at the murder site. Been a development.* Frank sent Rob a text and they met at the PD before driving out. What Layla had said the night before still bothered Frank. *Don't need advice from a climate change denier.* Yeah, she liked mind games and knew just when and where to strike at someone's psyche to be most effective. Layla had a hard, cruel spirit. He had expected something different from her. The fun-loving wild sex partner had faded, replaced by someone he no longer wanted to be a part of. Frank put what she said aside. Couldn't let her get to him. You either control your emotions or your emotions control you.

When Frank and Rob pulled up to the murder site on Municipal, the road was crowded with police vehicles, so they parked on the intersecting street, in the 3100 block of Valentine. Marked and unmarked vehicles lined the street as before, including a CSU unit. There were a couple of extra vehicles Frank didn't recognize as DPD. He didn't want to get out of the car. The bad memory of the woman hanging from the tree clung to Frank like a rotten scent he couldn't wash off. A large crowd of neighborhood types waited at the corner of Valentine and Municipal. No one crossed the road, only huddled in a wad on the edge, gawking at the show from the sidewalk.

Rob turned his way and, in a voice laced with concern, asked, "You okay?"

"Yeah."

There was no crime scene tape this time, but one lone uniform officer. As before, they guarded the entrance to the narrow path that led into this section of the Great Trinity Forrest. The crowd talked quietly amongst themselves, then one guy shouted.

"There been another killing?"

Rob just waved to the guy and took the lead toward the gloomy woods. It was another hot morning, getting ready to be another hot day, as they followed the winding trail through the thick brush. Rob rolled his sleeves up and kept a steady pace until they heard talking up ahead. The voices were coming from the exact area the dead woman had been discovered. Rob stopped and looked back at Frank. Frank nodded and they kept walking. As the voices got louder, Layla's and Alton's became clearer—another argument. Rob and Frank rounded the last corner and caught the conflict's climax.

"Why the hell wasn't a camera installed?" Layla shouted.

Alton stood with his fists posted on his hips and stared down at her. "We don't install cameras at murder scenes after the fact."

Layla's scarlet red complexion almost lit up the darkness of the woods. "But this was a serial killer murder scene, you idiot!"

Alton took a step back at the insult but came back strong. "Well, I'm sure we didn't know that until you informed us the following day. If you thought a camera should have been installed, you FBI guys had plenty of time and resources to install one."

Layla lifted her arms and shook her head as she paced back and forth. "I always assume I'm working with professionals until something proves otherwise."

Alton planted his legs wide and his nostrils flared. "So that's what you think! You don't think I'm a professional. Well, you can just pucker up those rosy, red lips and kiss my big, black ass, bitch, and go to hell while you're at it."

That made Frank grin. Other than the OCD, Alton did have one other peculiarity. He never took crap off anyone. Guy wasn't hard to work with until you crossed the line. Alton's line was thin—real thin. All you had to do was question his professionalism or try and tell him how to do his job. Frank once overheard him tell a captain he was full of shit a few years ago during an all-unit detective meeting. Incidents such as that had led to numerous counseling sessions from Alton's supervisors. Probably more than Frank and Rob's total, but counseling Alton did little good. He always admitted his sins, promised to never do it again and went about his business as before until the next time.

"Your supervisor's going to hear about this," Layla said, pointing her finger at Alton.

A quick, evil grin spread across Alton's mouth. "You want to talk to my supervisor, be my guest." He snatched his cell from his pocket and started dialing, mumbling obscenities under his breath.

"Forget it, it's too late, already lost our chance," she answered turning away.

Rob bumped Frank's shoulder and pointed to the limb that had held the dead woman the other day. A large black dog hung from it, dissected the same way the woman had been. Frank had never been much of a pet lover, but something about the poor animal hanging and cut up that way touched him. You butcher animals for food, not thrills.

"There's nothing more I can do here," Layla said.

When she caught a glimpse of Frank and Rob, her expression registered surprise. But just as quickly, the cold, dead-eyed looked returned as she walked toward them.

Frank thought she was going to talk, but she brushed past him without a word, followed by her pal, Agent Sanders. They marched down the trail back toward the cars.

Alton noticed Frank and Rob for the first time. He strolled over and grimaced before speaking. "Dispatch got a call last night about someone shining a flashlight in the woods. They sent a unit to check it out. Cruiser drove by and shined its spotlight, but no one around. They cleared the call at 10:10 PM. This morning, the guy who called it in took a stroll to this spot, and that's when he found the dog." Alton frowned and gazed down the trail as Layla and Saunders disappeared around a corner. "Poor bitch."

Rob rested a hand on his shoulder. "Don't let her get to you—she's like that with everybody."

Alton's eyes narrowed and he rubbed his chin. "Huh?"

"Layla," Rob said. "Don't let her get to you."

Alton's brow relaxed and he chuckled. "No, not Layla. The dog. It's a bitch—you know, female."

"You seeing the symbolism here," Frank said. "Female with black hair, killed with throat cut and hung from a limb. A female dog with black fur done the same way? Either one of the locals has a sick sense of humor, or the suspect returned to the scene of the crime—scary."

"So, you setting up a camera?" Rob asked.

"Damn tooting. Not going to be second-guessed again by the FBI —or our bosses," Alton said.

Frank glanced over at the CSU techs crawling in a straight line with their eyes focused on the ground. Kelly wasn't among them. One tech stopped, pulled down his mask, and jerked the hood from his sweaty hair. Frank figured, in full Tyvek suits, they were close to a heat stroke. "Anything so far?" Frank asked.

The tech shook his head. "We got nothing. Too many tracks from sightseers to make any definitive conclusions. No new semen, fibers, or hairs, yet."

"Shoot us a copy of your report when you've finished," Frank said. He looked at Rob.

"Okay, we're out of here," Rob told Alton. "Drop us a copy when you're done."

"Hey," Alton said as they started to leave. "Is Layla getting worse, or is it just my imagination?"

Last night flashed back into Frank's memory. "Getting worse."

FRANK AND ROB made it back to CIU about mid-morning. After briefing Terry on the dead dog, Frank settled himself in his cubicle and checked emails. Since they officially had nothing to do until evening, he Googled serial killers. He'd never worked a serial killer case. The research was informative, but there wasn't a clear agreement among the experts. Several posts expressed a belief that serial killing was a particular type of insanity because they didn't meet the diagnostic criteria for schizophrenia and bipolar disorders. Serial killers were calculating and organized, showed no feelings for their victims, and might even appear charming. But the sobering fact that surprised Frank was the numbers. The FBI calculated between fifty and two hundred serial killers were operating in the United States at any given time, killing between ten to twelve persons a day. There was no clear prediction of early serial killer behavior, but there were clues—bed wetting, mutilation of animals, and setting fires.

Frank read the last post, and a queasy feeling fluttered deep in his gut. There was a theory that serial killers were born to kill. An extra male Y chromosome had been noted in a number of them. The other common trait—extra strength.

Frank closed his computer as Rob slipped on his jacket.

"I'm out of here. Doing lunch with Carmen and grabbing a nap before this evening," Rob said.

Frank didn't answer. He still hated working a case when he couldn't direct the investigation. In Layla's defense, she was probably doing as much as could be expected, but it still bothered him that he was only the hired help of the feds. No one needed to tell Frank that you often didn't get the answers you want when you wanted them in an investigation. Or for that matter, an answer that even made sense. Now and then, you just have to keep doing what you believe is right. Sometimes you run, sometimes stagger, and sometimes crawl to the right conclusion. But sometimes it evades you. That's how some cops arrest the wrong person while letting the real culprit go free. When you attempt to force the facts to fit the crime, the wrong person gets prosecuted. And when you aren't open to alternative explanations for the crime, that's how you lose a case in court, or worse, convict the wrong person.

This guy would kill again. Somewhere right now, a woman went about her daily activities. A woman who resembled Layla. A woman under a death sentence. She didn't know it, so it didn't bother her. Problem was... Frank knew it, and that bothered him.

SEVENTEEN

Perry finished his sandwich under the massive oak in front of the house under renovation. He took the last swallow of Coke, and that's when the soap taste hit him. He grimaced and glanced at the top of the can. A drop of liquid soap somehow ended up there and he'd just now tasted it. How did it get there? Probably someone from the food truck got sloppy while washing their hands. The taste almost made him gag. He looked at the can and remembered that night so many years ago.

His dad had been dead a little over a year, and eight-year-old Perry woke to some weird sound coming from down the hall. Things had been hard the last couple of years. His mom had to go on public assistance and used a special government card to purchase food. Not able to afford the nice home Perry had grown to know and love, they'd moved across town to an old house in a neighborhood Perry didn't like. The streets had ugly, gaping holes that rattled the car, no one cared enough to plant flowers or even mow their yards, and a feeling of uneasiness seemed to hang in the air like an invisible fog. There were lots of night sounds in the creepy old house they lived in now. Perry's mother ran the register in a convenience store and still kept late hours with her gentlemen friends, but this noise tonight came from deeper down the dark corridor, not in the living room. A bumping and moaning sound. Perry wiped the sleep from his eyes and stared into the darkness but couldn't figure out what the noise was. He swung his legs over the side of the bed and tiptoed into the blackness along the cold wooden floor. A thin sliver of light appeared from his mother's bedroom door. It was *her* moaning. Was she sick? Hurt? What was bumping? He eased to the door and put his eye to the narrow crack.

His mother had on no clothes and lay on her back with her legs straight up in the air against the chest and shoulders of a man with a hairy back who was also naked. His butt moved back and forth, pushing against her. Her breath came in quick pants, and she moaned, *"Yes, yes, yes,"* to an unasked question from the man. He wasn't hurting her, but he looked in agony. He gritted his teeth and had the most terrible expression of pain little Perry had ever seen. The harder the man pushed, the louder his mother repeated her chant. *"Yes, yes, yes!"*

Not able to contain his curiosity any longer Perry pushed the door a little farther open. The top hinge released a loud squeak. His mother's head sprung from the pillow and she met eyes with him. Perry never forgot the flash of surprise and anger in those eyes. He dashed down the hall and back into his room, pulling the covers over his head. He waited—wondering what would happen. His mom had become meaner since his father passed, and she'd begun taking more pills. It never used to be that way, but something changed in her. Heavy footsteps of someone sounded from the hall—*the man leaving.* Perry waited a long time. His stomach ached at the thought of getting another whipping. She'd beat him so hard last time with the belt buckle that blood stained his pajamas. The waiting for her to do something that night was one of the longest and scariest in his short life. A feeling of complete helplessness. His stomach twisted so much he wanted to puke. After a long time, her soft footsteps entered his room. Perry shook with fear and anticipation over his punishment. He'd covered his head and lay as still as a rock.

The cover was yanked from his head and just the dark shadow of her stood there silhouetted by the open door and hall light. She was a small woman, but the way she appeared and the fear Perry felt made her ten feet tall.

"You decided to spy on me, eh?"

Perry had seen dozens of horror movies, but the vision of that dark shadow, hateful voice, and not knowing what to expect made the movies pale in comparison. It was the scariest thing he could remember.

"No, mama. No, mama. I wasn't spying, I promise, I wasn't spying."

"And it lies, too, doesn't it?" she hissed. Her voice had taken on a spooky, malevolent quality.

Perry curled into as small a ball as he could, waiting for the belt, but it never came. Her shadow just stood over him like a looming, silent monster.

"Well, looks like a whipping doesn't do much good. Have to try something else. I'll just bet—"

When her voice stopped, Perry felt the ice-cold finger of dread run up his spine. A tingle that still made him shiver when recalling it. She dragged him from the bed and down the dark hall, his feet barely touching the floor as she almost pulled his arm from the socket, directing him into the bathroom. His cries still lingered in his conscience to this day. The fear of the unknown. She turned the water on in the sink and held his head with one hand as she rubbed a wet bar of soap across each of his eyes, and then shoved it in his mouth. He gagged and spit it out which only resulted in her rubbing his eyes and mouth harder. Her liquor breath drifted down to him as she screamed, "Dirty little eyes and lying little mouths need to be cleaned and washed out."

Perry screamed in fear, but also pain. The soap burned his eyes with an intensity that felt like they were melting. "Please, mama, stop. Please, mama, stop."

When she finally did stop, she dragged him back to his bed and tossed him in like a bag of trash. She never allowed him to wash the soap from his eyes. He cried with pain for the rest of the night. Something else happened to Perry that night. Something he couldn't explain. A feeling toward his mother. A feeling about other people. That night, for the first time since he was five, Perry wet his bed.

ROB MET Frank in the police parking lot that Tuesday evening, and Frank slipped into the passenger seat without a word. He had a beat down expression of boredom.

"Feeling okay?" Rob asked.

Frank effortlessly eased into his favorite riding position—knees on the dash and head on seat rest. He let out a tired breath. "Yeah."

They pulled out of the parking garage and headed north on Lamar.

"Called the other team members earlier," Frank said.

"Oh, yeah?"

"Yeah. They're not doing any better than us. Just riding around, drinking, and chatting up the hired help in the bars on their list. No sightings of the suspect from anyone they've talked to."

Rob chuckled. "Bet Dexter in Vice loves that—already a borderline alcoholic. Biggest bitch I've heard is no group knows what's going on with the other groups unless they call the individual detectives. Layla's not that great about keeping everyone in the loop."

Frank shifted to his *one knee on the dash and one leg stretched in the floorboard* riding position. "Layla has her agenda. Communication isn't a big part of it."

Rob's voice quieted, "I know you're doing this more out of a sense of wanting to help me with closure over my uncle's death than anything else. But don't you believe this guy needs to be taken off the streets?"

Frank rolled his head toward Rob. "Of course, I do. Don't worry about me. Besides, in the long run, all this will probably help us build character."

Rob smiled. One of Edna's favorite sayings when she assigned them something she knew they hated—*it builds character*. "We've finished all the places on our list. Nothing to do but start with the first place and visit them all a second time."

Frank had grown quiet, and his eyes were closed. Rob adjusted the visor against the blazing western sun. Was Frank already asleep? "Hey, you hear me. I said we've finished all—"

"I heard you," Frank mumbled, "but no more Grovite or Tushhog joints. Let's swing back by Ruby's."

FRANK WAS on his last stages of dropping into a deep nap when Rob shook his shoulder.

"Up and at 'em, killer. We're here."

Frank slowly opened his eyes to the sun's blinding glare and pulled himself up. He rubbed his face and pulled his hand through his brown hair. "I've got to get more sleep. This evening shift is kicking my butt."

In a chipper voice, Rob said, "One good thing about this assignment: we'll never get thirsty this summer."

Frank gazed into Rob's guiltless face and hated what he was about to do. He understood Rob took great pride in his appearance. That's why he got in a workout every morning before work. Rob had a tendency toward pudginess if he didn't work out often—beer had always been his dietary downfall. Since this assignment didn't allow Frank the opportunity to play mind games with suspects in interrogations, he still believed he needed to keep his hand in. Poor Rob must become his victim. Frank shook his head before saying, "You're getting fat, drinking all that beer."

Rob frowned. "Huh-uh." And immediately checked his belly.

"Un-huh, you looked at yourself in the mirror lately? Those jeans feel just a little bit tighter than usual?"

Rob got out and tucked his shirt in, taking an extra few seconds to feel his stomach. "You're so full of crap, Frank."

Frank fought the grin as he strolled to Rob's side of the car. "And to think, just a few short days ago you were an Olympic god." Frank cast an accusatory eye Rob's way before finishing with, "And now just a fat little Mexican."

Rob trailed Frank to the door. "Cracker, you are so full of shit..."

From the corner of his eye, Frank caught him feeling his stomach again. The cool darkness of the club put Frank in a slightly better mood as they strolled up to the bar. Ruby had just taken a bite of a grilled cheese sandwich when she spotted them.

"Oh, my god. The apocalypse is upon us," she exclaimed. "Frank Pierce coming by twice in one week."

"Hey, Ruby. What'cha eating?"

She held up the half-eaten sandwich stained with lipstick and a wedge of what appeared to be a wilted dill pickle. "Dinner. To what do I owe the pleasure of two visits, sweetheart?"

Rob and Frank plopped down on the barstools. "Just stopping by to see if you may have seen that guy we asked about a few days ago."

Ruby smiled. "Frank, I know how this thing works. No need to remind me. No, he hasn't stopped by." She turned to the young woman they'd met the other day, Lucia. "You haven't seen that guy, have you?"

Lucia's face darkened and she shook her head before turning away.

"Anyway," Ruby said, "I'm happy you stopped by. How about something cool to drink?"

Rob rubbed his hands together in expectation. "Great idea, I'll have a Mic?"

Frank sighed. "You got a petite Syrah or a smooth malbec?"

Ruby gave him the stink eye. "No, Frank. Still only cabernet and merlot."

"Merlot, please."

Lucia cast a strange sideways glance at Frank as she served Rob his beer. She poured the merlot for Frank and slid the glass to him without making eye contact. Something had changed between them. Had he somehow offended her? Did she take offense at his joke about the Syrah and malbec? Frank couldn't tell, but clearly, she now felt uncomfortable around him. This would probably drive him nuts the rest of the evening, but he didn't say anything. Most likely his imagination anyway.

They visited with Ruby as they finished their drinks and Lucia excused herself to the back, citing the storeroom needed tidying.

The rest of the shift was boring. Eight more stops at various clubs and honkytonks, with no one having seen a thing. Layla's remark about Whisper's DNA came back to Frank—he's invisible. Someone somewhere knew something, but talking to the cops wasn't a thing people in this part of town were comfortable with. Most of them, or someone they knew, had had a bad confrontation with the law in the past, and now their distrustful nature kept them from reporting suspicious activity. Getting someone jammed up with the cops was a reputation killer in most South Dallas neighborhoods.

By the time Frank made it home, his exhaustion and wine intake hardly allowed him to make it to the bed. Didn't even take his clothes off, just his shoes. But sleep wouldn't come. He stared at the ceiling with his mind racing a mile a minute. Too much happening, but nothing that led them any closer to the suspect. Layla's bad behavior, Rob's concern over his uncle's closure, Lucia's strange behavior all rushed back through his conscience. Nothing made sense. Frank liked to index and catalog information in his mind, looking for similarities—or anomalies. Nothing gelled together as he'd expected. This in itself was not unusual for a complicated investigation with a bunch of moving parts, but since Frank didn't control it, he knew he wasn't seeing the whole picture. Just pieces and parts knitted together from what information he'd gathered. It wasn't enough to gain a clear understanding. He briefly considered asking Layla to allow him to look at the full FBI file and put him in the loop on what was going on locally. That's what he was best at, figuring things out. Driving around canvassing joints and ice houses was a waste of his god-given abilities. But Frank knew the request wouldn't be granted. That's the way the feds worked. Advice from local cops was neither sought nor desired.

EIGHTEEN

Wednesday morning at eleven o'clock, Frank's phone rang. He cracked his eyes open, and shards of sunlight sliced through the miniblinds in his bedroom. That faint smell of Layla's perfume still lingered in the air. *Or was it his imagination?* He leaned over and checked the caller ID—Terry's cell number.

"Morning, Terry."

"Sorry if I woke you, but there's been a couple of developments you and Rob need to be made aware of. Can you guys swing by around two?"

Frank rubbed sleep from his eyes and yawned. "Sure. Want me to call Rob?"

"Just talked to him," Terry said. "See y'all at two."

It wasn't until Terry hung up that it dawned on Frank. Terry didn't sound right. Frank had been half asleep and not noticed earlier. But Frank had worked for Terry so long that he could detect even a slight change in the tone of his voice. The one he heard this morning was Terry's worried voice.

Frank drank coffee while doing his yoga. He showered and made a Greek salad using the *Awsamic* balsamic vinegar Rob loved so much. By the time Frank made it into CIU, it was one forty-five. Rob was already there.

He looked up from his computer when Frank sat down. His eyebrows were drawn together. "Check out Edna's office."

Frank casually shifted his gaze to the glassed-in office. *Oh, crap!* Major Higgins sat in Terry's chair, and he sat on the sofa. Edna sat ramrod straight as Higgins lectured her and Terry. Frank couldn't hear the words, but it was clear from their expressions, it wasn't good. "How long has this being going on?"

Rob kept his voice low and stare glued to his computer screen. "Don't know. I got here fifteen minutes ago. They were already there. What have we done? Is this about us?"

Frank shrugged. "Can't be."

"So, this is just a coincidence? Higgins being here just before we have a meeting with Terry? You're not much of a detective, Frank, if you really believe that."

Of course, Rob was right. It had to be about them. But they'd done nothing to warrant the attention of the major. The meeting lasted another ten minutes before Higgins stormed out, casting a dagger look in their direction. Frank glanced back to Edna's office. Terry had reclaimed his traditional chair near the door, and he and Edna still talked another five minutes before Frank's phone rang.

"Frank, could you and Rob step into my office for a minute, please." Edna's voice had an exhausted quality like a meeting with Higgins usually produces.

"On our way."

Rob stared at him and didn't speak.

"Showtime," Frank said.

When they walked in, Terry stood and closed the door behind them. Edna had regained a little of her composure and slumped in her executive chair. She squeezed the stress ball with a white-knuckled grip. If it had been Higgins' throat, the guy would be dead already.

"Take a seat, guys," she said.

Terry spoke first. "It appears we, that is I, miscalculated on the funeral arrangements for the mayor's father." Terry cleared his throat and continued, "I assumed since the old man had lived in Dallas so many years, and still maintained a membership at the First Methodist Church, that's the place the funeral would be." He shot a glance at Edna. "I badly miscalculated." The chief was informed by the mayor's office early this morning the burial will not be in Dallas but at the mayor's father's ranch. It's a closed service, just family, and he'll be buried at the family cemetery there on his ranch."

"They're burying him at a ranch?" Rob asked.

"Correct. You guys will still be involved in the funeral, but not in the way we first envisioned."

Again, reading Terry's hesitant voice tone, Frank was certain he wasn't going to like what he heard next. He braced himself for the bad news. His sergeant did not disappoint.

Terry crossed his legs. "You're being assigned to drive the mayor's children to the ranch from Dallas. The mayor will fly his King Air with his wife, other family members, and the family attorney. Sergeant Miller on the mayor's protective detail has a pilot's license and will act as co-pilot for the flight. He'll be in command of all DPD protective operations during the trip. We need at least one DPD detective vehicle out there. You're it."

Rob's relief at not being in a jam shined on his face. Frank was still worried—very worried. "Why don't the children just fly out with the mayor?" Frank asked.

"No more room on the plane," Edna replied.

"Where's the ranch?" Rob asked.

"Leakey," Terry answered.

Frank had heard of Leakey, Texas, but had no idea where it was. Sounded like one of those quaint little Hill Country towns in Central Texas. The ones native Texans went dreamy-eyed over. But this didn't explain why Higgins had been meeting with Edna and Terry. The funeral stuff could have been covered in a memo.

Edna spoke up. "Now to the other thing." Her stare bore in on

Frank. "The mayor has requested to meet with you personally." She paused, and that hard stare had now turned into a bug-eyed gaze. "Any idea what that's about?"

Oh, crap! Frank was positive it had to do with the mayor's daughter, Katrina. But no use confessing to something until he knew the details. Frank shrugged. "Me?"

Edna showed an aggravated look, probably the kind reserved for her young daughters. "Yes, *you!*"

Frank shook his head. "I got nothing. Did he say what it was about?"

Edna's lips puckered and her stare intensified. "No, but he requests the meeting be private and not in a city building."

A tight knot grew in Frank's gut. "Is it case related?"

Edna drummed her fingers on the desk. "Don't know."

For the first time in a long time, Frank was stumped. Had to be about Katrina. What else did he and the mayor have in common? "I can be home this evening if I'm released from bar hopping."

Edna glanced at Terry, and he nodded.

"Okay," Edna said. "I'll pass the word."

Terry turned to Rob. "You need to be there, also."

"What?" Rob asked. His shining relieved expression dulled into a mask of worry.

"The mayor's request was to meet with the CIU detectives working the serial killer case," Edna said.

Relief washed over Frank like a hot shower on a cold night. So, it probably was case related. Had nothing to do with Katrina.

"You guys are relieved from any further task force work until the old man dies. We'll let you know about the final arrangements when we know—won't be long now," Terry said. "Meanwhile, enjoy a little downtime on the city this evening. Just be home before too late. Wouldn't want to keep the mayor waiting—I'll let you know."

Edna still had a look. A look that said she didn't believe this was happening, and she didn't believe Frank's story about not knowing what was going on. Higgins's meeting appeared to have left her a little on edge. The bun in her hair had loosened, and a few rogue strands drooped around her ears and neck. She absentmindedly raked them back with the side of her hand as she said, "You guys be cool tonight with the mayor. Not sure what it's about, but be on your guard. Okay?"

Rob let out a long breath and nodded. When Frank didn't answer, Edna turned her gaze to him.

He showed his familiar smile and said, "Relax, Edna, you know me."

Edna closed her eyes, lowered her head, and whispered, "Yes, I do."

AFTER LEAVING EDNA'S OFFICE, Rob and Frank caught up on a few police emails and bounced around ideas about what to do for the next few hours. They settled on meeting at Frank's place for dinner and waiting to hear if the mayor would come. Rob told Frank he'd bring pizza when he came. Frank hated most takeout pizzas, but he only wanted to get home and relax before the meeting, so he didn't raise any objections.

The day had turned weird with the news they would travel out of town when the old man died and transport the mayor's children to the funeral. Even weirder that the mayor wished a private meeting with them. Frank thought of a dozen reasons the mayor might want to meet, but none made any sense without Katrina playing a major part. There was something he didn't know. A tiny piece of the puzzle he hadn't considered.

Frank arrived back at his loft around three. Nice beating the five o'clock traffic for a change. Walking down the hall, Layla's scent again greeted him. He needed to get her out of his head—move on. Frank showered, changed into fresh clothes, and poured a glass of 2018 Louis Jadot Beaujolais-Villages. Putting on some jazz usually relaxed him, but he wanted to watch the news first. He managed to catch the beginning of the weather report.

"Okay, folks. Here's something the people along the Texas coast need to keep in mind."

The screen switched to a map of the Gulf Coast states and a large weather system just entering the Gulf of Mexico through the Florida Straits.

"Tropical Storm Kate has just been upgraded to hurricane strength. Hurricane Kate has maximum sustained winds in excess of seventy-five miles an hour. This storm has undergone rapid intensification in the last twelve hours."

The meteorologist pointed to the middle of the weather system and circled his finger counterclockwise. *"You can see this distinct eye developing as its central pressure drops."* He drew a northward sweep with his hand and rested it on Texas. *"Still has a long way to go, and lots could happen, but several models have it slamming into the Texas coast."*

A dozen multicolored lines appeared on the map showing possible landfall between Texas and Gulfport, Mississippi. Most appeared to end somewhere on the Texas coast.

"Still a big rainmaker, so it bears watching. It's slowed down its forward movement, but with the extra warm waters of the Gulf, that's not necessarily good. The last thing we need is to have it churning out there, gaining strength every hour. We'll keep an eye on it and let you know. Now for what's happening locally. More hot weather today with—"

Frank turned off the set. He was too antsy about the mayor's meeting to concentrate on the news. He switched on an old Babs Gonzales album, one of his favorite jazz vocalists. In his early forties, Frank was still a relatively young man, but he also recognized he had an old soul. Old songs, old people, and old recipes fascinated him. This started Frank to thinking about his grandma again and women in general. Frank loved women. He loved their feel, smell, and just being around them. Many of his most cherished memories centered around the women in his young life. After puberty, his thoughts turned less matriarchal and more sexual, but the familiar things he loved about women remained. Probably one of the things that led him to cooking. Probably the reason he wanted to take home economics and not go out for football in high school. His dad quashed that idea, but Frank still hung around the kitchens of his mom and grandma more than your average Florida schoolkid.

Rob knocked on the door at 6:30 with a large to-go box from Serious Pizza off Elm Street and a six-pack of Michelob. "Hey, hope you like lots of meat."

Frank preferred little meat. More of an all veggies guy, but Rob was a total carnivore. Frank poured another glass of red as Rob opened a Mic and they dug into the five-meat pizza. Frank's cell rang ten minutes after they finished.

"Hey, Frank." It was Terry's voice. Had a strained quality. "You at home?"

"Yeah, Rob and I—"

Terry interrupted, "Edna just called. The mayor will be there at eight."

Frank checked his watch—less than twenty minutes. "Thanks, Terry."

Frank had expected Terry to give some advice or encouragement before he hung-up. He was surprised by what Terry said next.

"Good luck." And the line went dead.

A cold cube of ice inched its way up Frank's spine as he spoke to Rob. "Mayor's en route."

This was the first time Frank had noticed how many beers Rob had drunk. During their dinner conversation, they discussed the reasons the mayor might have called this meeting, and Rob always seemed to have a beer in his hand, but Frank never dreamed he'd have drunk the whole six-pack in under an hour. When Rob was stressed, he drank more—and faster, it appeared. Now he had that goofy smile and sleepy-eyed look plastered to his face. Yeah, *plastered* described it.

Rob yawned and waived Frank's information away, flashing a cocky grin. "Great, about time he showed up."

Oh, brother! Frank made a pot of strong coffee and poured a large cup for Rob just before the knock on the door. Rob snapped his head in Frank's direction and all the cockiness disappeared. "He's here."

"Act natural," Frank muttered.

Rob straightened up in his chair, probably thought better of the idea, and stood beside it, tucking in his shirttail. He tucked his shirt-tail a second time as Frank opened the door to find Sergeant Novack from CIU – Dignitary Protective Squad waiting in the hall. His beady eyes were pinched together, and a scowl settled on his lizard lips. Frank always thought Novack looked like a high school gym coach he'd once had. Neither Novack nor the coach smiled very much.

"Evening, sergeant."

Novack leaned closer and muttered, "Don't know what this is about, but watch your ass, Pierce."

The mayor stood behind Novack with an all-business look in a navy-blue suit, white shirt, and a yellow and green striped tie.

Frank nodded over Novack's shoulder. "Your Honor, welcome to my home." And he opened the door wider.

Novack stepped aside as the mayor walked in. Frank closed the door in Novack's face as he stood in the hall. Frank turned back to the mayor. He stood in the living room, gawking at the wall of windows overlooking downtown. He'd arrived at the perfect time. The last traces of sunset streamed through clear skies and filled the loft with a warm, yellow glow. Soft, pink clouds hung to the west, and their colors enhanced the downtown skyline, casting long shadows through the canyons between the buildings.

Mayor Wallace's jaw dropped, and he slowly swiveled his head in Frank's direction. "Christ, how much do we pay you guys?"

A giggle sounded from the bar, and the mayor glanced at Rob.

Rob steadied himself with one hand on the bar and another on the barstool. He was fundamentally still drunk, but at least he'd started sipping the coffee. Couldn't shake that intoxicated, goofy look he sported after a few too many.

"He inherited it, sir," Rob said and snickered again.

Mr. Mayor faced Frank. "Is he drunk?"

Frank shrugged, "He was a little stressed over the meeting, sir. May I offer you something to drink? Have a fresh pot of coffee and iced tea."

Mayor Wallace strolled toward Frank's full wall library with his hands in his pockets, trying to look casual. "Anything stronger than tea and coffee?"

"I have wine. That's about it."

The mayor scanned the shelves of books without replying. Spent quite a few tense seconds checking out each shelf. He was a distinguished-looking man. The stylish graying hair swept back over the ears, and his signature walk gave the appearance of someone in total control. Someone you could have faith and confidence in. A quick grin formed on the mayor's lips as he scanned the books. After a few more long seconds, he said, "Can always tell a lot about a man by the books he reads." His expression hardened as he turned his gaze toward Frank. "But I can't tell a damn thing about you from your books. Why's that?"

Frank swallowed. "Diverse interests."

The mayor nodded and took a silver flask from his inside jacket pocket. "Yes, of course." His eyes held a look of suspicion or doubt Frank couldn't interpret. The mayor slowly twisted the cap and opened the flask. He took a long pull, exhaled, and motioned to Rob with the flask. "Is he working with you on this case?"

Frank walked to where Rob now sat at the bar. "Yes, sir. We're partners."

Rob slurping coffee was the only sound in the place.

Mayor Wallace nodded and pointed at them. "I remember you two. You're the guys that pulled Katrina out of that god-awful cave."

Rob's voice had a more sober sound when he said, "Frank almost died that day."

The mayor's features softened before saying, "I know, and I'm eternally grateful for what you guys went through to save her." He took another quick swig from the flask and screwed the cap on before sliding it back into his pocket. His soft features vanished, and he eyed Frank with intensity. "I know you and Katrina are in a relationship."

Frank fought to keep a straight face. *So, this was all about Katrina.* The mayor had no power to fire him, but he could arrange for Frank to be sent back to night shift patrol at a station across town, with Tuesday and Wednesday off.

Mayor Wallace nodded. "I want you to know I'm fine with it. All young people have to find their own way in their own time, even Katrina. But don't get too comfortable. This is a passing fancy for her. You're a new, bright, shiny toy. Katrina always tires of new toys." He raised his brow and wiggled a finger at Frank. "And she'll tire of you. I don't expect to see you sitting across from me at Thanksgiving dinner, ever."

That rebuke angered Frank. He and Katrina had never talked of marriage—he didn't even want to get married—he was too old, she too young. But what had she said to her father? What did *she* think?

Mr. Mayor took the flask from his pocket again. "If my daughter wants to sow a few wild oats, I'll let her." He took another long pull from the flask, then paced the floor, rubbing an eyebrow for a while. He cleared his throat. "Speaking of wild oats, I have something I need to share for the good of the investigation." He paused just long enough, and his expression gave Frank the idea that he might reconsider the thought. Finally, he said, "The chief told me a man came into the police department and said he might have met the killer on the road one night near Atlanta. Said the killer told him his dad was the mayor of Dallas."

Frank nodded. "Yes, sir. His name was Tom Price. I interviewed him."

Mayor Wallace grimaced. "There's an outside chance he might be right."

Frank sucked in a sharp breath.

The mayor kept pacing, keeping his head lowered, never making eye contact. "When I graduated from college, my dad decided he wanted to diversify my knowledge of the business world. By that time, I'd already learned the oil and gas side of our energy company to the point there wasn't much more I could do. But he wanted me to get experience in real estate. To that end, he sent me to Atlanta to work in the investment real estate firm my Uncle Dalton founded."

The mayor shrugged. "I was up for a little adventure after college, so I embraced the idea, and off to Atlanta I went. This was just before the big boom they saw in the eighties. I was in the right place at the right time to learn how to buy and sell office buildings and apartments." He looked around Frank's living room and smiled. "Could have picked up this building a decade ago but screwed up. Let someone outbid me—lesson learned. Anyway, I spent a year as my uncle's assistant. Seeing everything he did and how he did it. Better than any college course I ever took."

Frank's stomach twisted in knots, afraid of what the mayor might say next. He was stalling, getting up his courage to confess to god knows what. Frank knew how these things worked. Watched criminals go through the same ritual just before spilling the works.

For the first time in his dissertation, the mayor made eye contact. "We were all young once. Made our share of mistakes. I made a big one, night after a party in Buckhead. It never came back on me, so I figured I was in the clear, but..."

Frank remained quiet. When you had someone offering a confession, be it criminal or politician, you never rushed it. People have to get comfortable baring their souls in public. They have to hear themselves speaking the words, admitting the wrong, and accepting responsibility.

The mayor kept his eyes lowered, shook his head, and smiled. "Some associates I knew employed the company of a couple of hostesses to keep us entertained after a business get-to-together one evening. I'd had a lot to drink and—" Mr. Mayor cleared his throat and looked away. "Anyway, I went into the back bedroom with one of 'em—we all did. Weeks later, a friend from that night called. Said one of the girls contacted him. Said she was pregnant. He told her, if it were true, that was her problem. Never heard any more about it until the chief briefed me the other day. Started me thinking."

"Do you recall the woman's name?" Frank asked.

"No."

"Anything description-wise?"

"Mid-thirties, petite, with the blackest hair I've ever seen."

Layla's description.

"Know anyone who might still have contact with her?"

The mayor chuckled. "No one keeps up contact with a hooker for over thirty years. Especially one who tries to shake 'em down. No."

The mayor stopped pacing and stared at Frank. He released a long breath before saying, "So, now you two know my deepest, darkest secret. Something that could ruin me politically, socially, and alienate me from my family. I may have helped create this monster. I'm only telling you this because my family is the most important thing to me. I'd like to keep it confidential. But if push comes to shove, reveal it to whoever can help put a stop to this."

Frank glanced at Rob. The mayor's story appeared to have fully sobered him up. Rob said, "Revealing it might not be necessary, sir. But first things first. You'll need to give a DNA sample. We can compare it to the killer's. See if there's a match. Don't worry, we'll make sure the paperwork says it's submitted from an anonymous donor."

"What if there's a match?"

Frank spoke up. "Then we'll know if he's your son, but that won't help us find him if he's not listed in the DNA database. Quite unusual not to get a DNA hit. Not unheard of, but unusual."

"So, we'll just have to wait, I guess."

Studying the mayor, Frank had to admit something he never thought he would. While he didn't particularly like the man, he did respect him now. He was correct when he said it could ruin his political career. They now held the secret that could be the guy's undoing.

But Mr. Mayor was willing to trust them for the safety of his family. Couldn't help but respect a man like that. "Yes, sir. Sooner we send in the DNA, the better. I'll make sure it's expedited."

The mayor nodded and began walking toward the door. "I'm only sharing this information with you guys and the chief." He stopped before opening it. "When I tell this to the chief tomorrow, I'll instruct him that you and your partner are to be treated as special investigators working on my behalf on a highly personal matter. If anyone tries squeezing you for information about this meeting, let me know." The mayor handed Frank a business card with his cell number printed on the back. "When my dad passes, I understand you two will be driving the kids to his ranch."

"Yes, sir. When's the last time you saw your father?"

"Katrina and I slipped out there for a couple of days last week when it looked like he might go at any minute. He was in and out of consciousness. Rallied a bit and recognized us before we had to leave. Now they say he's headed back down again." Mayor Wallace's forehead pinched, and he stared at the floor. "Got a lot on my plate. You squared away on what I want?"

"Yes, sir. And thanks."

Wallace eyed him. "For what?"

"What you did tonight took courage. I respect courage in a politician."

The mayor patted Frank on the shoulder and offered a crooked smile. "Well, don't get used to it."

PERRY STARED into the flames and took in the scent of the burning wood. The fire lit the small area around the creek where he sat drinking his beer. He wiped away a bead of sweat easing down his neck. Way too hot for a fire on a warm night like tonight, but Perry liked fires—always did. Still recalled the ass whoopings he got as a kid when the adults caught him secretly building one. He stilled and recalled his last big fire. The way it crackled as the furniture lit up. The screams and pleas imprinted on his memory.

An owl broke the silence, hooting in the distance. Its sound echoed down the creek as Perry poked the fire with a stick and took another swallow of beer. The slow swish of water running under the train trestle relaxed him as he settled back and enjoyed the evening. His dad, the dentist, had taken him camping a few times. Didn't matter if the guy hadn't been his real dad. He left Perry with what few good memories he had from childhood. Perry didn't have many good memories after that summer in Biloxi with his cousins. The rest of his life was living in one down-and-out place after another. Most times with a man his mom had taken up with. Someone who would eventually beat her up and toss them out. Using food stamps, not going to school for weeks at a time, and his mom trying to keep a roof over their heads became young Perry's new memories. Those and his mom's bad behavior were the ones that ate away at his soul.

But all that would have been okay if only his mom hadn't changed so much. If she hadn't taken all those pills and shot-up with whatever drugs men offered her. Perry could have easily weathered the smaller storms if only his mom had cared about him. Her personality had changed so much from the time she was married to the dentist. To her dying day, his mom swore she had slept with a rich man from Dallas, and he was Perry's true father, and now that man was the mayor of Dallas. Didn't know if it was true, but Perry had to find out. He knew who the man was, Mayor Wayne Wallace.

Perry had waited long enough. Needed a plan to meet him. Barging into his office wouldn't work—too many cops. He needed to catch him at an event the mayor would for sure attend. Not at home or his office, but a place he could just walk right up to the guy without being challenged. Perry wasn't much of a book smart man. But he was clever. He glanced at the train trestle, looming tall and dark against the night sky with the firelight outlining the girders, and grinned. He could talk a woman he'd never met into going anywhere, anytime, with the false promise of anything that popped into his mind. And ninety percent of the time, they'd go. That was the incredible part. They'd go just to see what the action was. That's what she did. That was the only way he'd ever be able to meet the mayor, using his gift of gab—his ability to lie. Deception and deceit were what he knew well. Those would get him close to the mayor without dealing with the cops.

Perry checked his watch and opened the last beer. He took a deep breath of the rich humid air and swatted a mosquito that landed on his hand. Yeah, his mom had been a real mystery to him when he was younger. Her death didn't bring the kind of closure Perry expected or wanted.

The thick woods along the creek scared him a little. Perry hated confined spaces—anything tight and dark. The memory of being locked in the small closet when he was a kid made him shiver.

Perry stared again at his night's handiwork hanging from the trestle. Did she have a family? Local girl or new transplant? Why did she get into the truck with him? He couldn't take his eyes off her face. Of all of them, she most resembled his mom. Not the way his mom looked when she was married to the dentist, but what she became later. Her beauty in her younger days was beyond words. She'd done her best to hang on to it for as long as she could, but her lifestyle finally took its toll. But only in her later years did Perry truly see who she'd been all along. As they both aged, he recognized the true hideousness that lay beneath the makeup. A hideousness that still haunted him.

NINETEEN

Thursday morning at 8:57, Rob parked behind the last patrol car at the end of Japonico Lane in far South Dallas. A low ground fog still lingered, waiting for the sun to vaporize it. The routine had become familiar. Patrol vehicles, detective cars, and a couple of CSI vans lined both sides of the isolated street. There were new additions to the line-up this morning. Lots of new additions. A half-dozen unmarked cars Rob didn't recognize as DPD vehicles and a van with the words FBI-ERT on the side. Rob put the car in park before saying, "We're here."

Frank, as usual, rode in his favorite position.

Rob was still a little shaken from their meeting the night before with the mayor. Rob hated drama and always felt uncomfortable around political types, especially the mayor and his staff.

Frank opened his eyes, sat up, and let out a tired breath. "Where the heck are we, anyway?"

Rob motioned over his right shoulder with his thumb. "Lemmon Lake is behind us, and Simpson Stuart Road is over there," he said, pointing to the left through the woods.

Frank unscrewed his water bottle and took a long swallow. Rob had noticed a change in his partner. This case ate at him. Frank was the idea guy. The one who always figured things out before the rest. Using them the way the FBI did didn't give Frank the latitude needed to do much figuring out. If Frank wasn't using his brain, this always led to a more lethargic attitude. Guy had no energy—looked washed out.

"Ready to do this?" Rob asked.

Frank grunted and opened his door.

As Rob walked to Frank's side of the car, he motioned toward the new van and vehicles. "Looks like the Bureau will be joining us again today."

The uniform officer waited at a grove of trees about a hundred feet from where the dead-end street stopped. Today, the uniform was joined by a guy in a gray light-weight wool business suit, sunglasses, and an all-business expression. Rob and Frank left their jackets in the car and strolled toward the yellow evidence tape marking off the grove of trees. About a dozen onlookers from the neighborhood waited outside the evidence tape, chatting among themselves. The serene cooing of a mourning dove from the open field around the trees welcomed them as they approached. The gray suit guy stepped forward.

His voice mechanical, he asked, "Can I help you?"

Rob slightly turned so his badge, attached to his belt, was more visible and said, "DPD Criminal Intelligence."

"Do you have any identification?"

Rob was usually a patient man, but the absurdity of the question took him aback. He turned and pointed again at the badge next to his pistol and kept walking.

Gray suit moved to block his path. "Do you have any *official* credentials?"

Rob stared at the guy and smiled, "Yeah, but they're in the car. And I don't plan to go back to get them."

The uniform standing behind gray suit stifled a snicker.

Gray suit had his mouth open to say something, but Frank stepped up and said, "We were called. Is Supervisory Special Agent Layla Barbee on the scene yet? We were told to meet her here."

The wrinkles in gray suit's forehead relaxed a little, and he spoke into a sleeve mic. "Have two CIU detectives to meet Barbee?"

The faint murmur of a voice sounded from his earpiece as he kept his stare on Rob and Frank. He said, "Roger. Sending them in."

Gray suit stepped aside, and Rob led the way into the woods. It appeared pretty much like the first scene, except the ground was bone dry and it took a slight downhill dip with each step. The rumble of an approaching northbound train drowned out any other noise as they followed the narrow lane deeper into the forest. The overhead train rumbled its way across the trestle, leaving a burnt diesel scent in the air as the first person came into view. It was Alton. His face was contorted, and he spoke rapidly while waving his arms to Kelly, standing beside him. Kelly and a six-person DPD-CSI team dressed in white Tyvek coveralls gazed at the crime scene with their hands in their pockets, speaking quietly to each other. Rob's stare followed Kelly's to the corpse.

The young woman was naked and hanging with her arms spread wide from the top of the trestle. Looked like a crucifixion. A wire was wrapped around each wrist and affixed to bolts in the wooden trestle above. Her head hung down, chin resting on her upper chest. But there was no blood. Not a scratch on her as far as Rob could tell. She looked older than the first one—a face that said *rode hard and put up wet.*

Layla and a male FBI agent, the guy from the club the other night, Sanders, looked on as a dozen FBI/ERT members dressed the same as Kelly and his team, searched the area, each with an evidence bag and tweezers. Two FBI still photographers and a third guy with a video camera recorded every square foot of the scene.

Frank spoke into Rob's ear to be heard over the noise of the departing train. "This could be the work of a copycat. MO doesn't fit the previous crime."

Rob nodded and headed toward Alton and Kelly. As they approached, the faint whiff of burnt wood hung in the humid morning air from the embers of a dying campfire.

Alton looked their way and nodded. His eyes had a cold, hard look. He'd also left his jacket in the car. His blue dress shirt's sleeves were rolled to his elbows, and he wore no tie.

"Welcome to FBI land," Alton said loud enough that all heads turned.

"Who reported it?" Frank asked.

Alton flexed his fingers a few times, staring at Layla before pointing up the hill. "Guy who lives at the end of Japonico Lane. Works the early shift. Left home at six o'clock this morning when he smelled smoke coming from the creek. Called 911 on his way to work. Patrol unit found the body a half hour later."

"What's with the Bureau?" Frank asked.

Kelly answered. "We got a stand-down order from the chief's office after making our initial sweep. Said the Bureau would be *assisting us.*"

Kelly's glare came to rest on Layla and Sanders. She looked up from taking notes long enough to nod Rob and Frank's way. Frank strolled to the narrow, muddy creek and scanned the banks. His sensitive nose twitched, probably from the strong fishy smell before motioning for Rob to follow him toward Layla and Sanders. The last time Rob encountered those two had been that night in the club's parking lot. Not sure he wanted another encounter so soon, but he followed Frank.

Layla and Sanders looked up again as Frank walked up. "Is this the same guy?" Frank asked.

Keeping her voice low, Layla said, "That's what we've been discussing."

Frank looked around the creek and stared up at the dead woman.

"Why did he leave her whole? Guy likes using a knife on people and animals. Why leave this one in one piece?"

Sanders mumbled something into Layla's ear and walked away. Rob got the impression Sanders didn't care for them any more than they cared for him.

Layla closed her notebook and took a patient breath. "Our guy has been changing and evolving his MO since we started tracking him. The fact he didn't cut her up means nothing by itself. We have to determine if she lost any teeth before making a final decision."

Members of the ERT were pulling the dead woman up on the train tracks. Two others had a black body bag open and ready. A couple of Kelly's CSI team members observed from a few feet away, also taking notes and photos.

"I'm going to nail this son of a bitch," Layla mumbled as she watched the corpse being laid out in the bag.

Frank moved closer. "Listen, don't go to any more clubs looking for him dressed the way you were the other night."

Layla snapped her head in his direction.

Frank dropped his voice. "You're playing his game, and he's better at it than you think."

Layla stepped back from Frank and crossed her arms. A smirk eased across her lips. "And what makes you such an expert on my case and how I investigate it?"

Frank kept his voice just above a whisper. "Because I have a feeling about this one. A bad feeling. You're taking chances you don't have to. This guy is smart, or he'd be caught already."

Layla's nostrils flared, and her stare bored into Frank. She turned and pointed above to the ERT guys carrying the corpse down from the tracks. "And while we all just sit on our collective hands waiting for him to make a mistake, the body count rises." Her voice rose with each word.

Frank didn't answer. He had that look that showed he knew he'd lost the argument but didn't want to admit it.

Layla was still wound up. She moved in closer, eyes bulging. "In case you hadn't figured it out yet, I was sent down here to put an end to this guy." She flashed a condescending smile. "And you know what? That's exactly what I plan to do—one way or another."

Rob's memory went back to the conversation they had with their FBI pal, David Ford, in the FBI parking lot. *Enjoys blood sports.*

Frank gave her his fatherly stare. "Good luck, Agent Barbee." He whirled around and marched back up the path toward their car.

FRANK LED the way into CIU. He and Rob settled into their cubicles, and Terry walked from his office and stood beside Frank.

In a hesitant voice, Terry asked, "How did it go with the mayor last night?"

Frank understood what he wanted—details. He met eyes with Terry. "The mayor had a piece of personal information related to the case he wants investigated. He's asked Rob and me to handle it, confidentially."

Terry nodded. "Figures." He leaned closer and whispered, "Edna and I got a call from Higgins earlier. Said you guys were acting as the mayor's personal investigators on something." Terry grinned. "Major Higgins is bouncing off the roof with frustration. Kind of fun to watch him from a distance."

Frank glanced toward Edna's glass office. She sat with her back to them, writing something on her desk calendar. Frank motioned in her direction. "How does she feel about it?"

Terry shrugged. "She's okay. Likes seeing Higgins squirm, whether she'll admit it or not. What about the dead woman by the creek this morning? Any ID? Same guy?"

Rob stuck his head above the short cubicle wall and answered, "Won't know until the ME has a chance to check her. At least she wasn't dissected."

Frank interlaced his fingers and slid them behind his head. "Bureau was out in force today. Alton and Kelly were fit to be tied."

"See Layla?" Terry asked.

"Yeah." Frank let out a long breath. "She was there."

Terry stuck his hands in his pockets and strolled back to his office.

Just before 11:00, Frank received a call from the first floor visitor's lobby. He took the elevator down and walked toward the desk. The lobby was bustling as usual with people gazing at the registry on the wall, trying to figure out what floor to go to or asking questions of the officers manning the information desk. Before Frank got there, a tall, skinny millennial in a suit intercepted him. The guy had short, blond, spiked hair and his hazel eyes appeared larger behind the gold, wire-rimmed glasses.

"Detective Pierce?"

Frank stopped walking. "Yeah, I'm Pierce."

The millennial didn't introduce himself but held out a cigarette-pack-sized package wrapped in plain, brown paper and tied with white cotton string. "I was instructed to give you this by the mayor."

Frank took the package from the gofer/staffer want-to-be. "Any message?"

The millennial shook his head. "Mayor said you'd know how to handle it."

"Thanks," Frank said before heading back to the elevator. He took the package directly to the forensic lab. As he opened the door, Kelly stood behind the counter and looked up from writing something in a large black ledger. Frank seldom saw him inside the PD. Most of their encounters were outside when he was geared head to toe in white Tyvek coveralls. Kelly looked funny in jeans and a DPD Polo with the words CSI Team Leader stenciled above the left breast.

Frank laid the small package on the counter and said, "Need this sent out ASAP and analyzed, then forwarded to CODIS for a DNA comparison with the killer's."

The Combined DNA Index System enables federal, state, and local forensic laboratories to exchange and compare DNA profiles electronically. Makes tracking serial offenders easier.

Kelly raised an eyebrow. "Who recovered it from where?"

"It's not evidence, not recovered, but donated."

Kelly picked up the package. "Donated? From who?"

"Whom," Frank said.

"Whatever. Whose is it? What is it?"

"DNA cheek swab from an anonymous source."

"You're kidding, right?"

Frank knew he'd have trouble getting the mayor's DNA tested as an anonymous source but didn't figure it would start with Kelly. "I'm not at liberty to explain. Call Edna if you need more authorization. Tell her it's related to my meeting last night."

Kelly chuckled. "All right, I'll bluff it up the chain, but you have to file a report to cover it."

"No report."

All humor left Kelly's face. His eyes zeroed in on Frank's for several long seconds. Finally, he said, "Okay, but it'll have to be signed in." Kelly pointed to an open space in the ledger.

Frank scribbled his name, date, and time on the line, and under the column that read *Evidence*, he wrote *DNA sample*.

When he finished, Kelly gave him another long stare. "Don't know what the hell you're up to, Frank, but don't let it bite you in the ass."

Frank spun around and headed for the door. Over his shoulder, he said, "Thanks, owe you one."

Kelly's reply of, "Damn right you do," echoed down the hall as Frank left the confines of the musty lab.

PERRY relaxed on the tailgate of his truck and tried to catch a small breeze as he munched on his tuna and cheese sandwich from the food truck. The half hour lunch break hardly gave the crew time to eat, but Perry didn't mind. He was nothing if not easy to get along with. The boss strolled up, holding a Dr Pepper can. Droplets of sweat dripped off the bottom. The boss took a long swallow before leaning against the truck beside Perry.

"We're wrapping up the sheetrock job here tomorrow. You interested in staying on to finish the carpentry end of it?"

Perry considered the offer.

The boss said, "Or if you want, I can refer you to another drywall job not far from here. They're just about to start a new project—could use a good guy like you."

Perry knew sheetrock better than other jobs. He found basic carpentry more difficult than it should be. Probably some kind of mental block. Perry had made it all these years doing what he knew, not learning new skills. Didn't have the time or patience for new stuff. *Play to your strengths* had always been his motto. He took another bite of the sandwich and nodded.

"Thanks. If it's all the same to you, I'll move on over to the new job if that's all right."

The boss stood. "Okay, finish the garage and bedroom today. Tomorrow, you can do touch-ups, and start hauling drywall trash to the dumpster. Load the extra sheets for return on the flatbed. I'll have your final check ready when you're finished."

Perry and the sheetrock crew finished the last bedroom late that afternoon. As he collected his things, Diego and Alejandro strolled his way.

Alejandro said, "Hear you're dragging up."

Perry took a swig of ice-cold water before answering. "Yup, the boss is setting me up with another drywall job, starts Monday."

Diego laid a hand on Perry's shoulder. "We haven't forgotten what you did for Pedro—saved his life. You ever need something, we're here for you, friend."

Perry was touched. He loved praise and admiration, especially from his coworkers. Made him feel appreciated and respected. Feeling appreciated was something Perry never felt as a kid. Anyone who gave him that feeling was his friend for life. He'd decided a long time ago not to tolerate people who took him for granted. He'd been taken for granted long enough.

He shook hands with Diego and Alejandro. As he walked to his truck, he smiled to himself. The first day on the job, they'd called him *gringo* and wanted nothing to do with him; the last day, he was their friend.

Perry drove slow to Mrs. Cleveland's boarding house. He always drove slowly and observed all traffic laws. Made sure the inspection and registration were current on the truck, and never gave any cop a reason to stop and question him. Perry drove with a Mississippi driver's license. Never bothered getting a new one in Texas. Lived and worked in several states across the south for the last few years. Didn't make sense to change licenses every time you changed states— still the same country.

When Perry arrived at the boarding house, he parked in the back. The garage was open, and Mrs. Cleveland and Raul were wrestling with a large, ancient chest freezer. Sweat poured off them in the hot garage. Even with the doors open, still probably a hundred in there. Perry got out of the truck and walked their way.

"Oh, thank god you're home, Perry," Mrs. Cleveland said. She stopped fighting with the six-foot-long beast and wiped her brow with the corner of her apron. Raul was huffing and puffing on his end of the freezer. He leaned his arms on it, caught his breath, and nodded at Perry.

"Need help?" Perry asked. He liked winning favor with Mrs. Cleveland. When Raul moved out, Perry was next up for his larger room with the good view.

"Oh, lord, yes," she said. She pointed to the wall on the other side of the garage. "I need to move this freezer over there."

She had cleaned out an area just large enough for the freezer on the opposite wall, fifteen feet away.

Perry strolled into the garage and waived her to one side. He eyed Raul. "I'll push it from the front, and you keep it moving in the right direction from your end. Don't let it sway to the side."

Raul nodded and took a long breath.

Perry centered himself on the freezer and tested it. The thing was full and felt like it weighed a ton. He placed both hands on the front and leaned into it. He grunted and pushed off with his powerful legs. A grinding, squealing sound filled the garage as the old, rusty wheels that probably hadn't moved in twenty years began turning. Perry kept the forward momentum as blood pumped to his leg muscles. Raul scampered around from side to side, keeping the thing straight.

"Okay, that's it," Raul shouted.

Perry leaned against the freezer. A lot harder than it looked. He swallowed and wiped the sweat from his neck. He was ready for a cold shower and supper.

Mrs. Cleveland stood against the opposite garage wall with her hands on her hips, admiring his work. "Good job, boys. Now we have more room for storage."

Perry turned her way. *Boys?* Raul didn't do a damn thing.

"You guys get cleaned up. We'll eat after a while," she said.

Raul had a strange expression as he stared at Perry. Something was up.

Perry showered and slipped on a pair of cargo shorts and a T-shirt. He slicked his long, wet hair back to let it dry naturally and tucked the tooth necklace under his shirt. As he walked down the back stairs, the voices of Mrs. Cleveland and Raul in the living room drifted up to meet him. Perry stopped when he heard the subject of the conversation—him.

"When will you tell him?" Raul asked.

Mrs. Cleveland, keeping her voice low, answered, "After supper."

Perry couldn't imagine what they were being so secretive about. He stood in the dark stairwell listening for more conversation. There was silence for almost a minute before the sound of footsteps approached. Mrs. Cleveland turned the corner and let out a short scream at the sight of Perry in the stairwell's shadows.

She placed her right hand over her chest before saying, "Good lord, Perry. Almost scared me to death. Come on, supper's ready."

He followed her into the dining room. Raul was already seated and helping himself to a hot cornbread muffin. He cut the muffin in half and slathered the steaming thing with butter as they walked in. Perry was on his guard. They were planning something but weren't telling him. What could it be? They couldn't know about his late-night activities. What other secret was there?

Mrs. Cleveland took her seat at the head of the table and passed a bowl to Perry. "Try these peas, Perry. Made 'em the way you like."

Was she being intentionally nicer to him today because he'd helped with the freezer, or was she setting him up for something else? He took a couple of spoons of peas and passed them across the table to Raul.

She passed the mashed potatoes, gravy, and meatloaf while humming a church tune Perry had heard on the radio she kept on in the kitchen when she cooked. Perry's appetite was gone. He picked at his food. A sick feeling washed out his insides with the dread of the secret that hung over him. Why didn't she just tell him? Why torture him this way? Every few minutes, she looked at him and smiled while making small talk about the day and how blisteringly hot it was. Perry didn't eat any cherry cobbler with ice cream for dessert. He sat back in his chair, sipping iced tea and watching Mrs. Cleveland and Raul.

Mrs. Cleveland scooped up her last spoon of cobbler and wiped her mouth with the napkin. She shot a sideways glance Raul's way before saying, "Raul offered me a deal today to make an additional thousand dollars a month."

Perry eyed Raul. A slight smirk formed on the guy's lips. The kind of smirk that people showed just before they screw you over big time.

Mrs. Cleveland placed her hands on the table and interlaced her fingers. "Raul has a cousin and his wife who are newlyweds. They're moving to Dallas and looking for a place for a few months until they can both find work and get settled." She smiled a sweet smile. "You know, something in their price range. Say they can pay a thousand dollars a month for room and board." She twisted a ring on her finger without making eye contact. "Could use a little more money every month to supplement my Social Security. If I could rent out the last room, I wouldn't have to raise your rent to keep up with inflation." She stopped twisting the ring and met eyes with him. "What do you think about that?"

Perry was confused. What did he care if she rented the last room? None of his business. Her house—do what she wants. Was this the big secret he'd worried about? He felt silly, but at the same time relieved. "Sounds like a good idea."

Raul released a slow grin from the other side of the table. Mrs. Cleveland reached out and patted Perry's hand. "I'm so glad you approve." She let out a long breath. "But we have to make a few changes first. That's the reason I was moving the freezer. The couple has several large cardboard boxes that need storage in the garage while they're here. And of course, they'll need extra room to live, being two of 'em and all." She exhaled another long breath. "That last unrented bedroom's too small for two people. They'd be bumping into each other and knocking things around all over the place. We're just going to have to put them in your room and move you down the hall to the smaller one, you understand."

Perry thought he'd misheard her at first, but Raul's smirk grew wider. No, Perry heard her perfectly. "But, I don't want to move. I'm a big man. I need a larger room, not a smaller one."

"Oh, don't worry. It won't be forever. Just for a few months, probably six at most, until they have steady jobs and can get an apartment."

Perry was numb. *Stabbed in the back by someone he'd trusted.* Just like his mom. His needs and desires were always ignored. Always second—never first. He pointed at Raul. "It's his cousin. If someone has to give up a large room, it should be him. His room's bigger than mine."

"Oh, no. That wouldn't be good," she said. "That would put the young woman too far from the bathroom." She smiled a knowing smile. "Us women need to be closer to the baths than you men."

All the affection and respect Perry once had for her vanished with that statement. Diego and Alejandro cared more for him than that old bitch. Perry left the table without saying another word and stormed up the stairs. He wasn't putting up with this. It was clear Mrs. Cleveland and Raul no longer cared about or respected him. *They just didn't know who they were dealing with.*

TWENTY

Rob relaxed in Sarge's and sipped his third beer. Place was quiet, only a half dozen customers scattered among the barstools and booths. Rob liked it when the noise was low. Hated drinking in most bars because of the commotion. Carmen was with her friends for their weekly girls' night out—no use hurrying home. Frank sat slumped in the booth across from him with his back against the wall and a half-full glass of red wine. When he asked Rob if he wanted to have a drink after work, Rob figured he wanted to talk about something, but he was wrong. Frank had the kind of look he got when a case wasn't going the way he wanted and he had no more interest or ideas. Sort of a dead-pan expression.

"Heard from Layla lately?" Rob asked.

"Nope."

"How long will the mayor's DNA test take?"

"I expedited it. It'll take as long as it takes."

Sarge meandered up. "Last call, boys."

Rob glanced at his watch. Sarge kept the place open from eleven to seven. Wanted to catch the lunch crowd and the "let's have a drink after work bunch." It was six-thirty, and the big German looked like he was ready to call it a day.

"I'm good," Rob said.

Sarge turned his attention to Frank.

Frank only shook his head.

Sarge pulled the bar towel from his shoulder and wiped something off the corner of the table. "You guys having any luck with the investigation?"

Rob said, "No."

Sarge rubbed his chin and dropped the bar towel back over his shoulder. "Let me get this straight. You guys are cruising the bars and clubs looking for this guy, right?"

No one answered, but Sarge continued. "And CIU's principal concern is protecting the mayor from this guy?"

Rob said, "Yeah, Alton's handling the homicide angle. We're concentrating on the mayor's security."

Sarge tilted his head from side to side, weighing the choices. "You might have to just wait for the guy to make his move on the mayor. Can't believe none of the bars have seen this guy if that's where he grabs his victims."

Rob took a slow sip of beer. "Yeah, well he doesn't exactly grab them, he's an enticer. They go willingly. Besides, you know those places, Sarge. Don't want to do anything that might bring the heat down on them or their clientele. Half are probably in violation of more than one city, county, or state liquor law. They hate calling the police."

Frank finished his wine and sat up in the booth. "Meanwhile, Whisper keeps killing right under our noses. He's like a predator—hunts out a certain area and, before the police catch him, moves on."

Rob grinned. "For a guy who doesn't hunt, you have amazing perception into the habits of animals."

Frank stared at him through sad eyes. "We're all animals at heart, Rob."

Rob jumped as his and Frank's phones dinged simultaneously.

Frank didn't move except to reach for the wine. "If it's another body, then I'm just staying here."

Rob fished his phone from his pocket. He felt the same as Frank. Nothing worse than a case with no end in sight and a never-ending body count. This case was eating their lunches one bite at a time. Rob read the text message and sat back in the booth.

Frank leaned closer and lifted a brow. "Well?"

Rob held the phone up. "Looks like we're finished in Dallas for a while. Mayor's father passed away at 5:46 PM today. We're heading to Leakey."

FRANK GOT into CIU extra early that Friday morning. He'd called Katrina the night before to offer his condolences, but she didn't answer and the call went to voicemail. Just before he hit the sack, she called back. She sounded composed and thanked him for his call. Frank heard the stress and tension in her voice but didn't acknowledge it. They chatted only a few moments before she said she had to go. Her voice, and composure, had started to crack. Frank wished he could just hold her, but she seemed in a hurry to end the call before she broke down.

Terry had called a meeting for eight o'clock. Frank had mixed emotions about the whole thing. On one hand, he was happy he and Rob would be doing something different, even if it was driving the mayor's children to South-Central Texas for a funeral. At least it would get them out of Dallas and away from the case and Layla. Frank understood this was a personality flaw on his part. When a case was rolling, he wanted to work it all day and night. When a case stalled, or he couldn't figure it out, he wanted a break. Not something a detective should admit, but the truth. Often, by just clearing your mind and taking a step back, a case took on a whole new perspective. Details you couldn't see before became clear. Perhaps that's what he needed. His head had become clouded with so many conflicting details, he was missing something important. In a case he couldn't control, he was at the mercy of the case detective, or in this case. Layla. Frank figured there might be things the FBI held back. Angles they wanted only their people to work. Frank figured something else—Layla had been right. *This case will work on you.* Every day, Frank felt a little more depressed, wondering how much longer before some investigative reporter discovers this is a serial killer. That's when it'll hit the fan. Frank was in favor of releasing information about the killer to the press right now. Put this guy's photo out there. Someone knew him. The public could work with them.

Rob and Terry strolled in, chatting.

"Need to make a couple of calls, boys. Give me ten minutes and come on in. Coffee should be ready by then," Terry said as he passed Frank's cubicle.

Rob had dressed full cowboy today, down to a bolo leather tie with an arrowhead at the top. Frank sometimes wished he had some fashion statement he could make to the world like Rob. Rob's attire and bearing said, "I'm a cowpoke, pure and simple. Not looking for any trouble but won't put up with any crap." Since Frank had no such fashion proclamation he could share with the world, he'd have to be content with just making fun of Rob.

"Hope you left the AC on in the car for your horse. He'll die in that parking garage."

Rob didn't answer while he carefully stretched and smoothed his jacket over the back of his chair before sitting down.

Frank went back to reviewing emails until Terry called them in.

After everyone had a seat and a fresh cup of brew, Terry began. "Funeral arrangements are being finalized, but you guys should be ready to drive out to Leakey starting tomorrow." He sighed. "Realistically, I don't expect it'll be until Sunday, but we should know more by the end of the day."

"Still driving the kids?" Rob asked.

"That's the last we heard. Have the garage do a complete check of your vehicle. Belts, hoses, fluid levels, and tires. Be ready to shove off when we get the final word."

Rob sipped his coffee before asking, "How far?"

"Close to four hundred miles," Terry said. "Should be able to cover it in seven hours, even stopping for lunch."

Frank liked the idea of traveling to the hill country with Katrina. He'd like it even better if her brother and Rob weren't going.

Something else had been troubling Frank. He'd had an uneasy feeling about Layla the last couple of days. Ever since that scene in the club parking lot, Frank harbored the idea she was putting herself in too much jeopardy. The second murder scene yesterday only confirmed it. She was driven by career, reputation, or something Frank didn't fully understand. Something that pushed her to take extreme chances. Frank had killed men and almost been killed more than once, but he always left gunplay as the last option. He avoided violence whenever possible. Layla sought it out, embraced it, lived for it. She'd been caught twice. How many more times had she gotten away with it that no one knew about? Frank didn't understand people like that.

"Frank? Frank! You still with us?" Terry was talking to him.

Rob stared at Frank and grinned. "Just went on another mental walk-about, didn't ya?"

Frank sat straighter in the chair. "Sorry, Terry. You were saying?"

Terry said, "I said you guys finish off any reports before you leave. If we have something break while you're out of town, I want to be able to answer any questions about what you've been up to."

Frank nodded and took a sip. "Got it—will do."

Frank and Rob typed the rest of the morning until Frank's phone rang around eleven o'clock.

"Frank, you need to come back out here."

"That you, Ruby?"

Ruby's smoky voice dropped lower. "How many other sexy women do you have calling you this time of the morning?"

"Ruby, we're buried in paperwork over here and looks like—"

"This is important, Frank. Lucia came into work this morning and completely broke down. Keeps saying it's all her fault—she killed her."

"Killed who?" Frank asked.

"It's better you hear it for yourself, Frank."

"Okay, we'll swing by."

"Thanks."

Rob popped his head over the cubicle wall. "Was that Ruby?"

"Yeah."

"Somebody get killed?"

Frank stood. "Let's find out what's going on."

A half hour later, Rob and Frank walked into Ruby's club. The usual lunch crowd was there. Well, Ruby didn't actually serve lunch like Sarge's. Usual lunch crowd in her place meant people who drank their lunches and snacked on nuts and chips at the bar.

Ruby leaned on the bar with one hand and had her other planted on her hip, listening to a story from one of the construction workers. When she noticed Frank, she walked away from the guy telling the story in midsentence.

"What's going on?" Frank asked.

Ruby took him by the arm and led him and Rob to the door in the back of the bar. Just before stepping into the storeroom, she turned and said, "Gleeson, cover things out front for a minute."

To Frank's surprise, one of the patrons, an old skinny guy wearing a Rangers baseball cap, calmly dismounted his barstool and walked behind the bar. When they went into the storeroom, Lucia was holding a clipboard and pen, inventorying cases of liquor on the shelf. She fixed eyes on them, and tears ran down her cheeks. She sat the clipboard on a desk and took a seat.

Frank had no clue. He'd only met this girl twice. What could have upset her so? And who had she killed?

Ruby eased beside Lucia and laid a motherly hand on her back. "Okay, they're here. Tell them what you told me."

Lucia wiped her eyes and looked up at Ruby.

Ruby nodded. "It's okay. They're friends."

Lucia wrung her hands in her lap and didn't meet eyes with Frank. She kept her stare on the floor, and in a quiet voice she said, "I think I may have seen that guy you're looking for."

Frank moved closer and took a knee directly in front of her. "Tell me."

"A few days ago, I picked up my brother, Diego, from where he worked. I dropped him off at a garage—his truck was being worked on." Lucia shuddered and took a deep breath. "I saw him... had to be him," she whimpered.

"The guy we're looking for, you saw the guy?" Rob asked.

Lucia rubbed her arms with both hands and nodded.

"Where was he?" Frank asked.

"There's a house my brother is working on. The guy you're looking for was sitting against a tree eating a sandwich. I asked my brother, and he said he was a drywaller."

Rob's stare widened.

Frank almost smiled but maintained a straight face. This was the break he'd been waiting for. They always came; all you had to do was wait them out. "Why didn't you call us?"

Lucia lowered her head into her hands and wept uncontrollably for several moments. Ruby rubbed her back softly, giving her time to compose herself.

Lucia looked up, and through red eyes, shook her head. "Didn't want to get someone in trouble that might be the wrong guy. Especially a friend of my brother. If I'd said something earlier, that woman by the railroad tracks might still be alive."

Ruby interrupted. "Lucia's family has had bad luck with the police in the past. Not a lot of trust there."

Frank took Lucia's hand. Had to quickly establish a level of trust she'd feel comfortable with and get whatever information she had. "Do you trust me?"

She wiped her eyes again and nodded. "I guess. Ruby said I could."

Frank stood. "We'll need you to come to the station and give a statement. You can ride with us. Is that okay?"

Lucia glanced at Ruby, and she nodded.

"Sure, okay, I guess," Lucia said.

"We'll drop you off back here in a couple of hours."

Lucia's voice broke when she asked, "Am I in trouble?"

"No, Lucia. You did just fine," Frank said. No use agreeing with her about her lack of candor. Certainly, the other woman might still be alive, but that was Lucia's burden to carry. A life sentence of wondering. "Get your things together," Frank said.

Frank leaned over and whispered to Rob, "I have a phone call to make. Take your time bringing her out."

Rob nodded.

Frank began dialing Alton's cell when he left the storeroom. By the time he got to the front door, Alton answered.

"Frank here. We're bringing in a witness who claims to have seen the suspect. Put a surveillance team together. We'll give you the guy's work address in a few minutes. We're doing a quick drive-by and see if we can spot him at the location, but get your team headed to South Dallas."

"Don't get burned on the drive-by," was all Alton said.

Rob walked Lucia to the car, and Frank asked, "How far is the house from here?"

Lucia pointed southeast. "A couple miles."

"We'll swing by there on the way so you can make a firm identification of the address. If the guy you saw is around, point him out to us."

Lucia's face contorted, and she looked from Rob to Frank. "We're not going to stop, right?"

"Right, just a quick drive-by so we'll know the correct address," Rob said.

Lucia hesitated a moment before getting into the unmarked police car. She looked back at the club's door. Ruby stood in the doorway and gave her the thumbs-up sign. Frank understood. In

Lucia's neighborhood, if you were seen in a cop car and not being taken to jail, you were a snitch plain and simple. Snitches often had bad accidents. They became the victims of hit-and-runs, drive-by shootings, and aggravated assault.

Lucia directed them to the 1600 block of Bannock, just off Hatcher and Lamar. Rob drove extra slowly as he turned onto Bannock.

"Get low in the seat, Lucia," Frank said. "When we get close to the place, describe it to me so I know what it looks like."

Frank leaned forward and stared down the street. A construction dumpster came into view on the right. "Is that it on the right up ahead?"

Lucia's shaky voice came as a small whisper from the back seat. "Yes, that's it with the big tree in the front yard. That's where I saw him."

Frank copied down the street address as they drove by and noted the description of the house. There was no one in the yard or around the dumpster, but workers' trucks lined the street. That meant there was still a crew on site. Frank noted the time—one o'clock exactly. He called Alton and passed on the information for the surveillance team.

They were back at the PD fifteen minutes later and heading to Homicide where Alton waited.

"Team's just arrived at the house," Alton said as Rob, Frank, and Lucia walked through the door of Homicide.

They all went into an interview room and Alton got the details from Lucia. Fifteen minutes later, they were back at Alton's desk. Someone had just started a new bunch of popcorn at the coffee bar. Rob stared at it and licked his lips.

"Do we need a warrant?" Rob asked.

"Exigent circumstances," Alton said, "No warrant." He dialed a number on his cell. "Yeah, what are you guys seeing out there? Is the suspect around?"

Alton nodded at the response and said, "Okay, it's a go. I'm calling Lieutenant Gunn to deploy the team."

"Using SWAT?" Frank asked.

Alton dropped the phone back in his pocket. "You bet. Lieutenant's call. Not taking any chances. You guys want to be there for the takedown?"

"Wouldn't miss it," Frank answered.

After giving her statement, Rob and Frank delivered Lucia back to Ruby's and drove to a convenience store in the twenty-seven hundred block of Hatcher Street near Malcom X Boulevard, about a half-mile from the house. The corner parking lot of the store was overflowing with patrol vehicles, unmarked cars, and the SWAT battlewagon. Small groups of uniform officers stood around waiting for the go sign and trying to avoid the blazing sun. Lieutenant Gunn from SWAT had a dozen of his guys in an impromptu briefing off to the side. Looked like they'd deployed the whole team. Spotters, snipers, and assault officers in black combat gear stood in a circle, getting their instructions. They were in soft caps, but each carried an impressive array of weapons, equipment, and a Kevlar helmet.

The meeting broke up as Rob and Frank approached. Gunn turned around, and they were right behind him. He jerked his head back and did a double-take.

"Jesus H. Christ! Don't tell me you two are involved in this?" Gunn said.

Rob had worked for Gunn during his SWAT days, so he answered. "Hi, Lieutenant. What's the latest?"

Gunn squinted and pointed at Rob and Frank. Every time you have an occasion to show up at a SWAT event, something is always screwed up. Why's that?"

"Just lucky," Frank mumbled.

Gunn shot a stare at Frank.

"We're the guys who provided the location where the suspect works," Rob said.

Frank cleared his throat, lowered his head, and spoke softly. "Criminal *Intelligence*."

Gunn's expression tightened at Frank's comment. "In answer to your question, we're assaulting the house as soon as the snipers get into position to give cover."

"Think he'll try and take a co-worker hostage?" Rob asked.

Gunn leaned his athletic frame against a marked car, took off his cap, and wiped sweat away from his graying stubble before saying, "We're ready if he does. Time, talk, and tear gas."

"Has the surveillance team spotted the suspect yet?" Frank asked.

"Mostly Hispanics in the work crew, but the team caught a glimpse of an Anglo guy for a second walking past a window."

A voice called from across the parking lot, "Lieutenant Gunn."

Gunn eyed Rob and Frank. "Good work on the identifying the house, boys. Have to go."

"Want anything to drink?" Frank asked, walking toward the convenience store.

"Cherry Coke," Rob answered.

Frank showed a grin as he opened the door. Five minutes later they sipped their bottles of water and waited for the assault convoy to depart. Frank had been on several takedowns with Gunn and the team. It always began with a stealthy approach and ended with a dynamic entry. Seldom were shots fired. The team trained and worked so well together, they usually brought things under control before the suspect could act or react.

Gunn climbed on the back ladder of the battlewagon and waved his cap to the assembled troops as he spoke into the walkie-talkie. "Blocking units—shut down both ends of the target street. Surveillance teams—sound off if you spot the suspect. Snipers— watch for weapons on the guy. Don't take chances with a life—take the shot." He climbed into the SWAT armored battlewagon, and it roared down the street with a line of police vehicles in tow. No sirens screaming, nothing to give away their surreptitious approach.

They got to the house much faster than Frank would have thought. The SWAT perimeter team deployed off the running boards of the battlewagon at a run and surrounded the house. The assault team stacked against a wall only feet from the front door, with

Sergeant Burns in the rear. The rest of the unmarked vehicles stayed a safe distance back as uniform officers ran to fortify the perimeter fifty yards in every direction.

Rob tuned the police radio to the SWAT channel and grinned as team members reported in. *"North side secure, east side secure, west side secure,"* voices said. The hushed voice of Sergeant Burns came over the air, "Ready to commence assault."

Gunn's voice answered, "Sergeant Burns, the operation is yours."

Frank and Rob rolled their windows down to listen. The only thing they heard was a deafening silence. No voices spoke on the radio. Frank didn't know what he expected. Shouting? Shooting? After what seemed like too long, an out-of-breath voice came over the speaker, "Objective cleared, three suspects in custody."

A few cars away, the driver's door of a gray sedan swung open, and Alton with another homicide detective bolted toward the house.

"Let's go," Rob said.

The outer perimeter appeared to collapse in on itself as a dozen uniforms descended on the house from every direction, with Rob and Frank bringing up the rear. As they got closer, loud voices sounded from the back rooms of the house. Smells of sheetrock and wood shavings hung in the air as they entered the front door. Work tools, trash, and building materials were strewn on the floor, causing Rob and Frank to negotiate an obstacle course to the back rooms of the house. Place had been gutted, and with a new ceiling and interior walls, looked like it had been under renovation for a while. In the hall, SWAT officers had a Hispanic man on his stomach, hands cuffed behind his back. In a back bedroom was another Hispanic man and a large Anglo dude face down on the floor.

Alton squatted beside the Anglo and shouted, "Look at me."

The guy slowly turned his head and stared Alton's way.

He had a lean face, with two-day stubble, and dark brown eyes.

Alton stood when Rob and Frank approached.

"Who are you?" Alton asked the Anglo on the floor.

The man on the floor, sweating heavily, mumbled, "Never

figured having outstanding warrants for unpaid traffic tickets would come to this."

From the hall, another voice screamed, "We're all legal here, man. I've got papers."

Alton held the FBI Snapshot photo he received at Layla's briefing in front of the guy's face. "Are you this guy?"

The man on the floor wiggled and stared at the photo. He didn't speak at first, but let loose a hysterical laugh. "No, I'm Dean Bradshaw. That's a picture of Perry."

Everything stopped. No one moved or spoke. Frank held his breath. Finally, Alton asked, "Who is Perry, and where is he?"

The man said, "These cuffs are too tight—can't feel my fingers anymore."

Alton motioned for a SWAT officer to remove the cuffs.

The big guy named Dean sat upright and rubbed his wrist, staring at the dozen officers around him.

"Now, where is Perry? Does he work here?" Alton asked.

Dean rubbed his wrist again and flexed his fingers before saying, "Used to. Cut him loose a little after twelve. Going to another job."

Frank let out a breath and his mind drifted back to the drive-by with Lucia. They identified the house and called it in at exactly one o'clock. *Shit!*

The boss, Dean, and the two Hispanic guys were all taken into custody. Everyone got a trip downtown for a full interview. Didn't do much good. All Alton got out of them was a better description of Perry and a good description of his truck. But they didn't discover Perry's true last name. Dean thought it might be Cartwright—didn't know for sure. He always paid the crew in cash. That kept things simple. No taxes, no insurance, and no minimum pay regulations applied to contract guys working for straight cash. A police team even went to the new job site to see if Perry might have checked in early— no dice. The rest of the afternoon, everyone burned up computers, checking local, state, and federal criminal indices looking for anyone with a name even close that fit Perry's description. By five o'clock, everyone had come up empty.

Rob rubbed his temples with his index fingers. Frank knew he always did that when he felt a dull headache coming on. The kind he got when he went too many days with too much on his mind. The kind he got when Carmen was going through the worst of her depression years ago.

Rob pushed back from his computer. "I've checked everything. Think I'm calling it a day."

Frank yawned and stretched. He also pushed his computer aside. "Me too. I've checked that name through all the states where there's been a murder. Looks like Perry Cartwright might be an alias."

Frank's phone rang and he put it on speaker.

"Pierce," he answered.

"Forgot to tell you," Alton said. "Woman hanging from the train tracks has two missing molars."

"Thanks." Frank placed the phone into the cradle and told Rob.

"Big surprise," Rob mumbled. He stood and glanced toward Terry's office. He was on the phone and had a pen in his hands, taking notes. He noticed Rob's stare and held up his index finger, indicating *wait*.

"Hey," Rob said. "Something's up."

Frank also stood and did a lower back stretch.

Terry got off the call and headed their way, notepad in hand. "Okay, boys. Go home, get a good night's sleep, and pack. Leaving tomorrow for Central Texas."

"Still taking the kids?" Rob asked.

Terry nodded. "Yeah, be at the mayor's home tomorrow morning by nine o'clock. Pack for a two to three-night stay. By the way, the press has already picked up on the funeral arrangements at the ranch. Must have a source inside the mayor's office." Terry looked up. "Any questions?"

Rob shook his head. Frank headed for the door.

TWENTY-ONE

Frank walked into his loft, flopped on the sofa, and released a slow breath. Layla still haunted his thoughts. Needed to forget about her and this whole wretched case for a while. If they were lucky, the FBI would catch the guy before they returned from Leakey. Either way, Frank vowed to avoid Layla from now on. Started messing with his head the first moment he met her and hadn't stopped.

Frank took a shower and changed into shorts and a polo shirt. Felt like something different for dinner tonight. He dug in the freezer and took out a small, frozen cheese pizza. Ordinarily, he'd make the dough himself, but he didn't feel like doing that much work. Besides, he knew how to make the store-bought pizza taste great. You must first find one made with sourdough. Gave it a tangy flavor. After pouring a glass of 2017 Coppola Claret, he diced a red onion, sweet pepper, and olives. He dropped them in extra virgin olive oil and put it over a low flame before starting the oven. Halfway through the bake time, Frank loaded the top of the pizza with his vegetable confit. A couple of minutes before he took the pizza out of the oven, he dashed out to his patio herb garden and plucked a few sprigs of lemon basil. Frank tore them in quarters to release the aromatics before scattering them over the baked pizza. He listened to a vintage Mary Lou Williams record as he ate dinner.

Frank finished packing for the trip and was about to settle in for an evening of reading when the phone rang.

"Can I please come over for a while?" Katrina asked.

"Sure."

A half hour later, he and Katrina lay on the sofa, curled up together watching TV. Frank kept the volume low. The local PBS station had an English murder mystery playing that Katrina appeared interested in watching at first, but as the evening rolled on, it became apparent she didn't care about watching TV, just wanted to be held by Frank and talk. Katrina did all the talking. She was devastated over the loss of her grandfather and just wanted someone to share his memory with. Frank learned the story of Poppy Wallace as Katrina knew it from her childhood.

Matthew Charles Wallace was born in the early twenties in Houston. Served as a mechanic in the Army Air Corps during World War II in England, and after the war, went to college on the GI bill and receive a degree in petroleum engineering. He married Mary Helen Lewis and somehow ended up in Midland around 1954, teaming up with a future president. George HW Bush hired him as an engineer with Zapata Petroleum Corporation. Poppy Wallace read everything he could get his hands on about oil and gas geological sites in West Texas. He studied the newest exploration and drilling methods and had a keen intuition about marketing and distribution. In the mid-sixties, when future president Bush sold out his shares of Zapata Petroleum, Poppy Wallace mortgaged the family home, drained the savings account, and borrowed as much as his credit would allow, grabbing shares of Permian Basin oil production sites. For the next decade, he put his family on a near-starvation diet to buy as many shares and oil leases as possible.

By the seventies, he had moved to Dallas and started his own energy company, Wallace Energy Corp. That's where Mr. Mayor grew up and learned the oil and gas industry before venturing off into investment real estate in Georgia. In 1986, Mary Helen died of cancer, but Poppy lived in Dallas until the mid-nineties. He retained a controlling interest but sold Wallace Energy for an unknown amount. Estimates put it between five hundred million and one billion dollars. The Permian Basin to date has produced an estimated 35 billion barrels of oil and one hundred and nineteen trillion cubic feet of natural gas. No one knew for sure what Poppy was worth except the family attorney. Poppy's will would be read after his funeral at the ranch.

Poppy had enjoyed deer hunting as a kid, and he and his dad traveled to Real County, Texas to camp and hunt every season. They hunted just north of a sleepy little town named Leakey. Poppy always said he felt closer to his father there than anywhere else on earth. So, after retiring, he left the city and moved north of Leakey. Bought a Texas-sized ranch and built a home large enough for all the family to visit. He'd been generous with his money in his new county—built a library, new school, and first-rate hospital. The name Wallace showed up a lot in Real County, especially Leakey.

Katrina shivered and pulled Frank's arm a little tighter around her. "I never knew my grandmother. Poppy's the only one from my dad's side of the family I felt close to. He was a kindly, loving old gentleman."

Frank had done a little reading on his own about Poppy Wallace. Everything Katrina said was true, but there was much more to the story. Mr. Wallace had been an aggressive, ruthless businessman—especially in his younger years. Hated unions, was a workaholic, and made sure to befriend the right people in political circles to maintain his business interests. Big Republican contributor for congressional and presidential campaigns. Had the personal cell numbers of Saudi oil princes and Russian oligarchs. But one thing stood out. He was never accused of doing anything illegal. Morally questionable, perhaps, but not illegal. Someone who could accumulate as much wealth as old man Wallace and stay on the right side of illegality was a rarity.

Katrina sniffled and pulled his arms even tighter around her. "I'm going to need you, Frank. I don't think I can get through the next few days without you being around."

Frank hugged her tighter, kissed the back of her neck, and said, "I'm here. It'll be okay."

Frank wasn't a good consoler, and he knew it. He tried, but he had become so emotionally numb after his wife's death and years on the PD, he just couldn't convincingly pull it off. The loss of his wife had burned out Frank's feeling receptors in his soul. He had to help Katrina as much as he could but feared he wasn't up to the task.

She stayed until a little after ten. "I'll see you tomorrow, okay?" Katrina said as she stood at the open door.

Frank gently kissed her. "Nine o'clock. Good night."

PERRY LAY in his bed and listened to the silence of the old house. Seldom was the place ever quiet—never silent. But tonight, the silence lulled Perry into a relaxed state. Perry liked quiet. Enjoyed being alone with his thoughts. But his memories were another thing. Bad memories about the years his mom was at her worst. Memories about the small, cramped closet under the stairs. About being locked in there for days with only a loaf of bread, a gallon of water, a roll of toilet paper, and a bucket. During those days when his mom was off on a trip with some man, Perry allowed his mind to leave his body. He traveled to imaginary places, met nice people, and had exciting adventures. Perry loved those trips, even if they were imaginary. Anything to get away from the dark scary confines of the closet.

But one day after traveling on an out-of-body trip, he wasn't sure his mind ever returned to his body. He was about nine years old and recalled going to a mental place with lots of pretty colors. A place where cinnamon and peppermint filled the air. A place with soft music playing from all sides. That was the most wonderful place of all. Perhaps his mind enjoyed it so much it just decided to stay.

Perhaps he was still there but just didn't realize it. Maybe his present life was all just a crazy dream.

Something creaked downstairs, and Perry bolted upright and strained to listen. Wasn't Mrs. Cleveland or Raul, he was sure of that. But old houses make sounds.

Perry had hit a roadblock in his efforts to introduce himself to his dad, the mayor. The mayor's father was dead now and the whole family would be going to the funeral. Hey, that was Perry's grandpa, too. Anyway, according to the news, the mayor would be traveling out of town to a place called Leakey, wherever that was. Pretty much put the mayor out of reach for the time being. Or did it? Perry had been looking for a time and place he was sure to catch the mayor. Looking for an opportunity to introduce himself to his dad. What better time or place than the funeral of a blood relative?

TWENTY-TWO

Rob strolled into CIU at eight o'clock Saturday morning. Following Terry's instructions, he had worn his best dark business suit and left his cowboy attire in the closet. Long drives in suits were a pain. At the end, you always looked like you'd slept in them. Neither Edna nor Terry were in. Frank sat slumped at his desk, eyeing his computer and talking on his phone as Rob approached.

Frank said, "Okay, keep us in the loop. We're leaving in the next hour."

Frank placed the phone back into its cradle and looked up at Rob. "That was Alton. Wanted to know if Layla had called us about leaving her out of the raid we did yesterday."

"Have you heard from her?"

Frank kept scrolling on his computer, "Nope. You?"

"Nope," Rob said. "Did she call and bitch at Alton?"

Frank stopped scrolling, tilted his to the side, and squinted. In an uncertain tone he said, "No, she didn't. Figured she'd be all over him for leaving her out."

Rob shrugged. "Probably just as well since the bust was a flop."

Frank studied the computer another second before kicking back in his chair with his fingers interlaced behind his head. "You want to go the scenic route or the boring route?"

Rob understood what he was talking about. Taking I-35 South or 377 South out of the DFW Metroplex were the best choices for Leakey. Not much difference in the times, but 377 took you through some of the prettiest scenery in the hill country, with quaint colorful towns and breathtaking vistas, while I-35 was hours of dreary freeway. "Already decided on the route—377."

Frank glanced around the office. "Anyone coming in today?"

"Terry said he'd be in by nine. We can shoot him a call when we leave, and he'll make the necessary notifications."

Frank had a giddiness in his voice Rob hadn't heard in days— sounded like the old Frank. Yeah, this was probably a good time to ease away from the case and let things settle in. Whisper had outmaneuvered them at every turn. Both Rob and Frank needed time to think, and with all the crap rolling downhill, no one could think in Dallas anymore. Well, no original or useful thoughts, anyway.

Rob stood and unscrewed the lid on his Copenhagen tin. He grabbed a big pinch and shoved it in his lip. "You ready?"

Frank had worn the same suit he did to the FBI meeting. Probably his class A dress uniform. He showed a neutral expression and nodded. "Yeah, let's go."

Rob and Frank had last been to the mayor's house a couple of years ago when Katrina was kidnapped. Rob pulled up to the two-acre corner lot and stopped at the metal gate. The stone wall was covered in fig ivy, giving it a softer, less institutional look.

It was exactly ten to nine when Rob pushed the button on the speaker box. Instead of the formal voice asking their business as before, the metal gate creaked open slowly as if welcoming them to a special land. The mammoth English country house at the end of the driveway always fascinated Rob. The two-story, solid rock structure with Boston ivy cascading to the ground looked like something from an English travelogue.

"Still can't get over the size of this place. Who needs this much room?"

Frank sat as still as a statue, staring at some point on the dash. Just as they pulled through the gate, he dialed his phone. His lips flattened, waiting for an answer. Frank disconnected and dropped the phone in his pocket.

"Layla?"

Frank nodded.

"Didn't answer?"

Frank shook his head and blew out a long breath. "No. Let's go to work."

As Rob pulled up to the house, Sergeant Miller from the mayor's CIU protective detail got out of a black sedan with another plainclothes officer. Miller wore a dark suit and serious expression. He was short with bushy eyebrows and mustache. Miller was seen as only marginally competent by the rest of the department. He'd taken the lieutenant's exam four times and never passed, even when his seniority points were figured into the final score. The fact he held a private pilot's license gave him the edge. The mayor flew everywhere in his private plane. Miller was always included because he could co-pilot. Must have something on the ball to get a license, but Rob would never fly with the guy; however, he still liked Miller. They'd worked together during Rob's Homicide days. Miller got promoted to sergeant and transferred to CIU – Dignitary Protection.

Rob strolled his way. "Hey, Sarge."

"Hi, Rob," Miller said. "Hear you and Pierce are driving the kids out."

Rob shrugged. "Looks that way."

Miller allowed his gaze to drift to Frank who was just getting out of the passenger seat.

Miller said, "I'll be with the mayor and his guest on the plane. We'll leave later this morning, after the mayor ties up a couple of loose ends. Should arrive before you guys."

Rob stared up at the sky. "At least you have clear flying weather."

"Here, maybe," Miller said. "Not so much as you get closer to the coast."

"Huh?"

Miller grinned. "Don't tell me you haven't been listening to the weather."

It had been a while since Rob had bothered listening to the weather. No use, nothing but hot and dry in the forecast. "Well…"

"Hurricane Kate made a wild turn north and intensified even more this morning, headed directly for the lower Texas coast. Padre Island looking like the most probable landfall target. I need to get the mayor going. Flying conditions south of here are deteriorating every hour."

"Oh, yeah. I recall hearing about that. Looking bad for Padre Island, huh?"

Just then the front door opened and an older man wearing a suit carried out two suitcases and set them beside the door.

The detective with Miller looked at Rob. "Those are for the kids."

Rob popped the trunk and fitted the suitcases inside, beside his and Frank's.

***

FRANK NEVER CARED FOR MILLER. Never worked for him, but his reputation was what kept Frank away. The guy was in that class of supervisors who had been promoted above their abilities. He was best known for being wrong on everything he'd ever done. How he got promoted to sergeant and kept his assignment on the mayor's detail remained a departmental mystery. Frank assumed it had to do with politics. That's what usually kept screw-ups in places they had no business.

Frank kept his eyes on the front door. He crossed his arms while leaning against the car. Just as he got comfortable, his cell rang.

"Morning, Frank," Kelly said. The sound of munching drifted

over the line. "Got that return on the super-secret DNA you dropped in my lap."

Frank held his breath and walked to the rear of the car, out of earshot of the group waiting near the door.

"Sorry, no hit. Couldn't match it to the suspect."

"You sure?" The second Frank asked that stupidest of stupid questions, he regretted it. Kelly hadn't run the test. He was just reading an email from the lab that performed it. "Sorry, Kelly."

Kelly chuckled, and the sound of more munching drifted over the line. "You okay, Frank?"

The front door opened, and the mayor escorted Katrina and her brother outside. Ms. Mayor followed. She wore a loose-fitting pair of white linen pants and a bright red blouse. She'd gained a few pounds since last they'd met. Her hair was still the sickly shade of red-orange he remembered, and her eyes were a bit overdone. She shot a sideways glance his way and frowned.

"Kelly, have to go. Thanks again for expediting the DNA. I owe you a beer."

Another chuckle sounded from Kelly's end. "Don't worry about it. You already owe me so many beers we'll both have to work 'til a hundred to repay the debt."

Katrina stared at Frank. She looked especially beguiling today. Lowcut pink blouse, and white shorts with sandals. Her little brother, Gerald, who was named after his mother's father and everyone called Jerry, wore jeans, yellow-and-green striped T-shirt with some logo Frank didn't recognize, and tennis shoes. Kid reminded Frank of himself at that age. Lanky and awkward, with long, thick chestnut brown hair. Frank had never met the kid, but Katrina assured him Jerry was the biggest nerd in Dallas. Seventeen years old, and all he did was play on the computer except when called to eat, and then right back to the latest game.

Frank gave a discreet nod to Katrina before she received a hug from Mr. and Ms. Mayor.

Katrina's smirk confused Frank. Was she still saddened at the thought of losing her grandfather, or excited at the prospect of going on an ultra-chaperoned road trip with him? He tried not to stare at her. No sense in drawing the ire of Ms. Mayor any more than necessary, but Frank found it difficult not to gaze her way. God, she reminded him so much of his wife.

Frank didn't have an epiphany very often, but staring at her smiling back at him, he had a big one. She was counting on him to *be her rock* for the next few days, to get her through the funeral. He'd promised he would. Wasting another thought on Layla was useless. Frank had done all he could for her. She neither desired nor appreciated his help and advice. Whatever happens, happens. Katrina was not only his primary job the next few days, but also the only living woman he could say he loved other than his mom. Katrina must be the one he concentrated on. He wouldn't let her down.

Frank opened the back door for Katrina, resisting the temptation to hug and kiss her.

"May I sit on the other side?" she said and winked.

"Certainly." Frank understood why she wanted to sit in the other seat. She could at least have a profile view of him instead of looking at the back of his head for the next seven hours.

The mayor turned to Frank, and Frank motioned with his head to the rear of the sedan. When Mayor Wallace met him, Frank said, "Got the DNA back."

The mayor blanched and shifted his feet shoulder wide, leaning one hand on the trunk.

"No match. Whoever that monster is, he's no relation to you."

Mr. Mayor let out a slow breath. "You sure?"

Frank couldn't resist a grin. "Yes, sir. On high profile cases like this, the test is checked and doubled checked, and then signed off on by the lab manager. No mistake."

The mayor lowered his head and muttered, "Thank god." Then he shifted closer and glanced in the backseat at his children. "Keep them safe, Frank."

"We will."

Rob cranked the car and put the AC on high before strolling over to Sergeant Miller. The sergeant motioned for Frank to join them in a quick meeting.

"Okay, guys. Every state trooper between here and Leakey has been notified there are dignitaries traveling through their district. Any car trouble or something more serious, just switch the radio to a DPS band and call for assistance. Once you get to Real County, you've got it made. The sheriff's department is rolling out the red carpet. They'll have a patrol vehicle at the ranch entrance. Deputy knows your license plate number, and he'll let you in when you pull up to the gate. Keep your speed down. As long as you're there by four, you're golden."

"Thanks, Sarge," Rob said.

Frank nodded.

"Mr. Mayor," Sergeant Miller said. "We should get a move on." He looked to the south. "With that storm building offshore—might be a little bumpy."

Rob and Frank got in the car, and Rob looked in the rearview mirror. "Hey, Katrina."

"Hey, Rob."

"You guys buckle up," Rob said. He interlaced his fingers and popped his knuckles, "We're riding."

Frank laughed to himself. Just had to throw in that little cowboyism for good measure. Frank dialed Terry's desk at CIU.

"Yeah, this is Terry."

"Terry, we have a departure. Make the notifications," Frank said.

"Will do. Drive safe."

Rob drove to the front gate before Jerry spoke. He'd been fooling around on his cell since he got in the car with a concentration equal to Robert Oppenheimer trying to unlock the secrets of the atom. "I'm hungry."

Katrina shot him a scolding glance. "Don't be silly, you just ate breakfast."

Jerry mumbled, "Didn't eat breakfast."

"Then that's your problem. If you'd stop playing those stupid games long enough to eat, you wouldn't be hungry, would you?"

Frank smiled at Katrina's chiding of her little brother. Teenagers were never a group Frank had much patience with. But kids were kids, no matter how rich or poor their parents were. Only thing, poor kids had to grow up faster and harder.

Frank wasn't looking forward to the long drive. He hated driving or even riding great distances—too boring. Rob loved driving. He could drive all day and never complain. Thank god he was Frank's partner.

"Could you turn up the air conditioner?" Jerry said, never taking his eyes off the iPhone as he pecked away.

Rob didn't answer, only dropped the temperature five degrees and directed the middle vent to the back seat.

As Rob turned on the freeway entrance ramp, Jerry dropped his phone in the seat and searched the rear floorboard area looking for something. After a minute, he said, "Where's the backseat AC vents and controls?"

Before Frank could answer, Rob said, "There aren't any. This is a police car, not a limo. No fancy stuff like that—lowest bidder." Rob had a slight grin after saying it. Rob hated whiners. Being a Marine and having undergone the horrors of war, Rob had no use for someone who complained too much. *Get tough or get out* was his motto.

Jerry showed a scowl, picked up his cell, and began playing again. Katrina had a book on her lap but hadn't opened it. She sat solemn faced, looking out the window with a pensive expression. Was she thinking of her grandfather or Frank?

Frank tried not thinking about them, but Layla and the case popped up in his head again. Still left a bad taste in his mouth that he was leaving town without a final resolution. No cop or investigator wants to walk away from something, leaving it undone. But that was exactly what he and Rob were doing—walking out. Well, technically they were still providing security for the mayor's kids, but they were no longer involved in the day-to-day effort to locate the killer. After yesterday's debacle at the renovated house, Frank took it as a sign. A sign they should just step away for a while. But leaving town still felt wrong.

Rob wound his way through the canyons of downtown Dallas. The familiar skyscrapers glistened in the sunlight as Frank placed his palm against the window—hot. Best just settle in for a long ride. Might even catch a quick nap after lunch.

The trouble started as Rob turned off on I-30 West toward Fort Worth and points beyond. He slipped his Copenhagen can from the armrest and thumped the top a couple of times for a fresh dip. He twisted the lid off one-handed with the precision of a Swiss watchmaker. Rob got an extra-large pinch of snuff and tucked it into his lip. As he replaced the lid, Jerry spoke.

"Hey, can I try some of that?"

"Huh?" Rob said.

"I want to try some," Jerry repeated.

In an exasperated tone, Katrina said, "Don't be a jerk. It'll make you sick. Besides, that's a man thing."

"You saying I'm not man enough?" Jerry asked, in a challenging tone.

"No, I'm saying you're an idiot if you do," Katrina answered.

Frank lowered his sun visor and opened the mirror cover to better observe the disturbance in the back seat.

"I'm serious, I want to try some," Jerry repeated.

Rob glanced Frank's way and grinned.

Frank knew Rob had a mischievous side that loved to teach people how stupid they were with hard life lessons, but he never figured Rob would do it to the mayor's kid. But this morning, there was something in Rob's smirk that made Frank very uncomfortable.

"If you try that stuff, you'll be barfing all the way to Leakey," Katrina warned.

Rob again glanced at Frank and slowly twisted the lid off the Copenhagen can again.

Frank furrowed his brow, shook his head, and mouthed the word, *NO!*

"Here you go," Rob said, handing the open can back to Jerry. "Have some."

Jerry snatched the can and smelled it. "Kind of smells funny. It's not past its expiration date, is it?"

Rob chuckled. "No such thing with Copenhagen."

Katrina had opened her book, but she wasn't reading. She kept her gaze on Jerry.

He sniffed the can again and asked, "So, how do I do this?"

Rob looked into the rear mirror and said, "Just get a pinch and tuck it between your cheek and lower gum."

"What do I do then?"

Rob smiled at Jerry. "Just enjoy the fresh, satisfying flavor."

"Jerry," Katrina said, "if you get sick, you're cleaning it up."

Jerry got a pinch and stuffed it in his lip. "I won't get sick."

Frank closed his eyes, lowered his head, and waited. It didn't take long.

In less than two minutes Jerry mumbled, "I'm feeling a little dizzy. You sure this stuff wasn't spoiled?"

"You're looking bad, Jerry, really bad," Katrina chimed in.

Frank again glanced in the visor mirror. The color had drained from Jerry's face, and he took deep breaths through his nose while staring at the floorboard. Some muscle in his throat pulsated, looking like an alien ready to break out of his neck.

Jerry pulled in a deep breath and said, "Don't worry, Kat, I've got this," then immediately gagged and vomited in the back floorboard behind Frank's seat.

Katrina scooted closer to the door. "You are GROSS and an idiot!"

When the smell hit Frank, his breakfast began rising in the back of his throat. He took a quick swallow of water and choked it down.

Rob showed a satisfied expression as he rolled down all the windows. They had just passed through Grand Prairie and were crossing Highway 360 when Jerry dropped his head to the back of the seat and moaned. Rob got off at the Division exit in Arlington and quickly found a service station. Katrina sprang from the car like it was on fire, cursing Jerry with every breath. She stomped toward the ladies' room still mumbling obscenities under her breath. Jerry slowly pulled himself from the backseat with vomit still on his pants and holding on to the car door for support. Frank gave him his half bottle of water and sent him to the men's room to clean up.

Frank was more than a little pissed. "We did not need this the first half hour of the trip."

Rob didn't answer. Just pulled out the rubber floorboard liner and hosed it down. He got a ratty towel from the trunk, soaked it, and scrubbed down the splatter on the back seat.

"That's not going to help with the smell," Frank said.

Rob returned to the trunk, produced a can of Lysol and sprayed down Jerry's side and floorboard.

"Wouldn't it have just been easier to tell the boy no?" Frank asked.

Rob threw the towel away, returned the Lysol to the trunk, and replaced the rubber liner before saying, "Probably." He headed to the men's room to wash up.

Frank leaned against the car in the blazing sunshine, waiting for everyone. The overpowering odor of Lysol mixed with Copenhagen and vomit wafted from the car's interior. His hatred of long drives was only surpassed by his hatred of smelly long drives.

***

ROB STROLLED into the men's room as Jerry was walking out. He lowered his head as they passed. After washing up, Rob went inside the convenience store and bought an air freshener. He had to admit he felt a slight tinge of remorse at the *life lesson* he'd taught Jerry. Figured the boy would be too embarrassed to tell his dad.

Everyone stood outside the car with the doors open as Rob

approached. He cranked the car, torqued up the AC, and rolled up the windows, then attached the pine tree air freshener to the rear mirror. Frank gave him a *Really?* look, and they were back on their way. Rob sniffed, the car didn't smell all that bad, especially if you worked in a hospital or jail. Frank readjusted the visor mirror to catch a better look at Katrina in back. Rob had noticed a change in Frank as of late. Seemed a little more settled in his relationship with Katrina. While he and Katrina both dated other people, Frank didn't seem to share his bed with as many women as before. Were he and Katrina more involved than Rob suspected? Frank had been enamored with the girl for almost two years since they had investigated her kidnapping. The fact she looked identical to his deceased wife was what drew him to her at first, but something deeper, more evolved had taken hold. Since Frank never discussed their relationship, Rob could only guess.

Frank worked his way into his favorite riding position and readjusted his sunglasses before taking a swallow of water. Katrina read a book, and Jerry laid his head on the seat with his eyes closed. He'd bought a Coke at the convenience store to settle his stomach. It rested between his legs. He took a sip every few minutes.

"Anyone care if I turn on the radio?" Rob asked.

"Just don't make it country and western," Jerry mumbled.

Country and western was exactly what Rob had in mind. He had an oldies C&W station he listened to driving to and from work. But he decided to take pity on poor Jerry this time, so he dialed the radio to a classic rock and roll station. The lyrics of Eric Clapton's *Layla* filled the car.

Frank rolled his head in Rob's direction and pulled down his sunglasses with his finger. From his expression Rob understood.

"Think I know a better station," Rob said and quickly changed the digital dial to a Rolling Stone's tune.

Once they got on I-20 heading to Weatherford, Rob relaxed. He never enjoyed driving in the city, but on the open road, he slipped into the zone. Especially when the open road was west of Fort Worth.

As the saying goes, where Fort Worth ends, the old West begins. This was the country Rob dreamed about. Being a cowboy or lawman in the mid-nineteenth century, maybe even a Texas Ranger. Camping on the open prairie, eating out of a chuckwagon or saddlebag, and riding horses all day. No long commutes in traffic, no long reports sitting at a desk. Yeah, that was a life he could embrace. Of course, he'd miss taking a hot shower every night, microwave popcorn, and ice-cold beer every evening, but he figured he could get used to not having all that.

A whimpering sound drifted from the back seat. Frank sat up and turned to Katrina. Rob tilted his head toward the rear mirror to see what was going on. She had stopped reading, and big tears slid down her cheeks. She let out a sniffle and placed a hand over her mouth.

"You okay?" Frank asked.

She didn't answer but nodded as more tears appeared in the corners of her eyes.

Frank kept eying her until she whispered, "Just thinking about Poppy." Her voice cracked on the last word.

Frank slid his left hand into the backseat area and Katrina grabbed it and held on for dear life.

Jerry's brow rose, seeing this sign of affection. He opened his mouth to speak, probably thought better of the idea, and laid his head back on the seat, closing his eyes.

This pretty much confirmed what Rob had suspected. Frank and Katrina had entered a new phase in their relationship.

The next couple of hours were fairly uneventful until Jerry awoke from his Copenhagen induced coma and announced he was hungry again. Katrina didn't chide him, so Rob suspected she was also hungry. The road sign indicated Comanche was twelve miles ahead. Rob bumped Frank's shoulder and he grunted.

"Ready to eat?" Rob asked.

Frank sat up, ran his hand down his mouth and chin, and then looked around with a confused expression. Rob was always amazed Frank had made it so long in law enforcement with such poor situational awareness. Cops were always supposed to know where they were so they could summon help. But Frank depended completely on Rob to keep up with such trivial things as current location while he napped.

"Where are we?" Frank asked.

"Just outside Comanche. Ready for lunch?"

Frank turned to the back seat. "You guys about ready to eat?"

"Great idea," Jerry agreed.

Katrina nodded before saying, "Fine with me."

Frank opened his smartphone and typed for a minute before saying, "Mexican food fine for everyone?"

"I'll say," Jerry said.

Katrina said, "Yup."

Rob smiled. "Proves you still love me, Frank."

Rob parked in front of Lozano's Mexican restaurant in Comanche just before noon. The place was almost full, but they found a table near the window and ordered. Rob sat beside Jerry while Katrina and Frank sat across from them. Katrina let her hand slip under the table and onto Frank's leg. He placed his hand on hers.

"We have about another two hundred miles to go. Should make it in three hours," Rob said as he looked at the menu.

Jerry stared at Rob. "Can I see your gun?"

Rob slowly turned his head Jerry's way. "What?"

"What kind of gun do you guys carry. Can I see it?"

Rob pursed his lips before saying, "NOOO!"

"Why? I like guns. I know how to shoot."

Rob had turned back to Jerry, but before he could answer him, Katrina spoke.

"He does know a lot. Shoots every week at the gun club."

Rob was shocked. A gamer nerd who was also a barrel sucker. Who would have thunk? "We carry the Sig Sauer P226, and I am not showing it to you in a restaurant full of people."

"Oh, yeah. I've shot one of those," Jerry said. "German 9mm, right?"

"Yeah," Rob answered, and another tinge of embarrassment crept into him at having played the Copenhagen trick on the poor kid. This boy wasn't all bad if he was a barrel sucker like most cops. Most cops, that is except Frank. Guy hated guns, which was unusual because he was a great shot. Never practiced, but outshot Rob and most other detectives at every scheduled qualification—a natural.

They snacked on chips and salsa until the meals arrived. Katrina kept them entertained, reminiscing about her grandfather. Everyone ordered the Lozano's lunch plate, which consisted of pork with tomatoes, onions, and jalapeños served over rice and beans. The white corn tortillas were easily the best Rob had eaten since leaving home as an eighteen-year-old kid to join the Marines.

This trip wasn't turning out to be as bad as he'd feared.

TWENTY-THREE

Perry silently opened the door and peered into the almost dark room. Only a dim floor lamp shined from the desk by the wall. Place had a rich, old leather smell. Could make out shadows of other pieces of expensive furniture around the room, but Perry's concentration centered on the desk and man writing something in a notebook-looking thing. Complete silence filled the place as Perry eased the door further open and approached his dad, Mayor Wayne Wallace.

He didn't notice Perry's approach at first, writing furiously in the notebook. The man did resemble Perry a little, or did Perry resemble him? He didn't speak, only walked softly, so as not to disturb whatever his dad was working on. A board creaked underfoot, and Perry froze.

Mayor Wallace's head rose from his writing and turned Perry's way. His mouth flew open and the voice rose to a high pitch when he asked, "Who are you?"

This was the moment Perry had planned for most of his life, but he couldn't think how to answer. Silly, really. Something this big, something he'd worked this hard to achieve, and he was tongue-tied.

Should he tell the mayor he was his son first and then introduce himself, or introduce himself and then tell the mayor he was his son. For someone who could always think of something to say, Perry was at a complete loss for words. He smiled, stepped forward, and in his quiet voice said, "It's me, Dad. Your son, Perry, from Georgia."

His dad's brow wrinkled, and he stared at Perry for what seemed like minutes but was probably only a couple of seconds. A broad smile broke out on his dad's lips. He walked over to Perry and threw both arms around him, pulling him into a strong embrace. "Thank god, I've finally found you, son."

The slamming of a car door awoke Perry from the best dream he'd ever had. He never had good dreams, only nightmares. The morning was already hot. Sweat trickled down his cheek as he slowly opened his eyes and the filtered sunlight reflected off the windshield of the police car parked behind him. Perry straightened up in the driver's seat and eyed the officer as she strolled up to the driver's side of his truck. She wore the gray uniform of a DPS Texas State Trooper. Her brown hair was pulled up in a bun that rested behind her head. Her hand rested on the pistol she carried in the black holster.

This wasn't the first time Perry had been rousted while sleeping in a public park. He seldom spent money when traveling, even on cheap motel rooms, if sleeping in his truck was an option. He always made sure before he napped that if a cop woke him, they'd find nothing to arrest him for. That's why, when he arrived in the quiet city park earlier this morning, he'd dumped all the empty beer cans in the trash can before settling down to sleep. He'd driven through the night, and the day before had been a hard one. Must have been tired. Couldn't believe he'd slept so long. Perry had his story set as she walked up to the window.

"Morning officer," Perry said in his quiet voice.

"More like afternoon," she replied.

Perry checked his watch—12:34. *Shit.* "Yes, ma'am, good afternoon."

The trooper cranked her neck, catching a glimpse inside the truck before asking, "What are you doing?"

Perry had learned a long time ago how to tell a convincing lie. Hell, most of his life had been one big deception. He understood from her expression that she must realize he'd been sleeping. *Never start a police interview with a lie you can get caught in.*

"Just catching a few winks before finishing my trip, officer."

The trooper's eyes pinched. She stepped back from the door and unsnapped her holster. "Please step out of the truck."

"Yes, ma'am."

Perry knew why she wanted him out of the truck, so he couldn't grab a hidden gun. Perry knew a lot about the police. Watched every cop show on television. Knew how they thought. Understood their procedures. Heck, he could probably pass himself off as a cop if he needed to. She should be more concerned about him grabbing her. Perry didn't need a gun. Never owned one—terrible shot anyway. As powerful as he was, he could attack or defend with just his bare hands, or if needed, his knife. He stood erect outside the truck, towering over the short trooper and stared at her. Didn't need any trouble from this one. Perry was on a mission. *Just leave me alone and let me be on my way. No one has to get hurt today.*

"You have any identification?" she asked. "A driver's license, maybe?"

"Yes, ma'am." Perry quickly pulled out his wallet and produced a Mississippi driver's license.

The trooper studied it a moment before asking, "This your current address?"

"Yes, ma'am."

She glanced again into the open door of the truck before asking, "Were you drinking last night?"

"Oh, no ma'am."

She glanced at the license, grinned, and squared her shoulders. "Why are you sleeping in a park in Texas if you live in Hattiesburg, Mississippi?"

Perry had told some version of this lie to so many people he didn't have to think about it—rolled off his tongue with ease. First Perry had to set the stage. He showed his best embarrassed expression. This usually meant a grimace first and a foot shuffle next. He spoke slowly in his best aw-shucks tone.

"Figured you ask about that."

She raised her eyebrows and waited.

"Fact is, just drove in from Clovis."

"What you doing out there?"

"Working, doing carpentry, mostly sheetrocking."

She cocked her to the side. "What?"

"It's true. Just left one job, heading to another."

She moved back a step and cocked her head again. "I think you should explain."

This was Perry's favorite part of the lie. He changed it up enough to suit the circumstance but kept the basic story. "Well, it all started when I got divorced. Wife kept the house and kids. I moved in with my mom for a while, until we got on each other's nerves. Heard about a job in Tulsa, big apartment project. So, I loaded up all my tools and headed out. Have to do something to keep up child support." He flashed his most innocent grin. "Sort of enjoy traveling, seeing and living in different parts of the country. Anyway, the job played out last month and I heard about another one in Clovis. When it ended, got the word about a new project in San Antonio. Another big apartment job."

"Are you telling me you work all over the southwest?"

Perry shrugged. "Have to go where the high-paying work is. Nothing much going on east of the Mississippi."

She nodded, still studying his license. "So, this address in Mississippi is your permanent address?"

"Yes, ma'am. Well, my mama's, anyway."

Her tongue poked inside her cheek as she considered his story. "Okay, if you become a permanent resident of Texas, you'll need a new license. I think I understand—divorces can be tough."

She handed him back his license, whirled around, and headed back to her patrol car.

Perry let out a sigh and got back into his truck. He carefully placed the genuine Mississippi license on the right side of his wallet beside his genuine Social Security card. Perry lived by rules: Always present your genuine identification with your real name to cops. They had the training to spot fakes. Always live and work under fake last names. Getting a counterfeit driver's license and social security card was easy. That's all he needed at most check cashing places. Besides, he usually looked for cash-paying jobs.

Perry cranked his truck and backed up. He glanced south at the billowing clouds rolling in—looked like rain. Must be part of the storm hitting the coast he'd heard about on the radio last night. He shifted into gear and drove toward the main road. As he took a left on Highway 83, he glanced at the sign outside the park entrance. Never noticed it as he drove in before dawn this morning—Frio Canyon Park, just inside the city limits of Leakey.

AFTER THE MEAL, Frank led the way outside. He stopped and stared at the southern sky. A dark horizon looked back at him.

"Wow," Rob said. He stood beside Frank. "Looks nasty."

"Yeah, might switch on the weather," Frank said.

Rob cranked up the air conditioner to full before turning in the seat and drawing his pistol. He held it up for Jerry to see.

Jerry smiled. "Nice, is that a fifteen-round magazine?"

Rob pushed the magazine release button and held up the magazine. "Yup, and hollow points."

Jerry stared wide-eyed with his mouth open. "Are those night sights?"

"Yeah," Rob answered.

"A sweet set-up. Shot one like it a few months ago. That's what I'm asking for when I turn eighteen."

Frank tuned the radio to a news station before staring at Rob with a disinterested expression. Like the one you showed someone when you already knew the punchline to a joke but allowed the person to keep telling it just to be polite. Frank was ready to talk about anything other than guns. "Ready to go, Rob?"

Rob replaced the magazine in the pistol and slipped it back into its holster. Just as he pulled back on the highway, the forecast came on:

The National Weather Service announced Hurricane Kate has just made landfall on the lower Texas coast between Port Aransas and Corpus Christi. The eye passed over Mustang Island only moments ago, and the storm is tracking due northwest as it approaches Ingleside and Portland. This is a dangerous category four hurricane with maximum sustained winds of 147 miles per hour. Residents are instructed to shelter in place and avoid low-lying areas because this is a rainmaker. Catastrophic flooding is expected as it moves inland. This slow-moving storm could spawn tornados in its wake. Stay tuned to this station for updates as they become available.

Frank turned off the radio and caught Katrina's worried expression from the back seat. "Don't worry. We're over two hundred miles inland. The storm probably won't affect the graveside service tomorrow."

Katrina shook her head. "Service isn't tomorrow. It's this evening after we arrive."

"Huh?"

"Yeah, thought you knew," Katrina said. "We arrive at four, clean up, change clothes, and drive over to the family cemetery. Service is at six this evening."

Crap! It aggravated Frank no one bothered to tell them when the service was. He and Rob had assumed it would be the following day. He checked his watch and looked over at Rob.

Rob must have read his mind. "No problems. Got plenty of time."

This was why Frank hated working dignitary protection assignments. It was always a hurry-up and wait situation. Always at the beck and call of the dignitary. This wasn't real police work. It was armed babysitting. Frank went out of his way to avoid every dignitary protection assignment. Didn't understand how those Secret Service types didn't lose their minds doing it for years at a time. Rob never minded the hurry up and wait. Probably because of his military days.

PERRY DROVE south on Highway 83 until it became Market Street inside the city of Leakey. He'd stopped at a McDonald's drive-thru before leaving Dallas last night but missed breakfast—wanted something heavy for lunch. When Hillside Barbecue appeared on the right, his mouth watered. He ordered a sliced BBQ beef sandwich with fries and a soft drink from the takeout window. There were tables under a metal carport-looking thing at the entrance, so he took his drink to a table and waited for his order.

The weather was hotter and more humid than Dallas. Perry needed a place to clean up and make himself presentable before meeting his dad. But he still had no real plan. He'd read in the paper before leaving Dallas that there would be a private graveside service at the family cemetery at the Wallace ranch. *Where was the ranch?*

As Perry pondered this dilemma, a Real County Sheriff's Department patrol vehicle pulled up. Perry tensed. Had the DPS trooper contacted the locals to keep a lookout for Perry's truck? Was this another roust, or something more serious? The deputy got out of the car and left it running. He walked directly toward Perry's table. Big deputy, at least Perry's size if not bigger. His biceps and triceps strained the material of the short sleeve shirt. He wore sunglasses and had a short buzz-cut. Just a brown stubble outlined his large head. As Perry considered standing up to meet the threat, the deputy veered to the left a little and approached the takeout window. Perry slowly released a breath, keeping his eyes on the big cop.

"Hey, Erik," the girl at the takeout window said. "Your order's almost ready, just another minute. Surprised you called it in and not eating here."

The deputy leaned against the counter, wiped a bead of sweat from under his chin, and sighed. "Yeah, well, just got the word. I'm doing a short change today. Have to go back in at midnight."

"Why are you doing such a crazy shift?"

"Sheriff's idea. Keeping a patrol car out at the Wallace place while the family is in the area. Looks like I'm pulling a couple of mids. Figured I'd eat lunch at home and grab a few winks."

Perry tilted his head toward the officer.

The girl said, "Yeah, heard the Dallas mayor's arriving today."

"Already there. Just flew in on a private plane. Waiting on the rest of the family to arrive later today."

"Sir, your order's ready... sir, sir, your order's ready."

Perry turned around as the girl at the takeout motioned for him. He walked to the window and collected his sandwich and fries. He nodded to the deputy a few feet to his right, and the deputy nodded. As Perry turned back toward his table, he glanced at the deputy's nametag—E. Therme.

Perry sat down just as the girl at the window said, "Here you go, Erik. Yours is ready."

The deputy took the paper bag back to his patrol car and left. Perry finished his sandwich and strolled back to the takeout window. Needed to handle this carefully. No need to rush, just play it slow. He flashed his best *nice guy* smile at the chubby redhead inside at the takeout window. She wore white shorts and a black T-shirt with Willie Nelson's photo blazed across the front. Her thighs stretched the shorts so much it left a red line around the bottom of her leg.

Using his quiet voice, Perry said, "Not from around Leakey, but want to ask a question."

She smiled. "Know you're not from here."

Perry leaned on the takeout counter. "Oh, yeah. Did my accent give me away?"

"No, never seen you before and you can't even pronounce the name of the town."

"Huh?"

"We don't pronounce it LEE-key. It's LAY-kee."

Perry made a mental note—this was important. "Hey, thanks for setting me straight. Couldn't help overhearing your conversation with the officer a minute ago. Y'all talking about Mayor Wayne Wallace from Dallas?"

"Sure was," she answered.

Perry drew a little closer. "Wow, I'm from around Dallas. Just down here for a little R&R on the Frio River. Never imagined the mayor would also be here."

"He's not here to party. Father died—having a private graveside service."

Perry frowned. "Really?"

"Yup, dad has a big ranch outside of town."

"I've never seen a big ranch before."

"Well, you can't do anything but drive by the Wallace place. But it's worth the drive. Beautiful spread." She scribbled a crude map on a paper napkin and slid it to Perry.

"Hey, thanks." He folded the map and stuck it into his shirt pocket.

ROB FELT bad about the way he'd treated Jerry earlier—not a bad kid. Jerry was back playing games on his phone, and Katrina's head started bobbing as soon as they got back in the car. She loosely held her book in her lap and her breathing had become slow and shallow. Her eyelids fluttered every so often. She'd be asleep in a few minutes. Fortunately, the Mexican food hadn't put Frank asleep. He stared at the maps app on his phone and ran his tongue along his lower lip. He looked Rob's way.

"Our best route is Highway 16 South out of Fredericksburg and hop over to Highway 41."

Rob had memorized the route before leaving Dallas. That was his gift—remembering road numbers. "Got it. We can catch 336 from there. Ranch is off 336, near the headwaters of the Frio River."

Frank said, "Now I understand why they told us suit and tie for the trip. Didn't realize graveside service was today."

Rob shrugged. "Who cares when it is? Today, tomorrow, the day after. Pays the same." He looked around and grinned at Frank. He knew it bugged the hell out of him. Frank hated surprises, always had. But to be honest, Rob hated them, too. Not getting all the necessary information in a timely manner aggravated him as much as Frank. No use letting Frank know. Let him stew awhile.

Frank shifted in the seat and kept scrolling on his cell's map. Probably double-checking the road numbers Rob just gave him. Frank's eyes narrowed and lips pressed into a white slash. He closed the app and rested his head against the seat. His gaze stayed on the darkening sky to the south. "Wonder what's happening on the coast?"

"I don't have to wonder, I know," Rob said. "We rode out several hurricanes when I lived there as a kid. When the weather guy uses a word like a rainmaker, that's not good. Most hurricanes deaths are caused by drowning."

PERRY NOW HAD the kernel of a plan developing in his mind. It would solve all his problems and get him close enough to finally meet his dad. But he needed to get cleaned up. His first stop was the barbershop, then the drug store, and finally checking into a private cabin at the Historic Leakey Inn. He showered, shaved, and worked on his hair.

Perry stepped back from the mirror and admired his work. Not bad. Hadn't looked this respectable in years. He propped up several pillows on the bed and relaxed while drinking a beer and reading the local paper. It was yesterday's edition, but Perry still found it interesting. That's the way Perry enjoyed getting his news—hated TV. He could pick up a paper anywhere and discover the local goings-on. Wouldn't hurt to know a little more about the Real County area. The paper said there would not be a formal funeral service for Mr. Wallace, just a memorial service at the Methodist church on Friday. Only the family would gather for a graveside service at the ranch later. *Damn, missed the memorial service by a day.* Perry turned the page and read about a house fire in the area. An unidentified body was found in the back bedroom. Tests were underway to determine the identity.

Perry sat the paper aside and stared at the opposite wall a moment, remembering the last time he saw his mom. He was fifteen years old, but because of his size, looked eighteen or older. Perry rode his bicycle home from spending the evening with some friends at their house. He never invited friends to his house; it was a wreck and smelled bad. Perry had already eaten dinner with his buddies; their mom was a great cook. All he wanted was to shower, watch some TV, and go to bed. As he walked up to the front door, an ugly, rough-looking man walked out. He had hard features, long unruly hair and beard, and eyes that scared you. The man nodded Perry's way and zipped up his jeans. Perry stopped short of the door and watched him march to his truck.

The house was dark and lonely. Only a dim light shined from his mom's room down the hall. Perry crept to the bathroom. If she knew he was home, she'd start fussing about something again—always did. He hated her fussing. She never had a pleasant thing to say anymore. Her beauty had abandoned her years earlier because of age and drugs. Her long stringy hair hung limp and had reverted to its natural blonde with streaks of gray. She'd lost so much weight, her cheeks had collapsed into her face, giving her a skeletal appearance. Sores sprouted from her neck and arms. Their only income was from men who visited in the evenings and welfare checks.

Perry softly closed the bathroom door and showered. After finishing, he opened the shower curtain, and she stood leaning against the door frame. She'd taken his towel from the top of the toilet, and he stood naked gazing at her. She grinned, looking just below his waist.

"You've grown into quite a boy."

Perry drew the curtain and covered himself.

His mother pulled her dress over her head, revealing her nakedness. Her glazed-over eyes and wobbly stance scared Perry. *Did she want him to...?*

She strolled to the shower and jerked the curtain from Perry's grip. "Come on, big boy, let's see how much of a man you are." She grabbed his hand and led him out of the bathroom, dripping water all the way. When she pulled him down the hall to her bedroom, his mind started to drift. He felt himself drifting toward the bubble of bright colors and soft music he loved so much when he needed an escape from the reality of life.

Perry was petrified. She was so small and weak he could easily pull away, but the hold she had over him was more mental than physical. She always knew how to manipulate him into doing whatever she wanted, and he hated her for it. But just like so many years ago, when he'd been terrified and locked away for days in the small, dark closet, his mind finally broke free from reality. It traveled to the wonderful land of beautiful sounds, vivid colors, and soft music. A place of refuge, a place he felt safe and protected and loved. A place he didn't want to leave. He didn't know how much time had passed before he came back to his senses. He and his mom lay on their backs, naked in her bed. His wet, sweaty body gave him a chill as he opened his eyes and ran his hand down his stomach to his crotch. Something gooey and slimy met his touch. He jerked his hand back. The shock and horror of what he'd done—what his mother had done to him— finally sank in. His chest tightened and it became hard to breathe.

Tears formed and clouded his eyes. The son of a crack whore who was no better than her. This would be his life until he left home. Perry had run away twice before, but they always found him and brought him back. But he'd learned from his past mistakes. He now understood what he must do to survive. Staying here wasn't surviving. He was disgusted by the woman and the life she'd forced on him. There was a freight train that blew its whistle every night at ten-thirty. Perry used to lay in bed and wait until the sound floated into his bedroom. Tonight, he'd be on that freight. Didn't know where it went—didn't care. As long as it was away from here.

While his mother dozed in her drug-induced slumber, Perry threw some things into the largest backpack he had. As he started for the back door, he recalled why he'd always been caught and returned home. The bitch called the cops and they made sure to bring him back to his abuser. He wouldn't let that happen this time; he couldn't let that happen. Perry collected all the stacks of newspapers, plastic bags, and dirty paper plates and hauled them into the bedroom. He wadded up the papers and built a waist-high wall of trash around her bed. She moaned once and rolled over as he constructed her funeral pyre. From her dresser, he snatched the lighter fluid and doused the trash. Perry took one long last long look at her. He loved her, and he hated her. They'd been so happy before with the dentist, and now here they were, together in their own miseries. He struck the match and walked around the bed, lighting the paper in a half dozen places before stepping back as the fire caught hold and spread.

Perry could never understand, much less explain, why he stood there so long, watching the fire lick the bottom of the sheets and blanket. The bright red and yellow flames fascinated and terrified him. Once the mattress caught, the room was so filled with smoke he could hardly see or breathe. The heat finally woke her. She screamed something and formed herself into a tight ball, crying for help. Perry's eyes burned and the smoke choked him, but still he stayed, mesmerized by the fire. She again screamed, over and over, louder and louder. Feeling light-headed, Perry dashed from the room and outside into the fresh night air. Their house was down an old dirt road in the country. No one to call 911 or hear the screams and pleas for help.

Perry stood back from the intense heat near the back door until the cries stopped. He didn't know how to feel—sad, liberated, or nothing at all. The numbness told Perry he'd done the right thing, the only thing he could do. The miserable bitch needed to be put down. Only decent thing he could do.

Perry hoisted the backpack onto his shoulder, turned toward the dark woods, and walked in the direction of the railroad tracks.

TWENTY-FOUR

Frank had just started becoming bored with the trip when Katrina touched Rob's shoulder.

"Two more hills and it's on the right," she said.

Frank checked his maps app on his cell again and confirmed the address of the ranch. He had been to the Texas Hill Country before. A few trips west of Austin, Fredericksburg, and even a winery in Luckenbach. But the scenery passing by his window was like nothing he'd seen. Deep gullies, tall hills, rock outcroppings that went on for miles. The sky had darkened to the point it resembled twilight. A light wind blew the leaves of the live oaks, and the rolling clouds gave the sky a surreal appearance.

Rob slowed down as they coasted to the bottom of the second hill and turned right. They drove another couple of miles before a stream of water trickled over a concrete low water crossing. On the other side, there was a police vehicle and an eight-foot-tall stone wall with a reinforced metal gate.

"This is part of the headwaters of the Frio River," Katrina said, motioning at the stream.

Rob eased over the low water crossing. The splashing water

against the underside of the car caused him to slow down. The officer in the patrol car waved and hung his hand out of the car window. He pointed a remote at the metal gate, and it slowly opened. On the door of the police car was a star and the words, Real County Sheriff's Department. Rob waved back his thanks to the deputy, and they drove through the gate and into the wilderness of the Wallace Ranch.

Frank craned his neck in all directions. Nothing but pasture with a few live oaks and post oaks scattered across the vast rocky landscape. "Your grandfather did like his privacy."

"Poppy loved this country. The deeper he lived in it, the better," she said.

Frank focused on a large oak they passed. Years ago, someone had nailed a metal cross onto the young tree. The cross was about a foot tall, and over the years the tree had begun growing around it. That in itself wasn't unusual. But someone had recently painted the cross blood red. A chill ran up Frank's back, but he didn't understand why.

After another five minutes of traveling down the gravel road, a house came into view. A house surrounded by dozens of live oaks, their limbs pruned high. A house that looked familiar to Frank.

Rob slightly turned his head to Frank. "You have to be kidding," Rob said under his breath.

The two-story English-style country house sprawled across a great lawn of buffalo grass. It was a replica of the mayor's house in Dallas, or to be more correct, the mayor's house was a replica of this house. Some kind of weird psychological father and son thing probably going on here.

"Not kidding," Frank mumbled back.

Katrina started unbuckling her seatbelt before the car stopped. Another sheriff's department car sat under a tree near the front of the home, and Sergeant Miller from DPD and an older man in uniform talked. There was a large piece of paper draped on the car's hood.

Katrina bolted from the car, and Jerry wasn't far behind. They greeted the older man in uniform like long lost friends. He was short, heavyset and had graying hair along the temples. His salt and pepper mustache widened as he laughed and hugged them.

"Almost didn't recognize you two—you're already grown."

Frank and Rob took their time strolling to where Sergeant Miller waited. Frank continued studying the great house. There were a few differences from the mayor's home in Dallas. This house was built with the native limestone found in Central Texas. This house had lightning rods strategically positioned around the roofline, and the roof wasn't slate like the mayor's house. It appeared to be some kind of brown metal alloy.

Miller said, "Guys, meet Sheriff Dwayne Garcia. Been sheriff around these parts longer than you've been on the PD."

Rob and Frank greeted the sheriff with a handshake, and Frank stared at the large paper on the car's hood—a map.

"Boys," Sergeant Miller said. "Sheriff Garcia was just going over the security arrangements. Looks like he has things well in hand. Not much for us to do."

Rob flashed a sideways look Frank's way. No telling what he and the sheriff had planned for them.

Miller wiped a bead of sweat from his cheek and waved his hand over the map. "This is the ranch, a little over twenty-five hundred acres." He pointed to a thin blue line. "The Frio River is its western boundary." He looked up. "You just crossed it a minute ago."

Frank studied the map as Miller spoke. While the two houses were the same basic layout, the grounds were very different. The mayor had a tennis court and pool. His dad had passed on that idea but instead constructed a guest cottage and an English-style maze and flower garden in the back.

"We'll keep a deputy at the ranch entrance to shoo away the curious onlookers during the visit," the sheriff said. He handed Miller a folded piece of paper. I'll be back here tomorrow morning. Deputy David Flores is out there right now on the gate, and Deputy Erik Therme will be here at midnight. Their cell numbers are listed here."

He pointed to the bottom of the paper. "Just call if you have a problem."

"Thank you, sheriff," Miller said. He eyed Rob and Frank. "The sheriff will attend the funeral at the cemetery—family friend. He'll keep an eye on everyone until they get back to the house. We'll do a tour of the residence while they're at the service and familiarize ourselves with the layout, ingress and egress points, and establish a hard room in case of emergencies."

Miller turned to the sheriff and extended his hand. "Thank you for your assistance."

Garcia shook it, hoisted up his Sam Browne belt, and said, "Sergeant, it's our pleasure. Mr. Wallace gave so much to this community, it's the least we could do. I met him thirty years ago when I was a young deputy. We became friends, and I watched those two grandchildren of his grow up during summer visits. You have the complete cooperation of the Real County Sheriff's Department. All you have to do is ask."

"I appreciate that," Miller said. He eyed Rob and Frank. "Pull around back to the guest cottage and we'll get you settled."

After following the driveway to the rear of the great house, Rob parked near a wisteria-covered arbor beside the English-style cottage. Giant oaks surrounded it, and numerous native plants, wildflowers, and roses filled the small, shaded yard, outlining the path to the front door.

"This guy loves the English, don't he?" Rob said as he unloaded the bags.

When Rob opened the cottage door, Frank said, "Yeah, he's an Anglophile."

"A what?"

"Anglophile."

"What's that?"

"A person who loves England."

Rob grunted. "Thought that's what I just said."

The interior of the cottage was what Frank expected, kitchenette and living room combination with a small dining area to one side. Cozy and rustic design with gently worn antique furniture. The lace window coverings allowed in just enough light to give it a quiet, soft feel. The air-conditioning was a welcome relief.

Sergeant Miller pointed to a door on the left. "That's y'all's room. I have this one," he said, pointing to the right.

Frank and Rob dropped their bags at the foot of their double beds.

"I'm grabbing a quick shower," Frank said.

Two hours later, Frank, Rob, and Sergeant Miller stood by the front door as the five vehicles drove to the cemetery. There were several people Frank didn't know in the funeral party. Probably brothers and sisters of the mayor. The look in Katrina's eyes before she left broke Frank's heart. She wanted him with her, to support her at the service. He wanted to be there, but it could never be. The full impact of a secret relationship with the mayor's daughter finally hit him. It could never work long term. Doomed from the start. Whatever Katrina's plan was for them wouldn't work with her family. *"I don't expect to see you sitting across from me at Thanksgiving dinner, ever."*

PERRY SAT on the high hill across the Frio River from the Wallace ranch. The bluff had a scenic-overlook feel. The land opened up for miles in all directions. The light wind cooled the evening, and the smell of rain hung in the air as heavy as the humidity. He kept the binoculars pressed to his eyes as the line of cars, led by the police car, weaved their way along a solitary road to a group of live oaks in an open field. The directions from the redhead at the BBQ restaurant had been pretty good. Perry shifted the binoculars to the sheriff's department vehicle parked just across the Frio River guarding the front gate—one guy inside. Hadn't figured on that, but it could all work to his benefit. He shifted back to the vehicles parked around the trees. He recognized the mayor and his family. Didn't know the others, all dressed in black, walking through the metal gate. A waist-high stone wall enclosed the place. *This was the private funeral service.* He should be there. A profound sadness coursed through him at the thought that his grandfather was being buried without him. Why was it always this way? Never included. Why, just once, couldn't he be a part of the group?

"What are you doing?" a voice behind him asked.

Perry swung around and eyed the man sitting on the horse thirty feet away—never heard him approach. The old guy had gray curls that almost covered his ears trailing from his well-worn brown cowboy hat. He wore a white cowboy shirt with the sleeves rolled to the elbows. Perry stood. This wasn't good, getting caught so early in the game—*be cool.*

"Oh, hello," Perry said. "I'm just doing a little sight-seeing, that's all."

"Sight-seeing, huh?" The man sat higher in the saddle and stared across the road toward the cemetery. "Don't look like you doing anything but snooping to me. This is private land."

"Didn't know that," Perry said.

The old man chuckled and pointed down the road Perry had driven up to get to the bluff. "You passed two NO TRESPASSING signs on your way here. What's the matter, can't read?" He pulled a piece of paper and pen from his shirt pocket and stared at the back of Perry's truck.

"What are you doing?" Perry asked.

"Sheriff said next time I caught someone trespassing to give the license plate number to him and they'll handle it."

Perry's gut tightened as he slowly closed the distance between him and the old man. As a distraction, Perry casually removed his wallet from his back pocket with one hand and smiled, offering it to the man. "I do apologize, sir. I'd be happy to pay for the privilege of being here if that's all right. Just take out what you think's fair."

The old guy glanced up from writing as Perry carefully approached.

With his other hand, Perry already had the knife ready to open.

———

FRANK, Rob, and Sergeant Miller walked from room to room in the main house as Miller pointed out security-related issues like which doors were to remain locked and which were kept unlocked. They toured the upstairs hall leading to the mayor's bedroom and talked about evacuation routes in case of a fire or other emergencies.

Frank had been in lots of wealthy persons' homes during his years with Dallas PD, but this wasn't what he expected. The furnishings and window coverings were expensive, but probably within the budgets of most of the non-wealthy. The place had a well-worn, homey look you see in many homes of the older generation. Unlike the mayor's home in Dallas, this place looked lived in and cozy. No leather furniture, but muted-design fabric chairs and sofas scattered near windows throughout the mansion. *Great reading rooms.*

Sergeant Miller ended the tour with, "I'm concerned about this weather. Listened to the forecast before you arrived. The remains of this hurricane are heading directly for us. They say it's dropping as much water as Hurricane Harvey did on Houston. Can't see much chance of us getting out of here by plane tomorrow. Might try driving if the mayor wants to, we'll see."

Frank's favorite parts of the tour had been the library and kitchen. The library had a formal, aristocratic look. Floor-to-ceiling mahogany bookcases with beautifully bound volumes of English and American authors. Antique world maps hung from the walls, and the centerpiece was a massive oak desk that was probably over a hundred years old. They were introduced to Felix and Delma in the kitchen. Felix was the ranch manager, and Delma was his wife and the cook. She was an attractive Hispanic woman, short and round, while Felix was a not-so-handsome Anglo, tall and skinny—seemed like the perfect match. She had dinner in the oven, and the place smelled like heaven to Frank—loved homemade Mexican cooking, even if that's what he had for lunch.

Miller told them all the domestic help had the weekend off except for Felix and Delma. Since they were the only house staff who lived on the ranch, it wasn't a big deal. They had a small home about a mile from the main house. Felix could fix anything that broke, and Delma would make sure everyone was properly fed.

Ten minutes later, the cars arrived back at the main house as the first drops of rain began falling. As everyone ran inside, the sheriff strolled up to Rob, Frank, and Miller. "Glad that's over," he said. He held up his phone. "Just got a text about a missing man I need to check out." He pointed toward the road Rob and Frank had driven down hours earlier. "Guy owns the property across the river. He went for a horse ride and never came back." Sheriff Garcia glanced at the low-hanging clouds. "I'd better get a move on. Call if you need something."

Frank also gazed at the sky. It had turned a light shade of green, with rolling puffs of black clouds rushing over at incredible speeds. Reminded Frank of the way the sky looked in the movie *Independence Day*, just before the aliens zapped the crowd of new-age greeters on the roof of the building. Frank lifted his sensitive nose and took in the scent of the approaching storm. A fresh, earthy, ozone smell greeted him. Frank had experienced this before as a kid in Florida and for sure in the tornado alley city of Dallas. Yeah, this one's going to be a doozy.

ROB AND FRANK followed Sergeant Miller at a trot around the side of the house as the rain picked up. Rob hated rain during protection assignments. Somehow, he always managed to get soaked by the end of the shift. At least they could work this assignment from inside. They made it under the small, covered porch of the cottage when

Frank's phone rang. Sergeant Miller went inside, and Frank dug his cell from his pocket.

"Pierce."

Frank's face registered confusion as he listened to the caller. "No, I haven't. When's the last time for you? Okay, if I hear anything I'll let you know. Shoot me a call if you find out anything."

Frank scrolled through past text messages and recent calls on his phone as he chewed his lower lip.

"Who was that?"

Frank kept searching his phone and said, "Sanders."

"Who?"

"Agent Sanders, FBI, Layla's partner."

Frank dropped the phone in his pocket. "Layla didn't make the eight o'clock meeting this morning. Doesn't answer her phone and not in her room."

Rob shifted his feet and stared at the sheets of rain sweeping across the lawn and splattering on the driveway. "What are you thinking?"

Frank didn't answer for several seconds. His eyes scanned the large house just as the drapes from a downstairs window pulled back. Katrina stared back at him, smiled, and offered a short, sad wave. He waved back. "Nothing... I'm not thinking a single thing."

Miller sat in the small cottage living room and tinkered with a walkie-talkie as Rob and Frank entered. The rain falling on the roof sounded like a stampede overhead. Miller had turned on the TV and the picture of a weather map, with warnings scrolling past the bottom of the screen, lit the room.

"This storm is going to be worse than we figured," Miller said as he pointed to the screen. "This is just the leading edge. The main show will roll in later tonight. Already, tornado warnings for us and the surrounding counties." He held up the walkie-talkie. "Keep this radio on channel three at all times. The mayor has a panic alarm on his person. If there's a problem, all he does is press the button on top or tip it to a horizontal position and we'll hear the alarm here," Miller said, waving the radio back and forth. "Keep the radios on even when you are sleeping. If there's a problem, we'll need everybody." Satisfied with his briefing, Miller sat back on the soft couch and studied the TV weather summary. "Okay, I've got things under control until ten o'clock, boys. You guys get cleaned up, rested, and fed. You'll handle things tonight. I'll pick it up again at eight tomorrow. Delma said she'd make sure we got supper after the rest eat."

"Fine, I'm hitting the showers," Rob said on the way to the bedroom.

WHILE ROB SHOWERED, Frank laid on his bed and thought of Layla. He didn't want to, but every time he let his mind wander, it defaulted back to her. *Where was she?* She wouldn't miss work unless... Nah, she'd never travel out here. What would be the use? Frank needed to concentrate on Katrina and not Layla.

Three soft knocks echoed from the corner of the room. Frank sat up and tilted his head. The storm was blowing debris everywhere. The bumps of something hitting the house and constant rumble of rain on the roof made it difficult to discern three individual knocks. Frank figured it was his imagination. A moment later another three knocks from the same location. Sounded like it came from inside the closet. Frank eased to the closet and opened the door. Another three knocks sounded from the other side of the back closet wall. Frank took a step back—he had no idea. Was Rob knocking from the bathroom adjacent to the closet? Not knowing what to do Frank asked, "Who's there?"

"Okay if I come in?"

Katrina! "Sure."

The rolling of wheels drifted from the back of the closet as the wood panel slowly moved to the right. Katrina stuck her head through the opening and grinned.

"Called ahead and told them to put you and Rob in this room."

Ducking under the closet clothes bar, she rushed into Frank's arms. Before he could say a word, she kissed him hard. Her grip on his shoulders and back seemed like she was holding on for dear life. Her voice choked with emotion. "God, this feels so right. Please just hold me, Frank."

It felt *so right* for Frank also. During the trip, he'd suppressed a desire to hold and kiss her. Not a sexual desire, but more of a love desire. Just being with her now would have to do for the moment.

The shower turned off as Frank and Katrina embraced outside the closet.

"This has been a hard day. A really hard day," she said.

Frank rubbed her back and whispered into her ear, "I know, but it's over. You okay?"

Katrina didn't answer, but the nodding of her head against his cheek was enough.

The door to the bathroom swung open and Rob emerged dressed only in boxers, whistling some country and western tune. He saw her about the time she saw him.

"Hi, Rob."

"Whoa!" Rob ducked behind the bathroom door and peeked around the corner. He glanced at the closed bedroom door leading into the living area where he'd left Miller.

"How did you get in here? How did you get past Miller?"

Frank motioned with his head at the closet.

Rob grabbed a shirt and pair of jeans and slipped them on in the bath. He meandered out and joined Frank and Katrina at the closet entrance. "You were in the closet?"

"Look closer," Frank said.

Rob stared at the missing back wall. "A secret door and tunnel?"

Katrina broke from Frank's arms and pointed inside the closet. "Poppy called it his priest hole, wine cellar, and storm shelter." She glanced outside at the blowing rain whipping the trees. "Might be a good place to know about if the storm worsens." She waved. "Follow me, and I'll show you around."

Katrina ducked under the clothes bar and squeezed through the opening. Rob and Frank followed. It was about this time Frank decided Poppy had taken the whole Anglophile thing a bit too far. Frank held the handrails as he eased down the stairs on the other side of the closet. LED lights in the seven-foot, arched ceiling revealed a tunnel made of ancient bricks. The place had an old, musty odor. The low sound of something mechanical drifted down the passageway.

"How long has this been here?" Rob asked.

"Since the house was built, over thirty years ago," Katrina said.

Frank was impressed. Except for a few cobwebs and a colony of ants moving around a crack in the bricks, the place was exceptionally well maintained. "Who knows about it?" he asked.

Katrina laughed as she led them deeper into the hole. "All the family. Jerry and I used to play down here when we were kids."

After about a hundred feet, they entered a small room lined on each wall with racks of wine, cognac, and Scotch whisky. The mechanical sound Frank heard earlier emanated from a huge humidifier in the corner. A loud rumble of thunder shook the ground above them.

Frank perused the collection of spirits in the head-high wine rack. Nothing within his price range. He picked up a bottle of Chateau Pontet-Canet Grand CAU Classic, Pauillac. Saw this Bordeaux at a wine shop awhile back, almost three hundred dollars a bottle. This collection was probably worth ten thousand plus. Heck, most likely twice or three times that much.

"Follow me," Katrina said and headed up a flight of wooden stairs.

Rob appeared awestruck. Hadn't said a word since entering the space. He turned back to Frank. "We found something very much like this under one of Hussein's palaces in our operational area during the war." He wetted his lips and released a breath while shaking his head. "Filled with dead Iraqi civilians. Men, women, and children. All shot in the head and dumped." He let out another breath. Rob had seen terrible things during the war. Every so often, something triggered a memory and he became quiet and melancholy until Frank snapped him out of it.

Katrina waited until they were all on the stairs before pushing on the edge of a wooden wall at the top of the landing. The wall swung open, and she led them into the library of the main house. The tunnel door was disguised as the middle section of the bookcase Frank had admired earlier.

"Agatha Christie would love this place," Frank said.

Katrina's little brother, Jerry, sat motionless on the window seat. Sheets of rain pounded the glass, but it didn't distract him from playing with his phone. He didn't appear to notice he had company. His eyes and thumbs worked in perfect harmony with his concentration.

Katrina edged closer to Frank and whispered. "Can I come over tonight?"

Frank would be pushing the envelope if he said yes. With Miller and Rob just a few feet away, he hesitated before whispering back, "Eleven o'clock."

They left Katrina in the library, and Frank and Rob strolled back through the tunnel to their bedroom. The rumbling thunder, hard rain, and lightning caused the lights to flicker.

"We going to tell Miller about this tunnel?" Rob asked.

"Suppose we have to."

When they entered the small cottage living area, they found Miller relaxed on the sofa. The TV was on a different weather channel out of San Antonio. A map of Southwest Texas with a massive counterclockwise rotation in red and yellows filled the screen.

Miller looked up. "This thing is stalling just south of here." His lips flattened into a thin, sharp line. "What we're getting is just the opening act. The worst is yet to come." He pointed in the direction of the TV. "At the speed this thing is going, I doubt it will—"

The TV picture disappeared, and a dark blue color filled the screen.

"Well, shit! Just what we need. No TV weather updates," Miller said.

Frank checked his phone's weather app. "I still have Hi-Def radar."

Miller also checked his. "Thank god for small miracles."

The three of them sat in the living area, and Frank dozed as Miller and Rob chatted. The ringing of a phone an hour later woke Frank up. It was Miller's cell that disturbed him. Miller nodded as he spoke.

"Okay, thanks—be right over. That was Delma," Miller said. "Everyone's just about finished eating. Delma will set up the dining room to feed us."

Another flash of lightning lit up the living room wall, and a loud explosion of thunder sounded nearby. Rain lashed the cottage, and it sounded like they were going through a car wash.

Miller pointed to a coat rack near the front door consisting of several hooks with knee-length black rain jackets lined in a row. "Got those for us, but hell, we'll still get soaked just running to the house," Miller mumbled as he stood.

Rob perked up. "Have I got a surprise for you, sergeant. Follow me."

Rob led the way back into their room and pointed at the hidden door in the back of the closet.

Miller leaned over with his hands on his knees. "What the—?"

Rob took the lead through the tunnel proudly reciting what Katrina had just told him moments earlier. Pretty clear Miller was impressed. Rob was especially happy to share the secret with him. Rob always liked impressing supervisors.

As they mounted the stairs at the other end of the tunnel, Miller asked, "Where does this thing come out?"

"Surprise," Rob answered, as he opened the hidden door into the library.

There sat Mr. and Ms. Mayor, another couple, and an older woman still in her black funeral dress holding a martini glass. They stared at the newcomers with open-mouth expressions. Especially the woman with the martini glass. She studied them with a critical stare like a high school girl dissecting a frog.

An evil smirk spread across Ms. Mayor's lips before taking a sip of her wine. "Well, well... what do we have here?"

Sergeant Miller blanched, stammered something unintelligent, and took a step back before saying, "Excuse us. We had no idea we were intruding."

Mr. Mayor chuckled. "See you discovered the family secret. My dad was fond of cloak and dagger. Liked to slip away down there in the afternoons for a quick nap. Used to keep a bed down there." He turned to the others. "Allow me to introduce my brother, Kermit, and his wife Earline."

Kermit toasted them with a good-natured grin without standing. He was in his early sixties and had long salt and pepper hair combed straight back. Looked like a doctor or senator. Earline was a mousey younger woman with a straight figure and plain face.

"Of course, you know my wife," Mayor Wallace said.

Ms. Mayor maintained her evil smirk.

"And my sister, Dedra."

The old woman, Dedra, with the martini glass, twisted a ring on her finger and gazed at them with mild disgust.

Frank got the feeling they had been discussing some sort of family business.

The mayor continued. "This is Sergeant Miller and detectives Soliz and Pierce from the Dallas Police Department."

Miller took another step back to the hidden door before saying, "Very sorry for the intrusion, folks. We were called by Delma. We'll just go back down and go outside—sorry."

Mr. Mayor waved them in. "Don't be silly. Please come on through. Pouring buckets out there."

Sergeant Miller nodded in agreement, and Frank and Rob

followed him into the hall. "Nice job, Soliz!" Miller grumbled as they walked toward the dining room. He turned, giving Rob a nasty look.

Delma served them in the main dining room. They feasted on steak fajitas, refried beans, and Spanish rice. Sergeant Miller scanned his cell phone during dinner. His worried eyes pinched before saying, "The storm has stopped advancing north—sitting right on top of us. No way we're flying out of here tomorrow. Might need to drive out."

TWENTY-FIVE

Perry drove slowly down the gravel road leading to the entrance to the ranch. He kept his lights off and made sure not to tap his brakes. The lightning flashes were all the light he needed to drive. The worn-out wipers on the truck barely kept up with the heavy rain. From his vantage point high on the bluff a couple of hours ago, he got a good look at how things were set up. Ahead was the Frio River. A low water crossing led to the ranch entrance on the other side. With this much rain, it would soon become impassable, if it wasn't already. He had to get past the sheriff's department car guarding the gate and climb the fence to get to the road that led to the house. Perry hated getting his nice clothes wet. He needed to look presentable when he met his dad and extended family. But it couldn't be helped. The big problem would be all the cops. Needed a way to avoid them. No problem killing them—he'd done that before—but best to avoid it for as long as possible. But sooner or later, they'd all have to go. That was the only way he could finally meet his dad and have the long talk necessary for him to understand what it meant to Perry to be a small part of such a great family. Yeah, that's exactly how he'd put it when he saw them.

Perry had thought his plan through several times. The odds were fifty-fifty, but if he could pull it off... Best wait 'til later. He'd wait for the sheriff's department deputies to do a shift change before making his move. While on the bluff, he'd spotted an area he could park just off the road in the trees without drawing attention from vehicles coming in or going out. That's what he was looking for. He leaned forward and strained his eyes to the right—searching for that area as his truck coasted further down the road toward the low water crossing.

<hr>

ROB COMPLIMENTED Delma on the dinner in Spanish—tasted as good as Carmen's. Mexican food for lunch and dinner. If this wasn't heaven, it was as close as he could get.

Frank appeared to also enjoy the meal, but Rob knew Frank was a Mexican food once-a-week kind of guy, not a Mexican food twice-in-one-day person.

By the time they made it back to the cottage, it was closing in on nine o'clock. Miller started yawning as soon as his butt hit the couch, but he still wanted to have an impromptu meeting.

"Okay, guys. Here's the way I read it," Miller said. "We'll look at departing tomorrow by car if that's what the mayor wants. We'll use your vehicle as the limo and a ranch SUV as the follow-up. Should be able to fit most of them in the limo and all the luggage in the SUV."

"What about the river?" Rob asked. "We'll never get across the Frio on that low water crossing tomorrow after this much rain."

Frank hadn't said a word. Had a blank look. Was he thinking about Layla, Katrina, or the ingredients to make his favorite pot roast? Hard to read a guy like Frank.

Miller continued, "So, there is another entrance to the ranch." He spread out the map he'd shown them earlier onto the coffee table and smoothed the creases. He pointed to a road on the ranch that led east, away from the main house. "This road leads to the entrance the ranch hands and utility vehicles use. There's a bridge that crosses a deep ravine behind the ranch. Puts you out on Highway 83." Miller looked up and tapped the map. "That's how we'll drive out if that becomes the plan. Who knows, the mayor might decide to wait it out and let this thing blow over. Then we can fly out. Plane's protected in a hanger, so we at least have options."

Rob grinned. That was Miller's big thing, *options*. Used that line in every briefing.

Frank still hadn't spoken. He studied the map with mild interest and only nodded.

"Okay, guys." Miller stood and stretched his back. "Last, but not least, we'll use the tunnel as the hard room." Another explosion of thunder rocked the cottage. Miller glanced at the ceiling. "Or storm shelter if it comes to that. If you got this, I'm hitting the sack—long day. Sorry there's no TV, but try and stay awake enough to hear the mayor's panic alarm if it goes off. I'll relieve you by eight tomorrow morning."

Miller meandered to his bedroom and closed the door.

"I'll take the first shift if you want the second," Rob said.

Frank stood. "Fine for me. Wake me at three o'clock."

Once Frank went to bed, Rob scrolled through his cell for emails and messages. He sent Carmen a text: *Good night—love you.* She didn't answer, so he figured she had already retired. Rob picked up a fishing magazine off the coffee table and got comfortable on the sofa. Something bumped the side of the cottage. The wind had picked up, blowing larger chunks of limbs and debris. For reasons he couldn't explain, Whisper drifted back into his mind. Rob looked at the door as a flash of lightning lit up the darkness outside. He eased to the door and set the deadbolt lock before returning to the couch. He also drew his pistol from its holster and laid it on top of the table.

FRANK SILENTLY LOCKED his bedroom door, undressed, and brushed his teeth. Just as he drew back the bed covers, three knocks sounded from the closet. He opened the closet door and the back wall slid open. Katrina didn't say a word, just walked into his waiting arms. Frank checked the bedroom door lock again before slipping her oversized Dallas Cowboys T-shirt over her head. The curves of her naked body cast soft shadows in the lamplight. He kissed her tenderly, and she pulled down his boxers and pushed herself against him.

They made slow, wonderful love for over an hour. With the knowledge Rob was in the next room, Katrina stifled her moans. Afterward, they lay together, wrapped in each other's embrace.

"Where do you think our relationship is going?" she said, low and tentative.

Frank had expected they'd have this conversation sooner or later but hadn't expected it tonight. He didn't know how to answer it, so he just said, "I'm not sure."

She eased closer, pulling his arms around her tighter. "I know you love me, but is that enough? Can just love sustain us with all the adversities we'd face?"

"I'd like to think so, but that's nothing we can control. Whatever we do, we do on our own—opinions be damned."

She didn't answer, just gazed at him with sad eyes. After a minute, a tear trickled down her cheek and she sniffled. "I know."

They slept until almost three. Frank shook her awake. The low rumble of distant thunder vibrated through the room and the slapping of rain against the windowpane reminded Frank the storm wasn't near finished. He checked the weather app on his cell. Thing was lit up like an airport runway with more colors than a Picasso. Tornado and hail symbols dotted the area around the ranch.

Katrina slipped her T-shirt back on. "Guess I'd better be going."

Frank gave her a long hug. "We'll talk more when we get back to Dallas."

She only nodded before disappearing into the closet.

Frank opened the bedroom door at five to three, fully showered and dressed. Really could have used a few more hours of sleep. Rob sat droopy-eyed and perfectly still, staring at a magazine. *Was he even awake?* Frank tiptoed into the room, but Rob never acknowledged him. Rob had been an Eagle Scout, gone to war as a Marine, served in SWAT for three years, and always complained about Frank's sleeping on duty in the car. This was too good to pass up. Frank snuck closer to the couch and quietly knelt directly in front of Rob. He still didn't move. His breath was slow and even—eyes just half-closed slits. *Yup, out cold.* Frank held back a laugh. In the cop world, this is what's known as *wake-sleep*. Officers who do all night surveillances know it well. You believe you're awake, but you're sound asleep. Frank had experienced it several times. He dreamed he was awake, but he wasn't. That was the only explanation. A slight tinge of regret entered Frank's conscience as he pushed his face to within a couple of inches of Rob's.

"Good morning."

Rob's eyes sprang open, he jumped a foot off the couch and cried out. Then, just as quickly, glanced toward Miller's bedroom next door and clapped both hands over his mouth.

Frank stood, and a grin spread across his lips. "Okay, you're relieved. Any unusual activity during the night?"

Rob shook his head and muttered, "Asshole, cracker. No, there wasn't any unusual activity."

"Checked the weather on my cell," Frank said. "Looks like a half dozen tornados have developed in the wake of the storm."

Rob stood and stretched. "Any more updates?"

Frank pointed the remote toward the TV, but only the blue screen appeared with the message *Attempting to acquire signal.*

Frank dropped his voice. "Get some rest. No telling what Miller has planned for us today."

"Think we'll drive out?"

"If I were the mayor, that's exactly what I'd do."

"Aren't they supposed to read the old man's will this morning?"

Frank shrugged. "Guess so."

Rob closed the door on the bedroom, and Frank scrounged in the small kitchen area for coffee. He found some Folgers in the small freezer part of the refrigerator and started the pot. Coffee smelled like the freezer—*great!* The rest of the night gave Frank time to think about him and Katrina—what she'd said last night. Some kind of final decision would be made soon. The only question was who would make it first.

ALTON BRADY and his wife were early risers. After his years as a cop and his wife's years as a school teacher, they always awoke together at five o'clock and were out the door before seven. But this Sunday morning, Alton sipped his first cup of strong, black coffee at a quarter to six while relaxing in his reclining leather chair watching the weather. The volume was so low he hardly heard the newscaster. The remnants of the hurricane were advancing deeper into Central Texas and flooding rains had forced the closure of roads as far away as San Antonio. *Bet Rob and Frank are getting slammed. Happy to be in Big D.*

Alton took another slow sip and sucked in the smell of his wife cooking his favorite breakfast—a three-egg omelet with cheese and grilled onions. He rested his head back and relished the early morning ritual. He hadn't had a day off in two weeks, since this madness started, and the mental strain of the case—dealing with the feds and DPD supervisors and especially Layla—had taken a toll. He wanted to be waited on and pampered for a change, even if it was only his favorite breakfast.

"Come on, Alton. It's ready," his wife yelled.

Just as he stood, his cell on the end table rang—Homicide calling.

Christ, what now? "Yeah, this is Alton."

"Hey, Alton. Lieutenant Baker here. There's been a development."

Fifty-five minutes later, Alton pulled up to the 1940s two-story in South Dallas. His wife had folded his omelet into a huge hotdog bun, and he'd eaten it on the way. A grilled onion stain marred his freshly cleaned and pressed suit pants.

There were six police vehicles on the street and the CSU van. No sign of any FBI vehicles or Layla—*thank god!* Yellow evidence tape surrounded the yard and drive leading into the back driveway. Neighbors lined both sides of the quiet, shaded street that had suddenly turned into DPD Central. Alton nodded at the uniform on the sidewalk, sweating like a professional wrestler in the merciless sun.

As Alton headed up the drive, the officer spoke. "It's another bad one, Alton."

Alton didn't bother looking his way as he muttered, "Aren't they all?"

Alton smelled the crime scene before he saw the first detective— Chris Baggett. The whole back yard and garage had a dead, rotten odor.

Baggett and Kelly from CIU were huddled in the shade of the open garage in a discussion.

"What do we have?" Alton asked as he approached. He slipped next to Baggett and out of the relentless rays of the sun.

Baggett pulled out his pocket notebook and flipped the pages. "Two dead ones in the chest freezer." He pointed to a body bag on the garage floor. "Already pulled out a Mrs. Doris Cleveland—sixty-five. Owns this house. Rented it out to boarders. And this guy." Baggett led Alton to the open chest freezer. "We haven't got an ID yet, but looks Hispanic." Baggett turned to Kelly and pointed in the freezer. "Hey, your guys about ready to pull this one out?"

A CSI photographer snapped another picture of the stiff body in the freezer before Kelly said, "Getting the last shots now. One more minute."

Alton wiped his forehead and squinted as he looked around the garage. "What's that god-awful smell?"

Baggett pointed to a pile of something wrapped in white butcher paper, leaking what looked like blood, in the corner. The red streams wormed their way across the cracks in the garage floor, looking for the lowest point. "Whoever dropped these two into the freezer took out all the chicken, steaks, and roast and dumped them in the corner over there. With this heat, didn't take long for the neighbors to start complaining."

"Okay, we're ready over here," Kelly said.

Alton and Baggett moved closer to the freezer as the four CSU guys positioned themselves to lift the Hispanic body out.

"Okay," Baggett said.

Another CSU tech stood by with the camera to capture the event.

"One, two, three—lift," Kelly said.

As the body cleared the top of the freezer wall, Alton did a double take. A hand and arm appeared at the very bottom of the freezer. *There was a third body under this one, completely hidden by the dead Hispanic guy.* Alton edged closer as Kelly said, "Holy shit!"

Alton put both hands on the top edge of the freezer and gawked at the dead woman. Her skin was gray and wrinkled. Tiny ice crystals covered her eyebrows and black hair. A dark blue cloth ligature was still around her neck. Her small breasts lay flat, but the nipples protruded. Layla stared back at him through wide-open, fearful eyes, her red lipstick smeared and her lips formed into a small circle.

Alton's breath caught and he stepped back. "Oh, no."

"Alton... Alton?" Baggett said.

Alton turned as Baggett passed him an 8"x10" plastic evidence bag, sealed at the top with red tape. "We found this in the computer printer tray of one of the upstairs bedrooms. That's why you were called—thought it might involve your investigation."

Alton took the bag and held it to the light for a better look. It was a Google Maps printout—directions to Leakey, TX.

"Oh, Christ, no," Alton muttered. He jerked out his phone and his hands shook as he called Frank's cell. It failed to connect and immediately went to voicemail.

———

FRANK SAT on the sofa reading his book and drinking coffee as the wind and rain continued pelting the cottage, sometimes from the east, sometimes from the west, and sometimes from both sides at once. Every so often, Frank tried the TV, but the thing remained dead. Frank checked his watch—seven o'clock. Last night after dinner, Delma had offered to fix them breakfast. She told them to drop in any time after seven. Frank collected his handheld radio and silently slipped into his bedroom. Rob lay fully clothed on top of the covers, snoring like a Russian submariner. Katrina had left the tunnel door open when she departed last night, so Frank eased down the stairs and strolled toward the door on the other side. He took in the musty air of the tunnel, laced with a whiff of old wood and masonry, as he tried to recall what Delma said she would make for breakfast. He really just wanted a decent cup of fresh coffee. This stale Folgers stuff wasn't cutting it.

As Frank pushed open the back of the hidden door to the library, he had a sense something was different. A lamp in the corner of the room shined with just enough glow to cast the room in mostly shadows. The aroma of fresh coffee hung in the air. Frank closed the hidden door and turned toward the hall leading to the kitchen. The sense he was not alone stayed with him.

"Good morning, Detective Pierce," a female voice said.

Frank snapped his head to the right, and the vision of someone dressed in black, sitting in an over-sized chair in the corner, came into focus.

"You're up early, ma'am."

The mayor's older sister, Dedra, took a sip of coffee and said, "The storm—difficult to sleep. Please join me." She motioned him over with her finger.

Frank wove his way past furniture to the window where she sat. The shrill whistling of wind reminded him of some musical instrument he couldn't recall the name of.

She nodded to another chair. "Please, have a seat."

She wore a black robe and had her hair up in a loose bun. Without her makeup, the lines in her face reminded Frank of photos from space, outlining the different tributaries to a great river. He never figured on encountering someone other than Delma, certainty not the mayor's sister. Why would she want him to sit with her?

Dedra showed a half-grin before saying, "You know, I've never met a policeman. You're the first."

Frank settled back into the soft cloth chair. "Really? Never been pulled over for a traffic offense."

"What little I drove in my younger life was in New York. Mostly took public transportation and cabs." She smiled. "I've had a driver for most of my life."

Frank wanted to ask if by driver she meant a chauffeur, her late husband, or a friend, but decided to drop the idea. All he wanted was a fresh cup of coffee and perhaps a little breakfast. Conversation with a stranger didn't rate high on his list of important things on a morning like this.

"What's it like... being a policeman? I enjoy detective programs and novels, but I'm sometimes afraid the authors I read don't truly understand real police work."

Her voice had a nasal snob quality Frank found aggravating. He had been asked this question so many times he'd lost count. He used to try and explain the confusion, doubt, and fear officers felt more often than not when faced with a serious crime or a criminal. But people didn't understand. How could they? They were preset to believe books, movies, and the media about how the police did their jobs. This old girl's idle curiosity was no different. She wanted something from a *real cop* to hang her hat on so she could feel she now possessed some secret, inside knowledge few did. Frank could have sugarcoated it but decided to just tell the truth. He stood.

"Ma'am, very few people who haven't done the job can accurately understand and describe what it's really like. I've done it for over sixteen years, and I still can't. The closest I can come is, it's a screwed-up mess. Can't see how they get so many good men and women to do it with the low pay and inherent dangers. Every major company is looking for the type of people who go into law enforcement each year. But they all want to be top cops, not junior business executives."

Her expression sagged in confusion, and she slowly shook her head. "Then why do you do it?"

"To tell you the truth. I don't know, ma'am," he said and walked away. He hoped he hadn't appeared rude, but it was a subject he no longer wanted to think about, much less try and explain. Years ago, after Carly's murder in New York, he could have explained it. He'd stayed on at the restaurant for months after her death but couldn't handle the stress and memories. Hours of loneliness and depression, and every place he went, her ghost seemed to be waiting. He couldn't bear to live there any longer; too much had happened. And part of those memories was being a chef. She and his unborn child had been murdered while he was working at the restaurant. Joining a police department across the country seemed like a good change way back then. Now, he got so little satisfaction from the work he could no longer explain to himself why he even stayed.

Just as Frank entered the dining room, something caught his eye. A dim glow in the corner by the floor in the dark room. Frank eased toward it, and Jerry sat crossed-legged, playing some game on his iPhone.

He looked up and said, "Morning, Frank."

Christ. This family doesn't sleep. Why was everyone awake?

"Hey, Jerry. Catching up on some games?"

Jerry went back to the iPhone and said, "Uh-huh," giving the phone his sole attention.

Frank swung toward the kitchen. Just before he walked through the door, the mayor's panic alarm sounded, a shrill hi-low scream over his handheld radio. The alarm had never sounded the few times he'd filled in on other protective details in the past. The first thought that flashed in his mind—Whisper. Frank tore through the foyer, around the corner, and took the stairs three at a time, his long legs pumping blood into the half-asleep muscles. As per protocol, the key to the mayor's door was propped above the door frame. Frank grabbed it with one hand while knocking with the other and saying, "Is everything all right in there?" When no immediate answer came from the room, Frank unlocked the door and charged in, gun in hand.

The mayor stood in the middle of the room, bare-chested, wearing only white pajama bottoms and a royal blue robe, open at the front. His usually well-kept gray hair resembled a bird's nest. Frank caught a glimpse of Ms. Mayor's backside and negligee rushing into the bath, and the door slammed shut.

"Is everything okay, sir?"

The mayor cinched the belt of the robe and ran his hands through his hair. "Sorry about that—our bad. My wife accidentally knocked over the panic alarm. Everything's fine, Detective Pierce."

Frank reholstered his weapon. *Figures!* "Sorry for the intrusion, sir."

The mayor showed a sheepish look. "No apologies necessary. I appreciate your prompt response."

As Frank left the room, the sound of feet running up the stairs drew his attention. Sergeant Miller and Rob topped the stairs before Frank said, "False alarm—accidentally tipped over the alarm."

Both were out of breath after having run from the cottage, through the tunnel, and up the stairs. Miller had a coughing fit trying to catch his breath. He held onto the banister and sucked in air. His face had an unhealthy scarlet shine. He stammered before getting out the words. "You sure he's okay?"

Frank nodded. "I spoke to him. He and Ms. Mayor are fine."

Rob sneered. "Nothing like a morning sprint to wake up."

Miller kept up his loud coughing all the way down the stairs. Anyone who wasn't awake before was up by now.

Just before they turned the corner into the kitchen, Delma's scream and the breaking of a dish sent hairs on Frank's neck to attention. They ran into the kitchen and found her in a corner near the refrigerator. When she saw them, she pointed at the kitchen door leading outside, the look of terror still on her face.

It was a half-windowed door. Through the darkness, lightening flashed in the distance, outlining the head and shoulders of a big hulk of a man outside, with rain dripping off his head. Rob pulled his gun and pointed it at the figure. The man outside raised his hands and a pitiful voice spoke above the wind and rain, "Don't shoot."

Miller and Frank both had their pistols out, and Miller motioned for Frank to open the door. Frank eased his hand to the doorknob and swung the door wide open with one fast motion.

The figure stood shivering. He was huge, and his sheriff's department uniform was soaked. The name tag on his breast pocket read E. Therme. Frank knew that name.

Miller motioned the man in. You can put your hands down. "Who are you?"

The poor wretched creature wiped water from his face, and a flush crossed his cheeks as his feet shuffled. "Deputy Erik Therme, Real County Sheriff's Department."

Everyone holstered their pistols and Frank shut the door.

Miller searched the pockets of his jacket before asking, "What are you doing out there?"

Deputy Therme again shuffled his feet a moment, and his ears turned red. "Had a little accident with my car."

Miller found what he was looking for in his pocket—a piece of paper. He eyed it a second and passed it to Rob. He read it and passed it on to Frank. It was the list of officers guarding the front gate and their cell phone numbers that the sheriff had given them yesterday. The midnight shift deputy's name—E. Therme.

From out of nowhere, Delma appeared with a large, white towel and handed it to Deputy Therme.

"Thank you, ma'am."

"What kind of accident?" Miller asked.

Therme's chin dipped and he rubbed the back of his neck. He met eyes with Miller. "The kind that will probably get me suspended or fired, most likely. I went to sleep, and the water came up faster than I expected at that low water crossing by the front gate. Next thing I knew, I was floating down the river. Barely got out before the car got completely swept away. I walked in the rain from the front gate. Bad out there." He shrugged. "Sheriff's going to be pissed."

Frank would like to have laughed, but he knew weird things happened on night shifts in all police departments. And in weather like this, anything was possible. Rob grinned, covering his mouth, and turned his back before Therme saw him.

"Get dried off and have breakfast, deputy," Miller said.

Therme wiped the towel across his face and buzz-cut hair. "Thank you, sir."

Delma handed him a steaming mug of hot coffee and he sipped it.

"If you want to slip out of those wet clothes, I'll wash and dry them. We have a robe around here somewhere."

Therme smiled and nodded. "Thank you, ma'am. That would be nice."

Frank opened his cell phone to check the latest weather information and stared at Miller. "My phones got no signal—dead."

Rob checked his. "Mine, too."

"Crap," Miller muttered. "Delma, is there a landline I can use?"

"We have one in the kitchen and the hall," she replied.

"I'll use the hall one." Miller strolled out of the kitchen.

"Here, have a seat," Rob told Therme.

"Thanks."

Rob extended his hand. "I'm Rob Soliz and this is Frank Pierce. We're detectives with Dallas PD."

"Happy to meet y'all," Therme said as he shook their hands.

Frank was surprised at the size and strength in Therme's hand. Frank's was big with long slender fingers, but Therme's were larger and hard as steel.

Rob said, "You must work out a lot. Nice build. I don't have time for bodybuilding anymore, just a few workouts a week with the free weights."

"I've not been hitting them as much as I should. Need to get back into a routine."

Frank found the whole bromance weightlifting conversation amusing. The gym was the last place he'd go. Poor Therme, just another good old boy sheriff's deputy from a small county department who allowed his cruiser to be washed away while he napped inside. Yeah, he'd probably be suspended, and depending on his record, perhaps even terminated. But he was young, he'd find something else better, making more money.

When Miller reentered the kitchen, he had a smile. "Good news and bad news." He motioned toward Therme. "Good news is, I spoke to the sheriff, and he says he's just glad you're safe, deputy. Bad news is, things are shit all over the county. Roads washed away, bridges flooded, trees down, and cell towers torn up by high winds and tornados. I'm going to advise the mayor to not even think about leaving today. The emergency services here are overwhelmed. Several high-water rescues already and it's barely seven o'clock. Our best bet is to see what this storm does and plan for departure tomorrow." Miller turned to Therme. "Sheriff asked if you're okay staying here until we leave? Doesn't have anyone he can spare to relieve you until tomorrow, anyway."

Therme's lips thinned and he nodded. "Sure, anything the sheriff thinks best. I'm good 'til tomorrow."

Both Rob and Frank checked their cells.

"Don't bother," Miller said. "The sheriff said one cell tower is down and another badly damaged—no service in Real County, period."

Delma handed Therme a soft white robe. "Shuck those clothes and put this on. I'll have those wet things washed and dried in a jiffy." She pointed to a door in the kitchen. "Use that half bath."

"I appreciate it, ma'am."

After Therme closed the bathroom door, Miller said, "I'll talk to the mayor after breakfast." He scratched the side of his head. "Our best bet is to hunker down and wait for the county to clear the roads and this wind and rain to be over. You guys get a bite to eat, and I'll see you back in the cottage. No use all of us staying awake. Get some rest if you can."

"What about Therme? Where will he bunk?" Rob asked.

"Hmm, good question. We'll put him on the sofa tonight," Miller said. "By tomorrow, he should be out of here and hopefully us, too."

TWENTY-SIX

Rob hadn't planned on staying more than one night in Leakey. He did not welcome the news from Miller of being there for another night with much enthusiasm. The fact they now had a stranger thrown in their cottage also pissed him off. He leaned closer to Frank and whispered, "This is going to suck."

Miller was back in the hall making another call, and Delma finished up breakfast as Therme walked out of the bath wearing the robe and carrying an armful of soggy clothes.

"Here, let me take those, hun," Delma said.

Looked like she adopted the tall stranger. She grabbed the uniform and slid around the corner to the laundry room just as her husband, Felix, came in from outside. He took off his cowboy hat and hung up his dripping raincoat by the door.

"Hadn't seen rain like this in a spell," Felix said. "Y'all better not leave in this weather."

"Already made that call. Staying another night," Rob said.

Felix nodded and glanced outside. "I told the ranch hands to stay inside. Can't do a damn thing but get stuck in this mess."

As Felix finished his last sentence, the kitchen lights flashed twice and the room was plunged into darkness. Just as quickly, a cranking noise, like a diesel truck, sounded from outside the laundry room; the lights flickered again and came back on.

Felix motioned with his head. "Emergency generator. Figured this would happen. Don't worry, the thing's big enough to power a small town—we're okay."

Delma made huevos rancheros on fresh tortillas for breakfast. Rob was quickly falling in love with her cooking. Mexican food three meals in a row.

When everyone finished eating, Miller said, "I'll stay in the main house today. There's an unused bedroom upstairs. Still have to talk to the mayor. When Therme's clothes are finished, I'll send him down the tunnel to you guys."

Which was Miller's way of saying *get lost until tonight when I'll need you.*

Rob and Frank went back through the underground passageway to their cottage, and Frank dropped on his bed. "I'm going to grab a nap."

Rob wasn't sleepy, so he wandered into the living area. He pushed his face to the window. Hard rain still fell in big drops with no clearing in sight. The dark twilight outside was depressing. No sun today. About a half hour later, Miller and Therme strolled into the cottage living area through the room where Frank slept.

"And we're using this room as our command post," Miller told Therme.

Therme had this expression of disbelief at the whole set-up. He was back in his cleaned, pressed uniform, courtesy of Delma. The shirt sleeves and pants legs were a little short, but what did you expect from a small county in southwest Texas.

"Wow, never worked with a big city police department before," Therme said. "Closest I came was when I was an escort car for the governor's visit here during his last election. Man, there were Texas Rangers, DPS units, and the whole sheriff's department turned out."

Miller had a smile of satisfaction and self-worth glued to his lips. "You're in the big league now, kid." He walked to Rob. "By the way, since they've offered me a room in the main house for tonight, Therme can have my room in the cottage tonight." He patted Rob's shoulder as if to assure him everything was under control. "They've just started the reading of the will in the library, so we'll give them some privacy."

Miller began to get on Rob's nerves. The guy was a suck-up in the worst way. Most officers attained advancement through hard work and tests; some, like Miller, thought making a political play was the way to go.

Just before lunch, Frank appeared in the doorway. He looked like crap. Dark circles under his eyes and his clothes had that wrinkled appearance like he'd slept in them, which he had.

Miller stood and checked his watch before saying, "Let's see what Delma's fixed for lunch."

"I'm grabbing a shower and change of clothes first," Frank said.

Miller headed toward the tunnel. "Don't be long," he called over his shoulder.

Rob followed him, but Therme headed to Miller's bedroom. "You coming?" Rob asked.

Therme said, "I'll be along. Got to hit the john first."

FRANK TOOK A LONG HOT SHOWER, scrubbing the sleep crud from his eyes and rinsing his long hair under the heavenly flow of hot water. One of Frank's secret pleasures was showering. Something about the water rhythmically beating against his skin calmed and relaxed him after a long day. He dressed and went back into the cottage living area to make sure everyone had left. The room was empty. As he turned to leave, the wet raincoat hanging by the front door dripping water caught his attention. *Who used that? Why go outside?* Frank shrugged and followed the tunnel to the library door on the other side. This time he slowly opened it, making sure no one waited in ambush.

Frank skirted the dining room where the family dined and walked into the kitchen as Felix and Delma placed plates of food on trays. The aroma of roasted meat filled the area. Rob and Miller had finished eating, and Therme was about halfway through. Frank took the last seat at the small table in the corner. His roast beef sandwich, chips, and lemonade waited.

Rob chuckled. "Good thing you got here when you did. Ol' Therme was eying your sandwich."

Therme grinned. "That thought did cross my mind."

Just then, Felix and Delma came back into the kitchen to grab another round of plates to serve the family in the dining room.

Felix said, "We're cut off."

Miller looked up. "Cut off from what?"

"Phone's out. Probably a downed pole or tree across the line." Felix placed several more plates of food on his tray and he and Delma headed back toward the dining room.

Miller sighed. "Wonderful, things keep getting better and better."

Frank ate without comment. Miller was a minor irritant on this trip. He would be out of Frank's life soon enough. For the first time that day, Frank thought about Katrina. A wave of guilt passed over him for not thinking about her sooner. Wondered what, if anything, Poppy left her in the will. The girl was already set for life with her dad's fortune. What more could she need?

Miller spoke up. "I don't like this... I don't like it one bit." His eyes squinted, and he pinched his lower lip with thumb and index finger.

"Like what, sergeant?" Rob asked.

"Being out of communication. I contacted Major Higgins a couple of hours ago and gave him this number. If he tries to call me back, it won't go through."

"Don't you think he'll figure it out?" Rob asked.

"That's not the point," Miller said. "It's my job to stay in communications with headquarters at all times."

Frank sucked in a slow breath. *Here we go!*

Felix and Delma came back into the kitchen and ate their sandwiches standing up by the counter.

"Excuse me, Felix," Miller said, "but do we have any way to communicate with the outside world in case of emergency, you know, other than the landline?"

Felix took a swallow of lemonade before answering. "Sure—the shortwave."

Miller's brows shot up. "Shortwave?"

"Yeah, Mr. Wallace was an avid HAM radio operator. Talked to people all over the world."

Miller's smile grew. "Do you still have it?"

Felix nodded. "Yup, in his room, upstairs."

Fifteen minutes later, Miller had briefed the mayor on the phone problem and the need to get back into communication with the world. He, Rob, Frank, and Therme looked on as Felix attempted to transmit from the dusty HAM set. The ancient unit came on without a problem, but something appeared wrong with the transmit mode.

"KKD3433 to anyone monitoring this frequency," Felix repeated over and over into the mic. After five minutes of trying other frequencies, Felix said, "We're not transmitting or receiving. I'd bet it's the antenna."

"Where's the antenna?" Miller asked.

Felix pointed to the ceiling. "Directly above us, on the roof."

"Can you fix it?"

"If the weather was dry, perhaps. No way I'd go up there in the rain—too dangerous."

Miller looked at the floor a second and pursed his lips. "Could you tell my guys how to fix it?"

Rob's head snapped toward Miller.

"Probably just a wire came loose from the mounting with all this wind," Felix replied. "Shouldn't be that big a deal."

Miller faced Rob and Frank. "What about it, guys. Will you give it a try?"

Frank was just about to tell Miller he was crazy to his face when Therme spoke up.

"I'll go."

Miller stared at Therme a second before saying, "You know anything about antennas?"

"Not much, but shouldn't be all that hard to figure out."

"He'll need someone to help him. Count me in," Rob said, more as an exasperated admission than a voluntary statement.

Frank saw nothing good coming out of climbing onto a steep, slippery metal roof during a torrential rain and lightning storm.

ROB NOW HAD second thoughts about his decision to help Therme. They were in the dimly lit attic, winding their way past rafters and wires strung across the floor on the way to the roof access. Rob didn't care for heights. Sure, he was airborne-qualified during his Marine days, but it took all his courage to make each jump. Therme didn't seem to give the whole crazy idea a second thought. The guy was young and strong—bulletproof, he thought.

Frank brought up the rear, his silence signaling his thoughts that the whole idea was nuts.

When they were about halfway through the attic, Therme stopped and took a few deep breaths, his white-knuckle hold on a rafter causing Rob to pause.

Rob touched Therme's back. The muscles were hard and tight. "You okay, man?"

Therme swallowed and grinned. "I don't like tight, confined spaces. Especially dark ones like this."

"Want to go back?"

Therme took a couple more deeper breaths before shaking his head. "No, I'm okay."

The access door to the roof had a metal ladder leading up from the floor of the attic. Rob took the lead and climbed to the hatch door. Felix had provided Rob with splicing wire, electrician's tape, wire cutters, pliers, and screwdrivers. He kept them in a bag around his neck under his long raincoat. He looked down at Therme. "Ready to do this?"

Therme wiped his hand across his mouth and buttoned the top button of his rain jacket before saying, "Yeah."

"What do you need me to do?" Frank asked.

"Just stand by in case we need help." Rob pulled the jacket hood over his head and pushed open the hatch. The wind almost yanked it from his grasp. Rain hitting his jacket felt like he was showering with his clothes on. He slowly climbed onto the slippery roof and moved away from the hatch enough for Therme to get through the access door. They both straddled the peak, and Rob couldn't help but stare at the sixty-foot drop to the soggy ground below. As per Felix's suggestion, Therme tied himself off to the hatch handle, and then tied Rob off to him with an orange nylon climber's rope.

Rob wiped rain from his face and swiveled his head in all directions. "Well, this sucks."

Therme appeared more relaxed now that he was in the open air. He nodded then said, "But the view's great."

Through the downpour, the usually drab, sandy Hill Country view looked like it had a dull green filter draped over it. The air was fresh, and the wind had died just enough for them to keep their balance without too much trouble. "Yeah, it is... isn't it?" Rob said.

The antenna problem was obvious. Some flying debris had torn the thing loose from its mounting. The whole roof was pock-marked with dents from hail or god knew what. The best option looked like reattaching the antenna to the hatch handle they were tied off to. Nothing else was close enough that had any stability. Rob stretched out so that his chest was flat with the wet roof, reached down, and grabbed the loose antenna flopping in the wind. He pulled himself back to a seated position and handed it to Therme. Over the falling roar of the rain, Rob yelled, "We'll wire it to the handle. You go back inside, and I'll follow. I think I can wire it back while standing on the ladder inside." Rob was happy to be able to do the job inside the hatch with both feet firmly on something steady. The wind had increased again, and the rain slammed harder against his face, almost blinding him. The dangers of remaining on the roof increased with each second.

Therme gave the okay sign with thumb and index finger and wiggled backward, closer to the hatch. He slid his legs inside and just his upper body now showed above the roofline. He untied himself from the handle so he could descend the ladder.

Rob eased backward, his feet searching for the hatch opening. When his left foot bumped the frame, he released a relieved sigh —*almost there.* Rob lifted his right leg and dropped his boot through the top of the hatch. Just then, a rogue gust of wind caught him when he was most off balance. It swung him hard to the right, and he spread out both arms and dropped his palms to the roof for support, but it didn't help. He began sliding head first off the right side of the roof.

Rob screamed just before his safety line tied off to Therme took up the slack and snapped him to a stop. He tried pushing with his hands and boots to gain any traction, but it was useless—too steep an incline and far too wet. Just before he called for Frank, the line tightened and he began being pulled back up the roof. Rob looked over his shoulder, and the vision of Therme's bulk appeared. The guy was standing inside on the ladder and pulling the rope hand over hand, slowly easing Rob back up. Rob closed his eyes, thanking god for Therme's strength. Frank would never have been able to do that alone, and Rob wasn't sure he could have either.

After what seemed like forever, Therme latched onto Rob's boots with a vice grip and finished tugging him back into the hatch. Rob's body felt like his liver and stomach had traded places. He took a minute, once both feet were on the ladder, to calm down. His legs were shaking and so weak he feared he didn't have the strength to crawl down. The adrenaline rush died away, leaving Rob totally spent.

Two strong hands locked around his waist and Therme's reassuring voice spoke up. "Just relax, I've got you, partner."

Rob allowed himself to be lowered down by Therme. Rob sat on the attic catwalk catching his breath and settling his nerves.

While Therme climbed the ladder to secure the hatch, Frank knelt in front of Rob. "Thought we'd lost you for a second." His boyish grin told Rob he'd been concerned.

"Yeah, thought I was a goner there."

Therme climbed off the ladder and joined Rob and Frank.

"Think you're up to walking?" Therme asked.

Frank gave Rob a hand and pulled him to a standing position. "So, did you get the antenna reattached?" Frank asked.

Rob felt like a fool as he shook his head. "No, I tore it loose even more. Last I saw of it, the thing slid off the roof and is probably banging against an eave right now."

Frank showed his bad-boy grin. "We'll just let Miller reattach the damn thing if it's all that important."

Five minutes later, they were sitting in the kitchen drying off and reporting their failure to Sergeant Miller.

"I still don't like it," Miller said. "Being out of communication with the outside makes me nervous."

Rob glanced Frank's way in time to see one of his famous eyerolls. "More nervous than having an officer fall to their death?" Rob asked.

Miller crossed his arms and in a weak voice said, "No, probably not."

FRANK HAD HAD JUST ABOUT ENOUGH of Miller. Didn't care about anyone or anything except the mission and his own advancement. If he was this gung-ho, he should have joined the military. Rob talked Frank out of the idea of telling the guy to go screw himself as Therme showered in Miller's bath.

Just then, Miller walked back into the cottage living area, trailed by Felix. They had concerned expressions.

Oh, Christ. What now?

Miller's eyes were vacant when he said, "Guys, Felix discovered what's wrong with the hard phone line." Miller turned to Felix and nodded. "Tell 'em."

Felix cleared his throat and shot a furtive glance around the room. "I was walking around the house checking for damage and happened by the phone box. Looks like the wires have been ripped away from it. No way to splice a line and make them work without a phone tech."

Frank didn't rattle easy, but what Felix said caused a cold chill to rush down his arms and legs. "Could this have happened with all the debris flying around last night?"

Felix shrugged. "That's what I figured, but the house isn't damaged near the box. If some flying thing tore it loose, it didn't damage the house."

Rob stared at Frank and slowly shook his head. "Can't be."

"Can't be what?" Miller asked.

Rob turned to Miller. "The serial killer who's after the mayor and his family."

Felix's eyes widened.

"Impossible. Has to be another explanation," Miller muttered.

The blood from Felix's cheeks drained and he stepped back a few paces. "Is this the guy who murdered those two women we've been hearing about on the news out of Dallas?"

Miller squared his shoulders and said, "I still find it difficult to believe." He shoved his hands inside his pants pockets and offered a slight nod to Felix. "But better not take any chances. I'll brief the mayor." He pointed at Felix. "Can you instruct the ranch hands to do a thorough search around the grounds. Anything looks unusual or out of place, I want to know about it, understand?"

Felix stammered, "Most of the help lives off the ranch. Only a few young guys we bring in as seasonal workers are staying in the bunkhouse, but I'll let them know."

The shower turned off in the bath, and Miller lowered his voice. "Let's keep this between just us until we know more." He motioned to his bathroom. "No sense giving Therme something to worry about he doesn't need to."

Rob stood. "Sergeant, if Whisper's out there, we'll need all the help we can get to secure this house. This cottage command post set-up might not work."

Miller's head cocked to the side, and he lowered his brow. "Let's just see what the search turns up first. We might have a better idea of what we're up against." With that profound statement, Miller spun around and headed for the tunnel.

Frank was ashamed to admit it, but until Rob mentioned Whisper, Frank had hardly thought about Katrina that day. Where was she? Of course, she couldn't call because there was no phone service. He assumed she'd attended the reading of the will earlier that morning, but it was almost dinner time. He wanted to see her —hold her.

Frank gave Miller a head start before following him back through the tunnel. Frank liked the wine rack in the tunnel. If he owned a house like this, that was exactly what he'd do. Every time he passed the rack, he wanted to pull out a bottle and sample it.

Frank pushed on the hidden bookcase door leading into the library and peeked inside. In a chair by the cold fireplace the mayor's son, Jerry, sat with one leg hanging over the arm of the chair. His complete concentration was on his iPhone, playing video games again. Kid was a loner, didn't like to mix with the crowd, might find him anytime in any room, pecking away on some Apple device. The sound of a video game drifted from the phone. He didn't notice as Frank walked past. Frank avoided the kitchen and drifted toward the sound of voices coming from the formal living room. Everyone but the mayor was gathered on sofas and chairs, enjoying late afternoon cocktails. Miller probably had the mayor in another room for the briefing.

Katrina's perfect face was silhouetted by the window. Just enough light shown across her features to stir a memory. God, she resembled Frank's deceased wife, Carly, more every day. Katrina sat in a straight back chair with a bored expression, holding a wine glass with both hands. Frank couldn't explain it, but seeing her gave him peace. He took a long breath, and just before he decided to head back to the kitchen, her head turned and their eyes met.

The wide, full-tooth smile he loved so much spread across her lips and she stood.

"Please excuse me, everyone," she said and casually walked into the hall.

Frank flattened himself against the wall as the group's stares followed Katrina from the room.

Katrina eased to Frank's side in the hall and took his hand. "I've missed you. Where have you been?" she whispered.

"Long story. You okay?"

She nodded, looked both ways, and gave him a quick kiss. "I'm good. Can I see you tonight?"

"Probably not a good idea. We picked up a local deputy today. The schedule will probably change. Not near as much privacy as last night."

Katrina gave him a longer kiss. "Then I'll see you when I can."

"Happy with what Poppy left you in the will?"

Katrina grinned. "I'm now officially the fifth richest person in Dallas."

"Good, when we get back, lunch is on you."

She kissed him again and turned to leave, but he grabbed her hand.

"Lock the door to your room tonight. Don't unlock it for anyone but me, okay?"

Katrina blinked several times and leaned closer, cocking her head. "I know that look. What's going on, Frank?"

Frank's fist clenched. "Probably nothing, but just do it for me, okay?"

In the dim light of the hall, her expression darkened. "Okay, but you'll tell me why later, right?"

"Promise."

A flicker of a smile flashed across her lips as she headed back into the family gathering.

Frank wandered into the kitchen, and the aroma of cooking seafood met him. "Whatcha cooking, Delma?"

Delma stirred a large pot. She started to answer him but caught herself. "I overheard them say you were once a professional chef. Is that true?"

"Guilty as charged," Frank said and offered a small salute.

"Guess what it is from the smell," Delma said. She had a smirk.

Frank stopped walking and sniffed. Definitely not a Mexican dish. He eyed the pot again. "Well, it could be a lot of things." He gazed at the ingredients on the counter. Dried basil, dried oregano, dried thyme, empty can of crushed tomatoes, and bottle of white wine. He sniffed again. But there was a distinctive fish smell. "If I had to guess, I'd say seafood cioppino."

Delma's smirk faded before giving the pot another long stir. "You're good... really good. It's a family favorite. Mr. Wallace Senior had me make it at least once a week."

Frank felt vindicated, but his silly back and forth with Delma couldn't undo the knot in his gut. *Who tore out the phone wire? And why?* He headed back to the cottage through the tunnel. The maddening rat-tat-tat of rain on the cottage roof welcomed him as he entered his bedroom.

When he wandered into the living area, Rob and Therme were sitting on the couch talking. Rob was so short and Therme so tall they looked like mismatched bookends.

"... and I have an application in with the San Antonio Police Department. Sure hope losing my patrol car doesn't screw that up," Therme said.

Rob relaxed deeper into the sofa cushions and gave his best fatherly advice. "Don't sweat that. Besides, the sheriff didn't appear all that upset when Miller spoke to him."

Therme leaned closer to Rob. "What's it like, you know, being a big city cop?"

Therme's hopeful, boy-like expression amused Frank.

"Paperwork out the ass. Spend more time typing than investigation. Everything has to be documented," Rob said.

Frank didn't speak but flopped into a chair. He needed to figure out the phone wire situation. Had to be a reasonable explanation.

Miller charged into the room from Frank's bedroom. "I explained things to the mayor. He didn't seem all that concerned. Said we'd probably depart by motorcade after lunch tomorrow. Maybe even fly out, depending on the winds. Wanted to give the storm time to play itself out a little more." Miller assumed his supervisor's stance—hands on his hips and his chin jutted out. "So, here's the deal. Before lunch tomorrow we'll do a recon of the roads leading into and out of the ranch." He gazed at Therme. "Might need you to help out with that."

Therme perked up like a kid who'd just won a spelling bee. "Sure, be glad to."

Felix reported the search turned up nothing. "There isn't a soul in the outbuildings, barns, shops, or anywhere inside a mile of this house, which means we have to also consider the phone wire problem as some anomaly of nature and the storm."

"What's wrong with the phone?" Therme asked.

Miller waved away the question. "Oh, nothing. Think the storm tore the lines out of the phone box. Some freak occurrence."

Frank allowed his stare to settle on Rob. He slowly shook his head, and Frank nodded.

"Anyway," Miller continued, "we'll have security on His Honor one more night in the house and depart early tomorrow afternoon." Miller smiled at Therme. "You could help us out if you'll willing to work tonight. We'd appreciate it."

"Sergeant," Therme said, "nothing would give me greater pleasure."

"Then it's settled," Miller said. "I'll throw together some kind of rotation schedule for tonight." Miller left the living area and made a beeline for Frank's bedroom and the tunnel.

"Wow, working the mayor's security detail. Maybe I should also apply to Dallas PD," Therme said. "Could I put you guys down as references?"

Rob grinned. "Sure."

"I'm grabbing a nap before dinner," Frank said.

He went into his bedroom and closed the door—needed to think. There was a feeling in the air. An uncomfortable feeling that he couldn't put his finger on. Miller was an idiot to willingly dismiss the phone wire incident. Only Frank and Rob could see it. But if Whisper was involved, where was he? Things just didn't add up. And just to further complicate things, Frank was almost sure he recognized Therme from somewhere. Couldn't quite put his finger on it... but somewhere. Frank's mind was so tired from lack of sleep. He just needed a short nap to reset his brain. He lay on the bed and closed his eyes. Sleep didn't come immediately. Couldn't turn off his thoughts. At some point, he must have drifted off, because he awoke to the sound of someone stomping up the stairs from the tunnel on the other side of his open closet.

Miller came in and stared at Frank. "Sorry if I woke you, but is Felix here? Need to talk to him."

Frank rubbed sleep from his eyes and tried to wake up. *Miller's an idiot.* Frank looked around the room and, in his most sarcastic voice, said, "Do you see him?"

Miller's head snapped back, and he turned toward the living area, mumbling, "Well, you don't have to be snotty about it."

As Miller left the bedroom, Frank understood he'd gotten all the sleep he was going to get today. The room was dark except the glow from a lamp in the corner. Sounded like the wind had laid down and the rain wasn't near as intense as earlier. Frank checked his watch—

quarter to eight. He sat on the side of the bed and took a minute to get it together before washing his face with cold water. As Frank walked out of the bath, the sound of the front door of the cottage slamming vibrated through the small house. Frank checked the living area to see who came in. Place was empty. A rain jacket was missing off the hook by the door. Apparently, Miller didn't want another encounter with Frank and decided to walk in the rain back to the main house.

Frank glanced at the wall by the door and did a double take at the rain jacket hooks. *Two* jackets were missing. There had been four, but now only two. Miller had one. Where was the other? Frank berated his thoughts. *What damn difference did it make?* So a rain jacket was missing—big deal. He needed more sleep if he wanted to keep a focused mind. At this point, it probably wouldn't happen until they got back to Dallas.

TWENTY-SEVEN

Rob dipped a piece of garlic toast into the bowl of seafood cioppino and popped it into his mouth as Frank meandered into the kitchen. The guy looked ragged out. "Sorry we started without you, but you were still sleeping."

Miller and Therme scooted their bowls and drinks tighter on the small kitchen table as Frank approached.

Frank yawned and flopped into a chair. "That's okay."

Delma brought him a big bowl of steaming seafood stew and laid a thick, golden piece of garlic bread on a saucer beside it. The aroma was mouthwatering.

"You want iced tea?" she asked.

"Yes, please."

"Say," Rob asked, "you see Felix? We can't find him."

"He's probably off checking the barns and shop for damage," Delma mumbled from the counter as she poured Frank's tea.

At the mention of Felix, Frank lifted his eyes and stared at Miller. Miller dropped his chin and dipped his spoon into the cioppino, ignoring Frank.

"Haven't seen him," Frank said.

Miller said, "Therme saw him leave about an hour ago in his truck—no sign of him since, but the truck is parked behind the cottage."

Frank shrugged and took the first bite of stew. *Wow.* He intended to get the recipe before he left—much better than his. The remainder of the meal was spent in small talk. No one appeared to have much to say. Rob figured they'd be back in Dallas by this time tomorrow, but still wished he could call Carmen and check on her.

Miller finished eating and stood. He used his thumb and index finger to smooth his bushy mustache before saying, "It looks like the worst of the weather is over, just a little rain. I want to do a recon on those roads now and then again before we leave tomorrow afternoon. If there's a problem with a tree down or part of the road washed out that might obstruct our passing, I want to know about it sooner rather than later. Shouldn't take all that long—fifteen or twenty minutes.

Rob looked across the table at Frank. He rolled his eyes, and Rob hid a smile.

Delma loaded the last of the dishes into the dishwasher and told them good night. Said she'd be back by six the next morning and had a special surprise for breakfast. Said Felix was probably already home eating a sandwich.

Thirty minutes later, Rob and Frank prepared to do the road recon. In Rob's humble opinion, it was pure, unadulterated madness. Waiting until after dark to drive down unfamiliar roads in the rain was only an idea a fool like Miller could come up with. Rob would take the DPD car they'd driven to the ranch and check the primary road to the entrance of the gate near the low water crossing. No one figured the crossing would be passable with all this rain, but Miller insisted it still be checked. Frank had the much saner assignment of checking the other road leading to the automatic gate at the other end of the property. The one that you went through before crossing the bridge over the deep gorge that took you to Highway 83. If clear, that exit looked like the only sure bet due to all the rain. Since Felix still hadn't shown up, Frank would take Felix's truck on the recon.

Miller hadn't given Therme an assignment, and from his hang-dog expression, it disappointed him. Just as they were about ready to leave, Therme said, "Sergeant Miller, you think I could go with one of 'em?" Therme squared his shoulders and stretched his neck from side to side. "Need to get out of the house for a few minutes."

Miller grinned. "Cabin fever, huh?"

Therme nodded and flashed an embarrassed grin. "Something like that."

"How about it guys? Anyone want company?" Miller asked.

Frank didn't say a word as he turned his back on the group while slipping on a rain jacket.

"Sure," Rob said. "Can always use a local who knows the ropes." He winked at Miller, and Miller winked back. Rob said, "Grab a rain jacket from the cottage, I'll wait for you."

"Got one right here," Therme said. He strolled into the mudroom off the kitchen and came out with a rain jacket still damp with moisture.

With those words, Frank's eyes narrowed as he turned and stared at Therme and the wet rain jacket. Looked like he was confused—probably still groggy from his nap.

As Rob and Therme drove down the gravel road toward the low water crossing, Rob said, "I wish you luck with your applications. Hope it works out for you."

"I'm excited," Therme said. "Can't wait to hear back from the recruitment officer. I could start in the October class if everything falls into place just right. Not doing much around here. Worked a house fire last week. Most excitement in months."

Rob increased the speed of the wipers just before the car's head-lights showed the stone wall and gate ahead. Rob pulled up slowly, and the gate automatically creaked open. Rob pulled through and stopped at the low water crossing. It wasn't so low water anymore.

Looked like a white water rafting river Rob had gone down last year with Carmen on vacation in Colorado.

"Well, this is a bust. No one's going to cross here for a week," Rob said. He put the car in reverse and started backing back through the open gate. He glanced back to the front for a second, and that's when the car's headlights reflected off something shiny to the left. Rob stopped and gazed at the object. He put the car in drive, swung the wheels to the left, and pulled up a few yards to get a better look. The outline of a police car materialized through the misty haze coming off the water. "Hey, is that your patrol car?" Rob asked Therme.

Therme didn't answer immediately like he was surprised or something. In a subdued voice, he said, "I guess."

Rob slammed the car in park before grabbing his flashlight. "Let's check it out." He rolled out of the driver's seat and shined his light in the direction of the patrol vehicle. It was halfway submerged in the rushing water and had wedged between two huge boulders about thirty yards downstream. Limbs and other debris were piling up against it as the relentless surge of water washed around and over the top. Rob wiped rain off his face and followed the current to where the car rested. Therme's footsteps on the graveled riverbank followed.

"Man, it's totaled," Rob said as he bent down and shined his light through the open window. "You're lucky to have gotten out."

Therme didn't reply.

Rob moved his flashlight beam across the interior of the patrol car and the head and shoulders of someone appeared. He jumped back. "Holy, shit! Someone's still in there."

Therme didn't respond.

Rob turned toward him and said, "You have a partner or—"

Therme stood higher on the bank with his gun pointed at Rob. In a low voice he said, "Real sorry about this, Rob. Nothing personal... ya' know?"

Rob stiffened. "Whisper!"

Therme showed a confused, pensive expression. "Wish Frank had invited me to go with him. Don't like him as much as you."

Rob stopped breathing as a weakness flowed through his limbs. *This wasn't possible—how?* When Therme cocked the pistol, Rob found his motivation. The fast-moving water was only feet behind him. How deep was it? What were the chances? Rob planted his left foot firmly on the rocky bank. Needed to time this just right. He quickly spun to his right as the shot sounded and the impact of the bullet tore into him.

FRANK STOOD in the light rain and tugged the jacket tighter as he stared at the automatic gate control box at the opposite end of the ranch. It had been smashed, and the battery and internal circuitry were destroyed. Frank pulled against the gate—didn't budge. He walked to the rim of the gorge and peeked over the side. Sixty or seventy feet straight down. The gorge acted as an outlet for thousands of gallons of water rushing downstream. No one's getting through here without an acetylene torch. But who wrecked the control box? Same person who wrecked the phone box? Let's see how Miller explains this.

Frank still had questions—lots of questions, but few answers. Who tore up the phone box? What happened to Felix? Who smashed the gate box he was standing beside? But the question he really wanted to be answered was a silly one. It had to do with raincoats. He'd figured out that Miller and Therme had taken the two missing coats from the cottage. Miller walked back to the house in the rain wearing his to avoid Frank, but why had Therme taken one, and why was it wet when he put it on in the kitchen a moment ago? Where had he gone while Frank slept? Frank didn't understand why, with all the other bigger issues and questions they were dealing with, that one small detail still nagged him, but it did. Obviously, he missed something during his nap. Something important.

The muffled sound of several gunshots echoed in the direction Rob and Therme had driven. Frank jumped in the truck and raced down the dark gravel road toward the low water crossing. With the cloud cover, darkness came early, but Frank charged through the night at full speed.

Just before he reached the house, headlights from another vehicle reflected in the distance, coming straight at him. But the vehicle stopped at the house and someone ran inside through the kitchen door. Frank couldn't tell who it was, but only one person left the car. He pulled alongside the sedan that Rob and Therme took to check the front gate. Frank put the truck in park but kept the engine running. He ran to the kitchen door and sounds of excited voices drifted outside. Frank swung the door open to Miller trying to calm Therme down. The guy was sitting in a kitchen chair babbling a mile a second about something—making no sense.

"Just slow down and tell me what happened," Miller said.

Therme shivered and rubbed his arms. He gasped for breath, and in a shrill voice, stammered, "He's out there. He ambushed us!"

Miller grabbed Therme's arms. "Who ambushed you?"

"Where's Rob?" Frank asked.

Therme shook uncontrollably as he faced Frank. Therme's face contorted and he whispered, "He's dead, Frank. Shot in the head."

The air left Frank's lungs in a sudden breath and he took a step back. A numbness raced through him, and he couldn't speak.

Therme lowered his head. "I tried getting him in the car, but someone had me pinned down."

Frank found his voice and shook Therme by the shoulders. "How do you know he's dead?" Frank shouted.

Therme put his head in his hands, and a whimpering noise sounded deep in his throat. "Has to be. Blew half his head off."

Frank let go of Therme and stared at Miller. "Need any more proof?"

Miller's ashen expression meant he now understood the danger.

Frank tried to arrange his thoughts, but they were a jumble of emotions and disconnected ideas. He decided to just act on pure instinct as he eyed Miller. "Get everyone into the tunnel. Only two ways in. You and Therme cover the entrances. I'll be back." Frank turned to leave.

"Where you going?" Miller asked.

Frank stared him down. "I'm going to get Rob."

Miller's chin stuck out, and he said, "No, you're not. There's nothing we can do for the man—he's dead. We need you here with us."

Frank raised his voice, his hands fisted, saying, "He's not just a man. He's my partner and my friend! I'll be back. Until then, I suggest you do what I said. I don't know how long it will take the guy to get here from the front gate, but you have time—use it wisely." Frank didn't wait for an answer as he wheeled around and opened the kitchen door.

"Stop," Miller commanded. "I order you not to go."

Frank looked back. "Your idiotic idea is what got them ambushed. I'm finished taking orders from you."

Frank rushed outside and hopped into the truck. The thought that Rob was dead was not one he wanted to process right now. He had bigger problems, like, was Whisper waiting down the road in the dark shadows of a tree for him to drive past? The first indication would probably be his window shattering and him being shot. Frank had been shot before—it hurt. He didn't care. He would get Rob and return to the house. If Whisper or anyone else tried to stop him, Frank would kill them.

Emotion swelled in his chest at the loss of Rob. How could this happen? Frank's mind was still fogged with confusing facts and unanswered questions. Why didn't anyone see this coming? He'd failed Rob, and now his friend was dead. Living with that thought the rest of his life would drive him insane.

As Frank neared the front gate, he strained his eyes for any sign someone was in waiting. The rain was only a light mist now—didn't even need his wipers, but rushing rivulets of water still flooded the ditches, looking for an outlet. Frank slowed the truck and searched the area for movement. The gate was open leading to the low water crossing. Frank put the truck in park and killed the engine. He slid from the seat with his Sig Sauer in hand and, wading through the soggy ditch, dashed to a near-by tree. He took a knee to keep as low a profile as possible. A thought came to him. *Stupid me!* Didn't think to ask Therme where Rob had fallen. Frank's heart pounded as he ran to the stone wall supporting the metal gate. He did a quick peek around the wall. The night was so dark only the sound of racing water across the low water crossing confirmed it was actually there. *If I can't see Whisper, he couldn't see me.* Frank drew in a deep breath and leaped through the gate, waiting for the shot he figured would probably come—nothing. He knelt beside a wall column and slipped his flashlight from his rain jacket. Turning it on would give away his position and draw fire, but he had no choice. He had to find Rob. Frank switched it on and at the same time pointed his pistol, ready to return fire. He scanned the beam around the outside wall and bank of the swollen river—nothing. Frank licked his lips, swallowed hard, and shouted, "Rob, are you here?"

ROB HAD ALMOST LOST consciousness more than once. He gritted his teeth against the pain that coursed through him like a hot coal. He hung onto the passenger side mirror of the almost submerged sheriff's patrol car. He'd lucked out, well almost. When he did his spinning dive into the muddy water twenty minutes ago, he never figured on being shot, but shot he was. He'd ducked below the dark waters, and they carried him to the car, slamming him against the driver's door. Coming up for air meant death, so he felt his way underwater until an opening appeared under the car. Rob stuck both legs through. Using his hands, he'd edged his way under the car feet first, with the current trying to tear his grip lose. When he popped out on the downstream side, he latched onto the mirror and held on for life. Therme—*Whisper!*—stood on the bank, searching the water with a flashlight, pistol still in hand. Luckily, Rob's head was behind one of the large boulders the car was pinned against, and the rushing water must have camouflaged him with just enough spray. After what seemed like hours, Whisper walked away. Rob only had two thoughts in mind—surviving, and killing that SOB. He wasn't certain he'd be able to do either.

Rob had just started on the final prayer of the Rosary:

Oh, God, whose only-begotten Son, by His life, death, and resurrection, has purchased for us the rewards of eternal life; grant, we beseech Thee, that, meditating upon these mysteries of the Most Holy Rosary of the Blessed Virgin Mary, we may imitate what they contain and obtain what they promise...

The sound of a vehicle approaching stopped the prayer in midsentence. Oh, no. Guy had come back to finish him off. Rob had to let go with one hand to slide his other to his side and unsnap the holster on his belt. Didn't know if the bullets would fire after being in water this long, but he wasn't going down without a fight. Gushes of nasty water splashed over him when he released the hand and his mouth filled with the stuff. He spit it out, gagged, and held his breath, increasing his grip on the mirror. When the pistol released from the holster, Rob used both hands to grab the mirror again, and waited his chance. The loss of blood and cold rainwater, together with the strain of holding onto the car, had zapped all his strength. All he wanted was one good shot. Even if he drowned and his body washed up in a heap of rubble later, at least he would have gotten Whisper.

Rob steadied his nerves and gripped the pistol tighter just before a familiar voice shouted, "Rob, are you here?"

Frank? What the hell?

"Yeah," Rob shouted over the roaring sound of the river. "I'm over hear."

Moments later, the beam of a flashlight slashed through the darkness. "Where are you?" Frank called.

"Here, I'm here." Rob raised his gun hand and waved toward the flashlight.

"Oh, crap," Frank screamed. "I see you. Hang on. I'll get something to haul you in."

Rob had no memories as an infant. But the words Frank just spoke felt as comforting as a baby being rocked asleep in the arms of its mother. *Thank you, God.*

TWENTY-EIGHT

Frank ran back to the truck and drove through the gate, cutting his wheels hard to the left, illuminating the almost submerged patrol car in the rushing water. He searched behind the truck's seat for something... anything... he could use as a rope. This was a ranch vehicle with farm tags. There had to be something. Felix kept the truck spotless inside and out. Nothing tool-related in the front or back seats of the cab. *Shit!*

Frank wheeled around to the bed of the truck. It had a rollup bed cover. He dropped the tailgate and pushed back the cover.

The body of Felix lay in the back, his throat slashed.

When the realization of what happened hit Frank, it was like a hard slap. That's why the rain jackets were important. Therme's disappeared just before the hard line phone was disabled. An unexplained missing rain jacket was the only evidence. Therme said he watched Felix drive away in his truck as Frank slept. Again, a rain jacket dripping beads of water in the mud room the only evidence. It had stared Frank in the face from the start, but he couldn't put it together until now. Sure, he recognized Therme! That was the face of the big guy with long, blond hair leaving the club that night before

Frank and Layla had their encounter in the parking lot. He'd gotten a haircut and colored his hair brown, but it was the same face. *Christ.* Therme was back at the house with Miller, and no one knew who he was.

But first things first. Frank used his light to search the bed of the truck. Plenty of tools back there—too many. Posthole diggers, wire, wire stretchers, staples, tow strap. *Yes.* Frank snatched up the rolled, yellow, nylon strap and eased himself into the edge of the wild water as far as possible. "Get ready when I throw this," Frank yelled.

"I'm ready, throw it," Rob yelled back.

Frank held one end and threw the rolled-up tow strap in the direction he'd seen Rob earlier. When the line went taut, Frank knew Rob had it.

"Pull!" Rob screamed. "I'm letting go of the car."

There was nothing Frank could tie the strap off to and not enough strap left even if there was, so Frank braced his feet in the muddy gravel bank, and the dark outline of Rob at the end of the bright yellow strap appeared downstream. Frank tugged against the swift current. It pulled him down the river bank until his heel found a stone sticking up and he finally got a good toe hold. Frank's muscles burned, and he almost lost his grip on the wet strap more than once before slowly dragging Rob to the bank. Frank reached down, grabbed him by the belt, and finished pulling him out. Rob was all dead weight, and Frank was spent. He collapsed beside Rob, gasping for air.

Rob lay face down, still holding the pistol, also gasping. After a moment he mumbled. "You call that pulling, Cracker? You pull like a twelve-year-old girl."

Frank grinned. "Had me worried. Though he'd killed you."

Rob rolled onto his back grimacing in pain. "He tried. You know Therme's Whisper, right?"

Frank took Rob's pistol from his hand and tucked it into his own waistband. "Yeah," Frank said. "A little late figuring it out, sorry."

Rob pulled up his shirt and pointed, "Shine the light on my side."

Frank flicked on the flashlight to a mess of jagged skin with blood oozing out. "What happened?"

"What do you think happened? The bastard shot me."

Frank said, "Roll over."

Rob rolled to his other side, and Frank checked his back before saying, "Lucky, went clean through. Didn't hit a bone or any organs. Just lost a little tissue around your love handle." But Frank was worried. The blood had drained from Rob's face and he shook uncontrollably. Purple lips twitched in the light of the flashlight beam. Looked like he might be going into shock. The pull from the water had used up his last reserves. Needed to get him to a warm, dry place.

"Come on, we're getting you out of here," Frank murmured.

He threw an arm around Rob's shoulders, and they staggered to the truck. Rob collapsed beside it, taking Frank down with him. Frank had seen a first aid kit in the bed of the truck. He left Rob's side long enough to retrieve it.

When Frank kneeled by Rob, he showed a faded, shallow smile. "Got a shot of morphine in there?"

Frank unwrapped packages of sterile pads and gauze. "If I did, I'd use it on myself."

Rob's chuckle was weak. More color had drained from his face, and the shaking increased.

The interior truck light outlined a grimace on Rob's lips as he sat in mud by the open door.

Frank cut off Rob's wet shirt and bandaged the wound as best he could. It had almost stopped bleeding. Frank found an old, thick towel matted with what looked like horse hair in the bed of the truck and threw it around Rob's shoulders. He helped him into the truck and turned the heater on high. Frank took Rob's pistol from his waistband and tossed it on the seat between them. Rob leaned against the passenger window with his eyes closed. As Frank passed through the gate heading back to the house, Rob spoke.

In a shaky voice, he asked, "What are you going to do?"

Frank didn't answer immediately. He had no good answer that

made any sense. What could he do? Finally, he said, "Kill Whisper." But the real thing on Frank's mind wasn't killing. Saving Katrina was the only reason he had to return to the house. No matter what, he'd get her and Rob to safety. Those were his only concerns.

Rob didn't say anything else. He slumped lower in the seat and his head lolled to the side. Frank felt his neck for a pulse. It was there, but weak. Needed to get him some help.

As Frank pulled up to the house, his heart sank. There were no lights inside or out. He glanced at Rob one last time and slid from the truck, leaving the engine running and the heater on. When he'd left a half hour ago, the place had been lit up like a circus. Frank listened, but the steady hum of the emergency generator no longer sounded from outside the utility room door. The house had a cold forbidding appearance. Frank understood the term *skin crawl*. He'd experienced it before. Inside the cave that day, waiting on the killers to enter. He eyed the dark house and pulled in a slow breath. Death lurked within, and Frank had no choice but to enter. He ran to the emergency generator and lifted the top cover. Shining his light inside, it was clear the generator ran on propane or natural gas, but he had no idea how to restart it. After a few seconds, he discovered it didn't matter. A copper tube that handled airflow was smashed in half. The jagged edges sparkled in the beam of the flashlight.

Frank took a second to have a *come to Jesus* moment, drew in another breath, and opened the utility room door. He leaped inside, expecting a shot—nothing. He squatted and strained his eyes down the dark hall. Easing toward the kitchen in the dark, his foot bumped something on the floor. Frank nudged his foot against it again but couldn't figure out what blocked his path. He felt in the dark, and his hand found cloth. Someone's clothes? He patted the cloth and only then discovered it was a body. Frank held his breath and ran his hand to the neck to check for a pulse. Warm, sticky blood coated his fingertips. The neck had a major gash and no pulse. When Frank touched the face, the bushy eyebrows and mustache caused him to jerk his hand back in disgust. The guy was an asshole and had gotten Rob shot, but no one deserved to die like this. As Frank's night vision improved, a dim reflection of light shined from down the hall, leading to the dining room and library.

Frank slipped behind the kitchen island and stared at the flickering light in the hall. *A candle?* He moved to the hall entrance and studied the light. Definitely a candle. Frank stayed close to the wall and tiptoed into the dining room. The candle sat in the middle of the table. The old saying, moth to a flame, drifted through his mind. He took a slow, even breath, and sweat trickled down his cheek, tickling his neck. He moved around the room, making sure he was alone before stopping at the door leading to the library. Another candle glowed from the small table next to the bookcase. The secret door in the bookcase stood wide open, welcoming him to enter. No one needed to tell him he was being led into a trap. But it was a trap he might be able to control. Frank backed out of the dining room, through the kitchen, and out the kitchen door. He ran to the cottage and slowly opened the door. He quickly entered and squatted. His heart beat against his chest so hard it was difficult to catch a breath. He stayed crouched, listening for several minutes. *Have to settle down.* Frank moved through the door into his bedroom and listened again. A long silence met him.

His plan was simple. Before he left to get Rob, he'd advised Miller to evacuate the mayor's family to the tunnel. Most likely, Miller and Whisper had done just that. At some point, he'd lured Miller back into the utility room and murdered him. If Frank was correct, he'd then confined the family in the tunnel, lit candles, and waited for Frank's return. Saving Katrina meant going into the dark abyss, no way around it. But Frank didn't have to follow the lighted path set for him. If he could approach from a direction Whisper wasn't expecting, he might still have a chance of taking him by surprise. *Might* was the operative word here. Frank had no idea what awaited him in the dark hole. His mind again drifted back to the day he and Rob defended Katrina and the other girl in the pitch-black cave. The day he came closest to losing his life.

Today, Whisper was the one defending. That gave the crazy bastard most of the advantages.

Frank approached the closet and stared into the gloom. *Can't turn on the flashlight.* He kept his gun pointed to the front and his finger tight on the trigger. If the guy jumped out of the darkness, Frank intended to unload the whole magazine into him. Frank felt inside the closet's back wall. It was still open. His fingers brushed over the edges of the rough, wooden panel and he duck-walked to the opening.

Frank shook and his breath caught. Walking through that dark door into the tunnel would most probably be the end of him. The guy waiting on the other side was smart. Perhaps smarter than Frank. And he was a clever killer. Knew how to fool someone into thinking one thing when they should be thinking about something entirely different. But Katrina was also on the other side. That day in her apartment, he'd promised her she'd never be in a dark, dangerous place again without him by her side. Keeping that promise became his life's goal now, for whatever life he had left.

Frank crept through the blackness. Only the white and green night sights on his pistol oriented him to the muzzle's direction. When his foot touched the stair landing on the other side of the secret closet door, he gazed into the void. An almost invisible flicker of light radiated far ahead in the darkness. Frank stopped and studied it a moment, taking deep breaths. Yes, it was a light of some kind, not his eyes playing tricks on him. He took the stairs one slow step at a time, stopping halfway down to listen—no sound. He reached the base of the stairs and had to make a decision. Which side of the black corridor would he walk down? *Think logically. Americans tended to walk to the right.* But how logical was Whisper? Frank did a mental coin toss. Taking the left side of the wall won—just as well.

Frank took slow, silent breaths through his nose as he eased deeper into the tunnel. He slid his left hand along the rough brick wall keeping him walking in a straight line. He stopped every few steps and listened. Frank wiped more sweat from his eyes and waited in the darkness, straining his ears. He had to go on. As he got closer and could see better, his eyes widened. In the shadows, sitting on the cold stone floor, blindfolded with their hands tied, were the mayor and his family. A candle sat atop the wine rack, its flame swaying in some invisible breeze Frank couldn't feel. He stared at Katrina, sitting motionless with the others. He fought the urge to rush and embrace her—this was *still* a trap.

Frank didn't want to, but turning on his flashlight was the only option to check under the dark wooden stairs leading into the library. He extended the flashlight, pointed the pistol in the direction the beam would shine, and flicked on the switch. Frank almost took a step forward but hesitated. He directed the beam under the staircase to make sure Whisper wasn't waiting there in ambush. It was all clear. Frank froze and his blood seemed to stop flowing, giving him a chill. He shook—in his excited state of mind he'd failed to check the underside of the staircase he'd just gone down at the opposite end of the tunnel.

A cold, hard piece of metal pushed against the back of his head.

"If you so much as twitch, I'll kill you," a firm, quiet voice whispered. "Drop the gun, and no tricks."

Frank never heard the approach. The guy moved with absolute silence. The blindfolded heads of the family all turned in Frank's direction as Whisper spoke those soft words. Several whimpers and moans drifted from the group sitting on the floor. Frank should have been scared, but amazingly he felt a sense of relief. His mind became less jumbled, and he was ready to accept whatever happened next. But what happened next was also unexpected. As Frank gazed at the group on the floor, something didn't add up. He blinked a couple of times and shook his head. Couldn't figure it out, but the whole thing looked wrong. He allowed the pistol to fall from his hand to the floor and raised his hands.

"That's better, Frank. Now turn around."

Frank twisted his head and faced Therme, or whatever his real name was.

A grin crossed Whisper's lips before saying, "Always had you figured for the smartest one, Frank. Knew if I were going to fool you, I'd have to come up with something smarter."

Disappointed moans sounded from the mayor's family in the corner.

Frank didn't answer, just stared at him.

"Way I figure it, we don't need you around anymore, Frank. Never did. It was always going to end this way. You just weren't clever enough to figure I'd drive all this way, were ya?" Whisper motioned to the stairs. "You first, and don't try anything. If you do, I might have to take it out on her." He nodded toward Katrina. "Wouldn't want to do that, but you'll make that call."

Frank had never felt more helpless. He slowly mounted the stairs, with Whisper's footsteps close behind. The last sound he heard before stepping through the door into the library was Katrina's whimpers. A profound sadness coursed through Frank. His gut knotted, and more sweat streaked his cheeks with each step. He tried taking a deep breath, but it felt like all the air had left his lungs and he couldn't restore it.

Halfway through the library, Whisper said, "That's far enough. Grab a chair."

Frank sat in the desk chair, and the killer moved to his rear. There was nothing Frank could do. This guy was going to kill him. Frank had no chance against a man that outweighed him by sixty pounds, twice as strong, and holding a gun behind him. Frank had never been all that good at self-sacrifice. Like most people, he was selfish at heart. This would have to be his last great selfless act. Don't resist an impossible situation. Don't chance Katrina paying for some ridiculous stunt he'd done as his last desperate attempt to survive. *Relax, just close your eyes and let it happen.*

"We can do this one of two ways," Whisper said. "Your choice."

Frank waited as sickening stomach acid flowed up his throat, making him want to puke.

"I can use the gun or knife, Frank. Which will it be?"

Frank pulled himself together and straightened in the chair. He was deathly afraid of knives ever since being stabbed by the whore. But he wasn't going to give this son-of-a-bitch the satisfaction of knowing that. "Get it over with, asshole. I'm bored with your talking."

A low chuckled sounded from behind. "In that case, I'll use the blade. Always enjoy the blade better—lousy shot with a gun. Besides, wouldn't want to disturb the others. I'll just tell them I tied you up. Shame about them. Before you came back, I tried telling the mayor about being his son, but I could see in his eyes he didn't believe me. They'll never accept me into their family. Looks like they're not giving me much choice anymore. Hate it, but nothing I can do."

That settled it. Whisper intended to kill them all. Frank couldn't wait. He'd hoped he'd hear the pistol slid back into its holster. That might be the chance he needed. Needed to do what? Frank didn't know—escape, attack the guy? Frank's thoughts clouded again. But instead of the pistol being returned to the holster, the sharp snap of a knife blade being deployed tore through the silence. Frank braced himself for action. *Okay, here goes.*

When the crack of a pistol's report exploded from behind him, Frank assumed Whisper had changed his mind, but Frank felt no impact from the bullet. He opened his eyes. He was still alive. He swung his head around and Whisper stood behind him, pistol in one hand and knife in the other. He did a slight head shake and his eyes narrowed, staring into the dark room. He no longer cared about Frank. All his concentration was focused on a corner of the library. A red stain marred his uniform shirt almost center mass. He gazed at it with a curious expression. Frank jumped from the chair and faced him as Whisper raised the pistol and pointed it in the direction he'd been staring.

Four more quick shots sounded from the darkness. The muzzle flashes lit up the room like a strobe light, enough that the shooter's identity was revealed. Whisper didn't make a sound. He staggered back a couple of steps and tripped over a footstool, collapsing to the floor.

Frank rushed the prone figure and kicked the pistol from his grip. In the candle's dim light, Frank could just make out Whisper's facial features. He turned his head toward Frank and a bloody grin formed on the mouth. Acted like he wanted to say something. His lips moved, but no sound came out. After a moment, his eyes closed, and the facial muscles relaxed. Looked like he drifted off to sleep.

Frank stood and faced the shooter. He'd stepped forward into the light. He still had the pistol pointed at Whisper, but his whole body shook so badly Frank figured he'd better take the gun to be safe. Frank walked over and took the weapon. Frank laid a reassuring hand on his shoulder and in a low voice said, "It's okay now, Jerry. It's okay."

EPILOGUE

Frank led Jerry into the kitchen. Once he had him settled into a chair with a glass of water, Frank released the rest of the family, starting with Katrina. Her embracing him surprised everyone except the mayor. He appeared to have a look of acceptance and didn't make a big deal of it.

Rob had regained consciousness by the time Frank made it back to the truck. The truck's heater was what he needed most to keep the shock of being wounded under control and revive him after being in the cold waters of the Frio River for almost an hour. Frank recalled only after the fact that Frio was the Spanish word for cold.

It was only after helping Rob inside, wrapping him in blankets, and getting some hot coffee in him that something marvelous happened—Frank's phone pinged with a text message from Alton. *Call me immediately!* Cell phone service had been restored. It took just over an hour to get an ambulance to the house after first having to cut the gate off its hinges with a torch. Rob made a quick recovery, as did Jerry from the trauma of killing a man.

Once the full story came to light, it sounded crazy. Jerry had been playing games on his phone in a cozy corner chair of the library when he drifted off to sleep. He awoke at some point during the night and decided he needed to go to bed. Looking out the library window, there was a vehicle in the drive, engine idling with the lights on, so Jerry wandered outside to see what was up. He found Rob wrapped in a towel and barely conscious in the front seat. Rob told Jerry that Frank was inside and explained what was going on. Jerry spotted Rob's pistol on the seat. He reached over and picked it up, promising he'd be right back. And that's how the kid came to be in the shadowed corner of the library that night. Jerry heard voices from the tunnel and surmised what was happening. He waited in the dark until Whisper and Frank came into the room.

The FBI, Texas Rangers, and local police swarmed the ranch later that day. They discovered Whisper's truck hidden off the road leading to the low water crossing. Finding his wallet, fake IDs, and genuine IDs was a bonus. They quickly figured out his true name was Perry Eugene Hansen. He was wanted for questioning in Georgia regarding an arson and murder investigation five years earlier. The victim had been his mother.

While everyone rejoiced that the menace had been taken down, and Jerry was publicly commended by police chiefs and sheriffs across Texas, Frank still had trouble with the whole thing. Trouble sleeping, trouble working, and worst of all, trouble even thinking. Since Rob was still on the mend and off work, Frank took up the department's offer for two weeks paid leave and traveled to Cruz Bay on St. Johns. Katrina had been disappointed he didn't ask her to join him, but he explained this had to be a "head-clearing trip," and he couldn't do that with anyone else there.

Frank checked into a small beachfront hotel a few days after Labor Day. The weather was still too hot for Frank's taste, but he sat under the shade of his patio every morning and sipped coffee as the sun crested the eastern horizon. He did a lot of walking along the beach and swimming in the Caribbean, resetting his mind and coming to terms with what happened.

During the hottest part of the day, he found a shaded cafe in town, drank dark rum and Coke, and had lunch. Always found time for an early afternoon nap. In the evenings, he drank wine on his patio and waited for the sun to make its final appearance. Frank drew emotional, spiritual, and psychological energy from the sun. Every night, Layla came to mind. Her death was inevitable. Frank had called it right. She'd played a dangerous game and suddenly found herself outmatched. By the end of the week, Frank found peace. His mind cleared, and his thoughts now made more sense. He settled with himself the illusion it could have ended any differently.

As for Whisper, he'd been a creature of the night. Who knew what mental disease or past traumas drove him? The idea there were probably thousands of Whispers in the world caused Frank to recall an incident. When he was a young rookie, he rode patrol with an older and wiser cop on the verge of retirement. Dude served three tours in Vietnam as a Ranger, wounded twice, and had every medal a Ranger could get except the Congressional Medal of Honor. Something the guy said one night now drifted through Frank's memory. He'd asked Frank if he believed in monsters.

Frank had laughed and said, "No, of course not."

His partner had leaned closer, and his expression hardened. "Well, you should. They exist—always have. They don't have long fangs and claws. Don't creep through the woods in the shadows after dark. No, they walk upright in the daylight, wear clothes like the rest of us, and act perfectly normal until something sets them off. You'll understand after a few years. We're all formed by our environment, and there are some truly horrible crucibles in this world."

ACKNOWLEDGMENTS

Writing a book is a team effort. I'm most grateful to those who took their valuable time helping me.

To my beta-readers--Daryle McGinnis and Brian Tracey—your comments and suggestions on the plot and characters are much appreciated.

To my editor, Twyla Beth Lambert—as usual, your keen eye for detail never fails.

To the DFW Writer's Workshop—your critiques were on the money.

And, as always, to Fawkes Press and Jodi Thompson for believing in the book and seeing it through.

ALSO BY LARRY ENMON

Class III Threat

Worst Case Scenario

More Rob Soliz and Frank Pierce Mysteries

Wormwood (UK)

The Burial Place

City of Fear